With the Procession

CHICAGO IN FICTION
SAUL BELLOW
ADVISORY EDITOR

HENRY B. FULLER

With
the
Procession

INTRODUCTION BY MARK HARRIS

CHICAGO AND LONDON
THE UNIVERSITY OF CHICAGO PRESS

Fuller and
the American Procession

A NEW INTRODUCTION BY

Mark Harris

Shall we be consoled by the idea that the luxurious misery of the principal persons of *With the Procession* is the continuing misery of American society—was and will be with us forever —or shall we renew our indignation that such a country was ever begun? The events which pained Henry Blake Fuller, seeming to motivate the composition of this novel, pain us now. His lament is ours.

On the other hand, our dilemma is deepened by our paradox, for we too celebrate this Procession; this *march*, as Fuller also calls it; this *caravan*, he says—the very word of Henry Adams in the very connection.

Where will this Procession lead? For one Irish family it has led to the White House. Perhaps that family is related to the Irish cop we meet in Chapter I. The Procession is a dream of that sort of success, and our expectation may be, as we read, that it marches the right way toward the best of history's alternatives.

The Procession is that principle of American freedom promising opportunity for men formerly without hope, political power for men formerly voiceless; wealth, of course; ascension in a single generation to that social class next above one's own. Give us your tired, your poor, yearning to be . . .

And yet if we can almost see justice, equality, human dignity, and more sweet abundance than any men ever consumed we see also conspicuous anxiety. Tyrannized by mediocrity, something within us may question democracy, making us sound a little snobbish when we ask whether a less flexible society might not improve our anxieties.

Whichever way we stand, we must know at least that the opposite idea exists before we approach *With the Procession,* for Fuller may be engaging us in a cause not quite our own. Perhaps he has been somewhere we have not—has had his own experience of the Procession, been tempted to join it, detected its dangers to the independence of his art, rescued himself. He was at mid-career, in age near forty, and he had remained alert, observing that increasing powers of workmanship do not necessarily excite popular admiration. His business honestly transacted along the lines of the old ethic—the old art—he nevertheless saw his trade diverted to practitioners who, like the spiritual enemies of his hero, David Marshall, speculated in quick returns.

The year of the novel is sometime in the early 1890s. The place is Chicago, called by Fuller a "great and complex city," but still sometimes referred to by his characters as "the town," so youthful is it: its population is two million; twenty years earlier it had been only 300,000.

The action of the novel begins with David Marshall, to whom Fuller gives an extended paragraph, then drops with a line— "But this is no way to begin." Perhaps this pretense at a false beginning was an afterthought. No matter, the uncertainty warns us that Fuller had in mind another hero, not David. David, after all, is a merchant ("teas, coffees, spices, flour, sugar, baking-powder"). He and Fuller had neither wandered the same routes of the world nor followed similar trades. David was hardly an author's logical disguise.

Presumably, then, it is to David's son, Truesdale, whom we look for Fuller's statement, who ought to assert the meaning of the events through we shall live. Truesdale, we are told, is an artist; like Fuller, he has been enormously impressed by sights abroad. Our logical expectation is that it is he, not his father, who shall tell us our story.

It was also Fuller's logical procedure. But Truesdale, as either an artist in spirit or a painter in practice, fails to persuade. His response to his own outrage is too often limited to the ejaculation *Ouf!*, as if the author were reluctant to entrust to Truesdale a mature articulation which would have been incongruous against Fuller's fidelity to realism. Where Truesdale at last rises to coherent protest against esthetic chaos it is not in his own language at all, but with an interior monologue paraphrased by the author. Truesdale ironically views a respectable proposal for "a piece of actual architecture":

Then he festooned it with telegraph wires, and draped it with fire-escapes, and girdled it with a stretch of elevated road, and hung it with signboards, and hedged it in with fruit-stands, and swathed it in clouds of coal smoke, and then asked them to find it; that was the puzzle, he said.

Significantly, this passage is instantly followed by Fuller's recognition that father and son "were dangerously near to the common ground upon which they had never yet met." Why *dangerously?* The word is truly inexplicable at that point, and may in fact more accurately refer to the danger Fuller escaped in transferring his sympathies from Truesdale to David than to relationships within the novel.

The speculation is worth the risk, for unless the book is seen as David's we fail to appreciate some of the force of Fuller's dedication to the life of his characters, even at the expense of his own intention. His rescue of himself from his miscalculation is surely a first achievement of *With the Procession*, and a signal of Fuller's loyalty to craft. (We may also support the speculation by noting the shift of the designation *Marshall* from Truesdale to David, and the reduction, after the early pages, of *Marshall* to the boyish *Truesdale*.)

It is David whose decline and death span the book, and David who utters its cry and appeal, not in the author's voice but in the more difficult voice of a civilized merchant drawn to life. "To David Marshall, art in all its forms was an inexplicable thing ..." Yet it is David whose art is true.

David established, Fuller turns to the Procession itself, and to Truesdale Marshall. Truesdale, younger son of David, is returning at twenty-three from three years of "culture and adventure" abroad, "to catch up again ... rejoin the great caravan." From Truesdale's viewpoint, as we re-enter the city we see an actual caravan suggesting the figurative:

... a long line of waiting vehicles took up their interrupted course through the smoke and the stench ... first a yellow streetcar; then a robust truck laden with rattling sheetiron, or piled high with fresh wooden pails and willow baskets; then a junk-cart bearing a pair of dwarfed and bearded Poles ... then, perhaps, a bespattered buggy ... then a butcher's cart loaded with the carcasses of calves ... an express wagon with a yellow cur yelping from its rear; then, it may be, an insolently venturesome landau, with crested panel and top-booted coachman. Then drays and omnibuses and more street-cars; then, presently, somewhere in the line between the tail end of one truck and the menacing tongue of another, a family carry-all ...

This carry-all belongs to the Marshall family, and it is likened to them, as a writer a generation after Fuller might liken a family automobile to its owners. But the carry-all personifies David, not his son. David persists in the language of the author's description of the carry-all, where the emphasis falls upon the relationship between virtue and fashion:

It is very capable and comprehensive vehicle, as conveyances of that kind go. It is not new, it is not precisely in the mode; but it shows material and workmanship of the best grade, and it is washed, oiled, polished with scrupulous care. It advances with some deliberation, and one might fancy hearing in the rattle of its tires, or in the suppressed flapping of its rear curtain, a word of plaintive protest. "I am not of the great world," it seems to say; "I make no pretence to fashion. We are steady and solid, but we are not precisely in society, and we are far, very far indeed, from any attempt to cut a great figure. However, do not misunderstand our position; it is not that we are under, nor that we are exactly aside; perhaps we have been left just a little behind. Yes, that might express it— just a little behind."

Fuller's scene set, his materials felt, his workmanship is never less than the workmanship of the conscientious artisan who made the carry-all. Scornful of simplification, he creates both heroes and villains too real to bear if we indolently insist upon easy identification. The novel is purest for the impurities of its actors, heroes not purely good, villains never merely bad. Among the heroes, for example, Truesdale is a snob, and sister Jane is a plain girl without prospects. The character Paston, whom we ought not to like, wins a rich reward; Jane has no such luck; David dies; Roger endures. The Procession marches on.

Consider the villains! May we even call them that? Are Mrs. Granger Bates and Roger Marshall really so wicked, after all?

Mrs. Bates appears to us at first as only that passive Mrs. Jones we compel ourselves to keep up with. It was not Mrs. Bates who searched out Jane Marshall, to poison Jane's mind with restlessness; no, it was Jane who sought Mrs. Bates. "I declare, when I called on Mrs. Bates and went over the place and compared their house and their way of living with ours . . . When I saw that magnificent style she lived in . . ." At Mrs. Bates's house the gayest chapters of the book occur. We are disarmed. We find ourselves witness to the first hour of a friendship likely to survive long beyond the period of the book itself.

How can this be bad? Mrs. Bates would be astonished that we name her a candidate for villain. She is certain that she has in mind no thought but Jane's advancement. She teaches Jane to develop much that is best in her, converts her plainness to something closer to her potential beauty, and guides her to the Charity Ball.

Jane's first "glimpse" of Mrs. Bates, and ours, was of "one of the big, the broad, the great, the triumphant; . . . one of a Roman amplitude and vigor, an Indian keenness and sagacity, an American ambition and determination . . . one of the conquerors, in short."

There is no dissimulation, no fraudulence, no misrepresentation on the part of Mrs. Bates. She knows where she has been and where she wants to go.

". . . We weren't so very stylish ourselves, but we had some awfully stylish neighbors . . . 'We'll get there, too, some time,' I said to Granger. 'This is going to be a big town, and we have a good show to be big people in it. Don't let's start in life like beggars going to the back door for cold victuals; let's march right up the front steps and ring the bell *like* somebody.' . . . Well, we worked along fairly for a year or two, and finally I said to Granger: 'Now, what's the use of inventing things and taking them to those companies and making everybody rich but yourself? You pick out some one road, and get on the inside of that, and stick there . . .' We have fought the fight—a fair field and no favor—and we have come out ahead. And we shall stay there, too; keep up with the procession is my motto, and head it if you can. I *do* head it, and I feel that I'm where I belong. When I can't foot it with the rest, let me drop by the wayside and the crows have me."

There is nothing of subtlety to her except that subtlety which is worst of all because it remains unknown to Mrs. Bates herself: she lacks a knowledge not of her actions but of their implications. Not what she does, but what her doing means, remains inaccessible to her. How can she help but admire herself when all her activities are praised and publicized? To a vision so willingly obstructed what's good for one's own vanity takes on the aspect of beneficence.

Jane's initiative liberates Mrs. Bates's initiative, the innocent provoking the villain, though her villainy consists of nothing so patent as conspiracy with any forces except itself. Unconscious, subtlest of all, it characterizes not only Mrs. Bates but the entire Procession, shielding old settler and immigrant from the implications of their actions. With every best intention Mrs. Bates now goes to David Marshall to urge him to invest in a monument for himself:

"... Imagine a man disposed to devote two or three hundred thousand dollars to the public, and giving it to help pay off the municipal debt. How many people would consider themselves benefited by the gift, or would care a cent for the name of the giver? Or fancy his giving it to clean up the streets of the city. The whole affair would be forgotten with the coming of the next rain-storm. . . . You drive out to the University campus this time next year, David, and you'll see Bates Hall—four stories high, with dormers and gables and things, and the name carved in gray-stone over the doorway, to stay there for the next century or two. I think I shall name it Susan Lathrop Bates Hall . . ."

It is Mrs. Bates, not Fuller, who places Mrs. Bates on record. In this same disciplined way Fuller presents the second villain, working always within the limits his craft has set for itself. Perhaps he yearned for a more expansive vocabulary, a wider viewpoint. If so, he refrained from indulgence. (Jane's use of the phrase "historical and sociological" is sufficiently extraordinary for Fuller to make a point of it.)

Roger Marshall had none of the liberal advantages of his younger brother, Truesdale.

Roger was held by his family to be above all foibles and frailties; his aunt Lydia had once told him . . . that he had too much head and not enough heart. It is certain that he had marked out a definite course for himself, and that nothing, so far, had had the power to divert him materially from it; and he had a far-reaching contempt for the man who permitted the gray matter of his brain to be demoralized by the red matter in his veins. . . . His severe face was smooth-shaven, as he thought the face of a lawyer ought to be, and he could address the higher courts with such a loud and brazen utterance as to cause the court-loungers almost to feel the judges shrinking and shriveling under their robes. His was a hot and vehement nature, but it burned with a flame blue rather than red.

Selected by his father to serve as the family's attorney, Roger's is the final act of the book—the assignment of a portion of David's estate to Jane, rather than, as had been stipulated, to a monument of the sort recommended by Mrs. Bates. If Roger's act is questionably legal it is undeniably brotherly, and we view him here at the last, as we saw him earlier, the defender, the protector, saving his sister from her own sentimentality.

Shall we complain of such a man? How is he a villain? At worst he may be one of the wreckers of civilization, but within the terms of Fuller's novel he is only dull and uninteresting. Every family has its practical son, proud of his own hard code, seldom aware that his assumptions are merely assumptions or that his motivations extend beyond superficial consciousness. Roger is "tough and technical and litigious; his was the hand to seize, not to soothe." He is the Procession's unconscious theorist.

It may be a weakness of *With the Procession* that Roger is sometimes indistinguishable from the other men who compose those younger forces surrounding David Marshall, who will carry on the business of business but who are incapable of inheriting David's style. The architect Bingham, whose ambition is in the mold of Roger, argues with David that "the noblest mountain in the world, when you come right down to details, is only a heap of dirt and rocks strewn over with sticks and stones. But if you will just step back far enough to get the proper point of view—well, you know what the painters can do with such things as these."

But David cannot be deceived: "I can't step back, Bingham. I started here; I've stayed here; I belong here. I'm living right *on* your mountain, and its sticks and stones are all about me. Don't ask me to see them for anything else; don't ask me to call them anything else."

"Make your impression while you may," Bingham urges: "This is the time—this very year. The man who makes his mark here today will enjoy a fame which will spread as the fame of the city spreads and its power and prosperity increases. You know what we are destined to be—a hundred times greater than we are today. Fasten your name on the town, and your name will grow as the town itself does."

It is the ancient appeal to the artist to exploit, to reduce his vision, to barter his soul for name and fame "today." But the merchant was unable to be less than he was. "To David Marshall, art in all its forms was an inexplicable thing..." He had no language for it, only a passion, a devotion:

Why did he go to bed at half-past nine? In order that he might be at the store at half-past seven. Why must he be at the store by half-past seven? ... because it was the only thing he wanted to do; because it was the only thing he could do; because it was the only thing he was pleased and proud to do; because it was the sole thing which enabled him to look upon himself as a useful, stable, honored member of society.

David, like Fuller—or Fuller, like David—worked within the limits of the material at hand. Neither felt himself responsible for social consequences beyond the work itself: well-made, the object created was its own morality and its own reward. "We have enough to bother us," says David, "without reporters coming around." That was the ideal.

As David declined, we are told, the "dismay" of his family "was now such as might occur at the Mint if the great stamp were suddenly and of its own accord to cease its coinage of double-eagles and to sink into a silence of supine idleness." He is Mint, he is carry-all, the conscience and the clarity of the Procession, set slightly apart.

Conceivably, the values of David Marshall never reigned except within the imagination of Henry Blake Fuller. Conceivably, the Procession is the best of all possible processions, neither so ominous nor so destructive as we may fear. All that is finally certain is that Fuller, having described the conflict of values for himself in his own decades, describes it as well for us in ours. Few literary restorations are more to the present point.

With the Procession

I

When old Mr. Marshall finally took to his bed, the household viewed this action with more surprise than sympathy, and with more impatience than surprise. It seemed like the breaking down of a machine whose trustworthiness had been hitherto infallible; his family were almost forced to the acknowledgement that he was but a mere human being after all. They had enjoyed a certain intimacy with him, in lengths varying with their respective ages, but they had never made a full avowal that his being rested on any tangible physical basis. Rather had they fallen into the way of considering him as a disembodied intelligence, whose sole function was to direct the transmutation of values and credits and resources and opportunities into the creature comforts demanded by the state of life unto which it had please Providence to call them; and their dismay was now such as might occur at the Mint if the great stamp were suddenly and of its own accord to cease its coinage of double-eagles and to sink into a silence of supine idleness. His wife and children acknowledged, indeed, his head and his hands—those it were impossible to overlook; but his head stopped with the rim of his collar, while his hands—those long, lean hands, freckled, tufted goldishly between joints and knuckles—they never followed beyond the plain gilt sleeve-buttons (marked with a Roman M) which secured the overlapping of his cuffs. No, poor old David Marshall was like one of the early Tuscan arch-angels, whose scattered members are connected by draperies merely, with no acknowledged organism within; nor were his shining qualities fully recognized until the resolutions passed by the Association of Wholesale Grocers reached the hands of his bereaved—

But this is no way to begin.

The grimy lattice-work of the drawbridge swung to slowly, the steam-tug blackened the dull air and roiled the turbid water as it dragged its schooner on towards the lumber-yards of the South Branch, and a long line of waiting vehicles took up their interrupted course through the smoke and the stench as they filed across the stream into the thick of business beyond: first a yellow street-car; then a robust truck laden with rattling sheet-iron, or piled high with fresh wooden pails and willow baskets; then a junk-cart bearing a pair of dwarfed and bearded Poles, who bumped in unison with the jars of its clattering springs; then, perhaps, a bespattered buggy, with reins jerked by a pair of sinewy and impatient hands. Then more street-cars; then a butcher's cart loaded with the carcasses of calves—red, black, piebald—or an express wagon with a yellow cur yelping from its rear; then, it may be, an insolently venturesome landau, with crested panel and top-booted coachman. Then drays and omnibuses and more street-cars; then, presently, somewhere in the line, between the tail end of one truck and the menacing tongue of another, a family carry-all—a carry-all loaded with its family, driven by a man of all work, drawn by a slight and amiable old mare, and encumbered with luggage which shows the labels of half the hotels of Europe.

It is a very capable and comprehensive vehicle, as convey-ances of that kind go. It is not new, it is not precisely in the mode; but it shows material and workmanship of the best grade, and it is washed, oiled, polished with scrupulous care. It ad-

4

vances with some deliberation, and one might fancy hearing in the rattle of its tires, or in the suppressed flapping of its rear curtain, a word of plaintive protest. "I am not of the great world," it seems to say; "I make no pretence to fashion. We are steady and solid, but we are not precisely in society, and we are far, very far indeed, from any attempt to cut a great figure. However, do not misunderstand our position; it is not that we are under, nor that we are exactly aside; perhaps we have been left just a little behind. Yes, that might express it—just a little behind."

How are they to catch up again—how rejoin the great caravan whose fast and furious pace never ceases, never slackens? Not, assuredly, by the help of the little sorrel mare, whose white mane swings so mildly, and whose pale eyelashes droop so diffidently when some official hand at a crowded crossing brings her to a temporary stand-still. Not by the help of the coachman, who wears a sack-coat and a derby hat, and whose frank, good-natured face turns about occasionally for a friendly participation in the talk that is going on behind. Can it be, then, that any hopes for an accelerated movement are packed away in the bulging portmanteau which rests squeezed in between the coachman's legs? Two stout straps keep it from bursting, and the crinkled brown leather of its sides is completely pasted over with the mementoes used by the hosts of the Old World to speed the parting guest. "London" and "Paris" shine in the lustre of the last fortnight; "Tangier" is distinctly visible; "Buda-Pest" may be readily inferred despite the overlapping labels of "Wien" and "Bâle"; while away off to one corner a crumpled and lingering shred points back, though uncertainly, to the Parthenon and the Acropolis. And in the midst of this flowery field is planted a large M after the best style of the White Star Line.

Who has come home bearing all these sheaves?

Is it, to begin with, the young girl who shares the front seat

5

with the driver, and who faces with an innocent unconcern all the clamor and evil of a great city? There is a half-smile on her red lips, and her black eyes sparkle with a girlish gayety—for she does not know how bad the world is. At the same time her chin advances confidently, and her dark eyebrows contract with a certain soft imperiousness—for she does not know how hard the world is nor how unyielding. Sometimes she withdraws her glance from the jostling throng to study the untidy and overlapping labels on the big portmanteau; she betrays a certain curiosity, but she shows at the same time a full determination not to seem over-impressed. No, the returned traveller is not Rosy Marshall; all that *she* knows of life she has learned from the broadcast cheapness of English story-tellers and from a short year's schooling in New York.

Is it, then, the older girl who fills half of the rear seat and who, as the cruel phrase goes, will never see thirty again? She seems to be tall and lean, and one divines, somehow, that her back is narrow and of a slab-like flatness. Her forehead is high and full, and its bulging outlines are but slightly softened by a thin and dishevelled bang. Her eyes are of a light and faded blue, and have the peculiar stare which results from over-full eyeballs when completely bordered by white. Her long fingers show knotted joints and nails that seem hopelessly plebeian; sometimes she draws on open-work lace mitts, and then her hands appear to be embroiling each other in a mutual tragedy. No, poor Jane is thoroughly, incorruptibly indigenous; she is the best and dearest girl in half the world, as you shall see; but all her experiences have lain between Sandusky and Omaha.

Perhaps, then, the returned traveller is the elderly woman seated by her side. Perhaps—and perhaps not. For she seems a bit too dry and sapless and self-contained—as little susceptible, in fact, to the gentle dews of travel as an umbrella in a waterproof case. Moreover, it is doubtful if her bonnet would pass current beyond the national confines. One surmises that she

6

became years ago the victim of arrested development; that she is a kind of antiquated villager—a geologic survival from an earlier age; that she is a house-keeper cumbered and encompassed by minute cares largely of her own making. It is an easy guess that, for Eliza Marshall, London is in another world, that Tangier is but a remote and impracticable abstraction, and that all her strength and fortitude might be necessary merely to make the trip to Peoria.

There is but one other occupant of the carriage remaining— the only one, after all, who can or could be the owner of the baggage. He is a young man of twenty-three, and he sits with his back to the horse on a little seat which has been let down for the occasion between the usual two; his knees crowd one of the girls and his elbows the other. He seems uncommonly alert and genial; he focusses brilliantly the entire attention of the party. His little black mustache flaunts with a picturesque upward flourish, and it is supplemented by a small tuft at the edge of his underlip—an embellishment which overlays any slight trace of lingering juvenility with an effect which is most knowing, experienced, caprine, if you like, and which makes fair amends for the blanched cheeks, wrinkled brows and haggard eyes that the years have yet to accomplish for him. A navy-blue tie sprinkled with white interlacing circles spreads loosely and carelessly over the lapels of his coat; and while his clever eyes dart intelligently from one side to the other of the crowded thoroughfare, his admiring family make their own shy observations upon his altered physiognomy and his novel apparel— upon his shoes and his hat particularly; they become acquainted thus with the Florentine ideal of foot-wear, and the latest thing evolved by Paris in the way of head-gear.

This young man has passed back through London quite unscathed. Deduce from his costume the independence of his character and the precise slant of his propensities.

The carriage moves on, with a halt here, a spurt there, and

many a jar and jolt between; and Truesdale Marshall throws over the shifting and resounding panorama an eye freshened by a four years' absence and informed by the contemplation of many strange and diverse spectacles. Presently a hundred yards of unimpeded travel ends in a blockade of trucks and street-cars and a smart fusillade of invective. During this enforced stoppage the young man becomes conscious of a vast unfinished structure that towers gauntly overhead through the darkening and thickening air, and for which a litter of iron beams in the roadway itself seems to promise an indefinite continuation skyward.

"Two, three, four—six, seven—nine," he says, craning his neck and casting up his eye. Then, turning with a jocular air to the elder lady opposite, "I don't suppose that Marshall & Belden, for instance, have got up to nine stories yet!"

"Marshall & Belden!" she repeated. Her enunciation was strikingly ejaculatory, and she laid an impatient and unforgiving emphasis upon the latter name. "I don't know what will happen if your father doesn't assert himself pretty soon."

"I should think as much!" observed the elder girl, explosively; "or they will never get up even to seven. The idea of Mr. Belden's proposing to enlarge by taking that ground adjoining! But of course poor pa didn't put up the building himself, nor anything; oh no! So *he* doesn't know whether the walls will stand a couple of extra stories or not. Upon my word," she went on with increased warmth, "I don't feel quite sure whether pa was the one to start the business in the first place and to keep it going along ever since, or whether he's just a new errand-boy, who began there a week ago! August, are we stuck here to stay forever?"

The little sorrel mare started up again and entered upon another stage of her journey. The first lights began to appear in the store-fronts; the newsboys were shrieking the last editions of the evening papers; the frenzied comedy of belated shopping commenced to manifest itself upon the pavements.

The throng of jostling women was especially thick and eager

before a vast and vulgar front whose base was heaped with cheap truck cheaply ticketed, and whose long row of third-story windows was obscured by a great reach of cotton cloth tacked to a flimsy wooden frame. Unprecedented bargains were offered in gigantic letters by the new proprietors, "Eisendrath & Heide . . ."—the rest of the name flapped loosely in the wind.

"Alas, poor Wethersby, I knew him well," observed Marshall, absently. He cast a pensive eye upon the still-remaining name of the former proprietor, and took off his hat to weigh it in his hands with a pretence of deep speculation. "Well, the Philistines haven't got hold of *us* yet, have they?" he remarked, genially; he had not spent six months in Vienna for nothing. "I suppose we are still worth twenty sous in the franc, eh?"

"I suppose," replied his mother, with a grim brevity. She rather groped for his meaning, but she was perfectly certain of her own.

"I guess pa's all right," declared his sister, "as long as he is left alone and not interfered with."

The evening lights doubled and trebled—long rows of them appeared overhead at incalculable altitudes. The gongs of the cable cars clanged more and more imperiously as the crowds surged in great numbers round grip and trailer. The night life of the town began to bestir itself, and little Rosy, from her conspicuous place, beamed with a bright intentness upon its motley spectacle, careless of where her smiles might fall. For her the immodest theatrical poster drooped in the windows of saloons, or caught a transient hold upon the hoardings of uncompleted buildings; brazen blare and gaudy placards (disgusting rather than indecent) invited the passer-by into cheap museums and music-halls; all the unclassifiable riff-raff that is spawned by a great city leered from corners, or slouched along the edge of the gutters, or stood in dark doorways, or sold impossible rubbish in impossible dialects wherever the public indulgence permitted a foothold.

To Rosy's mother all this involved no impropriety. Eliza

Marshall's Chicago was the Chicago of 1860, an Arcadia which, in some dim and inexplicable way, had remained for her an Arcadia still—bigger, noisier, richer, yet different only in degree, and not essentially in kind. She herself had traversed these same streets in the days when they were the streets of a mere town. Jane, accompanying her mother's courses as a child, had seen the town develop into a city. And now Rosy followed in her turn, though the *urbs in horto* of the earlier time existed only in the memory of "old settlers" and in the device of the municipal seal, while the great Black City stood out as a threatening and evil actuality. Mild old Mabel had drawn them all in turn or together, and had philosophized upon the facts as little as any of them; but Rosy's brother (who had been about, and who knew more than he was ever likely to tell) looked round at her now and then with a vague discomfort.

"There!" called their mother, suddenly; "did you see that?" A big lumpish figure on the crossing had loomed up at the mare's head, a rough hand had seized her bridle, and a raw voice with a rawer brogue had vented a piece of impassioned profanity on both beast and driver. "Well, I don't thank that policeman for hitting Mabel on the nose, I can tell him. August, did you get his number?"

"No 'm," answered the coachman. He turned round familiarly. "I got his breath."

"I should think so," said Truesdale. "And such shoes as they have, and such hands, and such linen! Didn't that fellow see what we were? Couldn't he realize that we pay for the buttons on his coat? Mightn't he have tried to apprehend that we were people of position here long before he had scraped his wretched steerage-money together? And what was it he had working in his cheek?"

"I think I know," responded August mumblingly.

"Like enough," rejoined Truesdale, with his eye upon the coachman's own jaw.

His mother's sputter of indignation died rapidly away. It was, indeed, her notion that the guardians of the public peace should show some degree of sobriety, respect, neatness, and self-control, as well as a reasonable familiarity with the accents of the country; but her Arcadia was full of painful discrepancies, and she did not add to her own pain by too serious an attempt to reconcile them. Besides, what is a policeman compared with a detective?

Mabel, released from the arm of the law, jarred over another line of car tracks, whereon a long row of monsters glared at one another's slow advances with a single great red eye, and then she struck a freer gait on the succeeding stretch of Belgian blocks. Presently she passed a lofty building which rose in colonnades one above another, but whose walls were stained with smoke, whose windows were half full of shattered panes, and whose fraudulent metallic cornice curled over limply and jarred and jangled in the evening breeze—one more of the vicissitudes of mercantile life.

"Well, I'm glad the fire-fiend hasn't got Marshall & Co. yet," said the young man, restored to good-humor by the sight of another's misfortune. He used unconsciously the old firm name.

"But he'd get us fast enough if the insurance was taken off," declared Jane. "Do you know, Dicky," she went on, "how much that item costs us a year? Or have you any idea how much it has amounted to in the last twenty, without our ever getting one cent back? Well, there's ten thousand in the Hartford and eight in the Monongahela and eleven in—"

"Dear me, Jane!" exclaimed her brother, in some surprise; "where do you pick up all this?"

Rosy turned her head half round. "Mr. Brower tells her," she said, with a disdainful brevity.

Her face was indistinct in the twilight, but if its expression corresponded with the inflection of her voice, her nostrils were inflated and her lips were curled in disparagement. To Jane, in

11

her dark corner of the carriage, this was patent enough. Indeed, it was sufficiently obvious to all that Jane's years availed little to save her from the searching criticism of her younger sister, and that Miss Rosamund Marshall bestowed but slight esteem —or, at least, but slight approval—upon Mr. Theodore Brower.

"Supposing he *does* tell me!" called Jane, absurdly allowing herself to be put on the defensive. "It's a mighty good thing, I take it. If there's anybody else in the family but me who knows or cares anything about poor pa's business, I should like to be told who it is!"

"That will do, Jane," sounded her mother's voice in cold correction. "There's no need for you to talk so. Your father has run his own business now for thirty-five years, with every year better than the year before, and I imagine he knows how to look out for himself. Thank goodness, we are on a respectable pavement once more."

Mabel, turning a sudden corner, had given them a quick transition from the rattle and jar of granite to the gentle palpitation that is possible on well-packed macadam. The carriage passed in review a series of towering and glittering hotels, told off a score or more of residences of the elder day, and presently drew up before the gate of an antiquated homestead in the neighborhood of the Panoramas.

"Just the same old place," murmured Truesdale, as he writhed out of his cramped quarters and stood on the carriage-block in the dusk to stretch his legs. "Wonderful how we contrive to stand stock-still in the midst of all this stir and change!"

"H'm!" said Jane, under her breath; "just wait and see!"

II

It was at Vevey, one morning late in August, that Truesdale Marshall received the letter which turned his face homeward— the summons which made it seem obligatory for him to report at headquarters, as he phrased it, without too great a delay. He was pacing along the terrace which bounded the pension garden lakeward, and his eye wandered back and forth between the superscription of the envelope and the distant mountain-shore of Savoy, as it appeared through the tantalizing line of clipped acacias which bordered the roadway that ran below him.

"'Richard T. Marshall, Esq.,'" he read, slowly, with his eye on the accumulation of post-marks and renewed addresses. "They keep it up right along, don't they? I can't make them feel that initials on an envelope are not the best form. I can't bring them to see that 'Esq.' on foreign letters is worse than a superfluity." He referred once more to the mountains of Savoy; they seemed to offer no loophole of escape. "Well, I've got to do it, I suppose."

He made some brief calculations, and found that he could put himself in marching order within a month or so. There was the trunk stored at Geneva; there was that roomful of furniture at Freiburg—Freiburg-im-Breisgau; there was that brace of paintings boxed up in Florence; and there were the frayed and loosely flying ends of many miscellaneous friendships.

"I should think the end of October might do for them," he droned, reflectively. "They can't mean to cut me off any shorter than that."

He saw the steamer taking on passengers between the two rotund chestnut-trees that adorned the end of the stubby little stone pier. Voices of shrieking gladness came across from the coffee-tables on the terrace of the Three Crowns, his nearest neighbor to the right.

"Well, America is meeting me half way," he said; "I don't want to seem reluctant myself. Suppose we make it Southampton, about October 15th?"

Truesdale Marshall had been away from home and friends for about the length of time ordinarily required by a course through college, but it was not at college that most of this period had been passed. He had left Yale at the end of his sophomore year, and had taken passage, not for Chicago, but for Liverpool, compromising thus his full claims on nurture from an alma mater for the more alluring prospect of culture and adventure on the Continent. This supplementary course of self-improvement and self-entertainment had now continued for three years.

He had written back to his family at discreet intervals, his communications not being altogether untinctured, it is true, by considerations of a financial nature; and his sister Jane, who charged herself with the preservation of this correspondence, would have undertaken to reconstruct his route and to make a full report of his movements up to date on ten minutes' notice. She kept his letters in a large box-file that she had teased from her father at the store; and two or three times a year she overhauled her previous entries, so to speak, and added whatever new ones were necessary to bring her books down to the present day.

She pleased herself, on the occasion of such reviews, with the thought that her brother's long absence was so largely and

14

so laboriously educational. There, for example, was his winter and spring at Heidelberg, which she figured as given over to Kant and Hegel. This sojourn was attested by a photograph which showed her brother in a preposterous little round cap, as well as with a bar of sticking-plaster (not markedly philosophical, it must be confessed) upon one cheek.

Again, there was his six months' stay in Paris, during which time he had dabbled in pigments at one of the studios affected by Americans. Her vouchers for this period consisted of several water-colors; they were done in a violent and slap-dash fashion, and had been inspired, apparently, by scenes in the environs of the capital. They were marked "Meudon" and "St. Cloud" and "Suresnes," with the dates; both names and dates were put where they showed up very prominently. Jane was rather overcome by these sketches on a first view, and after she had pinned them up on the walls of her bedroom (she had made no scruple over an immediate individual appropriation) she was obliged to acknowledge that you had to step back some little distance in order to "get them."

Then there was his year at Milan, during which he was engaged in the cultivation of his voice at the Conservatory. "A whole year," said innocent Jane to herself; "think of Dick's staying in one place as long as that!" She made no account of the easily accessible joys of Monte Carlo, but figured him, instead, as running interminable scales at all hours of day and night, and as participating, now and then, in the chorus at the Scala, for which purpose, as he wrote her, he had had a pair of tights made to order. In another letter he sent her a pen-and-ink sketch of himself as he appeared while studying the last act of "Favorita." He explained that the large looking-glasses surrounding him were designed to give the disillusioned Fernando opportunity to see whether his facial expression was corresponding to the nature of the music he was interpreting.

All this completely overpowered poor Jane; it enveloped her

brother's head in a roseate halo; it wrapped him in the sweet and voluminous folds of a never-failing incense; it imparted a warm glow to his coolish summer in the Engadine, and it illumined his archæological prowlings through the Peloponnesus; it opened up a dozen diverging vistas to the enthusiastic girl herself, and advanced her rapidly in long courses of expansion and improvement. Above all, it filled her with a raging impatience for his return. "Between him and me," she would say to herself, "something *may* be done. Pa'll never do anything to get us out of this rut; nor ma. Neither will Roger nor Alice. And Rosy—well, Rosy's too young to count on, yet. But Richard Truesdale Marshall, the younger son of the well-known David Marshall, of Lake Street, recently returned from a long course of travel and study abroad"—she seemed to be quoting from the printed column—"*can.* Especially when assisted by his sister, the clever and intellectual Miss Jane Marshall, who—"

"Oh, bother this bang!" exclaimed Miss Jane Marshall, pettishly. She threw her comb down between pin-cushion and cologne bottle, and flattened a frowning and protesting glance against her mirror. "I guess I'll give up trying to be beautiful, and just be quaint."

David Marshall received his son with less exaltation. He had a vivid recollection of the liberal letter of credit which had started the young man on his way, and this recollection had subsequently been touched up and heightened by the payment of many drafts for varying but considerable amounts; and he was now concerning himself with the practical question, What have I got for my money? He felt his own share in the evolution of this brilliant and cultured youth, whose corona of accomplishments might well dazzle and even abash a plain business person; and he awaited with interest a response to the reasonable interrogation, To what end shall all these means be turned? He received his son with a dry and cautious kindness, determined not to be too precipitate in ascertaining the young man's ideas as to the future—a week more or less could make no great difference now.

David Marshall was a tall, spare man whose slow composure of carriage invested him with a sort of homely dignity. He wore a reddish beard, now largely touched with white—a mixture whose effect prompted the suggestion that his grandfather might have been a Scotchman; and the look from his blue eyes (though now no longer at their brightest) convinced you that his sight was competent to cover the field of vision to which he had elected to restrict himself. He seemed completely serious, to have been so always, to have been born half grown up, to have been dowered at the start with too keen a consciousness of the burdens and responsibilities of life. Coltishness, even by a retrospect of fifty years, it was impossible to attribute to him. You imagined him as having been caught early, broken to harness at once, and kept between the shafts ever since. It was easy to figure him as backing into position with a sweet and reasonable docility—a docility which saw no other course or career for a properly minded young horse, and which looked upon the juvenile antics of others in the herd as an unintelligible and rather reprehensible procedure. He knew what he was for, and his way was before him.

He had acted on his knowledge, and now, at sixty, he seemed still to be travelling over the same long straight road, blinders at his eyes, a high wall on either side, no particular goal in the dusty distance, and an air of patient, self-approving resignation all about him. His burden, too, had increased with the years— just as his rut had grown deeper. Counting his family and his poor relations, and his employés and *their* families and poor relations, five or six hundred people were dependent on him. Many of these, of course, had seats so low that they were almost choked by the dust of the roadway; but others, more pleasantly situated, were able to overlook the enclosing walls and to enjoy the prospect beyond. Among these last was his younger son, who sat in the highest place of all, and thence surveyed the universe.

The Marshall house had been built at the time of the opening of the War, and as far "out" as seemed advisable for a residence of the better sort. In those days no definite building-line had been established, so that it was quite a walk from the front gate to the foot of the front steps. Neither, at that time, was ground too valuable to make a good bit of yard impracticable —so that the house had plenty of space on all sides. It was a low, plain, roomy building with a sort of belvedere and a porch or two. The belvedere was lingeringly reminiscent of the vanishing classic, and the decorative woodwork of the porches showed some faint traces of the romantico-lackadaisical style which filled up the years between the ebb of the Greek and the vulgar flood-tide of Second-empire renaissance. Taken altogether, a sedate, stable, decorous old homestead, fit for the family within it.

In the back yard, behind a latticed screen-work, some shrubs and bushes survived from a garden once luxuriant, but now almost vanished. There had been a cherry-tree, too—a valiant little grower, which put forth a cloud of white blossoms late in every May, and filled a small pail with fruit early in every July. It was thus that Jane was enabled to celebrate her birthday (which fell about this time of year) with a fair-sized cherry pie; and in especially favorable seasons enough cherries were left over to make a small tart for Rosy.

But the atmosphere had years ago become too urban for the poor cherry-tree, which had long since disappeared from mortal ken; and the last of the currant-bushes, too, were holding their own but poorly against the smoke and cinders of metropolitan life. One of Jane's earliest recollections was that of putting on her flat and taking her tin pan and accompanying her mother out to pick currants for the annual jelly-making. Her mother wore a flat, too, and carried a tin pan—both of proportionate size. The flats had long since been cast aside, and the pans had become less necessary with the dwindling of the currant-bushes; but the jelly-making returned with every recurring July. A great many quarts of alien currants and a great many pounds of white sugar were fused in that hot and sticky kitchen, and then the red-stained cloths were hung to dry upon the last remaining bushes. Jane would sometimes reproach her parent with such a proceeding—which seemed to her hardly less reprehensible than the seething of a kid in its mother's milk; but Eliza Marshall had scant receptivity for any such poetical analogies. The cloths, as seen through the lattice-work, had a somewhat sensational aspect; they spoke of battle and murder and sudden death, and sometimes the policeman passing by, if he was a new one, thought for a second that he had stumbled on a "clew."

Eliza Marshall took this risk quite willingly; the idea of buying her jelly ready-made never crossed her mind. No; she made her own year after year, and poured it out into her little glass tumblers, and sealed each tumbler with a half-sheet of note-paper, and marked each sheet according to the sort of jelly it protected—sometimes she made grape or crab-apple, too. She doled out her products very economically during the winter and spring. Then she would discover, about the first of June, that she had a three months' supply still on hand. Then, during the summer, the family would live on jelly and little else.

But she remained, year after year, the same firm, determined, peremptory person in her kitchen; she never spared herself there, and she never spared anybody else.

She gave no more quarter at the front of the house than at the back. To get fresh air into her dim and time-worn parlor and to keep sun and dust and smoke out—this was her one besetting problem. There were those windy days at the end of autumn, after the sprinkling-carts had been withdrawn from the boulevard; there were the days (about three hundred and sixty-five in the year) when the smoke and cinders from the suburban trains made her house as untidy as a switch-yard; and there was her husband's unconquerable propensity for smoking —a pleasure which she compelled him to take outside on the foot pavement. Here, on pleasant evenings, he would walk up and down alone, in a slow, meditative fashion—having little to say and nobody to say it to—until bedtime came.

This came early—from a habit early formed. The Chicago of his young married life had given him little reason for being abroad after half-past nine at night, and he appeared to find little more reason now than then. It would not, indeed, have been impossible to make him see that, in the interval, balls, concerts, spectacles, and such-like urban doings had come on with increasing number and brilliancy, and that there were now more interests to justify a man in remaining up until half-past ten, or even until eleven. But you could not have convinced him that all these opportunities were his.

Yet the consciousness of festivities sometimes obtruded upon his indifference. Now and then on summer evenings, when the wind was from the west, certain brazen discords originating a street or two behind the house would come to advise him that the Circassian girl was on view, or that a convention of lady snake-charmers was in session. Then there would be weeks of winter nights when the frozen macadam in front of the house would ring with a thousand prancing hoofs and rumble for an hour with a steady flow of carriages, and the walls of the great temple of music a few hundred yards to the north would throw back all this clamor, with the added notes of slamming doors and shouted numbers and epic struggles between angry drivers and determined policemen; sometimes he would extend his smoking stroll far enough to skirt the edge of all this Babel. Then, towards midnight, long after all staid and sensible people were abed, the flood would roll back, faster yet under the quiet moon, louder yet through the frosty air. But he never met the Circassian beauty, and he would have found "l'Africaine," for example, both tedious and unreasonable. To him each of these publics was new, and no less new than alien. Besides, it would have seemed an uncanny thing to be abroad and stirring at midnight.

Why did he go to bed at half-past nine? In order that he might be at the store by half-past seven. Why must he be at the store by half-past seven? Because a very large area to the west and northwest of the town looked to him for supplies of teas, coffees, spices, flour, sugar, baking-powder; because he had always been accustomed to furnish these supplies; because it was the only thing he wanted to do; becaue it was the only thing he could do; because it was the only thing he was pleased and proud to do; because it was the sole thing which enabled him to look upon himself as a useful, stable, honored member of society.

But it need not be supposed that the Marshalls in their young married days had lived totally bereft of social diversion. Quite the contrary. They had had tea-parties and card-parties now and then, and more than once they had thrown their house open for a church sociable. But the day came when the church jumped from its old site three blocks away to a new site three miles away. And by that time most of their old neighbors and fellow church-members had gone too—some southward, some northward, some heavenward. Then business, in the guise of big hotels, began marching down the street upon them, and business in all manner of guise ran up towering walls behind them that shut off the summer sun hours before it was due to sink; and traffic rang incessant gongs at their back door, and drew lengthening lines of freight-cars across the lake view from their front one; and Sunday crowds strolled and sprawled over the wide green between the roadway and the waterway, and tramps and beggars and peddlers advanced daily in a steady and disconcerting phalanx, and bolts and bars and chains and gratings and eternal vigilance were all required to keep mine from becoming thine; until, in the year of grace 1893, the Marshalls had almost come to realize that they were living solitary and in a state of siege. But they had never yet thought of capitulation nor of retreat; they were the Old Guard; they were not going to surrender, nor to die either.

As the advance guard of all, old David Marshall frequently occupied the most advanced bastion of all, the parlor bay-window. Here, in the half-dark, he was accustomed to sit and think; and his family let him sit and think, unconscious that it would sometimes be a kindness to break in upon the habit. He pondered on the markets and on the movements of trade; he kept one eye for the shabby wayfarers who threw a longing look upon his basement gratings, and another for the showers of sparks and black plumes of smoke which came to remind him of corporate encroachments upon municipal rights. And here one evening he sat, some few days after his son's return, while a hubbub of female voices came to him from the next room. His sister-in-law from three miles down the street, and his married daughter from ten miles out in the suburbs, had come to show some civility to the returned traveller, and the conjunction of two such stars was not to be effected in silence. Nor was silence to be secured even by a retreat from one room to another.

"Well, pa, you *are* here, sure enough." A hand pulled aside the curtain and made the bay-window a part of the parlor again. "Poking off by yourself, and thinking—*I* know. When I've told you so many times not to."

It was Jane. It was her office to keep the family from disintegration. None of them realized it—hardly she herself.

She perched on the arm of his big chair, placed her hand on his forehead, and looked in his face with a quizzical pretence of impatience. These little passages sometimes occurred in **the** bay-window—hardly anywhere else.

"Well, what is it *this* time?" she asked. Her intention was tender, but her voice issued with a kind of explosive grate—the natural product of vocal cords racked by the lake winds of thirty springs and wrecked by a thousand sudden and violent transitions from heat to cold and back again. "Not Mr. Belden, I hope?"

"No, Jennie. That will come out all right, I expect. We had a talk with the builder about it today."

He looked at her with a kind of wan and patient smile. His own voice was dry, husky, sibilant—sixty years of Lake Michigan.

She smiled back at his "Jennie"; that was always her name on such occasions. "It isn't about Oolong?" she asked, in burlesque anxiety.

"No."

"Well, then, is it the—Sisters?"

"Not the Sisters. They were in last week."

"Guess again, then," said Jane, perseveringly. "Is it—is it the Benevolent Policemen?"

"No, not the Policemen. They won't be around for a month yet."

Her hand dropped to his shoulder and her eyes searched his. To another they might have seemed staring; to him they were only intent. "Poor pa; he's like a ten-pin standing at the end of the alley, isn't he? They all take a turn at him, don't they?"

"I'm afraid that's about it, Jennie." He smiled rather wanly again and smoothed her hand with his own.

"Well, what else is there?" pondered Jane. "Is it the Afro-American bishop raising the mortgage on their chapel?"

"No. I guess the Afro-Americans have about paid things off by this time."

"How lonesome they must leave you? H'm! is it the Michigan Avenue Property Owners assessing you again to fight the choo-choo cars?"

Her father shook his head and almost laughed.

"Is it 'The Wives of the Presidents'? Is it 'The Mothers of Great Men'?"

23

"What a girl!" he said, and laughed aloud. It seemed as if he wanted to laugh.

She eyed him narrowly. "There's only one thing more I can think of," she declared, screwing up her mouth and her eyes. "But I sha'n't ask you that—it's too silly. If I imagined for a moment that you could be thinking about old Mother Van Horn—"

She paused. Her father cast down his eyes half guiltily.

"Don't say you are, pa. That would be too absurd. You, with all the important things you have to carry in your head, to waste a minute on that frowzy old hag! It isn't worth it; it's nonsense."

"I don't know whether it is or not," responded her father, slowly. He passed a careful hand through the fringe of the chair. "That's what I'd like to find out."

"Oh, fiddlesticks!" rejoined Jane. "You sha'n't sit poking here in the dark and thinking of any such thing as that—not another minute. Come in and hear Dick tell how those students in Paris tied him to the wall and daubed him all red and green, and what he did to get even. *That's* worth while. And you haven't seen Aunt Lyddy yet, have you? So is *that*—isn't it? Then come along, do."

III

> " 'When I was a student at Cadiz
> I played on the Spanish guitar;
> I used to make love to the ladies'—"

This brief snatch of song ended with the obvious and, indeed, inevitable rhyme for "Cadiz," and the singer completed the stanza by throwing an arch and rather insinuating glance at the young man who was lounging negligently on the chair beside her own. She herself leaned back rather negligently too, with her feet crossed; her elbows were crooked at varying angles, her fingers pressed imaginary frets or plucked at imaginary strings, and the spectator was supposed to be viewing an Andalusian grace and passion abandoned to the soft yet compelling power of music.

It was thus that Truesdale Marshall was welcomed home by his aunt Lydia.

His aunt Lydia—Mrs. Lydia Rhodes—was a plump and vivacious little brunette of forty, with a gloss on her black hair and a sparkle in her black eyes. She still retained a good deal of the superabundant vitality of youth; in her own house, when the curtains were down and the company not too miscellaneous, she was sometimes equal to a break-down or a cake-walk. She was impelled by social aspirations of the highest nature, and was always lamenting, therefore, that she possessed so little dignity. She was a warm-hearted, impulsive creature, who believed in living while on earth, and she was willing enough to believe that others would live too, so far as opportunity offered. It seemed to Truesdale, just now, as if she might be engaged in a mental review of his probable experiences abroad—there, certainly, was an opportunity offered.

"But now that you are back again we expect you to settle down and be good—a useful member of society, you know." She threw a coquettish smile on the young man and banished the imaginary guitar.

"Oh, really—" began Truesdale, with a flush and a frown. He glanced over his shoulder; his mother and sisters were in animated converse on the other side of the room.

"Yes," his aunt proceeded; "you are old enough to think about marrying. You don't know how pleasant it would be to have a nice little home of your own, and your own little wifey to meet you every evening with a kiss!"

"Dear, dear!" thought Truesdale to himself; "and now she's singing that song to *me!*" He remembered these familiar strains; they had been directed many a time and oft to the ear of his brother Roger. Year by year their plaintive poignancy had grown more acute, along with Roger's strengthening determination to remain a bachelor.

Truesdale found himself wondering whether his aunt's intense allegiance to the idea of married life was the sincere expression of a nature overflowingly affectionate, or a species of sensitive dissimulation cloaking a disappointment which, by this time, might well have come to be numbered among the bygones. For it was now six years since Alfred Rhodes, the gay, the genial, had died. He had cost his wife many anxious moments and a few sleepless nights. He had left her a moderate fortune, an ample freedom, and a boy of eight. She had increased her freedom by sending the boy off to an Eastern school. He visited Eastern relatives during vacation time, and was doomed to a longer course of knickerbockers than it would have pleased him to forecast. His mother's heart still palpitated youthfully; she showed herself in no haste to take her stand in the ranks of the elder generation.

"Yes," Mrs. Rhodes proceeded, "you must get into business, and then we shall have to find some nice girl for you."

"The same thoughtful Aunt Lydia," he observed, ironically. He gave his mustache an upward screw, then dropped his eyes to his knees and his fingers to the rungs of his chair. His design seemed to be to figure a slave shrinking on the auction-block. "Do you mean to say you haven't got one for me already?" He ignored the business side of her proposal.

"Well, you needn't put it *that* way," she rejoined. "You know perfectly well that I am not a match-maker, nor anything like it. And it wouldn't please me at all to have anybody say so of me or to think of me in that way." She was quite sincere in all this.

Truesdale, however, held the opposite view, and, considering all the circumstances, liked his aunt none the less. She *was* a match-maker—a very keen and persistent one; but he felt that her excesses in this direction were to be viewed simply as an acknowledgement to fortune for having guided her own courses to such advantage. She had come out from Trenton some eighteen years before with a pretty face, a light wardrobe, a limited purse, and an invitation (extended by a benevolent aunt) to remain as long as she liked. She had never gone back. She met Alfred Rhodes, Eliza Marshall's younger brother; and from the slight foothold offered by her kindly relative she had advanced to an ample fortune and a complete freedom. She was grateful for all this, and gratitude took the form of her extending, in turn, unlimited invitations to other girls with pretty faces, light purses, and limited wardrobes. She almost always had some comely niece or younger cousin in the house. She drove with them, she shopped with them, she gave teas and receptions for them. She summoned young men in numbers;

she had her billiard-table re-covered; she could always produce sherry and cigars when really put to it; she almost transformed her home into a club-house. "For," said she, "I can never forget how kind Aunt Marcia was to *me!*"

Such wide-spread beneficence as this had not, of course, excluded her sister-in-law's daughters. It was really to her aunt Lydia that Rosamund Marshall was indebted for her year at the New York school; her mother had unquestioningly accepted Mrs. Rhodes's declaration that the institution was eminently fashionable and desirable, and her father had committed her with the greatest confidence and good-will to the conductor of the east-bound Lake Shore express. And it was to her aunt that the girl was now looking, after an obscure and wistful fashion, for an introduction into society, in which, according to the belief of the family, Mrs. Rhodes occupied a secure and brilliant position. Rosamund had been revolving matters in her pretty and self-willed little head, and in her proud and self-willed little heart she had decided upon a formal début.

Her mother was completely nonplussed; she would as soon have wrestled with the differential calculus. "Why, dear me," she stammered, "there's Alice; she never came out, and I don't see but what she's got along all right: good home, nice husband, and everything she wants. And Jane, now—"

"Oh, *Jane!*" said Rosy, in disdain.

Then she sulked, and reproached her mother with the flat and unprofitable summer that had followed her return from school, and asked pointedly if the coming winter was to be like it. "Ha!" exclaimed the poor woman to herself; "Lyddy is to blame for this; I wish she had never mentioned New York!" But the year at school was only a remoter cause; the more immediate one was a pink tea which Rosamund had attended (casually, as it were, and quite informally) a month back. This was the tigress's first taste of blood—a pale, diluted fluid, it is true, but it worked all the effect of a fuller and richer draught.

It developed in Rosamund a sixth sense—one which was to lead her to lengths that none of her kin could have anticipated. And to the rest of the family, clucking and scratching in their own retired and restricted barn-yard, there came the day when they discovered that their little flock contained at least one bird of a different feather—a bird that could paddle about the social pond with the liveliest, and could quack, if need be, with the loudest.

Jane—who had even yet no adequate sense of the strength and pungency of her younger sister's spirit, but who would not in any event have hesitated to rush on an individual martyrdom that might secure some consideration for the collective family— threw herself into the discussion at once.

"No, don't let's have any party or dance or reception or anything at all. Not even a two-by-four tea. Don't let's try to be anybody or know anybody, or give anything or be considered anything. Let's go right on rusting and vegetating; let's just dry up and shake apart and blow away, with nobody the wiser for our having been here or the sorrier for our having gone!"

Her mother heard this outburst with some surprise and not a little resentment. "Well, Jane, you're quite surpassing yourself to-night. What do you mean by all this?"

Jane exploded again.

"I mean that I'm simply tired of being a nothing and a nobody in a family of nothings and nobodies. That's what it comes to. I'm tired of being a bump on a log. I'm tired of sitting on the fence and seeing the procession go by. Why can't *we* go by? Why can't *we* know people? Why can't *we* make ourselves felt? Other folks do."

Mrs. Rhodes passed over in silence this imputation of nullity; she was not so closely related, after all, that she need allow herself to be disturbed by it. But sister Alice took up the cudgel with all the ardor of an immediate connection and all the sensitiveness of a suburban resident. She even forgot the real, essential object of her visit: to intimate to her father that if he would give her a carriage, her husband could pay for the keep of a horse.

She was a contentious blonde, with a thin, aquiline nose and a pair of flashing steel-blue eyes. Several wisps of straw-colored hair blew about her temples.

"Thank you, Jane," she said, hotly; "I don't know that I feel myself a nobody, and I don't feel that I'm exactly a social outcast—even if I *do* live beyond the city limits." She turned back a floating lock with a hasty wave. "It might be to your advantage if you moved somewhere or other yourselves. I don't see how you can expect to see anybody or know anybody as long as you are buried in such a sepulchre as this."

Alice was the radical, the innovator of the family. She often brought her conservative mother to the verge of horror. Hers was the hardy, daring, and unconventional strain of the pioneer. She liked the edge; if the edge was a little ragged, so much the better.

"Ho!" cried Jane, sarcastically. "To see anybody or to know anybody we ought to be out at Riverdale Park, perhaps. Riverdale Park!" she repeated, with scornful emphasis. "There isn't any river; there isn't any dale; there isn't any park. Nothing but a lot of wooden houses scattered over a flat prairie, and a few trees no bigger than a broomstick, and no more leaves on them either. In the morning the men all rush for the train, and the rest of the day the nurse-girls trundle the babies along the plank walks, while 'society' amuses itself. Society consists of Mrs. Smith, Mrs. Brown, Mrs. Jones, and Mrs. Alice Robinson. On Wednesday, Mrs. Smith gives a lunch to Mrs. Brown, Mrs. Jones, and Mrs. Robinson. On Thursday, Mrs. Brown gives a tea to Mrs. Smith, Mrs. Jones, and Mrs. Robinson. On Friday, Mrs. Rob—(no, Mrs. Jones—I'm losing the place) gives a card-party to Mrs. Smith, Mrs. Brown, and Mrs. Robinson—in the daytime, too, mind you. And on Saturday, Mrs. Robinson designs giving a breakfast to Mrs. Smith, Mrs. Brown, and Mrs. Jones, but finds that the cook is packing up her things to leave. Quiet in the suburb for a week. Then Mrs. Smith's sister comes out from town to spend a fortnight. Well, everybody is anxious to see Mrs. Smith's sister—a new face, you know. So, after Mrs. Smith has started the second round with another lunch, Mrs. Brown follows with a tea, as before, for Mrs. Smith, Mrs. Jones, Mrs. Robinson—and Mrs. Smith's sister. Then Mrs. Jones—but you've all played the game: for breakfast I had this and that and the other. That is society in Riverdale Park. It would be too rich for *me!*"

Alice flushed with vexation. Truesdale (who had not come home to treat local society with too great a degree of serious-ness, and who, indeed, was like enough to take his pleasures beyond any bounds that society might set) looked on and listened with a kind of indulgent curiosity—like an explorer listening to the excited pow-wow of some flock of natives in some remote African jungle.

"Yes," retorted Alice, "according to your own confession more happens with us in a week than happens with you in a year. And you might as well acknowledge, at the same time, that there are a few houses in the Park where the carpets are a little less than fifteen years old, and where they don't have hideous old what-nots loaded down with all the stuff accumulated since the year one."

She lifted the corner of a rug with her toe, so as to disclose the threadbare breadth that it concealed, and she threw an ironical eye upon a sort of massive and convoluted buffet which displayed a number of antique Dresden figurines and a pair of old candelabra compounded of tarnished gilt and broken prisms. "And in the Park," she added, "we always have new wall-paper at the beginning of every century—it's a local ordinance!"

"Alice," called her mother, tartly, "take your foot away from that rug. And don't annoy me about that worn breadth; you know very well I've tried everywhere to match it. And don't imagine, either, that I'm going to bundle my wedding presents out of sight for you or anybody else."

"Match it!" cried Alice, unabashed. "Match it? They used the last to carpet the ark." She trod down the corner of the rug with a firm step. Then, with her scornful nostrils and sharply critical eyes, she seemed to be lifting it again.

"Well, then," said her mother. "And now leave it alone." The old lady had not the slightest idea of replacing her time-accustomed patterns by anything more current. Nor was her husband, apparently, of a different mind as concerned the wall-paper. He had followed Jane in from the other room, and he now sat there, sending a careful eye slowly along the old-fashioned border, and finding it impossible to believe that any one could seriously judge it to be grotesquely out of date.

"The carpet's all right, as far as I can see," declared Jane. "What if it *is* fifteen years old? Have you got one at Riverdale that is even fifteen months old? You know you haven't; if you had you'd start a museum of antiques with it. And as for our budging from this dear old place, don't you look for it; we're attached to it, even if you're not. Besides, to move would be to throw away the one advantage that we really have. Why, think of it!" she continued with a gesticulating and wide-eyed eloquence. "We have lived right here in this one house over thirty years. How many families in this town have lived in one house thirty years? Or twenty? Or even ten? We've always had the same door-plate on the same door. We've always had the same number in the directory. We started in a good neighborhood, and we've always stayed here—the only one in all the town that has anything like an old-time flavor and an atmosphere of its own—the only one where nice people have always lived and do live yet. Isn't that better than a course of flats up one street and down another? Isn't that better than a grand chain through a lot of shingle-shangled cottages in the suburbs? I should say so. What are they doing in the East now? They're going back to their old neighborhoods, and the people who haven't left them at all are the ones who are right on the top of the pile. We might have some new furniture or something of the sort, perhaps; but that's different from asking the moving-wagons to come and cart us out on to the prairie."

David Marshall followed his daughter's harangue with an indulgent interest and a sympathy by no means scant. He had no profound apprehension of social values, and no clear-cut conception of a social career; but he appreciated her loyalty to her lifelong home and to all its belongings and surroundings. He had reason for supposing that this loyalty would extend to himself; but Jane was wound up to go, and had no idea of allowing anything to stand in the way of her disposal of the question in all its bearings.

"I suppose," she went on, inexorably, "that we imagine ourselves to be 'prominent citizens.' Well, we make a mistake if we do. We may have been ten years ago, but not now. We've just been falling, falling, falling behind—that's the amount of it. Now, honest, pa, dear, do the papers ever come to you nowadays to know what you think about political prospects or to ask your opinion on the last new street-car route proposed? Or do they send men around for trade statistics who jubilate in the issue of Jan. one because we sold five thousand more barrels of flour this year than last? Now, do they?"

Marshall could not escape the justness of this pointed presentation of new conditions. "We have enough to bother us," he said, with a slow reluctance, "without reporters coming round."

"There it is," continued Jane. "Yes, and who cares nowadays about the volume of the lumber trade or the mortality at the stock-yards? Why, just those people themselves. The fact is, the town has moved to a higher plane, and we've got to move with it, or else get left. Why, dear me, if it wasn't for an intellectual daughter who had the gift of language and who wrote papers and read them at the club, this family would have scarcely a connection with latter-day society."

"Good for you, Jane," called her brother. "Give me some of them to read."

"They're pretty good,' said their father, unruffledly judicial. Jane was in the habit of reading him passages that she considered particularly effective. In listening to her perorations he sometimes felt himself as assisting at the liquidation of the universe.

"Now, here we are,' proceeded Jane, with unabated exegetical energy, "an old family, with position and plenty of means and everything to make an impression. Why can't we do it? Why can't we manage to assert ourselves? I'm not speaking for myself, of course; I'm a back number"—this half hysterically, between a gulp and a giggle—"I'm 'gone beyond recall,' and nobody knows that better than I myself. No; I'm speaking for all of us. Besides, here's Rosy, just coming up, and—"

"Thank you, Jane," remarked Rosamund, with some acerbity. "You needn't mind me. I can look after myself."

"—and it seems to me," went on Jane, ardently, "that people who have succeeded might just as well give some outer token of it. I declare, when I called on Mrs. Bates and went over the place and compared their house and their way of living with ours—"

Her aunt looked up suddenly. "Mrs. Bates? What Mrs. Bates? Mrs. Granger Bates?"

"Yes. When I saw what magnificent style she lived in, and how she had about everything that—"

"So you know Mrs. Bates, too," her aunt again interrupted. "Pleasant woman, isn't she? Have I ever told you how she and I used to play backgammon together at St. Augustine?"

"*Have* you?" muttered Jane. "I should think you had—a dozen times over!"

"And what were you doing at *her* house, may I ask?" her

aunt queried further. The geniality of this interrogation hardly concealed its crudity; Jane felt herself accused of an incongruous and inexplicable intrusion into a region of unaccustomed splendor and distinction.

"Oh, she was collecting money for her working-girls' lunchroom," volunteered Rosy, with a cruel bluntness.

Jane threw an air of outraged dignity upon her younger sister. "So I was. And I spent a very pleasant hour with her," she said, with some stateliness. "And I am going there next Wednesday to lunch," she added.

Her aunt looked at her with increasing consideration. She herself had never been honored with an invitation to the house of Mrs. Granger Bates—though rather than fail to respond to such an invitation she would have crawled there (a trifle of some fourteen squares) on her hands and knees. "Have you known her long?"

"Since ten this morning," contributed Rosy.

"Always," corrected Jane, with a whimsical brevity.

"And how do you find her?" persisted Mrs. Rhodes, with a curious intentness. "Dear me!" she laughed, self-consciously, "how she did hate to be beaten! How vexed she always was when I began throwing off first! How she would bang her dice-box! How she would—"

"She's perfectly grand!" declared Jane, with the loud enthusiasm of a new and fervent loyalty. "She's the finest woman I ever met. She's the best woman in the world!" The poor girl attested her earnestness by a tremble in her voice and a tear in each eye. "And she spoke so nicely of you, poppy," Jane went on, turning to her father.

"Did she?" said her father, in return. And a quiet smile of reminiscence played round his lips for full five minutes.

"And she inquired about all of us," Jane proceeded. "She wants to renew the acquaintance, I think. And she asked about Rosy, too—whether she was pretty and bright; and I said she

35

was. I expect she's inclined to take an interest in you," said Jane, in conclusion, turning towards her sister and dropping these few coals of fire upon her head.

Rosamund caught the proper tone from her aunt and bowed in unaccustomed meekness to this shower. Alice, however, as a confirmed and condemned suburbanite, had no idea of exhibiting any great interest in one of the acknowledged leaders of urban society—an interest which, from the very nature of things, could have been but futile and unproductive. She accordingly toyed carelessly and absently with the evening paper, as it lay on the centre-table.

"H'm," she observed, presently, "those game-dinners at the Pacific are still going on, aren't they? To-night's the thirty-eighth. Nice things, too, as I remember them. That's the way I learned to like venison. Here are some of the people to be there—your Mrs. Bates among them." She looked across to her father. "Why didn't *you* go?"

"Give me that paper, Alice," her mother called, with a sharp and sudden cry. She ran her eye down its column and then turned to her husband. "Why, David, how did you happen to forget? You know I wouldn't have missed this for anything."

Marshall checked his lingering smile. He looked at his wife with an embarrassed pain, and then dropped his eyes to the carpet. "There must have been some misunderstanding," he stammered. "The invitation was delayed—or it miscarried. Perhaps it went to the store and got mixed up with the mail there," he ventured; any improbability would do to soften the shock.

"Delayed! Miscarried!" cried Jane, in an acute access of anger and indignation. "Don't believe it! We're dropped, that's all! Well, what else can we expect? How are we going to hold our own against all these thousands and thousands of newcomers if we don't *do* anything? That's what I've been telling you all along. We've got to wake up and make an effort. Give me that paper." She snatched it from her mother. "Yes, they'll all be there—the Hubbards, the Gages, and the whole crowd of

Parmelees, and Kittie Corwith and her father, and all the rest, and—and the Beldens! The Beldens—there!" She turned fiercely on her mother. "What do you think of that?"

Eliza Marshall was cut to the quick. For twenty years and more she had attended this annual dinner; she had attached herself there to former friends and neighbors, who listened indulgently to her narrow little dribble of reminiscent gossip— the gossip and reminiscences of the smaller town and the earlier day. This dinner was her sole remaining connection (little as she had realized it) with the great and complex city of the present day, just as it was the sole reason for her plum-colored silk and for her husband's dress-coat; and the cutting of this last cable set her completely adrift on the wide and forlorn sea of utter social neglect. And the Beldens!—that was the last straw of all. She seemed to see her husband crowded from his seat at that cheery board by a man whom he himself had taken up and made—a man who was trying to push him from the social world, just as he was trying to push him out of the control of the business which he had founded and developed. It was all more than she could bear.

Jane rushed headlong into another mood. "Oh, well, the end of the world hasn't come if we *are* frozen out. And perhaps we're not, anyway; the invite may get round to-morrow—who knows? So don't let's order our sackcloth and ashes quite yet awhile. Life is still worth living, and we have got several other strings to our bow.

"This one, for instance," nodding in the direction of Rosy, towards whom she seemed inexhaustibly forgiving. "I have the honor to present to the waiting world Miss Rosamund Marshall, the bud of the season and the success of the century. Also her brother, Mr. Truesdale Marshall, who has come home stuffed full of accomplishments, and who will now proceed to show them. He sings—"

She stepped across to her brother, slipped her arm through his, and drew him towards the rug in the middle of the room.

Her height was within an inch of his own. She bowed him over the edge of the rug as over a row of footlights, crooked his other arm so that his hand was placed over his heart, put her own hand sprawlingly in a like position, threw back her head, and abandoned herself to a shrill succession of scales and roulades.

"Why don't you begin?" she presently broke off to inquire.

"What a girl you are!" he said. He looked a bit sheepishly in the direction of his father; then he stepped behind his sister, laid a hand on each of her imperceptible biceps, and turned her face round to the wall.

But Jane faced about at once. "Well, then, he paints—"

She dragged him toward the centre-table, grasped his wrist, and forced him to make several dabs and passes at the fatal newspaper, which still lay there with a bland impassivity between drop-light and book-rack. "That's how we dash off our little sketches," she declared.

"Goodness, Jane!" cried Alice, "you've almost upset the whole inkstand!"

"And what else is there?" cried Jane, whose mood was mounting higher. She clamped her hand on her disordered bang. "Why, of course! He fences!—aha!"

To this address Truesdale allowed himself to respond. He had no wish to obtrude his musical and artistic doings upon his father until a more definite *modus vivendi* had been brought about; but he could no longer lend himself passively to being made an absurdity by the over-enthusiasm of his sister. Fencing, now, was a manly art of which his father might not disapprove.

"On guard!" he cried. With his right hand he snatched up a paper-cutter from the table, curled up his left arm behind him, threw one of his long legs out in front and landed it with a *flump!* on the floor five feet ahead of his initial stand-point.

"Hurray!" cried Jane, shrilly. "What other girls do you know who've got a brother like this?" She snatched up a brass-edged ruler that had lain alongside the paper-cutter. Mrs. Rhodes started back; Alice's husband, who had come in to lead the homeward march to Riverside Park, paused astonished on the threshold.

"On guard!" echoed Jane in turn. With a *flump!* of her own she threw herself into an imitation of the angular crouch that her brother had assumed. "Go it!" she called, and began to hack at the paper-cutter with her ruler.

Save for the clash of weapons there was a complete silence. Suddenly Truesdale reversed his position. Jane did the same, bringing a sudden and unaccustomed weight upon her other foot. Her knee cracked loudly. Everybody heard it. Rosy snickered.

Jane crossed the room and sat down in a shady corner. In that ten seconds she felt ten years older.

"Where's pa?" she asked her mother in a sour tone, after Alice and her aunt had left the house. "I do hope"—crossly—"that the next time you let any of those wretched old women take anything away you'll have them pay for it in advance."

"I guess your father isn't bothering much about a bedstead and a few old chairs," retorted her mother. "If you want to know what he's thinking about, it's that Belden again."

"Belden?"

"Yes. He has decided finally to let your father put on those two extra stories, and what do you think he wants in exchange? He wants to make the firm over into a stock company. He's fixing a place for that boy of his—that's what."

"Well, haven't we got a boy, too?" retorted Jane, severely. She went out, and gave the door a loud slam behind her.

But David Marshall, back again in the bay-window, was thinking neither of the sinuosities of Mother Van Horn, nor of the aggressions of his junior partner, nor even of the just-concluding courses of the annual game-dinner. His thoughts had slipped back into the early times; he and Sue Lathrop (the Mrs. Granger Bates of to-day) were sitting together in the old, long-vanished Metropolitan Hall listening to the "Nightingale Serenaders," and the year was 'fifty-seven.

39

IV

"Well, here goes!" said Jane, half aloud, with her foot on the lowest of the glistening granite steps. The steps led up to the ponderous pillared arches of a grandiose and massive porch; above the porch a sturdy and rugged balustrade half intercepted the rough faced glitter of a vast and variegated façade; and higher still the morning sun shattered its beams over a tumult of angular roofs and towering chimneys.

"It *is* swell, I declare!" said Jane, with her eye on the wrought-iron work of the outer doors and the jewels and bevels of the inner-ones.

"Where is the thing-a-ma-jig, anyway?" she inquired of herself. She was searching for the doorbell, and she fell back on her own rustic lingo in order to ward off the incipient panic caused by this overwhelming splendor. "Oh, here it is! There!" She gave a push. "And now I'm in for it." She had decided to take the richest and best-known and most fashionable woman on her list so start with; the worst over at the beginning, she thought, the rest would follow easily enough.

"I suppose the 'maid' will wear a cap and a silver tray," she observed further. "Or will it be a gold one, with diamonds around the edge?"

The door-knob turned from within. "Is Mrs. Bates—" she began.

The door opened half way. A grave, smooth-shaven man appeared; his chin and upper lip had the mottled smudge that shows in so many of those conscientious portraits of the olden time.

"Gracious me!" said the startled Jane to herself. She dropped her disconcerted vision to the door-mat. Then she saw that the man wore knee-breeches and black silk stockings.

"Heaven be merciful!" was her inward cry. "It's a footman, as I live. I've been reading about them all my life, and now I've met one. But I never suspected that there was really anything of the kind in *this* town!"

She left the contemplation of the servant's pumps and stockings, and began to grapple fiercely with the catch of her hand-bag.

The man, in the meanwhile, studied her with a searching gravity, and, as it seemed, with some disapproval. The splendor of the front that his master presented to the world had indeed intimidated poor Jane; but there were many others upon whom it had no deterring effect at all. Some of these brought art-books in monthly parts; others brought polish for the piano legs. Many of them were quite as prepossessing in appearance as Jane was; some of them were much less plain and dowdy; few of them were so recklessly indiscreet as to betray themselves at the threshold by exhibiting a black leather bag.

"There!" remarked Jane to the footman, "I knew I should get at it eventually." She smiled at him with a friendly good-will; she acknowledged him as a human being, and she hoped to propitiate him into the concession that she herself was nothing less.

The man took her card, which was fortunately as correct as the most discreet and contemporaneous stationer could fashion. He decided that he was running no risk with his mistress, and "Miss Jane Marshall" was permitted to pass the gate.

She was ushered into a small reception-room. The hard-wood floor was partly covered by a meagre Persian rug. There was a plain sofa full of forbidding angles, and a scantily upholstered chair which insisted upon nobody's remaining longer than necessary. But through the narrow door Jane caught branching vistas of room after room heaped up with the pillage of a sacked and ravaged globe, and of a stairway which led with a wide sweep to regions of unimaginable glories above.

"Did you ever!" exclaimed Jane. It was of the footman that she was speaking; he, in fact, loomed up to the practical eclipse of all this luxury and display. "Only eighty years from the Massacre, and hardly eight hundred feet from the Monument!"

Presently she heard a tapping and a rustling without. She thought that she might lean a few inches to one side with no risk of being detected in an impropriety, and she was rewarded by seeing the splendid vacuity of the grand stairway finally filled —filled more completely, more amply, than she could have imagined possible through the passage of one person merely. A woman of fifty or more was descending with a slow and somewhat ponderous stateliness. She wore an elaborate morning gown with a broad plait down the back, and an immensity of superfluous material in the sleeves. Her person was broad, her bosom ample, and her voluminous gray hair was tossed and fretted about the temples after the fashion of a marquise of the old régime. Jane set her jaw and clamped her knotty fingers to the two edges of her inhospitable chair.

"I don't care if she *is* so rich," she muttered, "and so famous and so fashionable and so terribly handsome; she can't bear *me* down."

The woman reached the bottom step, and took a turn that for a moment carried her out of sight. At the same time the sound of her footsteps was silenced by one of the big rugs that covered the floor of the wide and roomy hall. But Jane had had a glimpse, and she knew with whom she was to deal—with one of the big, the broad, the great, the triumphant; with one of a Roman amplitude and vigor, an Indian keenness and sagacity, an American ambition and determination; with one who baffles circumstance and almost masters fate—with one of the conquerors, in short.

"I don't hear her," thought the expectant girl, in some trepidation; "but, all the same, she's got to cross that bare space just outside the door before—yes, there's her step! And here she is herself!"

Mrs. Bates appeared in the doorway. She had a strong nose of the lofty Roman type; her bosom heaved with breaths deep, but quiet and regular. She had a pair of large, full blue eyes, and these she now fixed on Jane with an expression of rather cold questioning.

"Miss Marshall?" Her voice was firm, smooth, even, rich, deep. She advanced a foot or two within the room and remained standing there.

"Yes," responded Jane, in unnecessary corroboration. She rose mechanically from her meagre chair. "I have come to see you," she began, awkwardly, "about a charity that I am interested in —no, not exactly a charity, but—"

At the ominous word "charity" Mrs. Bates's eyes took on a still colder gleam. She faced poor Jane with the broad, even, pitiless glare of a chilled-steel mirror.

"Really," she began, "I have a great many demands of this kind made on me; a great many—more than might generally be imagined." She showed none of the embarrassed evasion peculiar to the woman on whom such requisitions are made but at infrequent intervals; she employed the decisive, business-like tone of a woman of whom such requests are made daily. Jane seemed to see negation coldly crystallizing before her eyes, and she gave a mortified groan to find herself drawn so near to the brink of humiliation. She had never begged before, and she registered an inward vow never to beg again.

"You don't know *me* from Adam," she blurted out, at her bluntest and crudest, "but you must know my aunt, Mrs.

Rhodes. I have heard her speak of you very often. She met you at St. Augustine, last winter."

"Mrs. Rhodes?" the other repeated, doubtfully. She made her eyebrows take their part in an inquiring glance, and bestowed the result upon her caller.

"Yes," insisted Jane; "Mrs. A. L. Rhodes. She lives on Michigan—near Thirtieth."

"Mrs. Rhodes?"—again thoughtfully repeated. She seemed to move her head in doubt. "I *do* go to Florida every winter, and sometimes, on the way to our place, I stop for a day or two at St. Augustine—yes."

She looked at Jane again, as if to say, "That is really the best I can do for you."

"She played backgammon with you there," Jane still persisted —"on the hotel veranda. I've heard her say so twenty times."

Mrs. Bates did not change her expression. "Backgammon? Yes, I am very fond of backgammon; I play it a great deal. Mr. Bates keeps a board in the car especially for me. I'm always glad to meet anybody who cares to play; and it's pleasant, I'm sure, to be on easy terms with one's fellow-travellers."

She laid one hand in the other and gave an imperceptible sigh; she wore a great many rings. "What more can I say for you than that?"—such seemed to be the meaning of the expression now on her face.

"My father"—began Jane; she was loud, slow, deliberate, emphatic. What could the woman mean by receiving her in such a fashion? Were the Marshalls mere upstarts, nobodies, newcomers, that they must be snubbed and turned aside in any such way as this? Jane's eyes blinked and her nostrils quivered. "My father," she began again, in the same tone, "is David Marshall. He is very well known, I believe, in Chicago. We have lived here a great many years. It seems to me that there ought to—"

"David Marshall?" repeated Mrs. Bates, gently. "Ah, I *do*

know David Marshall—yes," she said; "or did—a good many years ago." She looked up into Jane's face now with a completely altered expression. Her glance was curious and searching, but it was very kindly. "And you are David Marshall's daughter?" She smiled indulgently at Jane's outburst of spunk. "Really —David Marshall's daughter?"

"Yes," answered Jane, with a gruff brevity. She was far from ready to be placated yet.

"David Marshall's daughter! Then, my dear child, why not have said so in the first place, without lugging in everybody and everything else you could think of? Hasn't your father ever spoken of me? And how is he, anyway? I haven't seen him—to really speak to him—for fifteen years. It may be even more."

She seemed to have laid hands on a heavy bar, to have wrenched it from its holds, to have flung it aside from the footpath, and to be inviting Jane to advance without let or hindrance.

But Jane stood there with pique in her breast, and her long thin arms laid rigid against her sides. "Let her 'dear child' me, if she wants to; she sha'n't bring me around in any such way as that."

All this, however, availed little against Mrs. Bates's new manner. The citadel so closely sealed to charity was throwing itself wide open to memory. The drawbridge was lowered, and the late enemy was invited to advance as a friend.

Nay, urged. Mrs. Bates presently seized Jane's unwilling hands. She gathered those poor, stiff, knotted fingers into two crackling bundles within her own plump and warm palms, squeezed them forcibly, and looked into Jane's face with all imaginable kindness. "I had just that temper once myself," she said.

The sluice-gates of caution and reserve were opening wide; the streams of tenderness and sympathy were bubbling and fretting to take their course.

"And your father is well? And you are living in the same old place? Oh, this terrible town! You can't keep your old friends; you can hardly know your new ones. We are only a mile or two apart, and yet it is the same as if it were a hundred."

Jane yielded up her hands half unwillingly. She could not, in spite of herself, remain completely unrelenting, but she was determined not to permit herself to be patronized. "Yes, we live in the same old place. And in the same old way," she added —in the spirit of concession.

Mrs. Bates studied her face intently. "Do you look like him —like your father?"

"No," answered Jane. "Not so very much. Nor like any of the rest of the family." The statue was beginning to melt. "I'm unique." And another drop fell.

"Don't slander yourself," She tapped Jane lightly on the shoulder.

Jane looked at her with a protesting, or at least a questioning, seriousness. It had the usual effect of a wild stare. "I wasn't meaning to," she said, shortly, and began to congeal again. She also shrugged her shoulder; she was not quite ready yet to be tapped and patted.

"But don't remain standing, child," Mrs. Bates proceeded, genially. She motioned Jane back to her chair, and herself advanced to the roomier sofa. "Or, no; this little pen is like a refrigerator to-day; it's so hard, every fall, to get the steam heat running as it should. Come; it ought to be warmer in the music-room.

"The fact is," she proceeded, as they passed through the hall, "that I have a spare hour on my hands this morning—the first in a month. My music-teacher has just sent word that she is down with a cold. You shall have as much of that hour as you wish. So tell me all about your plans; I dare say I can scrape together a few pennies for Jane Marshall."

"Her music-teacher!" thought Jane. She was not yet so far appeased nor so far forgetful of her own initial awkwardness as to refrain from searching out the joints in the other's armor. "What does a woman of fifty-five want to be taking music-lessons for?"

The music-room was a lofty and spacious apartment done completely in hard-woods; its panelled walls and ceiling rang with a magnificent sonority as the two pairs of feet moved across the mirror-like marquetry of the floor.

To one side stood a concert-grand; its case was so unique and so luxurious that even Jane was conscious of its having been made by special order and from a special design. Close at hand stood a tall music-stand in style to correspond. It was laden with handsomely bound scores of all the German classics and the usual operas of the French and Italian schools. These were all ranged in precise order; nothing there seemed to have been disturbed for a year past. "My! isn't it grand!" sighed Jane. She already felt herself succumbing beneath these accumulated splendors.

Mrs. Bates carelessly seated herself on the piano-stool, with her back to the instrument. "I don't suppose," she observed, casually, "that I have sat down here for a month."

"What!" cried Jane, with a stare. "If I had such a lovely room as this I should play in it every day."

"Dear me," rejoined Mrs. Bates, "what pleasure could I get from practising in this great barn of a place, that isn't half full until you've got seventy or eighty people in it? Or on this big sprawling thing?"—thrusting out her elbow backward towards the shimmering cover of the key-board.

"So then," said Jane to herself, "it's all for show. I knew it was. I don't believe she can play a single note."

"What do you suppose happened to me last winter?" Mrs. Bates went on. "I had the greatest setback of my life. I asked to join the Amateur Musical Club. They wouldn't let me in."

"Why not?"

"Well, I played before their committee, and then the secretary wrote me a note. It was a nice enough note, of course, but I knew what it meant. I see now well enough that my fingers *were* rather stiffer than I realized, and that my 'Twinkling Sprays' and 'Fluttering Zephyrs' were not quite up to date. They wanted Grieg and Lassen and Chopin. 'Very well,' said I, 'just wait.' Now, I never knuckle under. I never give up. So I sent right out for a teacher. I practised scales an hour a day for weeks and months. Granger thought I was going crazy. I tackled Grieg and Lassen and Chopin—yes, and Tschaikowsky, too. I'm going to play for that committee next month. Let me see if they'll dare to vote me out again!"

"Oh, *that's* it!" thought Jane. She was beginning to feel desirous of meting out exact and even handed justice. She found it impossible to withhold respect from so much grit and determination.

"But your father liked those old-time things, and so did all the other young men." Mrs. Bates creased and folded the end of one of her long sleeves, and seemed lapsing into a retrospective mood. "Why, some evenings they used to sit two deep around the room to hear me do the 'Battle of Prague.' Do you know the 'Java March'?" she asked, suddenly.

"I'm afraid not," Jane was obliged to confess.

"You father always had a great fondness for that. I don't know," she went on, after a short pause, "whether you understand that your father was one of my old beaux—at least, I always counted him with the rest. I was a gay girl in my day, and I wanted to make the list as long as I could; so I counted in the quiet ones as well as the noisy ones. Your father was one of the quiet ones."

"So I should have imagined," said Jane. Her maiden delicacy was just a shade affrighted at the turn the talk was taking.

"When I was playing he would sit there by the hour and never say a word. My banner piece was really a fantasia on 'Sonnambula'—a new thing here; I was the first one in town to have it. There were thirteen pages, and there was always a rush to see who should turn them. Your father didn't often enter the rush, but I really liked his way of turning the best of any. He never turned too soon or too late; he never bothered me by shifting his feet every second or two, nor by talking to me at the hard places. In fact, he was the only one who could do it right."

"Yes," said Jane, with an appreciative sigh; "that's pa—all over."

Mrs. Bates was twisting her long sleeves around her wrists. Presently she shivered slightly. "Well, really," she said, "I don't see that this place is much warmer than the other; let's try the library."

In this room our antique and Spartan Jane was made to feel the need of yet stronger props to hold her up against the over-bearing weight of latter-day magnificence. She found herself surrounded now by a sombre and solid splendor. Stamped hangings of Cordova leather lined the walls, around whose bases ran a low range of ornate bookcases, constructed with the utmost taste and skill of the cabinet-maker's art. In the centre of the room a wide and substantial table was set with all the paraphernalia of correspondence, and the leathery abysses of three or four vast easy-chairs invited the reader to bookish self-abandonment.

"How glorious!" cried Jane, as her eyes ranged over the ranks and rows of formal and costly bindings. It all seemed doubly glorious after that poor sole bookcase of theirs at home—a huge black-walnut thing like a wardrobe, with a couple of drawers at the bottom, receptacles that seemed less adapted to pamphlets than to goloshes. "How grand!" Jane was not exigent as regarded music, but her whole being went forth towards books. "Dickens and Thackeray and Bulwer; and Hume and Gibbon, and Johnson's *Lives of the Poets*, and—"

"And twenty or thirty yards of Scott," Mrs. Bates broke in, genially; "and enough Encyclopædia Britannica to reach around the corner and back again. Sets—sets—sets."

"What a lovely chair to sit and study in!" cried Jane, not at all abashed by her hostess's comments. "What a grand table to sit and write papers at!" Writing papers was one of Jane's chief interests.

"Oh, yes," said Mrs. Bates, with a quiet toleration, as she glanced towards the shining inkstand and the immaculate blotting-pad. "But, really, I don't suppose I've written two lines at that table since it was put there. And as for all these books, Heaven only knows where the keys are to get at them with. I can't do anything with them; why, some of them weigh five or six pounds!"

Jane shrivelled and shivered under this. She regretted doubly that she had been betrayed into such an unstinted expression of her honest interest. "All for show and display," she muttered, as she bowed her head to search out new titles; "bought by the pound and stacked by the cord; doing nobody any good—their owners least of all." She resolved to admire openly nothing more whatever.

Mrs. Bates sank into one of the big chairs and motioned Jane towards another. "Your father was a great reader," she said, with a resumption of her retrospective expression. "He was very fond of books—especially poetry. He often read aloud to me; when he thought I was likely to be alone, he would bring his Shakespeare over. I believe I could give you even now, if I was put to it, Antony's address to the Romans. Yes; and almost all of Hamlet's soliloquies, too."

Jane was preparing to make a stand against this woman, and here, apparently, was the opportunity. "Do you mean to tell me," she inquired, with something approaching sternness, "that my father—*my father*—was ever fond of poetry and—and music, and—and all that sort of thing?"

"Certainly. Why not? I remember your father as a high-minded young man, with a great deal of good taste; I always thought him much above the average. And that Shakespeare of his—I recall it perfectly. It was a chubby little book bound in brown leather, with an embossed stamp, and print a great deal too fine for *my* eyes. *He* always had to do the reading; and he read very pleasantly." She scanned Jane closely. "Perhaps you have never done your father justice."

Jane felt herself driven to defence—even to apology. "The fact is," she said, "pa is so quiet; he never says much of anything. I'm about the only one of the family who knows him very well, and I guess *I* don't know him any too well." She felt, though, that Mrs. Bates had no right to defend her father against his own daughter; no, nor any need.

"I suppose so," said Mrs. Bates, slowly. She crossed over to the radiator and began working at the valve. "I *told* Granger I knew he'd be sorry if he didn't put in furnace-flues too. I really can't ask you to take your things off down here; let's go upstairs—that's the only warm place I can think of."

She paused in the hall. "Wouldn't you like to see the rest of the rooms before you go up?"

"Yes—I don't mind," responded Jane. She was determined to encourage no ostentatious pride; so she made her acceptance as indifferent as she felt good manners would allow.

Mrs. Bates crossed over the hall and paused in a wide doorway. "This," she indicated, in a tone slightly suggestive of the cicerone, "is the—well, the Grand Salon; at least, that's what the newspapers have decided to call it. Do you care anything for Louis Quinze?"

Jane found herself on the threshold of a long and glittering apartment; it was full of the ornate and complicated embellishments of the eighteenth century—an exhibition of decorative whip-cracking. Grilles, panels, mirror-frames all glimmered in green and gold, and a row of lustres, each multitudinously candled, hung from the lofty ceiling.

Jane felt herself on firmer ground here than in the library, whose general air of distinction, with no definite detail by way of guidepost, had rather baffled her.

"Hem!" she observed, critically, as her eyes roamed over the spacious spendor of the place, "quite an epitome of the whole rococo period; done, too, with a French grace and a German thoroughness. Almost a real *jardin d'hiver*, in fact. Very handsome indeed."

Mrs. Bates pricked up her ears; she had not expected quite such a response as this. "You are posted on these things, then?"

"Well," said Jane, "I belong to an art class. We study the different periods in architecture and decoration."

"Do you? I belong to just such a class myself—and to three or four others. I'm studying and learning right along; I never want to stand still. You were surprised, I saw, about my music-lessons: It *is* a little singular, I admit—my beginning as a teacher and ending as a pupil. You know, of course, that I *was* a school-teacher? Yes, I had a little class down on Wabash Avenue near Hubbard Court, in a church basement. I began to be useful as early as I could. We lived in a little bit of a house a couple of blocks north of there; you know those old-fashioned frame cottages—one of them. In the early days pa was a carpenter—a boss-carpenter, to do him full justice; the town was growing, and after a while he began to do first-rate. But at the beginning ma did her own work, and I helped her. I swept and dusted, and wiped the dishes. She taught me to sew, too; I trimmed all my own hats till long after I was married."

Mrs. Bates leaned carelessly against the tortured framework of a tapestried *causeuse*. The light from the lofty windows shattered on the prisms of her glittering chandeliers and diffused itself over the panelled loves and graces around her.

"When I got to be eighteen I thought I was old enough to branch out and do something for myself—I've always tried to hold up my own end. My little school went first-rate. There was only one drawback—another school next door, full of great, rowdy boys. They would climb the fence and make faces at my scholars; yes, and sometimes they would throw stones. But that wasn't the worst: the other school taught book-keeping. Now, I never was one of the kind to lag behind, and I used to lie awake nights wondering how I could catch up with the rival institution. Well, I hustled around, and finally I got hold of two or three children who were old enough for accounts, and I set them to work on single entry. I don't know whether they learned anything, but *I* did—enough to keep Granger's books for the first year after we started out."

Jane smiled broadly; it was useless to set a stoic face against such confidences as these.

"We were married at the most fashionable church in town— right there in Court-house Square; and ma gave us a reception, or something like it, in her little front room. We weren't so very stylish ourselves, but we had some awfully stylish neighbors— all those Terrace Row people, just around the corner. 'We'll get there, too, some time,' I said to Granger. 'This is going to be a big town, and we have a good show to be big people in it. Don't let's start in life like beggars going to the back door for cold victuals; let's march right up the front steps and ring the bell *like* somebody.' So, as I say, we were married at the best church in town; we thought it safe enough to discount the future."

"Good for you!" said Jane, who was finding her true self in the thick of these intimate revelations; "you guessed right."

"Well, we worked along fairly for a year or two, and finally I said to Granger: 'Now, what's the use of inventing things and taking them to those companies and making everybody rich but yourself? You pick out some one road, and get on the inside of that, and stick there, and—The fact is," she broke off suddenly, "you can't judge at all of this room in the daytime. You must see it lighted and filled with people. You ought to have been here at the *bal poudré* I gave last season—lots of pretty girls in laces and brocades, and powder on their hair. It was a lovely sight."

"It must have been. I believe Rosy would have looked real pretty fixed up that way."

"Rosy?"

"Our youngest; she's eighteen."

"Is she out?"

"Not quite; but I expect she's on the way."

"Is she pretty?"

"Yes," replied the just Jane. "Yes, Rosy is quite pretty. She's dark. She would look lovely in yellow tulle—with a red rose somewhere."

"Is she clever?"

"H'm," said Jane, thoughtfully, "I suppose so. She's beginning to understand how to get what she wants, anyway."

"And just the least bit selfish and inconsiderate?" insinuated Mrs. Bates, shrewdly.

"Y—yes, I'm afraid so."

"Well, she might be quite a success; we must think about her. Come; we've had enough of this." Mrs. Bates turned a careless back upon all her Louis Quinze spendor. "The next thing will be something else."

V

Jane's guide passed swiftly into another large and imposing apartment. "This I call the Sala de los Embajadores; here is where I receive my distinguished guests."

"Good!" cried Jane, who knew Irving's *Alhambra* by heart. "Only it isn't Moorish; it's Baroque—and a very good example."

The room had a heavy panelled ceiling of dark wood, with a cartouche in each panel; stacks of seventeenth-century armor stood in the corners, half a dozen large Aubusson tapestries hung on the walls, and a vast fireplace, flanked by huge Atlantes and crowned by a heavy pediment broken and curled, almost filled one whole side. "That fireplace is Baroque all over."

"See here," said Mrs. Bates, suddenly; "are you the woman who read about the Decadence of the Renaissance Forms at the last Fortnightly?"

"I'm the woman," responded Jane, modestly.

"I don't know why I didn't recognize you before. But you sat in an awfully bad light, for one thing. Besides, I had so much on my mind that day. Our dear little Reginald was coming down with something—or so we thought. And the bonnet I was forced to wear—well, it just made me blue. You didn't notice it?"

"I was too flustered to notice anything. It was my first time there."

"Well, it was a good paper, although I couldn't half pay attention to it; it gave me several new notions. All my decorations, then—you think them corrupt and degraded?"

"Well," returned Jane, at once soothing and judicial, "all these later forms are interesting from an historical and sociological point of view. And lots of people find them beautiful, too, for that matter." Jane slid over these big words with a practised ease.

"They impressed my notables, anyway," retorted Mrs. Bates. "We entertained a great deal during the Fair—it was expected, of course, from people of our position. We had princes and counts and honorables without end. I remember how delighted I was with my first prince—a Russian. H'm! later in the season Russian princes were as plentiful as blackberries: you stepped on one at every turn. We had some of the English, too. One of their young men visited us at Geneva during the summer. I never quite made out who invited him; I have half an idea that he invited himself. He was a great trial. Queer about the English, isn't it? How can people who are so clever and capable in practical things ever be such insolent tom-fools in social things? Do you know Arthur Paston?"

"No. Was he one of them?

"Not exactly. He lives here. We thought we had Americanized him; but now he has slipped back and is almost as bad as he was to start with. Arthur Scodd-Paston—that's the way his cards read to-day. Do you care for paintings?"

"Of course. Is Arthur Scodd-Paston like one?"

"You bad girl! Well, we might just stick our noses in the picture-gallery for a minute.

"We're almost beginners in this branch of industry," she expounded, as she stood beside Jane in the center of the room under the coldly diffused glare of the skylight. "In my young days it was all Bierstadt and De Haas; there wasn't supposed to be anything beyond. But as soon as I began to hear about Millet and the Barbizon crowd, I saw there was. Well, I set to work, as usual. I studied and learned. I *want* to learn. I want to move; I want to keep right up with the times and the people. I got books and photographs, and I went to all the galleries. I read the artists' biographies and took in all the loan collections. Now I'm loaning, too. Some of these things are going to the Art Institute next week—that Daubigny, for one. It's little, but it's good; there couldn't be anything more like him, could there?

"We haven't got any Millet yet, but that morning thing over there is a Corot—at least, we think so. I was going to ask one of the French commissioners about it last summer, but my nerve gave out at the last minute. Mr. Bates bought it on his own responsibility. I let him go ahead, for, after all, people of our position would naturally be expected to have a Corot. I don't dare tell you what he paid for it. If I did"—she pointed to their joint reflection in the opposite mirror—"we should have a fretful porcupine here in no time."

"Don't, then," pleaded Jane, looking at her own reflection and clasping her hands across her forehead; "this miserable bang gives me enough trouble as it is."

"There's some more high art," said Mrs. Bates, with a wave of her hand towards the opposite wall. "Carolus-Duran; fifty thousand francs; and he wouldn't let me pick out my own costume, either. You have never seen me on dress-parade; take a look at me now." She gathered up the tail of her gown and modestly scuttled out of the room.

Poor dowdy Jane stood in silent awe before this sumptuous canvas, with her long, interlaced fingers strenuously tugging at each other and her wide eyes half popping from her head. She was as completely overpowered and shattered as an uncouth and angular raft under the thunderous downpour of Niagara. Presently she turned; Mrs. Bates stood peeping in from without, her eyes all a-twinkle.

"And now," she said, "let's go up-stairs." Jane followed her, too dazed to speak or even to smile.

Mrs. Bates hastened forward, lightfootedly. "Conservatory—

that's Moorish," she indicated, casually; "nothing in it but orchids and things. Come along." Jane followed—dumbly, humbly.

Mrs. Bates paused on the lower step of her great stairway. A huge vase of Japanese bronze flanked either newel, and a Turkish lantern depended above her head. The bright green of a dwarf palm peeped over the balustrade, and a tempered light strained down through the painted window on the landing-stage.

"There!" she said; "you've seen it all." She stood there in a kind of impassioned splendor, her jewelled fingers shut tightly and her fists thrown out and apart so as to show the veins and cords of her wrists. "We did it, we two—just Granger and I. Nothing but our own hands and hearts and hopes, and each other. We have fought the fight—a fair field and no favor—and we have come out ahead. And we shall stay there, too; keep up with the procession is my motto, and head it if you can. I *do* head it, and I feel that I'm where I belong. When I can't foot it with the rest, let me drop by the wayside and the crows have me. But they'll never get me—never! There's ten more good years in me yet; and if we were to slip to the bottom to-morrow, we should work back to the top again before we finished. When I led the grand march at the Charity Ball I was accused of taking a vainglorious part in a vainglorious show. Well, who would look better in such a rôle than I, or who has earned a better right to play it? There, child! ain't that success? ain't that glory? ain't that poetry?— H'm," she broke off suddenly, "I'm glad Jimmy wasn't by to hear that! He's always taking up his poor mother."

"Jimmy? Is he humble-minded—do you mean?"

"Humble-minded? One of my boys humble-minded? No, indeed; he's grammatical, that's all; he prefers 'isn't.' Come up."

Mrs. Bates hurried her guest over the stairway and through several halls and passages, and introduced her finally into a large and spacious room done in white and gold. In the glittering electrolier wires mingled with pipes and bulbs with globes. To one side stood a massive brass bedstead full panoplied in coverlet and pillow-cases, and the mirror of the dressing-case reflected a formal row of silver-backed brushes and combs.

"My bedroom," said Mrs. Bates. "How does it strike you?"

"Why," stammered Jane, "It's all very fine, but—"

"Oh yes; I know what they say about it—I've heard them a dozen times. 'It's very big and handsome and all, but not a bit home-like. *I* shouldn't want to sleep here.' Is that the idea?"

"About," said Jane.

"Sleep here!" echoed Mrs. Bates. "I *don't* sleep here. I'd as soon think of sleeping out on the prairie. That bed isn't to *sleep* in; it's for the women to lay their hats and cloaks on. Lay yours there now."

Jane obeyed. She worked herself out of her old blue sack, and disposed it, neatly folded, on the brocaded coverlet. Then she took off her mussy little turban and placed it on the sack. "What a strange woman," she murmured to herself. "She doesn't get any music out of her piano; she doesn't get any reading out of her books; she doesn't even get any sleep out of her bed." Jane smoothed down her hair and awaited the next stage of her adventure.

"This is the way." Mrs. Bates led her through a narrow side-door, and Jane found herself in a small room where another young woman sat before a trim bird's-eye-maple desk, whose drawers and pigeonholes were stuffed with cards and letters and papers. "This is my office. Miss Marshall, Miss Peters," she said, in the tone of introduction.

The other girl rose. She was tall and slender, like Jane. She had a pasty complexion and weak, reddish eyes. Her expression was somewhat plaintive and distressed—irritating, too, in the long run.

"Step along," called Mrs. Bates. She traversed the "office,"

passed into a room beyond, pushed Jane ahead of her, and shut
the door. "I don't care if it *does* hurt her feelings." Mrs. Bates's
reference appeared to be to Miss Peters.

The door closed with a light click, and Jane looked about her
with a great and sudden surprise. Poor stupid, stumbling child!
—she understood at last in what spirit she had been received
and on what footing she had been placed.

She found herself in a small, cramped, low-ceiled room which
was filled with worn and antiquated furniture. There was a
ponderous old mahogany bureau, with the veneering cracked
and peeled, and a bed to correspond. There was a shabby little
writing-desk, whose let-down lid was lined with faded and
blotted green baize. On the floor there was an old Brussels carpet, antique as to pattern, and wholly threadbare as to surface.
The walls were covered with an old-time paper whose plaintive
primitiveness ran in slender pink stripes alternating with narrow
green vines. In one corner stood a small upright piano whose
top was littered with loose sheets of old music, and on one wall
hung a set of thin black-walnut shelves strung together with
cords and loaded with a variety of well-worn volumes. In the
grate was a coal fire. Mrs. Bates sat down on the foot of the
bed and motioned Jane to a small rocker that had been re-seated
with a bit of old rugging.

"And now," she said, cheerily, "let's get to business. Sue
Bates, at your service."

"Oh, no," gasped Jane, who felt, however dumbly and mistily,
that this was an epoch in her life. "Not here; not to-day."

"Why not? Go ahead; tell me all about the charity that isn't
a charity. You'd better; this is the last room—there's nothing
beyond." Her eyes were twinkling, but immensely kind.

"I know it," stammered Jane. "I knew it in a second." She
felt, too, that not a dozen persons had ever penetrated to this
little chamber. "How good you are to me!"

Presently, under some compulsion, she was making an exposition of her small plans. Mrs. Bates was made to understand how some of the old Dearborn Seminary girls were trying to start a sort of clubroom in some convenient down-town building for typewriters and saleswomen and others employed in business. There was to be a room where they could get lunch, or bring their own to eat, if they preferred; also a parlor where they could fill up their noon hour with talk or reading or music; it was the expectation to have a piano and a few books and magazines.

"I remembered Lottie as one of the girls who went with us there, down on old Dearborn Place, and I thought perhaps I could interest Lottie's mother," concluded Jane.

"And so you can," said Lottie's mother, promptly. "I'll have Miss Peters—but don't you find it a little warm here? Just pass me that hair-brush."

Mrs. Bates had stepped to her single little window. "Isn't it a gem?" she asked. "I had it made to order; one of the old-fashioned sort, you see—two sash, with six little panes in each. No weights and cords, but simply catches at the side. It opens to just two widths; if I want anything different, I have to contrive it for myself. Sometimes I use a hair-brush and sometimes a paper-cutter."

"Dear me," asked Jane, "is that sort of thing a rarity? 'Most every window in our house is like this. I prop mine with a curling-iron."

"And now," said Mrs. Bates, resuming, "how much is it going to take to start things? I should think that five hundred dollars would do to get you under way." She opened the door. "Miss Peters, won't you please make out a check for five hun—"

"Oh, bless your soul!" cried Jane, "we don't need but three hundred all together, and I can't have one woman—"

"Three hundred, then," Mrs. Bates called into the next room.

"Oh, goodness me!" cried Jane, despairingly, "I don't want

one woman to give it all. I've got a whole list here. You're the first one I've seen."

"Well, how much, then? Fifty?"

"Fifty, yes. That's quite as much as I expected—more."

"Fifty, Miss Peters; payable to Jane Marshall." She looked at Jane quizzically. "You *are* unique, sure enough."

"I want to be fair," protested Jane.

The door closed on Miss Peters. Mrs. Bates dropped her voice. "Did you ever have a private secretary?"

"Me?" called Jane. "I'm my own."

"Keep it that way," said Mrs. Bates, impressively. "Don't ever change—no matter how many engagements and appointments and letters and dates you come to have. You'll never spend a happy day afterwards. Tutors are bad enough—but, thank goodness, my boys are past that age. And men servants are bad enough—every time I want to stir in my own house I seem to have a footman on each toe and a butler standing on my train; however, people in our position—well, Granger insists, you know. But Minnie Peters—Minnie Peters is the worst of all. Every so often"—in a low voice and with her eye on the door—"she has one of her humble days, and then I want to die. That was what was the matter before you came—I didn't really mean to seem cross to you. I just have to take her and shake her and say, 'Now, Minnie Peters, how can you be so bad to me? How can you think I would do anything to hurt your feelings, when your mother was my very best friend? Why are you always looking for a chance to find a slight, when'—Oh, thanks, thanks!"—Miss Peters having appeared with the check. Mrs. Bates clapped on the signature at her little old desk. "There, my child. And good-luck to the club-room.

"And now business is over," she continued. "Do you like my posies?" She nodded towards the window where, thanks to the hair-brush, a row of flowers in a long narrow box blew about in the draught.

"Asters?"

"No, no, no! But I hoped you'd guess asters. They're chrysanthemums—you see, fashion will penetrate even here. But they're the smallest and simplest I could find. What do I care for orchids and American beauties, and all those other expensive things under glass? How much does it please me to have two great big formal beds of gladiolus and foliage plants in the front yard, one on each side of the steps? Still, with our position, I suppose it can't be helped. No; what I want is a bed of portulacca, and some cypress vines running up strings to the top of a pole. As soon as I get poor enough to afford it I'm going to have a lot of phlox and London pride and bachelor's buttons out there in the back yard, and the girls can run their clotheslines somewhere else."

"It's hard to keep flowers in a city," said Jane.

"I know it is. At our old house we had such a nice little rosebush in the front yard. I hated so to leave it behind—one of those little yellow brier-roses. No, it wasn't yellow; it was just —'yaller.' And it always scratched my nose when I tried to smell it. But oh, child"—wistfully—"if I could only smell it now!"

"Couldn't you have transplanted it?" asked Jane, sympathetically.

"I went back the very next day after we moved out, with a peach-basket and a fire-shovel. But my poor bush was buried under seven feet of yellow sand. To-day there's seven stories of brick and mortar. So all I've got from the old place is just this furniture of ma's and the wall-paper."

"The wall-paper?"

"Not the identical same, of course. It's like what I had in my bedroom when I was a girl. I remembered the pattern, and tried everywhere to match it. At first I just tried on Twenty-second Street. Then I went down-town. Then I tried all the little places away out on the West Side. Then I had the pattern put down on paper, and I made a tour of the country. I went to Belvidere, and to Beloit, and to Janesville, and to lots of other places between here and Geneva. And finally—"

"Well, what—finally?"

"Finally, I sent down East and had eight or ten rolls made to order. I chased harder than anybody ever chased for a Raphael, and I spent more than if I had hung the room with Gobelins; but—"

She stroked the narrow strips of pink and green with a fond hand, and cast on Jane a look which pleaded indulgence. "Isn't it just too quaintly ugly for anything?"

"It isn't any such thing," cried Jane. "It's just as sweet as it can be! I only wish mine was like it."

Mrs. Bates glanced from the wall-paper to the window-box, and from the window down into the back yard, where, beneath the week's washing, flapping in the breeze and the sun, she saw next summer's flowers already blooming.

"Did you read that paragraph last week," she asked, suddenly, "about my having been a washer-woman once?"

"No. What was it in?"

"One of those miserable society papers. Do you know there's a man in this town who makes his living by sending such things to New York? Something scandalous, if possible; if not scandalous, then libellous; if not actually libellous, then derogatory and offensive."

"I never read such stuff," said Jane; "especially about people I like. I always skip it."

"Yes, but it's true. I can't deny it. I *was* a washerwoman for a whole year. I washed all Granger's shirts and starched them and ironed them, and put them away and got them out and washed them again for months and months. Every one went through the mill pretty often, too; there weren't very many of them.

"Those are Granger's shirts out on the line there, now—the

big ones. Those in the other row are Jimmy's—the little ones."

"H'm!" observed Jane, standing beside her at the window; "which *are* the little ones?"

Mrs. Bates laughed. "Well, perhaps there isn't much difference. Jimmy is eighteen and large for his age, but of course his *seem* the littlest. I had them made in the house, but he set off to college before I could finish with them. Perhaps they're just as well here, until the Sophomores have finished with *him*.

"Yes," she went on, proudly, "I could wash shirts then, and I can make shirts now. A woman, it seems to me, may do anything for herself or for those belonging to her; and I've always tried to be a lady and a woman too. I made all Jimmy's buttonholes and worked all the initials on the tabs." She looked appealingly at Jane. "I know you think I'm a silly old thing. . . ."

"I don't either!" cried Jane, loudly, with a tremble on her lip and a hot tear starting in each eye. "I don't either; you know I don't! You know what I think! You're a dear, good, lovely woman; and I've been just as mean and hateful to you as I could! I don't see," she went on, in a great burst on contrition, "how you could talk to me; I don't see how you could let me stay one minute in your house. If you only knew all the mean, ugly, uncharitable things I have thought about you since that man let me in! How could you stand me? How could you keep from having me turned out?"

"I am used to being misunderstood," said Mrs. Bates, quietly. "I took you at first for your father's sake, and I kept you for your own. It's a long time since I have met a girl like you; I didn't suppose there was one left in the whole town. You are one of *us*—the old settlers, the aborigines. Do you know what I'm going to do some time? I'm going to have a regular aboriginal pow-wow, and all the old-timers shall be invited. We'll have a reel, and forfeits, and all sorts of things; and off to one side of the wigwam there shall be two or three beautiful young squaws to pour firewater. Will you be one of them?"

"Well," Jane hesitated, "I'm not so very young, you know; nor so very beautiful, either."

"You are to me," responded Mrs. Bates, with a caloric brevity.

"Nobody shall come," she went on, "who wasn't here before the War. Those who came before the Incorporation—that was in '37, wasn't it?—shall be doubly welcome. And if I can find any one who passed through the Massacre (as an infant, you understand), he shall have the head place. I mean to ask your father —and your mother," she added, with a firm but delicate emphasis. "I must call on her presently."

She fixed her eyes on the fireplace. "I suppose I was silly— the way I acted when your father married," she went on, carefully. "We were only friends; there was really nothing between us; but I was piqued and—oh, well, you know how it is."

"I!" cried Jane, routed by her alarm from her contrite and tearful mood. "I? Not the least bit, I assure you!" She blushed and gulped and ducked her head and half hid her face behind her hand. "Not the least in the world. Why, if I were to die to-morrow nobody would care but pa and ma and Roger and Truesdale and Alice; well—and Rosy; yes, perhaps Rosy would care for me—if I was dead. But nobody else; oh, dear, no!" She stared at Mrs. Bates with a hard, wide brightness.

Mrs. Bates considerately shifted her gaze to the front of the bureau. She ran her eye down one row of knobs: "I wonder who he is?" And up the other: "I hope he is worthy of her."

Doubly considerate, she turned her back, too. She began to rummage among the drawers of her old desk. "There!" she said, presently, "I knew I could put my hands on it."

She set a daguerreotype before Jane. Its oval was bordered with a narrow line of gilded metal and its small square back was covered with embossed brown leather. "There, now! Do you know who that is?"

Jane looked back and forth doubtfully between the picture and its owner. "Is it—is it—pa?"

Mrs. Bates nodded.

Jane regarded the daguerreotype with a puzzled fascination. "Did my father ever wear his hair all wavy across his forehead that way, and have such a thing tied around his throat, and wear a vest all covered with those little gold sprigs?"

"Precisely. That's just the way he looked the last time we danced together. And what do you suppose the dance was? Guess and guess and guess again! It was this."

Mrs. Bates whisked herself on to the piano-stool and began to play and to sing. Her touch was heavy and spirited, but her voice was easily audible above the instrument.

> " 'Old Dan Tucker, he got drunk;
>   He jumped in the fire and he kicked up a chunk
>   Of red-hot charcoal with his shoe.
>   Lordy! how the ashes flew-hoo!' "

Jane dropped the daguerreotype in time to take up the refrain:

> " 'Clear the road for old Dan Tucker!
>   You're too late to get your supper.
>   Clear the road for old Dan—' "

"Aha! you know it!" cried Mrs. Bates, gayly.

"Of course," responded Jane. "My education may be modern, on the whole; but it hasn't neglected the classics completely! Gentlemen forward!" she said, with a sudden cry, which sent Mrs. Bates's fingers back to the keyboard; "*gentlemen* forward to Mister Tucker!" Mrs. Bates pounded loudly, and Jane pirouetted up to her from behind.

"*Ladies* forward to Mister Tucker!" cried Jane, and Mrs. Bates left the stool and began dancing towards her. Then she danced back and took her seat again; but with the first chord:

"ALL forward to Mister Tucker!" called Jane again; and they

met face to face in the middle of the room and burst out laughing. The door opened on a narrow crack, and there appeared Miss Peters's plaintive and inquiring countenance.

Mrs. Bates banished her assistant by one look of pathetic protest. "There!" she said, transferring the look to Jane, "you see how it always is when I am trying to have a good time! Even at my own table I can't budge or crack a joke; with those two men behind my chair I feel like my own tombstone. Lock that door," she said to Jane; "I *will* have a good time, in spite of them! Sit down; I'm going to play the 'Java March' for you."

She struck out several ponderous and vengeful chords. "Why," called Jane, "is *that* the 'Java March'?"

She spread out her elbows and stalked up and down singing:

> " 'Oh, the *Dutch* compa-*nee*
> Is the *best* compa-*nee!*' "

"Right again!" cried Mrs. Bates. "You *are* one of us—just as I said!"

"Well, if that's the 'Java March,'" said Jane, "it's in an old book we used to have about the house years and years ago. Only, if you bring it up as an example of pa's taste—"

"He liked it because I played it, perhaps," said Mrs. Bates, quietly. "Besides, why should you put it to those shocking words? It *is* in that book," she continued, "and I've got one here just like it."

"Is it the one with 'Roll on, Silver Moon,' and 'Wild roved the Indian maid, bright What's-her-name'?"

"Bright Alfarata. Same one, exactly. Bring up another chair, and we'll go through a whole programme of classics—pruggrum, I mean."

"Let's see, though," said Jane, looking at her watch. "Mercy me! where has the morning gone? It's after eleven o'clock."

"Supposing it is after eleven; supposing it was after a hundred and eleven? You're going to stay to lunch."

"I'd love to so much; but I just can't. I've got too many other scalps to take. So many thanks for yours! I'm going to work north towards the Monument—another Massacre!"

"Well, Wednesday, then, without fail."

They retraced their steps past the mournful Miss Peters and through the vast state bedroom. On the stairs Mrs. Bates said:

"I *do* remember your aunt, Mrs. Rhodes, now," The conscientious creature had been taxing her memory for an hour. Jane felt that this was a tribute, not to her aunt, but to herself.

"Yes," Mrs. Bates went on, "she's a little, plump, dark woman, and when she sits down she wiggles and flounces and goes all in a heap—like this." Mrs. Bates illustrated by means of the window-seat on the landing.

"Yes," assented Jane. She could not reproach Mrs. Bates for thus indulging her sense of humor in order to recoup herself for the tax on her memory.

"And when she goes down-stairs, it's like this." She gathered up her gown and sidled down affectedly over the remaining steps.

"That's it," said Jane, joining her in the hall below.

Mrs. Bates opened the front door herself. "You can take the choo-choo cars at Sixteenth, you know, and get off at Van Buren. Oh, dear; excuse my baby-talk; our little Reginald— two months old, you know. I'll have Lottie home for that lunch of ours."

"Don't apologize," said Jane. "I often use the same expression myself."

"Why, is there a baby at your house!"

"Well," said Jane, rather lamely, "Alice has got a little girl three years old."

"So David Marshall is a grandfather? But what is there extraordinary in that?—I'm one myself." She stood in the big porch looking down the street—at nothing. "Well, now I *am* going to," she said, half to herself. "*That* settles it!"

She accompanied Jane half-way down the steps, bareheaded as she was, and in her morning-gown. A society reporter who happened to be passing originated the rumor that she had gone insane.

"Good-luck, my child. Use my name everywhere. Take all that anybody offers. Good-by! Good-by!"

Jane retraced her steps to kiss her. She had not kissed her own mother for ten years.

VI

Within a month after Truesdale Marshall's return home the understanding between himself and his father might fairly have been classified among the facts accomplished; and it was brought about, too, by those indefinite courses, those impalpable procedures through which, in actual life, so many understandings are really arrived at. Truesdale, therefore, never received word that his father "wished to see him in the library"—as in the story-books. Nor did the two ever draw their chairs together in the middle of the stage close to the footlights, and have it out —as at the theatre. When Truesdale spoke at all he spoke casually—with more or less of implication or insinuation—to his mother or his sisters. When he spoke not at all, he acted—and his actions spoke as loudly and effectually as actions are held commonly to do. His father, therefore, learned presently, and with enough distinctness to serve all purposes, that the filial back was no more ready now than ever before to submit to harness; that rules and regulations were sure to be resented; that dates and duties were fretful affairs at best; that engagements and responsibilities were far too irksome to be endured; and, above all, that anything like "hours" would be most emphatically beyond the pale of a moment's consideration. Truesdale professed to regard himself as having returned once more to the life of the frontier; and being thus placed, what could he be but a pioneer? Very well; he *would* be a pioneer—the pioneer of a leisure class.

He made, however, one concession to his father: he consented to a reduction in his allowance.

He had led himself to believe that now, at last, in the town of his birth the career of a man of leisure was completely practicable. During his long absence from home his family had sent him at intervals copies of the local newspapers—sheets whose utterances were triumphantly optimistic, even beyond their triumphant and optimistic wont. Furthermore, his courses over the Continent had brought him into contact with many travellers more lately from home than himself, whose strange and topping tales—carried, indeed, in a direction the reverse of that taken by most such reports—had told him much of contemporaneous achievement behind them, and had filled him with a half-belief that no expectations founded on such a base could be exorbitant. A great light had arisen; the city, notably a metropolis for many years already, had opened out into a cosmopolis; the poet had at last arrived, and the earth was now tolerable for the foot of man.

He visited on the South shore the great white shell from which the spirit had taken its formal leave but a week before, and he acknowledged the potency of the poet's spell. "It *is* good," he assented; "better than I could have thought—better than anybody over there could be made to believe. I might have tried to get home a fortnight sooner, perhaps."

He met half-way the universal expectation that the spirit of the White City was but just transferred to the body of the great Black City close at hand, over which it was to hover as an enlightenment—through which it might permeate as an informing force.

"Good!" he thought; "there's no place where it's needed more or where it might do more good." The great town, in fact, sprawled and coiled about him like a hideous monster—a piteous, floundering monster, too. It almost called for tears. Nowhere a more tireless activity, nowhere a more profuse expenditure, nowhere a more determined striving after the ornate, nowhere a more undaunted endeavor towards the monumental expression of success, yet nowhere a result so pitifully grotesque, grewsome, appalling. "So little taste," sighed Truesdale; "so little training, so little education, so total an absence of any collective sense of the fit and the proper! Who could believe, here, that there *are* cities elsewhere which fashioned themselves rightly almost by intuition—which took shape and reached harmony by an unreasoned instinct, as you might say?"

But let that pass; he must take the town as he found it. Between his own transplanted artistic interests on the one hand and his association with the great throng of artists that the *Aufklärung* had doubtless brought and held, he should do well enough. He figured mornings given over to music and painting —his own; and afternoons of studio-rounds, when fellow-artists would turn him their unfinished canvasses to the light, or would pull away the clinging sheets from their shapes of dampened clay; and evenings when the room would thicken with smoke and tall glasses would make rings on the shining tops of tables, while a dozen agile wits had their own way with Monet and Bourget and Verlaine. For the rest, *concerts, spectacles, bals;* if need be, receptions; or, if pushed to it, five-o'clock tea—with the chance that one other man might be present. Thus the winter. As for the summer: "No canoeing, of course, on the Lahn and the Moselle; I must fall back upon the historic Illinois, with its immemorial towns and villages and crumbling cathedrals, and the long line of ancient and picturesque châteaux between Ottawa and Peoria. No more villeggiatura at Frascati or Fiesole; I shall have to flee from the summer heats to the wild ravines and gorges of DuPage County—and raise turnips and cabbages there with the rest of them."

Putting aside for the present all thought of the coming summer, Truesdale set himself to the formation of a circle. He had gone away as a boy and had come back as a young man. He had grown beyond his old acquaintances, he thought, and apart from them—of which last there could be no doubt on either side; and it struck him that the easiest and simplest thing to do would be to drop them all and to start afresh. To drop everybody and to start afresh was something he was completely habituated to. He did it through the year at intervals of from three to six months; during the busy summer season among the Swiss pensions he had done it once every fortnight, or oftener. His nature was full of adaptability, receptivity, fluidity; he made friends everywhere he went, and snatched up acquaintances at every corner.

Among the first in his new batch were Theodore Brower and Arthur Paston. They were both older than he, but he declared, *net*, that his non-travelled compatriots of his own age were impossible. These two new acquaintances he appeared to like equally well; and Jane, whose kindling ambition had devoted her brother to a brilliant social career, and whose forenoon with Mrs. Bates had done little enough to quench the mounting flame, wondered how such an augury was to be read; for Brower was wholly out of society, while Paston was understood to be (save for some slight but inevitable business entanglements) wholly in it. She decided, finally, that, as Truesdale had met Brower in their own house—involuntarily, as it were—while he had met Paston outside (as a result, inferentially, of his own endeavors and advances), the brilliant future of her brother was in no danger of being compromised. Then she restored the just balance between the two by the thought that Truesdale had taken very kindly to Theod—to Mr. Brower, after all; much more so than Rosy, whose sauciness (she could think of no other word) Jane found herself unable to forgive.

Theodore Brower was some ten years older than Truesdale. His hair was beginning to retreat before his advancing forehead, and about his eyes were coming to appear those lines proper to the man who is in business for himself and pretty largely absorbed in it. He had a pair of shrewd but kindly brown eyes and a straightforward and serious manner. He held his hand more or less on the pulsing actualities of the town, and at one time or another he took Truesdale to most of his clubs—the Crepuscular, the Consolation, the Simplicity, the Universe. At most of these they dined moderately and discussed immoderately, except at the Simplicity, whose avowed object was to free Man from the tyranny of Things. There they discussed and did not dine at all.

Brower called at the Marshall house at discreet intervals; now and then, provided there was a plausible pretext for business, the interval was shortened. He looked after all of old Mr. Marshall's insurance interests, and the alterations in the business premises of Marshall & Belden seemed to furnish him with such a pretext. The various policies required various permits from various companies, and numerous changes to correspond with the changes in the building itself. True, Brower might have sent one of his young men to the store; but he preferred to come himself to the house.

His presence there, under this ruse, was attended by various phenomena. It was then that Jane would pant over the banister and palpitate in doorways, and start and hesitate and advance and retreat, and presently go gliding along the hall, and finally look in through the open door to say, with affected surprise and disappointment:

"Why, dear me, it's only Mr. Brower, after all!"

Then the humiliation which she joyfully supposed him to suffer through the infliction of such an indignity would be cancelled by a fifteen-minute talk which, as regarded Jane's intention at least, would be quite gracious and brilliant. Brower went through this ordeal serenely enough, and never hesitated to expose himself again.

To Rosamund these subterfuges were too obvious for comment; this she reserved for those other occasions when Brower's attentions were not made to assume the mask of business. She objected that he came generally in a sack-coat, that he sometimes presented himself too early, that he dispensed with the mediatory services of a card, that he asked at the door for "Miss Jane," and that she herself was always treated by him as a child.

"Doesn't he know," protested Rosy, "that Jane is 'Miss Marshall'? And does he think that I shall let him go on calling me by a mere nickname?"

She appeared to feel instinctively the point and the justness of these her various exceptions, though where she collected her data it might have been difficult definitely to say. She was served by intuition, perhaps; or by a sixth sense—the social sense—which was now rapidly developing from some recess hidden and hitherto all unsuspected.

Though Brower was out of Society, Truesdale did not find him on this account any the more in Bohemia; he merely occupied the firm and definite middle-ground of business. But Paston, on the other hand, while firmly set in the flowery field of society, was quite capable of lifting a foot now and then to put it within the borders of another and a different area. Truesdale first met him in a sculptor's studio, at the top of one of the great down-town office buildings; the young Briton was escorting a pair of young women of his own circle who seemed disposed to encourage art to the extent of seeing how the thing was done, and whose interest was largely exhausted with an understanding of certain mechanical processes. He and Truesdale subsequently grazed against each other at places where young women, again, were present, whose interest in matters æsthetic was in varying proportions, and whose social foothold was in the lower strata—or substrata, as the case might be. Paston handled life with the easy freedom of a man who, after all, was away from home; and Truesdale was not far behind. Home, with him, was everywhere—or, rather, nowhere;

he had a great capacity for gypsy-like jauntings and an immense abhorrence of superfluous luggage, and among the most superfluous of all luggage he included scruples first and foremost. As soon expect a swallow to carry a portmanteau.

During his first year abroad he had dabbled a good deal in French fiction; this was at Geneva, before his long and intimate sojourn in Paris. His taste had been formed, in the first instance, by the more frivolous productions of the Romantic school— by "Mademoiselle de Maupin," in part; by the "Vie de Bohème," more largely; and this taste had taken a confirmed set through the perusal of other works of a like trend—more contemporaneous and therefore still more deleterious. At Geneva he had permitted himself various fond imaginings of Mimi and Musette as they might disclose themselves in Paris—it was useless, all, to expect the encounter in this strenuous little stronghold of Calvinism; but Mimi and Musette, the actual, the contemporaneous, once met at short range, were far, far from the *gracieuse* and *mignonne* creations of Murger and of 1830. And if disappointing in Paris, how much more so in Chicago?— where impropriety was still wholly incapable of presenting itself in a guise that could enlist the sympathies of the fastidious. Truesdale, whether or no, found himself restricted within reasonable bounds by his own good taste. Nor was Paston permitted much greater latitude; whatever his taste, the condition of his finances would alone have checked him from straying too widely outside the beaten path.

Paston was less reticent about the worldly status of himself and his family than might have been expected; he treated the subject in a broad, free fashion, with a great pretense to openness. Few apprehended the general and essential cautiousness of his disclosures; most people fell easily enough into the notion that so much frank jocularity had no other object than to entertain them; the young man was doubtless exaggerating, possibly inventing.

"Absurd situation, isn't it?" he would set forth in his large and genial way. "Poor father! six girls to see married off; and five boys to start in life—quite as bad. One in the Army, one in the Navy, one in the Church, one in the Civil Service, and one —in America. No other way; somebody had to come to America —the youngest, naturally. And here he is."

"Fancy that, Bessie! Imagine that, Allie!" his hearers would cry. Then they would ask him about the fox-hunting in Bucks, and tease him for further particulars about his sister Edith, who had married Lord Such-a-one.

The subject of America he treated with some tact—with some forbearance, he himself may have thought. If asked point-blank whether he liked it, he would reply that his preference, naturally, must be for England. If asked further whether he liked Chicago—an inquiry which courtesy might well have with-held—he would answer promptly and plainly, No. And there the matter would end: he never gave detailed explanations. He was prepared, it came to be understood, to put the best face on a bad matter. He remained, however, a loyal subject of the Queen, and prayed for as speedy a sight of Boxton Park, Witham, Essex, as fortune would permit. And in the meantime he enjoyed such makeshift pleasures as came his way.

Among these was that of leaving his card at several good houses—the card of Arthur Gerald Scodd-Paston. People met him at functions as Mr. Scodd-Paston, but most of them found his name rather a large mouthful; after they had used it enough times to show that they had caught it and were not unable to wield it, they would dispense with the forepart and use the Paston alone. This usage received the approval of a certain few who had had the privilege of addressing royalty—or sub-royalty—and who remembered that, after they had used the expression "Your Royal Highness" a few times, they were en-titled to an occasional lapse into the simpler "you." At the office, where he was by no means a royal highness, he was always Paston, and Paston merely.

His father was a general in the British army, but lately retired. He never referred to this dignitary, as such, save twice. These early references, pointed but discreet he held to suffice; he estimated, properly enough, that his father's fame, once started, might be trusted to spread of itself; and it did—along with the son's modesty.

It was doubtless to his father's personal influence that he was indebted for his connection with a great mortgage and investment company, which extended, in a chain of many links, all the way from London to Colorado, and a foothold in whose Chicago office he had been fortunate enough to secure. The salary connected with the place was but so-so; yet the place itself, as agreed to among the Englishry of Chicago, was in no degree unsuited to a young man of good family, fair education, small resources, and limited prospects, and a desire to make a decorous and self-respecting figure in society—such society as Western conditions offered. They said the position was as good —socially—as any in one of the branch Canadian banks; some of the more intensely English (the Canadians themselves) were fain to acknowledge that it was even better.

So Paston did his "office work" of whatever kind during the day, and distributed his cards through the evening hours, and dined out with a good-will whenever occasion offered. This was often enough; he soon became known as one of the most persistent diners-out in town, and one of the most accomplished. His animal spirits were overflowing; his plump and ruddy person seemed to be at once grace, appetizer, and benediction; his fund of stories and anecdotes (constantly replenished from the most approved sources) was inexhaustible; he carried everything through almost single-handed, by reason of his abounding vitality and never-ending good-nature. Everybody wanted him who could get him; his presence lessened by half the rigors of entertaining. He therefore lodged quietly in a retired little house in the edge of a good neighborhood; they gave him his break-

79

fast there, and warded off those who came to spy out the lean-
ness of the land. He was thus seldom called upon to take thought
for the morrow—having once passed, that is to say, the crucial
hour of lunch.

He led germans and promoted other social industries. His
vacations he could have spent six times over at all manner of
desirable places. On Sundays, through the summer, he was
possessed briefly of the freedom of the scattered suburban
settlements along the North shore. He always got a hundred
cents out of every dollar, and in many instances he got the
hundred cents and kept the dollar too.

Truesdale was slow in making up his mind to introduce
Paston into his own household. But Paston presently made his
entrée there under other auspices; and within a month from
that day Rosamund Marshall was studying Debrett and was
taking hurdles at a riding-academy.

For a third new acquaintance Truesdale was indebted to his
aunt Lydia; he had felt certain, all along, that some such in-
debtedness would befall. His aunt lived two or three miles due
south from his father's, near the last brace of big hotels. Her
house had a rather imposing but impassive front of gray-stone,
with many neighbors, more or less varying the same type, to
the right and to the left and over the way. The house had never
the absolute effect of extending hospitality; but he understood
the possibilities of the interior, and knew that a cup of tea late
on a November afternoon was among them.

As he drew near he found this house and the other houses
combined in a conspiracy of silence against the musical addresses
of a swarthy foreigner who had a foothold a yard beyond the
curbstone, and who was turning the crank of his instrument
with all the rapid regularity of the thorough mechanician. The
whole street rang. " 'Ah, perchè non posso odiarti!' " hummed
Truesdale in unison with the organ, as the performer, after an
intricate cadenza, returned to the original theme. "That's the

only recognizable thing I've heard these fellows play since I came over. I wonder who puts together all the shocking stuff they are loaded up with nowadays."

The melody, so plaintive and cloying as a vocal performance, leaped forward briskly enough under the rapid lashings to and fro of the crank; the elbow of the organist moved with a swift rhythm as his searching eye tried vainly to wring a penny or two from some one of all these opulent façades. "Good Heaven!" cried Truesdale; "how little feeling, how little expression! Here," he said to the man in Italian; "take this half lira and let *me* have a chance. Bellini was never meant to go like that."

The man, with a cheerful grin, yielded up his instrument to this engaging youth who was able to address him so pointedly in his own language, and Truesdale, with his eye on his aunt's upper windows, proceeded to indulge himself in a realization of his ideal. His aunt was vastly susceptible to music, and he would heap upon her (in the absence of any other) all those passionate reproaches for cruelty and faithlessness proper to the rôle—welling crescendos and plaintive diminuendos and long, slow rallentandos, followed quickly by panting and impassioned accelerandos. In other words, he would show this music-cobbler the possibilities of his instrument and the emotional capacity of the human soul. Incidentally, he should earn his cup of tea.

> "Why, oh why do I strive in vain to h-a-te thee,
> Cruel creature, as deeply as I would?"

began Truesdale, blithely, with his eye on the one window whose shade was not completely lowered. But at the third or fourth measure he paused disconcerted. He had adopted a varying rhythm to express each last fine shade of the text, and the air was already littered with abrupt and disjointed phrases which began with a quick snarl or with a prolonged nasal wail, leav-

81

ing a sudden hiatus here, and giving there a long, lingering scream on some mere passing note.

"Dear me!" exclaimed Truesdale, "this won't do at all. Here, signor organista, just set that thing back, will you, and we'll start again."

"Why, oh why do I strive in vain to hate thee?"

More notes shattered themselves on the stone walls about him— singly, in bunches, in long, detached wails. The organ yelped and snarled as Truesdale, time routed and accent annihilated, abandoned himself to the expression and the phrasing of the true Italian school. Two or three passing children paused on the pavement; a park policeman, stationed on the next corner, walked his sedate iron-gray slowly along to the point of disturbance.

Presently the object of all this attention showed herself. Mrs. Rhodes appeared at the window with that expression of indignant protest which forecasts an appeal to the authorities. When she saw the offending cause her indignation did not greatly diminish; she refused to smile even when Truesdale extended his hat for the usual tribute. He saw her lips move, however, with a quick exclamation which brought a second person to the window. Then both immediately withdrew.

"Another niece, I swear!" said Truesdale; "and I've walked right into it." He gave the man a second dime. "I guess you understand it better than I do, after all," he said, magnanimously.

"What was your idea in making me ridiculous that way?" his aunt asked in severe reproach, as she advanced to meet him in the reception-hall. "Do you want to set me up as a laughing-stock for all my friends and neighbors? After all I've told Bertie about your music, too! I don't know whether I shall let you know her or not."

"It was pretty rocky, wasn't it?" Truesdale admitted, with

a cheery impartiality. "I'm afraid it takes more practice than I've ever had a chance to give it. And perhaps I don't understand the genius of the instrument. Where do you suppose they learn to do it? How long a course is necessary, do you fancy, to get a complete grip on the technique?"

His aunt's protest had been purely personal. With a broader outlook and a better understanding she might have protested on behalf of a slighted neighborhood, or, indeed, of a misprized town. A finer vision might have seen in Truesdale's prank a good-natured, half-contemptuous indifference alike to place and people. "I don't know *what* the Warners over the way will think," she emitted, as if that were all.

She presently relented as to the new inmate of her household. "Come, Bertie!" she called; "step up, like a good girl. This is my nephew Truesdale—you've heard all about him; Miss Bertie Patterson, of Madison."

Miss Patterson of Madison was a shy, brown-eyed little girl who, at a guess, had been in long dresses but a year or two; as she faced Truesdale she seemed to be wondering if she might venture to smile. She had never before been south of the Wisconsin State line; but Mrs. Rhodes, having exhausted the ranks of her own nieces, was now giving a tardy recognition to the nieces of her late husband. Bertie Patterson had come for the winter, and she was finding a great deal of pleasure and interest (slightly tinctured with awe) in a town which for some years she had favored with a highly idealistic anticipation.

"Nice little thing," admitted Truesdale, inwardly; "but Aunt Lydia has got to leave *me* alone."

Mrs. Rhodes took him into the drawing-room, and had Bertie Patterson make him his tea. She did this very nicely; she helped rather than hindered the effect by her hesitancy and lack of complete confidence. She had never poured tea many times before for a young man—never at all for just such a young man as this.

"Now," said his aunt, presently. She emitted this monosyllable with a falling inflection, and followed it by a full stop. She took his teacup from him. "You know what little Tommy Tucker did." She placed her thumb on one of the upper black notes of the piano and waved her fingers over the remainder of the keyboard. " 'Just a song at twilight,' " She quoted, with a coaxing smile.

"All right," said Truesdale, promptly. "Thanks for this chance to redeem myself. I'll show you now how it really ought to go."

And he did. At Milan he had seen reflected in his lookingglass not only Fernando, but Elvino, too, besides Edgardo and Manrico, and that whole romantic brotherhood. He resuscitated them all, with as much sentiment, romance, passion, drama, as each individual case required, while Bertie Patterson sat in the fading light behind the great three-cornered screen of the up-tilted cover and clasped her hands and brought her generous idealizing faculty into its fullest play.

Then he sang a few German lieder of a more contemporaneous cast. Then his aunt asked him for that last sweet little thing of his own. "I don't believe Bertie has ever heard a composer sing one of his own songs."

As he concluded, his aunt gave a long and appreciative sigh. "There!" she breathed. Then: "Why do you act like a crazy, when you can be so nice if you only will?"

VII

"Drive on a little farther, Martin," Mrs. Bates directed her coachman; "I can never work my way through all that mess." Beds of mortar and piles of brick half filled the roadway, and the posts of a kind of rough plank canopy, which formed a shelter for pedestrians, rose flush with the curbstone. Far above this improvised shelter bricklayers were adding the courses of a new story or two to the walls of a shabby and smoke-stained old structure, and immediately below it the march of traffic and the hubbub of trade proceeded upon the broad flag sidewalk as fully as contractors and their underlings would permit. "Right over there," Mrs. Bates indicated; "between that sand-pile and the row of flour-barrels."

Porters in blue overalls hurried boxes and tubs across the wide walk to the waiting carts of suburban grocers. Through the dingy windows there showed rows of shelves set with bottles of olives or cluttered with glass jars containing various grades of molasses. From the narrow window of a small, close pen, a few feet within the door, a shipping-clerk, wearing a battered straw hat of the past summer, thrust out bills of lading to draymen and issued directions to a gang of German and Swedish roustabouts.

"I have taken a great time to come," Mrs. Bates observed to herself. She rubbed a streak of lime from her fur coat, and stooped to pick a splinter from the hem of her skirt. "Who's the one to ask, I wonder?"

She secured the interest of a plump, round-shouldered young German, whose viscous hands had just left a syrup-cask, and whose wide blue eyes stared at this unaccustomed visitor with an honest wonder. He ventured to lead her as far as a door in a grimy glass partition which closed off a large room filled with desks, gas-shades, clerks, and account-books. Circles of teacups stood on the round tops of oak tables; little pasteboard trays of coffee were disposed on the wide window-ledges, and were also ranged on the top of a substantial balustrade that shut off two or three gentlemen in high silk hats from the other occupants of the place.

Mrs. Bates threw herself upon the guidance of a young office-hand—the sole person present who seemed sufficiently disengaged to notice her. He asked her, with a mixture of surprise and deference, what name he should give.

"Sue Lathrop, say," she responded, in an access of large and liberal recklessness.

She was led through another door, in another dingy glass partition, to a smaller room at one corner, and as she passed along she threw a general glance over her surroundings. "So *he's* here, then!" she said, under her breath, as one of the gentlemen took off his hat and set it carefully on top of a desk. "I'd forgotten all about his being in business with David. It's just as well if he didn't see me. No love lost," she added, grimly.

She paused on the threshold of this last doorway; apparently she had fallen upon the final moments of some small conference. A tall, spare old man was delaying the resumption of his correspondence to call a last word after a younger one, who had just set his hat upon the back of his head and was now moving towards the exit.

"Try a summons—yes," said the elder; "that would have been the best thing to start with, wouldn't it?"

"I don't quite see it that way,' replied the other, in the tone of heated defence. "She took the goods, and must have had them on the premises."

"You didn't find them, though. I don't quite see the use of your having gone with a writ of replevin after goods that were bought to be sold again as soon as might be."

"Such old stuff isn't worked off in any such haste as that. It's as I tell you—word was got around to her that the writ had been issued. The place was all turned upside down; the things had been hidden away."

"Who could have told her?"

"Who?" cried the other, with a scornful impatience. "Somebody connected with the court. Who else could? Who else knew? Well, I'll try the other thing; there is plenty yet to be learned about justice-court justice, no doubt." He passed out with snapping eyes and a curl on his lips, and the older man again bent himself over his desk.

It was a cramped little room with a breadth or two of worn oilcloth on the floor. Two or three shelves, set across the dingy window, supported a range of glass jars filled with nutmegs and orris-root. On the tilted flagging, outside, the tops of a row of blue gasoline barrels held each a half-pint of the past night's shower, and across the muddy street bunches of battered bananas hung from the rusty framework of several shabby old awnings.

"Poor David! twenty years and more of *this!*" Mrs. Bates stood within the doorway. It was easy enough to figure her as already forgotten—easier still when the old man's half-guilty start at length acknowledged her presence.

She stepped forward with an undaunted cordiality. "Well, David, here I am at last, you see. The mountain wouldn't come to Mohammed, so"—She tapped her foot smartly on the oilcloth. "Here stands Sue Lathrop, with a long memory and a disposition to meet the mountain half-way, or three-quarters, or seven-eighths, or to trudge the whole distance—even to the last yard. One, two, three!" she counted, as she stepped up to his desk and flung out her hand.

The old man rose with something like alacrity. He banished his slight frown of preoccupation and hastened to replace it by an expression of—so to speak—apologetic cordiality.

"Mrs. Bates," he murmured. "It's very kind of you to come here—very. My daughter—" he hesitated. He finished the sentence by drawing up a chair and clearing its seat of the ruck of morning papers.

"I take the chair," she said, as if in burlesque assumption of the guidance of some public meeting, "but not as any 'Mrs. Bates.' You know, David, that I haven't come here to be treated with any such formality as that."

He looked at her with a half-smiling wistfulness, as if he would be glad enough to take her tone, were the thing only possible. But for such a juncture as this he had little initiative and less momentum, and he realized it all too well.

Mrs. Bates seated herself and threw open her furs. Her affluence, her expansiveness, her easy mastery of the situation seemed to crowd this square and ineffective old man quite into a corner. She counted his wrinkles and his gray hairs; she noted the patient dulness of his eye and the slow deliberation of his movements. "He *is* old," she thought; "older than I should have imagined. I might have bestirred myself and come before."

She turned on him with a flash of her own magnificent and abounding vitality. "I want you to assure me that I am not in the way—that I am not interrupting business. This is not the 'busy day,' I hope, that the little placards in the offices tell about." She must meet his unreadiness with the fluency over which she had such a fortunate and unfailing command. "This isn't the busy hour of the day, nor the busy day of the week, nor the busy week of the year?"

Marshall smiled slowly. He felt himself coming to a better

adjustment with her mature and massive comeliness, her rich and elaborate attire, her full-toned and friendly fluency. "We are always busy, and are expecting to be busier still; but we are never too busy for a call like this." He considered that that was doing pretty fairly for an old man who was immersed in affairs and altogether alien to the amenities of the great world.

Mrs. Bates rubbed again at the lime-streak on her fur. "Expecting to be busier, yes; and preparing for it accordingly." But why "we"?—she was not calling on the firm. "I'm sure I broke in on something at the very start." She made him a determined tender of this handle—something or other, apparently, he must be offered to take hold of.

"Only a little matter with my son. It was ending as you came in."

"Your son?" Here was an opening, indeed. "Not the one just home from abroad?"

"Oh no. That's Truesdale. Roger, now, has stayed at home; and he has done the better for it, I think. He looks after my law business. He has never had any of the disadvantages of European travel," the old man concluded, with a kind of gentle grimness.

Mrs. Bates's eyes flashed; here, to her thinking, was a glimmer of the real David, after all.

"My boys haven't been over either," she responded. She cast aside any lingering fear that no "talk" could ensue; it must, it should. "No," she went on, "neither one of them; and I'm none too sure that they ever *will* go. But as for college—well, *that* I absolutely insisted upon. When my first boy was getting along to that age the question gave me a good deal of anxiety. Mr. Bates had his views and I had mine. Granger was for clapping him right into business; for a week I was positively alarmed. Up to that time my husband and I had staved forward abreast—neither had ever disappointed the other, nor lagged behind the other; but I was afraid that the point had been reached at last where I must drop him behind and go ahead alone. 'My dear husband,' I began—and when I begin like that he knows I mean business—'my dear husband, do you realize what the next twenty years are holding for this town? Do you know the promise they have for a young man of family who is properly qualified and started? Do we want our boys to get their manners from the daily hustle of La Salle Street? Do we want them to get their physique by doubling over books all day in a close, unwholesome office? What's the good of all our millions if we can't start our children in life with good health and good manners? Let them build up sound bodies and let them learn the usages of good society—how to associate on equal terms, in fact, with men of their own class. Give them a chance at tennis and baseball. As for their Latin and Greek, it won't do them any real harm—they'll forget it all in due season.' And so forth, and so forth," added Mrs. Bates, conscious of the growing length of her tirade. "Well, I had my way in the end—I usually do—besides the satisfaction of finding that Granger Bates was still capable of stepping right along with his wife. Billy came home—a big, handsome, gentlemanly fellow—and was put into the business on the very day he was twenty-one. He's doing well, and Jimmy will follow in due course. Your oldest boy is a lawyer, then. What's the other one?"

"He's a gentleman—so far," answered Marshall, rather ruefully. "I'm afraid he's almost too clever to be anything else."

"H'm," pondered Mrs. Bates, with a sympathetic thoughtfulness; "that's bad—bad. I'd sooner have a boy of mine dead than a mere gentleman. And I shouldn't want him too clever, either. My Billy, before we sent him off to college, showed signs of cleverness; it worried me a good deal. He wanted to write; and there was one time when he thought he wanted to paint. Of course we couldn't allow anything like that. I was willing enough that he should be posted on the best books, and be able to tell a good painting from a bad one—to be a patron of the arts, if so minded. But to do things of that sort himself—oh, really, you know, that was altogether out of the question. He's with his father now, as I say, and he's where he belongs. How old is your other boy—Roger? Twenty-eight? Twenty-nine?"

"Thirty. He went right from the High School to the Law School. No college, no Europe; yet for all that—"

"For all that, he's doing well, eh? He's got quite a practice, has he? He's a smart fellow? He's a good lawyer?"

Marshall hesitated. A week previous his affirmative would have come more promptly. "Yes," he said at length, "Roger is pretty good in his line. He does for himself; he never makes any demands on his father. He is practising right along, and—and learning. He does quite well—in some things." The old gentleman's tone and manner expressed a delicate and disappointed qualification; and his thought seemed gliding away to something in no wise connected with the present talk.

Mrs. Bates brought him back to the actualities of the moment; she had no idea of permitting her impromptu address on education (furthest of all things from her thoughts as she had entered) to be succeeded by an absolute hiatus. She therefore made inquiries of the customary civility about the other members of the Marshall family. She asked with a firm and ceremonial emphasis after Mrs. Marshall, and expressed herself as pleased at the prospect of renewed relations between the two families. "We are the old settlers, you know. There are only a few of us left, and we ought to hang together." She inquired further about his youngest daughter, whose social fortunes she seemed disposed to promote; she even made a civil reference to the remote dweller at Riverdale Park. And then, with every appearance of relish, she approached the subject of the other daughter who came between—"the girl who gave me an art course in my own house," she declared, with twinkling eyes.

Marshall smiled. "That's Jane, true enough. She has always been kind of literary and artistic, and lately she has become architectural too. She is down here once or twice a week to help Bingham put on these extra stories."

"Bingham? My Bingham? Tom Bingham? He's the one who built our house," she explained.

"That's the one. Jane held out, at first, for an architect and a design; she had an idea that here was the chance, finally, to make this old block an ornament to the city. But I thought differently. So I had Bingham's people take off the cornice and run up two stories like the others. To-morrow they'll put the cornice back again, and we shall be under cover before the snow flies."

"Well, between Jane and Tom Bingham you're in pretty good hands. Have you had him before for anything? He's a grand fellow. It'll do you lots of good to know him—as much good as it has done me to know your girl. David," she went on, with a little touch of solemnity, "she's a fine girl, she's a splendid girl; and she thinks everything of her father."

"So she does," admitted the old gentleman, with a guarded smile. His comments on his daughter's affection for him were never profuse.

"When she came to see me the other day," Mrs. Bates continued, "it was like a whiff of air from the old times. It was like one of the Old Settler receptions that the Calumet people used to give—only better. Why did they stop them, I wonder? Are the old settlers giving out? Or has the town become too proud and indifferent? Or what?"

"I'm afraid it's the fault of the old settlers themselves," responded Marshall, with a grave and quiet smile. "They won't stay to be received."

"Yes, I know," said Mrs. Bates, with a soft little sigh. "They are dropping off one by one. David!" she exclaimed suddenly, leaning forward with a wistful smile, "we ought never to have drifted apart as we did. We ought not to have lost sight of each other for all these years. I'm sure"—in earnest questioning

92

—"that we remember enough about the old times to care to see each other once in a while still?"

Marshall dropped his eyes to his desk, and his long, lean fingers picked out the border of its blue baize covering. He was half touched, half embarrassed. "I hope so," he said.

"What gay times we used to have!" she went on, still determined, despite his meagre response, upon an evocation of their youthful past. "Such dances and sleigh-rides, and everything! You were ever so good to me in those old days; I haven't forgotten how you took me to the Diorama and the Bell-Ringers and what all besides. And 'Uncle Tom's Cabin,' too—I'm sure I should never have seen it but for you; certainly I haven't had much disposition to see it of *late* years—especially since they have put the blood-hounds in! And there was Topsy and Eva, too—oh, dear, I believe I should like to see it again, after all; don't they give it over on the West Side now and then? You must remember how they wore those tall pointed hats and those red petticoats and those black velvet bands across themselves in front—not the blood-hounds—and how they had the bells on different little tables according to their size—not Topsy and Eva; I'm talking about the Peake family, you understand. And there was Adelina Patti, too—a mere slip of a girl, in the quaintest little old clothes. I go every time she comes; I wouldn't miss one of her farewells for anything. You go, too, I suppose?"

"The same old Sue," he said, smiling. "I? No; I haven't seen her since that first time, so long ago."

"Yes," she cried, "I *am* the same old Sue; and I always shall be to the friends of those dear old days! But you, David—how is it with you yourself?"

She looked at him closely, earnestly, studiously. He felt that she was disappointed in him, and he felt almost disappointed in himself. She had come to him extending, as it were, an olive branch—living, lustrous, full-foliaged; and in return he seemed able to offer nothing beyond a mere splinter-like twig—dry,

93

sapless, unpliant. He was conscious that he was not all she had expected to find him, nor all that she was entitled to expect to find him; he was even conscious, but more dimly, that he was not quite all that he had meant to be; no, nor all that, in her eyes, he should have liked to be. Yet, in the end, he was a successful man, and she must know it. True, he had not rolled up any such enormous fortune as that of Granger Bates, nor did he make in the public eye any such splendid and enviable figure. All the same, however, he could command the world to the extent of three million dollars; nor was he displeased that his caller should have come at a time when indications of future prosperity greater still were so patent all over the premises.

Mrs. Bates smoothed her gloves upon each other and cast her eye over the nutmegs and orris-root and the other furnishings of the apartment, and heaved a little sigh and rose to go.

"I am glad to have had these few minutes with you, David; but I feel that I have no right to take up any more of them. I am sure this *is* your busy day, after all."

She looked up into his face, which was coming once more to be overcast with its accustomed aspect of preoccupation, and gave him her hand. He took it kindly enough, and she bestowed on his a quiet little pressure. It was hardly cordial; it was far indeed from effusive. Yet she had hoped, half an hour before, to have it both.

"Ten years ago," she said, "I might have satisfied myself about you without coming here at all." She stood at the end of his desk, and stirred with an unconscious finger the loose memoranda in a wire basket on the corner of it. "The papers used to speak of you, and now and then something would come by word of mouth. But I am hearing less about you of late. Hold your own, David. Don't let the world forget you. You have done well, as I know, and you are entitled to your place in the public eye."

She looked him in the face, smilingly but very earnestly. "I had great hopes for you in the early days, and I find that I am

94

jealous for you even yet. You have made a good deal of money, they tell me, and you are getting ready to make a good deal more—*that* I see for myself. But doesn't it seem to you," she proceeded, carefully, "that things are beginning to be different? —that the man who enjoys the best position and the most consideration is not the man who is making money, but the man who is giving it away—not the man who is benefiting himself, but the man who is benefiting the community. *There* is an art to cultivate, David—the art of giving. Give liberally and rightly, and nothing can bring you more credit."

Marshall regarded her with a dubious smile. Nobody had ever before attempted to fit his head to such a cap as this.

"As I have said so many times to Mr. Bates, 'Make it something that people can *see*.' Imagine a man disposed to devote two or three hundred thousand dollars to the public, and giving it to help pay off the municipal debt. How many people would consider themselves benefited by the gift, or would care a cent for the name of the giver? Or fancy his giving it to clean up the streets of the city. The whole affair would be forgotten with the coming of the next rain-storm. 'No,' said I to Granger, 'it must be something solid and something permanent; it must be a building.' And it's *going* to be a building. You drive out with me to the University campus this time next year, David, and you'll see Bates Hall—four stories high, with dormers and gables and things, and the name carved in gray-stone over the doorway, to stay there for the next century or two. I think I shall name it Susan Lathrop Bates Hall (Granger is willing), and make it a girls' dormitory. They'll call the girls 'Susans,' I dare say; but I sha'n't mind, and I don't suppose they will either. Besides, boys would be sure to be called 'Grangers,' so what's the difference?" She smiled whimsically, and made a feint to depart.

"But there are plenty of other things," she paused to impart. "People are always running to us about schools and hospitals.

A few loose thousands, for example, would help the Orchestra guarantee—Granger has contributed there, too. And lately he has been approached about an endowed theater. There are plenty of ways."

"Your husband is fond of music?"

"Oh, well, he doesn't object to it. He can sit out an evening in our box very comfortably. But a man of his position is naturally expected to support a great artistic enterprise. Besides, Granger thinks a good deal of the reputation of the city."

"Yes, there are plenty of ways, as you say," the old man rejoined, with his preoccupied smile. "The 'charity' page of our ledger shows that. No man in business is allowed to forget his obligations to the 'public.' I am just beginning to become acquainted with the public—our public. A justice-court is a good place for us to learn what it is and who compose it, and what their attitude is toward us—the public that we are expected to do so much for."

Mrs. Bates, with her hand on the door-knob, felt herself obliged to decline this theme so tardily introduced—though the old man's tart tone promised great possibilities. She would have thanked David Marshall for a prompter contribution of conversational material; she felt that her own efforts during this interview had been out of all proportion to his. She made no response, and he stepped forward to conduct her through the outer office to her carriage. "You needn't go through all those porters again," he said.

Just inside the outer doorway stood two gentlemen; their faces were turned towards the street as they watched the preparations for the upward trip of a great length of metallic cornice. "Why," said Mrs. Bates, as one of them turned half round, "isn't that Tom Bingham, now?"

"Yes," said Marshall; "he looks in occasionally."

"How do you do, Mr. Bingham? she said, hastening up to him with a jocular cast in her eye. She knew the Bingham Construction Company as the builders of a score of handsome residences, and of as many of the vast structures which towered all over the business district. It seemed droll to her to find him here, giving personal heed to mere alterations and repairs. "What will be the next thing—building-blocks? Let me send you a box of them, I beg of you."

Bingham turned round altogether—a tall, stalwart man whose face was full of the serenity that comes from breadth and poise, but whose mind, as she herself knew well enough, was too habituated to the broad treatment of big matters to have any aptitude for repartee and chatter. She liked to disconcert him, and it was usually an easy thing to do. "And I wish, while you have your hand in, you would just come up and nail some weather-strips on my dining-room windows."

Bingham smiled slightly. "Send on your blocks," he said— "if you think they will help me any *there*." He pointed towards the cornices of the building opposite. Above their broken skyline a tall steel frame (on the next street behind) rose some two hundred feet into the air; along the black lines which its upper stage etched against the sky a dozen men swarmed in spidery activity and sent down the sharp clang of metal on metal to the noisier world below.

"Mine, too," he said, shortly, as if the vast monument were its own sufficient spokesman. He seemed proud of himself and of the town where such things could be accomplished.

Mrs. Bates flashed forth a look full of admiration for both man and work. "I'll take that all back about the weather-strips; but if you *could* bring up your kit to-morrow morning and make us an extra coal-bin in the furnace-room— Too proud for that, too? Well, then, just come up to dinner to-morrow evening— only the family. And bring your sister, if she'll accept on such short notice."

The other gentleman, whom Mrs. Bates had overlooked, and indeed forgotten, turned round. "You know Mr. Belden, Mrs. Bates?" was Marshall's introduction.

Belden was a man between forty-five and fifty. His costume

and countenance were alike much more contemporaneous than his partner's. His dress was self-consciously fashionable, and he wore a carefully trained mustache, whose dark brown was beginning to show threads of gray. His cheeks and his forehead seemed in their smoothness as if coated with some impermeable and indestructible hard-finish. He had a resolute chin and a pair of hard, steel-gray eyes, which were set much too close together to leave great room for any attribution of an open-minded generosity. He and Mrs. Bates, under Marshall's promptings, bowed icily, and a cold and chilling silence immediately ensued.

"Just like me," said Mrs. Bates, as she effected a hurried departure, "to blunder up against him as I did. I wonder if he and David get along at all well together. And the idea of my extending invitations to dinner under his very nose! Well, it can't be helped now."

She thought this the only offence of which Belden might accuse her. But he was piqued by her apparent disparagement of their building, and he was still more incensed by her having called on his partner at their place of business. For Marshall must know—everybody must know—that the Beldens, though neighbors of the Bateses, had never been admitted, and never were to be admitted, into their house.

Belden stood behind the vast spread of dingy plate-glass, and watched Bingham putting Mrs. Bates into her carriage. He found additional offence in the gay nod which she sent to Marshall through the carriage window.

"In spite of you," he muttered; "we are moving up in spite of you. Prevent us, if you can!"

VIII

Susan Bates drove homeward, filled with a vague dissatisfaction. "I expected too much," she said to herself, as she half opened the door again to free the skirt that Bingham had fastened there. "I ought to have chosen a different time and place. I might have known that he would be deep in his business—I ought not to have taken him with the harness actually on his back."

She sighed as she thought of all the things she had meant to say, but had come away without saying—the thousand and one minor reminiscences of those early days in the straggling and struggling prairie town. She had imagined a mutual evocation of the past, and it had not been accomplished. But presently consolation came: she realized all at once that her present mood was but one of those early reminiscences made modern. She recalled now how many times he had taken his departure from that little parlor, leaving her to feel just as she felt now—piqued, balked, impatient over his slow, taciturn, unresponsive ways. But her impatience and her pique had always passed off in due time, and he had always returned, his same kindly and inscrutable self. "I believe he meant to do the best he could. Anyway, I shall follow things up, all the same," she declared to the opposite cushions. Her thought deflected in the direction of Belden. "I wonder how they get along together. He is not at all the man that I should think of David being associated with—as a matter of choice. I never heard how the partnership began. I never understood why it kept up so long as it has."

The partnership, as a matter of fact, dated back twenty years, and had originated through a kind of crisis in the affairs of Marshall & Co.—the only weak spot in the history of the firm. After several years of unbroken prosperity, David Marshall (with thousands of others) had been overtaken by fire. A year or two later fire was followed by panic, and Marshall felt himself crowded towards the brink of ruin. In a moment of weakness he permitted himself a course to which only so great an emergency could have prompted him. The situation was saved by a species of legerdemain—of card-shuffling, so to speak—which was quite outside the lines of mercantile morality, and barely inside the lines of legality itself. An instrument willing to lend itself to this feat of juggling was needed, and was found in a pushing young fellow who left a rival house to play discreetly and shrewdly the rôle of figure-head that the juncture required Marshall had long ago made full amends to the men whose welfare he had temporarily sacrificed to his own salvation, but he had never shaken off Belden, who remained constantly as a reminder of his early and only lapse from rectitude. In moments when conscience became tender under the quickening touch of reminiscence, Belden was upon him not only as a punishment, but as an incubus.

Belden had never yielded a single inch of the foothold gained by his sudden intrusion upon the affairs of the concern. His first demand was for the headship of a department; he had required, next, an interest as a partner; he had exacted, more lately, the presence of his name in the style and title of the firm; and to-day he was moving towards the making of the firm over into a stock company. He was younger than Marshall, stronger, more aggressive, more ambitious, more adventuresome; nor was it difficult to imagine him as fundamentally insolent and selfish.

His standard of mercantile morality was never higher than at the beginning, and his standard of social propriety was felt to leave much to desire. His first entry into the firm seemed to have been accompanied by a clairvoyant confidence and assurance and ambition. He was understood to have divorced his first wife, an amiable, faithful, but limited little creature, under circumstances of some cruelty, and even barbarity, to form a second union more in harmony with his mounting ideas for the future. A subtle atmosphere of distaste and disapproval had enveloped him and his for many years, and the social advances of himself and his wife had been, however determined, but slow—almost imperceptible.

Finally, what could not be accomplished in the West was accomplished, to some extent, in the East. Statira Belden was of New England origin; her family had resided for years in a small town which the taste of a few Boston families of consideration was turning into a summer resort. They contrived their cottages, and she contrived hers. She discreetly renovated the old "homestead," as she called it, and arranged to reside in eastern Massachusetts through the summer season. She made a few careful acquaintances among her neighbors, and presently found it possible to spend a profitable and distinguished winter month in the Back Bay. One step more brought her to her goal. Social exchange between Boston and New York being practically at par, she passed from one town to the other with an unimpaired currency. In Manhattan she was received with sufficient frequency by people sufficiently distinguished, and announcements in correspondence with the facts were borne westward by various metropolitan dailies and weeklies. She herself followed, in due course; she had now conquered a certain foothold at home, and her progress there was distinctly perceptible.

The last stronghold of the opposition existed, much to her mortification, in her own immediate neighborhood, where a stubborn little clique (as she called it) continued, under the leadership of Susan Bates, to ignore her. The Belden carriage-block, measuring diagonally across the street, was three hundred feet from that of the Bateses, but the distance might as well have been three hundred miles. Mrs. Bates, who, on some occasion or other, had met her face to face, continued to hold sturdily the impression that her eyes were at once too furtive and too bold, and that her hair was too yellow for a woman of her age; "or, for that matter, too yellow for a woman of *any* age."

In view of these considerations and others, Mrs. Bates was the reverse of pleased when Jane, one morning, came up to her little room, sat down on the foot of the bed, and announced that Mrs. Belden, among others, was likely to be bidden to Rosy's coming-out.

"Ma doesn't like her so extra well," Jane admitted, candidly; "she thinks they might have done something for Rosy this past summer. But it would seem awful to pa if his own partner's wife wasn't asked; and, besides, we don't know so very many people *to* ask, anyway."

Mrs. Bates had made her advances in due form to the women of the Marshall family. Throughout the call the talk had been frankly, inevitably personal, and Susan Bates had treated Eliza Marshall, whose difficult and captious character she at once apprehended, with the most elaborate and ingenious simplicity. Rosy was passed in review and then dexterously dispensed with, after having aroused the caller's interest and approval; and the subsequent talk ran along quite freely on the child's deserts and prospects. Mrs. Bates was quite direct and unadorned; and, though Rosy's future was the only common ground upon which the two women could meet, yet she handled this material with such a sympathetic persistence that Eliza Marshall was fain to believe that she and her caller had been knit in a close community of interests from time immemorial.

Mrs. Bates divined readily enough that nothing would be

more galling to Eliza Marshall than a betrayal of her own social ignorance. "How glad we ought to be," she said, in an innocent, left-handed fashion, "that girls are no longer brought out at a crush. Imagine, once more, that crowd of people surging up and down your stairs, and trampling each other underfoot as they try to dance in a room not a quarter big enough, and ten times too many poor flowers wilting all over the house, and a big band of music going it for dear life, and fifty or a hundred carriages tangled up in a noisy crowd outside;—why go through all that for the sake of getting a new little girl acquainted with a few of her mother's friends?"

Eliza Marshall fastened her intent but inexpressive gaze upon her caller's face and said never a word. The function thus sketched by Mrs. Bates was the precise function that for the past fortnight she had been imagining and dreading. She had filled her secluded old parlors with the squeak and the blare of music; alien draperies in their swift gyrations had whisked her immemorial ornaments from her immemorial old "whatnot"; in the dining-room a squad of custard-colored waiters had opposed a firm front to the hungry hordes that assaulted the various viands on the table; and a thousand teasing points of form and usage had afflicted her with worry, uncertainty, and possible mortification and despair. She saw now that nothing like her imagined entertainment was desirable, or even tolerable, to-day, and she gave unconsciously a little sigh of relief.

Mrs. Bates divined further that, having instructed ignorance, she must now allay timidity. She must represent the coming function as a mere bagatelle for simplicity and informality.

"Isn't it pleasant to think that things are being made so much easier for us than they used to be? Otherwise, I should have been dead long before this. Nothing to do but for our little girl to stand up with her mother and two or three of her mother's friends in one room, and for two or three other people to look after the tea and other things in some other room off behind somewhere or other." Mrs. Bates waved her hand genially towards the rear rooms. "When Lottie came out I said to Mrs. Ingles, 'Now you must just take the tea part of it off my hands. Get some girls for me—you know about the ones I want—and see that their gowns are right; and then I shall be at peace, knowing that people are nibbling their biscuits'—or crackers" (this in a tone unconsciously expository)—" 'dawdling with their spoons, as they ought to.' A few, of course, really drank tea; but the others—well, they had had tea somewhere half an hour before, or expected to have it somewhere half an hour after. How tired we all get of this old rigmarole, don't we?"

Eliza Marshall bowed gravely. For her this tiresome old rigmarole was a complete novelty. "Lyddy's niece," she said, turning to Jane; "that girl from Madison—she could pour for one, couldn't she?"

"Sure," assented Jane. "*Our* niece, too—sort o'," she added, correctively; for Eliza Marshall made little of certain vague ties to a half-brother.

Mrs. Bates cast her eye round the dim, old-fashioned room. One might have fancied her as exploring for the portraits of two or three mature female relations of the Marshalls.

"I don't know whether I am right in asking it," she began, with a fetching pretence of hesitancy; "but I am an old friend of the family—in a sense—and so interested in Rosy, too. If I might help you receive—"

Mrs. Marshall heard this proposal with a second little sigh of relief, and accepted as a matter of course. Indeed, outside of Mrs. Rhodes—and possibly Mrs. Belden—she had absolutely no one to whom she could turn.

"And Aunt Lyddy for another," said Jane.

"Yes," assented Mrs. Bates, in the tone of indorsement. "Mrs. Rhodes and I are acquainted"—with a sly look towards Jane; "and there—with your other sister, perhaps—our little party is made up."

"And about the people to be invited," Eliza Marshall proceeded, with some little show of initiative. Her task was becoming less and less formidable; she felt herself approaching this supposed ordeal with something almost like buoyancy.

"Let's have it nice and little and cosey," suggested Mrs. Bates, with a cosey little air of her own. "Twenty-five or thirty at the outside." She wondered inwardly where even so small a number could be got. "Why, *six* would do—if they were the right six! And why should we want more than three carriages before the house at any one time?—not to have a man shouting numbers, I hope!"

She drew her wraps together and rose to go. "If I might ask for cards for one or two of my own friends?—nice, pleasant people, who would be glad to become acquainted among the old families," she added, diplomatically. "If she can only be kept from suspecting how swell they really are, till it's all over!" was the good creature's inner thought. "Of course Rosy's appearance here isn't public, nor any equivalent for it; that will come later. I myself shall want to do something for her on the South side, and there will be one or two good houses for her on the North side—oh, our little duck will swim, when once put into the pond, as you shall see. After *that*, we shall want only a kind papa to pay the bills and a patient maid to sit up until three or four in the morning."

Mrs. Bates got herself away in great good-humor and kept that humor until the following day, when Jane came to announce the participation of Mrs. Belden.

"Have her pour tea!" cried Susan Bates, without a moment's hesitation. "Let her come early, and let her stay late, and pour and pour and pour until the last cup is drunk. I can't promise your mother that I shall be there throughout, but I will be there for half an hour—during the middle, perhaps. And tea— well, I never drink it, even at home."

Jane looked at her in some surprise.

"And don't let your mother change her rooms any," Mrs.

Bates went on, rapidly. "They're right as they are—in perfect agreement. They have a quiet tone; and a low, quiet tone, after all, is the best thing—and the hardest thing to get. And not too many flowers."

"Never fear," said Jane, grimly. "She won't change anything."

"And don't let her have too much on the table. Give them tea and chocolate and sandwiches and Albert biscuits—that's plenty. And if your second girl shows, a cap would do no harm. Put a slice of lemon in every cup—that discourages lots of people."

Jane laughed. "But ma doesn't want to discourage her friends."

"My good girl," said Mrs. Bates, impressively, "this whole function has only one object. That object is to show your sister for five minutes to Cecilia Ingles."

"Oh, that's it?"

"That's it, and all of it."

Mrs. Bates's function came off on the appointed afternoon, and was so limited in size and so simple in character that Eliza Marshall would have reproached herself for slighting her own child, had not Susan Bates, before her early departure, whispered in the old lady's ear a word of complete approbation.

Rosy herself flashed and sparkled in the dim and depressing old parlor like a garnet set in dull gold. Indeed, it must be confessed that she showed some of the hard glitter of such a jewelled fabrication, as well as its splendor. Cecilia Ingles, who could not but admire her beauty and her readiness, thought that her tone was a little too hard, and that in her excess of aplomb she pushed self-possession to the verge of self-assertion. Rosy, in fact, entered society not with the tentative step and slow advance of one who cautiously feels an unaccustomed way, but by a single confident and intuitive leap. As she stood there beside her mother, dressed in a pale yellow gown and playing carelessly with her bunch of red roses, she shifted any embarrassment incident to the occasion from her own shoulders to those of her mother's friends—two or three of whom, retired and aging persons, withdrew feeling their own social rustiness quite keenly.

Jane, who had no definite rôle to play, but who did general utility all over the house, was enabled to observe various episodes from various points of view. When the actual test came she had little more aptitude for the social graces than her mother had, and she imitated her mother's own cautious reserve. She did not meet Mrs. Ingles at all, but she witnessed from a distant doorway the conjunction which Mrs. Bates effected between the leading luminary of the day and the newly-discovered asteroid. Jane ungrudgingly acknowledged Cecilia Ingles to be magnificently beautiful, and her dress to be a miracle of taste, and her advances to be most winningly gracious. "And she's just about my own age, too," thought poor Jane, in half-unconscious comparison. "And the way that little chit stands up there and talks to her! I couldn't, for a hundred worlds. Rosy acts as if she was just as pretty herself—well, I suppose she is; and of just as good position—h'm, *that's* all right enough, I'm sure; and just as used to the ways of the world—well, so she will be, fast enough." And the dear girl gave a long slow sigh—partly that the family had at last such a champion, partly that she herself should have been doomed to such complete uselessness in so high a cause. She quite failed to realize that she alone and no other was the real motive-power of her family's tardy spurt.

As for Mrs. Bates, Jane caught quite another side of her. She showed herself profoundly formal and punctilious. She seemed to have dilated for the occasion, with the express determination of dominating it. "She acts mighty queer," said honest Jane, who was the same to one and all, to-day and to-morrow; "but I suppose she knows what tone to take. If she acts like that, though, the next time I see her, I shall want to stop knowing her. She calls it a 'function,' and I suppose she's trying to make it like one. But one's enough."

Jane observed, furthermore, that her aunt Lydia was inclined to neglect her own part in the ceremony in order to perform pirouettes and pigeon-wings (so to speak) before the back-gammon-player of the tropics. "If Aunt Lyddy forgets, after all," said Jane, anxiously, "and *does* mention Florida, why, I've told a fib for nothing." Jane had informed Mrs. Rhodes that the Bateses had lost their youngest child at Jacksonville, and so could not bear the slightest mention of the South; though she knew perfectly well that the youngest child of the Bateses was a lusty youth of eighteen, with strong hopes of becoming one of the Yale football team next season.

In the midst of the ceremonial Truesdale sauntered in and passed through the rooms with a graceful indifference; he was the last to be disconcerted by an assemblage purely feminine. He had doffed for the hour most of his imported eccentricities in the way of dress, and had consented to appear, properly enough, in a double-breasted black frock-coat with extremely long skirts. He had an orchid in his button-hole—a large one, very vivid and flamboyant. Jane had looked, rather, for a chrys-anthemum—one of those immeasurable blooms worn by the young men in *Life*. "But Dick *will* be individual," she acknowl-edged. "Thank goodness it wasn't a peony, or worse. He *does* look nice, if he is my brother; and he's the only young man I know with violet eyes."

Truesdale drifted into the tea-room, and Jane presently saw him lounging in a chair alongside Bertie Patterson. The table was officered after the fashion that Mrs. Bates had suggested—by Mrs. Belden, who, in the absence of her own daughter, kept away by illness, had brought, instead, another girl, her daugh-ter's friend, a visitor from New York. Truesdale failed to catch her name.

Mrs. Belden herself was somewhat large and inclined to be a bit high-colored and full-blown. An excess of blond down lined her cheeks just below and before her ears, and her light-colored eyebrows spread themselves rather broadly and dispersedly on her forehead. A superfluity of straw-colored hair of a shade essentially improbable waved about her ears and temples, and a high gold comb emphasized the loose knot into which it was drawn behind. "She would do better on the stage," Truesdale said to himself; "she has gotten herself up for the photographer. And if all those rings are her own, she has more than any one woman needs."

The girl with her, whose name presently came to him as Gladys—"Gladys what?" he wondered—let herself loose on him at once with a fusillade of ready familiarities. The field was clear, for Bertie Patterson, at his side, had few words to interpose. Her large brown eyes rested half appealingly upon him in the intervals of her constrained and halting little service, and he readily divined the poor child as in a lonely and uncomfortable minority.

"To-day is only my second time," she said to him, with a kind of appealing protest; "you mustn't watch me and criticise me." She had just finished her ministrations on a pair of old-time family friends whom Rosy, in the fulness of her social efflorescence, had banished for consolation and reassurance to the tea-room. Somehow, the guests that had fallen to her side of the table had all been of this character.

"When was the first?"

"Why, don't you know? The day you—you—"

"Oh, that day!" laughed Truesdale. "I didn't know you were there, of course. You must have thought me absurd."

"No; not—not—absurd. But on such a long, wide street, with so many handsome houses all around—"

Truesdale smiled. "Poor little thing! I believe she admires Michigan Avenue; I believe she's impressed by it." To him this thoroughfare was not completely innocent of the cheap and vulgar restlessness which is the dominant note of all American street architecture. "But let her admire it, if she can. Think what I expected to find Piccadilly!"

"I enjoy driving down it so much," she continued, confidentially, yet with a shy little look as if trying to learn whether her confidence was misplaced. "Aunt Lydia and I go shopping almost every day."

"Ten kilometres down and back," estimated Truesdale; "ten kilometres of luxury and grandeur—don't let it overpower you. And you are learning where the shops are, I suppose, and the theatres, and the post-office, perhaps, and the hotels, and what all besides."

"No," said Bertie Patterson, proudly; "I knew all that before I came. There are books, you know—and maps. I studied them at home beforehand."

Truesdale had never seen any of the books, but he thought their existence probable enough. He remembered, to, his own maps—how he had become familiar with the London clubs long before walking through Pall Mall, and how he knew where to find all the Paris theatres years previous to his first stroll along the Boulevard. "And you have been to all the high places, I suppose?"

"I've been to the top of the Masonic Temple."

"And to the places were they have the sun-dials, and the gates ajar, and the American flag made of—of—Heaven knows what?"

"The parks? Yes, we have been to one or two of them, but we were a little late for all those lovely things; most of them had been dug up."

"Lovely things!" groaned Truesdale. "Fancy them in the Bois or along the Row—or anywhere but here!" Yet he felt sure that she had his own fondness for pleasure-grounds and points of view. She had doubtless anticipated the Masonic Temple and Washington Park, just as he had anticipated the Pincian and the Tower of the Capitol. His fellow-feeling forgave her this crudity; after all, she was praising what she had never seen.

"I've been to your parks myself," the other girl broke in, as she glanced round the vase of chrysanthemums from the other side of the table. "But if you want to see a park, come to New York." She was rather abrupt and boisterous; Truesdale wondered if she had not at one time been a tomboy.

"And I know where ever so many of the society people live," Bertie went on in a low tone, which implored him not to repeat, and above all not to laugh. "I saw a book once with all their addresses, and I marked the places on the map."

Truesdale did smile here—crumbling, the while, a biscuit on the corner of the table. He smiled, not because she had seemed to refer to society people as a distinct and unique order of beings, but from pure sympathy. He himself had placed Stafford House and Bridgewater House and all the other town residences of the English aristocracy in those same days when he had found sites for the Pall Mall clubs.

"Yes," she went on, "I know where Mrs. Bates lives, and Mrs. Ingles, and lots of other prominent people."

"Upon my word!" cried Truesdale, in generous emulation. "Just what I did in Paris. I went all up and down the Rue de Grenelle and the Rue St. Dominique trying to select the right sort of hôtels—houses, you know—for the Viscountess of Beauséant and the Duchess of Langeais and the Princess Galathionne, and all those great ladies in Balzac—in Balzac's novels," he added, considerately.

"But Mrs. Bates isn't in a novel?"

"Oh no; she's real, I hope. So you have covered the North side and the South side and all? You know us through and through?"

"This talk about 'sides'!" the girl opposite broke in again. She took the other way round the chrysanthemums. "We have 'sides' in New York, but nobody you know lives on them. Fancy nice people scattered in squads all over a city and having their shops and clubs and theatres all jumbled up in the middle along with everything else! It's horrid."

Truesdale nodded across to the girl and smiled brightly. He wondered if she were really quite second-rate.

"Where do you suppose I went night before last with Aunt Lydia?" Bertie resumed, as she fingered the remaining two or three of a row of shining teaspoons. "To the opera"—in an awe-struck undertone; "to *Rig-o-letto*. Aunt Lydia couldn't get a box—she said they were all taken for the season; but we had seats close to one side, just below the boxes. Such a grand place! Ever since the Auditorium was opened I've been hoping to see it, and now I have."

"Congratulations!" cried Truesdale, heartily, and Mrs. Belden turned round to see the reason for it. He remembered how he himself had panted for the Scala, and for the Apollo at Rome— that poor Apollo, razed to the ground before ever he could behold its historic stage.

"I've been to your opera myself," the other girl proclaimed. "What was the matter with all the box people, anyway? They seemed afraid to assert themselves. I never saw a lot of rich people so cowed-like."

"Do you mean that they kept quiet during the performance?" asked Truesdale. "The effect *was* rather primitive, wasn't it? Whenever *I* sing I always ask the whole room to shout— especially if somebody shows any sign of listening."

"And I thought they looked pretty plain, too," the girl volunteered further. "If you want to see style and display, take the Metropolitan on a real gala night. I didn't see half a dozen necklaces among your people—and not a single tiara."

"You should have worn yours," declared Truesdale, genially. "Every one would have helped." Yes, she seemed second-rate, truly, and the worst type of a second-rate person at that—the second-rate person away from home. "Let *her* have them," he whispered to Bertie, as a brace of new-comers crossed the threshold.

"She'll take them anyway," said Bertie, ruefully. She did not at all seem to realize the greater triumph of completely monopolizing the one man present.

"I wanted to walk in the foy—in the place where they promenade," Bertie went on; "such a lovely place, and such a grand crush under all those yellow arches! But we didn't have any gentleman," she concluded, lamely.

"Never mind; you'll have one next time," responded Truesdale; gallantly. "I'm awfully fond of that place, already—the whole of it. It's one of the few good things they've got here. It's the only place in town where you can see any number of nice people together."

"Oh, really," protested Mrs. Belden, speaking to him for the first time. She had decided that he was worth talking to, as well as concluded that his attentions had been given too exclusively to one side of the table. "Oh, really, now!" Her voice was thickly, sweetly sibilant. "I shall hope to show you that you are wrong. Gladys, child, remind me to send this young man a card for a week from Wednesday."

"Very well," answered Truesdale; "I'm perfectly willing to be convinced. Only don't ask me to a dinner—I can't sit through a dinner. A little bit of a tea—well, that's different." And he turned his friendly eyes in the direction of Bertie Patterson.

"It isn't a dinner," said Mrs. Belden, as brusquely as her vocalization would allow. "It's—" But a new-comer advanced, and she turned to manipulate her teapot with her large, fair, plump hands.

Bertie Patterson smiled at Truesdale in return. She seemed to consider herself indebted to him not only for that vague promise of future festivities, but for a certain degree of moral support at a juncture which might have brought her mortification, if not actual tears.

"What a downright nice little soul she is, anyway!" thought Truesdale. "There *are* nice good girls in this world, after all, and some of them are right here. And how she idealizes this brutal and ugly town! If only she doesn't idealize *me!*"

Truesdale had been idealized more than once before. Sometimes the result had been merely embarrassing, sometimes disastrous.

IX

It may be remembered that Truesdale, in making an estimate of the resources of his native town upon the occasion of his return to it, had scheduled the five-o'clock tea as the last resource of all. If we find him present, then, at such a function, we may imagine him to have found the possibilities of local entertainment much slighter than he had figured, and time already hanging somewhat heavily on his hands.

Nor need we make any allowance for the fact that the débutante was his sister, and the scene of her coming-out his own mother's house. The catholic tolerance of his sympathies was such as to make his interest in his relatives, as relatives, no greater than his interest in other people whose general qualities would be likely to receive equal recognition from the world at large; and his outlook was so broad as to make his father's house but one of many houses, and to subject happenings in it to the same criterion as would be used to judge and rate the happenings in any other house throughout Christendom. Truesdale considered himself as admirably and flawlessly a cosmopolite.

Yes, he had done his sister's tea, but not until he had done almost everything else. He went to the few good concerts that offered, he made a fortnightly visit to the art stores, and he patronized (so far as he could endure them) the theatres— the chief and final resource of the town. But the concerts were a factor far from constant; and the theatres offered scarcely once a month a play that a person of taste and intelligence cared to sit through. Abroad he had been a valiant first-nighter; but he learned presently that at home the house for a première was composed largely of people whose tickets came from the exposition of theatre "paper" throughout the week in their storefronts—it was on Monday evening that they were paid off; and he found himself little disposed to join in judgment with a raft of small shop-keepers, until he recollected that a première was not a première, after all—the play's footing having already been secured at some other place, at some other time, before some other audience.

As for the picture-dealers, he complained that a canvas of any importance was likely to be displayed after a fashion frankly mercantile, in the show-window of the shop—a step which met more than halfway the public demand for free art, but which unjustly caused many an original to be taken for a copy. "Perhaps, though," he would say, "the public has got so far along as to judge of a picture independent of its surroundings. Possibly the crimson draperies and the row of gas-jets have really come to be superfluous."

He missed, furthermore, many of his accustomed pleasures and conveniences. He was astonished to find a metropolis without a promenade. True, on Sunday afternoons there was a good deal of strolling up and down along a half-mile of the lake shore; but he never observed that the people whose houses overlooked all this strolling ever took any part in it, and he never learned that they enjoyed this diversion anywhere else. "Singular," he said; "no concerted walking or driving. No understanding as to any time for it; no understanding as to any place for it. Not the slightest social organization for out-door life; how much there must be"—(with a backward thought towards Rosy's début)—"in-doors—somewhere!"

He deplored the absolute non-existence of the institution

known as the café—all the more, in view of the long months of waiting that must intervene before he should be able to gain membership in some club. The café, that crowning gem in the coronet of civilization—the name was everywhere, the thing nowhere. Nothing offered save a few large places of general and promiscuous resort, which, under one ameliorative title or another, dispensed prompt refreshment amid furnishings of the most reverberant vulgarity.

"It's impossible!" he said in one of these places one day to one of his artists, a new-comer from Milan. "Either you stand here in front of this counter facing all that superfluous glass-ware, and that cheap young man with the dreadful hair, and the reflections of all those hideous daubs behind you, or else you retire to one of those cubby-holes along the side there and make the disposal of a bottle of light beer seem a disreputable orgy or a dark conspiracy, or a combination of both."

"Not one word against the pictures," replied the other. "How else here do I live?"

"No journals," pursued Truesdale; "no demi-tasse, no clientèle, no leisure. No," he added, with the idea of a more general summing up, "nor any excursions; nor any general market; nor any military; nor even any morgue. And five francs for a cab. *Quelle ville!*"

To Truesdale the café was the great social foothold; it was here that he was accustomed to meet on common ground the whole male section of society. It was to the café that he would like to lead his young water-colorist with the portfolio of views from rural Missouri, or his last new poet with his thin little volume so finely flattened out between the two millstones of journalism and literature—neither of which, alone, could have ground him out his grist in livable quantities. In the absence of the café he led two or three such to the house. It was like thrusting a lighted candle into a jar of nitrogen. The candle went out at once. And never came back. To David Marshall, art in all its forms was an inexplicable thing; but more inexplicable still was the fact that any man could be so feeble as to yield himself to such trivial matters in a town where money and general success still stood ready to meet any live, practical fellow half-way—a fellow, that was to say, who knew an opportunity when he saw it. The desire of beauty was not an inborn essential of the normal human being. Art was not an integral part of the great frame of things; it was a mere surface decoration, and the artist was but for the adornment of the rich man's triumph—in case the rich man were, on his side, so feeble as to need to have his triumph adorned. He himself had taken hold of practical things at an early age; he had made something out of nothing—a good deal out of nothing; and compared with this act of creation the fabrication of verses or of pictures was a paltry affair, indeed.

He was willing enough that his daughters should improve themselves; he was even proud, in a way, of Jane's ability to keep step with the general advance of female culture. But for any such turn in one of his sons he had no sympathy, no patience. He conferred with Truesdale on the possible reorganization of the business, and put before him the appositeness of his coming in at such a time; but Truesdale would lift his brows and suck his lips and study the pattern of the carpet, and mumble something about packing his trunk and "going somewhere."

His days, in fact, were becoming long—inordinately so; it was to his evenings that he was coming to look exclusively for diversion. He made the most of these; he drew them out as long as possible—to counterbalance the days. He seldom came home before midnight, frequently not before two or three in the morning; occasionally not at all. In company with three or four choice spirits, Arthur Paston and his like, he turned night into day, and was seen now and then at such conjunction of place and time as would well have justified an explanation to the sober-minded or even to the comparatively correct. Like his other associates on these occasions, he still retained the enviable faculty of being able to "be nice to nice people"; but he acknowledged his taste and his sensibilities both to be badly lacerated, and he confessed now and then with a sigh that he had never amused himself so indifferently in his life.

His sense of ennui was, in fact, driving him out upon society; and the hopes of his sister, which had drooped somewhat after their first leaving-out, now began to lift themselves again. Jane, on reviewing Rosy's début, had arrived at a juster estimate of her own share in it; she had launched one member of the family very satisfactorily, and she felt herself prompted to the launching of another.

Rosy was now in the full tide of success. The edge of the wedge had been set with singular acumen, and the two or three smart blows that followed had opened up society to her in a twinkling. She had appeared at a few of the best houses, and had at once entered upon a vogue. Her mirror was always full of cards, her cards were always full of names, and her own name was always filling the newspapers. She figured in boxes at theatre-parties, in booths at fancy fairs. She had already poured tea at six receptions, and had acted as bridesmaid at two weddings. An incessant stream had run from the six teapots, and nobody had looked at the two brides. Jane would sit up in the dim library through the small hours waiting for Rosy's ring and planning corresponding triumphs for Truesdale.

Her first and chiefest task was to get him to take society seriously. He had professed himself as unable to put his finger on it; he asked her where it was to be found—what was the general platform on which it met. At the Charity Ball, she had answered him—rightly, perhaps; wrongly, perhaps. Let us waive the point.

"Then to the Charity Ball I shall go," he had answered, promptly.

"Will you?" shrilled Jane. "Oh, goody! And you won't be disappointed, either. It's the one great, magnificent thing of the year. Everybody goes. And they have 'C-h-a-r-i-t-y' in electric lights, and palm-trees, and champagne, and two different places to eat supper in." Jane had never attended one of these entertainments; her wealth of picturesque detail was gathered from the newspapers.

"Ouf!" said Truesdale, indifferently, discounting the magnificence. He had been to one ball at the British embassy in Rome, and to another at the Hôtel de Ville in Paris, and did not expect to be impressed. He rather looked to find this coming occasion like the latter—a heterogeneous assemblage of elements whose value was doubtful separately and not much greater collectively.

Jane ran to her fairy godmother; through Mrs. Bates everything appeared possible. "You must put him on the committee," said Jane; "or you must make him a floor-manager or something." Jane's head swam with a social vertigo; she could call spirits from the vasty deep and feel perfectly sure of their coming.

"Very well," responded Mrs. Bates; "a floor-manager he shall be."

"He'll do it splendidly, too," declared Jane; "he's so alert, and so self-possessed, and so awfully graceful and good-looking. Just the right height, and a very handsome figure—don't you think?"

"Too slender."

"Well, of course he's no slugger," retorted Jane, whose thought turned suddenly towards the youthful footballist at Yale. "Yes," she went on, "he's got plenty of assurance and readiness, and he'll do beautifully—if he'll just be disposed to take the trouble. Only—only he doesn't know anybody, hardly," was her dubious conclusion.

"Never mind," returned Mrs. Bates, genially; "lots of 'em

he couldn't know—there's too many; and lots of 'em he wouldn't want to know. He can jump about, I imagine, and see that other people are kept jumping about too. The fewer he knows the better he'll do his work."

She looked at Jane steadily for a moment or two. "One thing more; I want you to come and sit in my box."

"Me!" squealed Jane. "Oh-h-h!" It was a complicated cry; it indicated surprise, gratitude, self-depreciation, and (before all) a sense of divided duty.

Mrs. Bates, all unsuspected by her subject, had taken Jane in hand a month ago, and had made her at length fairly presentable. Incidentally she had made herself a martyr. "But never mind," she would say; "the poor child doesn't know how to do herself justice, so somebody else has got to do it for her."

After a pretty thorough canvass of Jane—her hands, her hair, her dress, her carriage, her complexion—she began operations. She went, for example, to a widely celebrated beautifier, as well as to other dealers in those lotions and cosmetics which have secured the recommendation of various singers and professional beauties, and she took Jane with her. The good woman pretended alarm at the state of her complexion—as if her robust health, her careful table, her good allowance of sleep, her active circulation, and her hundred varied forms of daily exercise all went for naught. So she sat in "parlors" with cloths tied round her neck, and let people smear her with creams and prod her with electric needles and work their will on her for the removal of all the "facial blemishes" that flesh is heir to.

"My dear girl," she would call over her shoulder to Jane, "I know this is awfully tiresome to you, and it must be very painful to see your old friend suffering so; but if you will just wait patiently for ten or fifteen minutes more—"

"Oh, don't mind me," Jane would respond, outwardly bored, but inwardly interested. "I'm getting along all right. Go on enjoying your sufferings as long as you please." And after a few of these forenoons Jane had realized her own imperfections, and had learned the means of getting round them.

Then Mrs. Bates would convey her unconscious pupil to the hair-dresser's. She would abandon her gray tresses to the manipulations of operatives skilled to show the possibilities of the natural material and the magical supplementary powers of the unnatural; every frown occasioned by a tug, every tear produced by a tangle, was borne cheerfully for the sake of an ultimate good, and Jane acquired indirectly a complete knowledge of all those preparations and processes which her preceptress felt her needs required.

"Yes, my hair *is* thinning on the forehead," Mrs. Bates would admit. "If you should happen to have the precise match . . ."

The match was always difficult, but Jane did not fail to observe how easy the same would be for herself.

Then Mrs. Bates would have her manicure at the house twice as often as before, to increase the chance of her being on hand some morning when Jane should drop in. "Try it yourself—just to see what it's like," she would suggest; and her own plump and shapely hands would yield their place on the small red velvet cushion to the long and graceless fingers of her protégée. And presently the other processes—the soakings, the washings, the rubbings—would follow.

She also recommended exercise—dumb-bells, for example.

"What's the matter with fencing?" asked Jane. "Truesdale, you know; he's awfully good to me." She might have found it difficult to cite any definite example of Truesdale's goodness; perhaps she meant merely that he never snubbed her, never hectored her.

"Better yet. Fencing by all means."

Jane, moreover, always accompanied Mrs. Bates to the milliner's and to the dress-maker's. They priced things, debated things, and tried on things—on themselves, on each other, on the attendants. Mrs. Bates purchased lavishly for herself, and suggested lavishly in regard to purchases by Jane.

"You'd better have this," she would say. "It becomes you first-rate—you won't find anything nicer."

"But the price!" Jane would demur. For Mrs. Bates frequented the most expensive places, and spent money with a prodigal recklessness. "I can't; it isn't right; I couldn't think of costing poor pa so much—especially with Rosy and everything making such an expense for him."

"Nonsense. You're entitled to some of the good things of life, too. Your father can stand it, I should hope. If he hasn't learned how to spend money, it's high time he did. Have you any idea, you poor, simple soul, what's he worth?"

"I suppose he is pretty well off," Jane would acknowledge, reluctantly, indefinitely.

"Well off? I should say so! You ought to have twenty times what you do. Let them send this home for you—I'll take the risk."

Thus in the course of a month or two Jane, to the bewilderment and surprise of her mother and sisters and everybody else, became more presentable than ever before in the whole course of her life. She fully merited, in fact, the sincere encomium finally bestowed by Mrs. Bates herself:

"There, now! You're not the worst-looking girl in this town—not by a jugful!"

Jane was seriously affected by this unstinted praise, and she was almost overwhelmed when her monitress showed the courage of her convictions by offering a place in her box.

"Oh-h-h!" she mimicked, after Jane. "What does that mean? Will you or won't you?"

"If I only could," said Jane; "it's the first thing of any account I've had a chance at since I don't know when. But I've got another engagement for that evening. I'm going to the university extension lecture with— I'm going to the university extension lecture; it's my regular night." She ended with a heavy downward inflection which she hoped was pronounced enough to conceal the tell-tale dislocation that had preceded it.

"Indeed? Where does your lecture carry you?"

"Over on the West side—to that Settlement."

"Um. Bad neighborhood to be going into alone, at night."

"I'm not going alone," returned Jane, with a kind of fluttering joyfulness.

"Oh! with some girl friends, then? Not much better—that way."

"I'm not going with any girl friends"—this accompanied by a perceptible palpitation of delight. She looked at Mrs. Bates with eyes that seemed to say, "Please go on; don't stop right there."

"Oh, then, that kind, good brother, perhaps," suggested Mrs. Bates—going on.

"No, not that kind, good brother." Jane's face was fairly beaming.

"Some other kind, good young man, then."

"Yes," responded Jane, with a challenging light on her countenance; "some other kind, good young man."

"Ah! And when does your lecture end?"

"At nine."

"Before the other thing begins. Of course the lecture is much too instructive to lose, and then there's the fascination of a mile or two in a dirty street-car; but couldn't you look in on us between ten and half-past? The box is small, but I have a great fondness for those kind, good young men. Couldn't you induce one of them—any one at all, of course—to bring you, if he knew there was a place waiting for you both?"

"The gentleman who is going to escort me," began Jane, rising suddenly to a very formal tone, "is—well, in fact, he—he doesn't go out very much," she proceeded, lapsing back into her former manner. "He's kind of quiet and retiring. I don't believe he'd ever go to anything like this."

"Not when he's got a good place offered him—and a nice girl to take, with a brand-new dress of just the right sort to go in? I should want a beau of mine to have a little more spunk than that."

"How can you talk that way?" whimpered Jane, quite quivering with pleasure. "I can't sit here and listen to anything like that. What right"—with a feint of maiden indignation—"what right have you to say that Mr. Br—that anybody is—is my—"

"Beau," supplied Mrs. Bates, serenely. "Beau—that's what I said. Old-fashioned word, I know; but I can't think of a better one."

"You're just dreadful; you are," stammered Jane, trying to withdraw as best she might from too pronounced an attitude of protest. She fingered the length of ravelled bordering that drooped from the hair-cloth cushion of her chair and ran an eye, pretendedly speculative, up and down the pink and green stripes of Mrs. Bates's wall-paper.

"I'm pretty sure he wouldn't go—the gentleman who is to escort me to the lecture," she said, with another return to her vain paraphrase. "He's earnest. He's serious. Besides, he hasn't got a dress-coat."

"Hasn't got a dress-coat?"

"He doesn't approve of them. He thinks they're ugly and foolish and—and not right. He believes that society is—well, not exactly wrong, but—"

"All the same," declared Mrs. Bates, "he will receive a ticket, and I shall contrive to let him know that there's a place waiting for him."

"Oh, no! No, you mustn't! What would he ever think of me?"

"I shall, too."

"No! Don't—please don't. He wouldn't know what to think. He might think that I—"

"I shall, too!" repeated Mrs. Bates, more loudly and stubbornly. "I shall, too!" She knew that anything less marked than this would be a chilling disappointment to the girl before her. "And if he hasn't got a dress-coat, why, he can just get one. I'm sure if a young man cared anything for me—"

"Oh, don't talk that way—please don't!" implored Jane, half hiding her face with a kind of despairing joy. "Don't say such things, I beg of you!"

"—I should expect him to make some little sacrifice for me," Mrs. Bates completed. "Let him come and look at us; we may not be half so bad as he imagines."

"Sacrifice." What a delightful and comforting sound the word had to Jane. It vitalized in a moment all her story-reading of the past ten years. That anybody should ever be moved to make a sacrifice for *her!*

"But he used to live in the Settlement," persisted Jane; "he used to work there. He doesn't approve of Charity Balls; he thinks that isn't at all the way to do things."

"Well," said Mrs. Bates, thoughtfully, "it's *a* way; but there are better ones, no doubt. Come, cut that lecture altogether. He could pick up more in half an hour with me there at his elbow than he could learn in half a dozen courses of lectures, however extended they were."

"And have you act as you acted at Rosy's afternoon? You'd paralyze us both." Jane blushed at her "both."

"Oh, that's only my little way," returned Mrs. Bates, laughing. "You'd *both* understand." Jane blushed again. "A way," she repeated; "but there are better ones, no doubt." And she laughed once more.

X

Bingham half folded the newspaper, and laid it again on Marshall's desk. Then he settled his large, long figure back in Marshall's other chair, and placed a broad finger or two upon each of its curved and varnished arms.

"Yes," he observed, slowly, with a smile in the direction of the old man, "the younger generation are holding up their end."

"So it seems," said Marshall, in return, while he scanned the other's face closely to see what his precise meaning might be. Bingham's remark had been uttered with an even intonation; it was difficult to determine whether, after all, he had emphasized "younger" more than "generation," or "their" more than "end," or, indeed, whether he had given an undue stress to either.

"Yes," the old man repeated. He made another reference to the newspaper. "Yes; that is my child."

He fixed an eye, half fascinated, half protesting, upon a large cut which was set to fill the width of two columns. It was a portrait of Rosy—of "Miss Rosamund Marshall," as it read—with a line or two more, vaguely biographical in character, in italics, beneath. It was engraved with more than the usual care, and printed with more than the usual success.

This was the first time that any woman of his family had ever been exposed in the public prints. "And here are five or six lines telling how she was dressed. Is that right, Bingham?"

"Well, I'm no hand at describing. I suppose it reads correctly enough. At any rate, Rosamund was the handsomest girl there, and the best dressed—so several said—and the one who drew the most attention."

"Is that right, Bingham?" the old man repeated. He was accustomed enough to the public presentation of other men's daughters, but this was the first time that such a thing had befallen one of his own.

"Oh," replied Bingham; "you mean *that* way. Well, times change. Ten years ago this would have brought a protest, and twenty a flogging. And we change with them. However, if this is the Miss Rosamund Marshall who has begun lately to figure at teas and receptions and cotillons, and always contrives to be the bright particular— Is it?"

Marshall smiled slowly. All this was true enough, and he could not profess himself completely displeased. He nodded.

"Well, then, you'll have to stand it; you can't avoid it; it can't be helped. And there's one more thing, too."

"What?"

"There was a young man present on this same occasion," Bingham proceeded; "a decorative, diffusive young man—with a badge. Richard Truesdale Marshall—was that his name? Any son of yours?"

Marshall nodded again, but his smile was distinctly less complacent.

"I am beginning to meet his name in print quite frequently," pursued Bingham, serenely. "Is he the same Truesdale Marshall who has a collection of water-colors in the current exhibition at the Art Institute?"

"I believe so," responded the old man, with some lack of warmth.

"Is it the same Truesdale Marshall who sang last Friday at the residence of Mrs. Granger S. Bates, for the benefit of—of—"

David Marshall smiled broadly. "Our Jennie—what a girl she is coming to be! That Lunch Club is one of her pet notions; she pushes it at all times—in season and out."

"She seems to be pushing it to good purpose just now," commented Bingham. "By-the-way, I suppose she is the same Miss Marshall I danced with last night. She sat in one of the upper places, so to speak, but she was induced to go down on the floor for a few minutes."

"Well, Bingham," said Marshall, "I knew you went to that sort of thing once in a while, and I thought that that in itself was a good deal for a man like you; but for you to dance there— I shouldn't have imagined your doing it; well, no."

"I didn't but once," responded the other, apologetically. "Still, if you're going to get along in this world, you've got to be of it. Besides, I thought"—*argumentum ad hominem*—"that she was entitled to show that dress; hers was described, too."

"Um!" said her father, soberly, with a sidelong glance towards his pigeon-holes. "But no picture."

"Well, let that pass," responded Bingham, with a slight touch of pique. "Is this the Miss Marshall who read lately at the Fortnightly?"

"Yes."

"Is it the same one who is announced to lecture at Hull House on the Russian novelists?"

"See here, Bingham!" The old man wheeled about sharply in his chair, and fastened a keen scrutiny upon the other's face. Bingham had never talked to him like this before; he had never seemed so light-minded, so slanted towards the jocular. "See here, Bingham, what are you driving at?"

Bingham fitted himself solidly into the curved back of the chair, and laid his hands out ponderously upon its arms. He had something to say, and he wondered how best he might say it. "Marshall is twenty years older than I am," he thought, as his eye traversed the shelves of nutmegs and orris-root and lit upon the discolored awnings over the way, "and I must be careful. I'm young to him, of course; but I can't ask the indulgence due to a boy. How shall I work it?"

He felt that he had earned the right to speak. He had done well by Marshall, and he knew that Marshall was pleased. It was more as a personal favor than anything else that he had undertaken the work upon the warehouse; he had put it through more promptly than anybody else could have done, and with less interruption to the course of trade than either of the firm would have imagined possible. For the past month the business had been comfortably accommodated in its enlarged quarters, and the two new floors were already habituated to the occult processes which competition and a minutely graded scale of prices impose upon even the most righteous of the trade. It is but fair to say, however, that Marshall & Belden always saw that their sugar was as saccharine as a specified price would permit, and that their coffee-roasters met the lowered standard of cheap purchasers as well as the apparatus of any rival did.

Yes, everything was running smoothly, and Bingham felt that he might venture a slight trespass upon the friendliness and tolerance of his last client.

He looked at Marshall for a moment with a slow and cautious smile. "Yes, the young people are holding up their end; but how about the 'old man' himself?"

"Oh, that's it!" thought Marshall. He made an instant and intuitive application of this remark. He *was* declining towards the horizon; he *was* shining but dimly compared with the twinkling of his attendant satellites.

"Well, the 'old man' isn't altogether useless by a long shot. The young people dance—and the old people furnish the platform. See here, Bingham. I don't have to go to the papers to learn what my daughters wear to parties; I've got my own papers here right within easy reach." He contracted his brows as his eyes turned towards the pigeon-holes. "A better account, too, than the newspaper one—fuller, exacter, more detailed, backed up by figures—down three long sheets and half-way down a fourth. And I don't need to go to art-galleries to understand what opportunities my son has had to learn to paint; the foreign exchange man at our bank could tell me all about that. And I don't have to go to concerts, either, when I want to make my contribution to a benevolent object: I can sit right in this room and draw checks, and be told just how much to draw them for, too. Yes, Bingham, there are a great many ways for an old fellow like me to make himself useful, and I am not allowed to overlook any of them."

Marshall's tone and expression during this exposition had wavered back and forth between jest and protest. But his eyes wandered towards those pigeon-holes again, and his mien and accents drew on a shade of distinct melancholy.

These receptacles contained other bills than those of the dress-makers. There was one, for example, from a carriage-maker, and another from a horse-dealer. For Rosamund, at the very outset of her career, had set her face against old Mabel and the carry-all. She declined to appear in any such fashion among the landaus and broughams of her newly-chosen associates. She represented, furthermore, that it was extremely awkward to depend upon the equipages of friends; and she protested that it was far beneath their dignity to hire a conveyance from a livery-stable. Her father had succumbed. Along with the bills for the new carriage and pair were bills for a coachman's hat and cape-coat. Besides these, there was the first month's statement of board for Mabel and storage for the carry-all—both having been crowded out of the cramped stable to another across the alley.

"Yes," resumed Bingham, availing himself of Marshall's own figure, "the young people are dancing—though no more briskly than they should; but why may not the old people dance, too? When the young ones are making their youth and their beauty and their cleverness tell as they do, may they not *expect* the old ones to come forward as well? Aren't there times when they should do it in mere justice to themselves? After your children have led so many more germans and adorned so many more receptions and founded so many more clubs and really worked their way into the life of the town, they may look to their father to put himself in evidence also. One of them, I can swear, is already a little jealous on your account."

"Jane? Oh yes; she is always trying to make her poor old father toe the mark."

"She has plans for you—ambitions for you. If you meet the expectations that the future is likely to develop, you will be carrying through a pretty big contract. I was surprised, myself, to learn how many diverse opportunities this town offers— enough to extend through three dances. People may preside at banquets, I learned, and address political meetings, and head subscription papers, and found public baths, and build and endow colleges. And there are others who donate telescopes, or erect model lodging-houses, or set up statues and fountains, or give— Marshall," he said, suddenly, "do something for yourself and for the town; nothing that you are doing here"—he waved his hand towards the larger office outside—"is enough for a man of your means and standing."

Bingham was now speaking with increased confidence and with greater seriousness. He felt himself entitled to say these things by reason of their personal relations and by virtue of his own standing before the public. He was twenty years younger than Marshall, but he was twenty times as great a figure in the public eye. He had had no mean share in those two fast and crowded years through which the city had striven towards readiness for the coming of the world. Like the Christians at Ephesus, he, too, had "fought with the wild beasts"— with time, with the elements, with Labor, with National niggardliness, with a hundred-headed management; and he had expanded and ripened in the struggle. He saw the world with a wider vision; he inhaled the vast and palpitating present with a deeper breath. He beheld, too, a triumphant and wide-spreading future, and he felt with the utmost keenness the opportunities that the town offered even to the older and departing generation—crabbed and reluctant though it be.

Marshall listened to his remarks and indicated an unremitted attention by bowing now and then with a subdued gravity. The strain seemed familiar; where had he heard it before? Why, from Susan Bates, to be sure—and in this very place: strophe and antistrophe. Could it be possible that he was so remiss towards himself and towards the community? Could it be true that he was doing himself such scant and graceless justice? What answer had he to make to this new advocate? The old one—with additions.

"I have been thinking about these matters. I have been considering the public that so much is asked for. It is not the old public I used to know twenty years ago—it has changed a good deal. It is better organized against us—a banding together of petty officials with their whole contemptible following: steerage-rats that have left their noisome holds to swarm into our houses, over them, through them, everywhere—between the floors, behind the wainscoting—everywhere. Do you know anything about cheap law?"

"Justice courts? Don't let's go into that," said Bingham, quickly.

"I *am* in that," retorted Marshall, angrily. His blue eyes took on an unwonted gleam. "And I shall stay in until I have satisfied myself."

"Drop it," said Bingham. "It's a terrible thing—rotten, deplorable, an out-and-out curse."

"I will not," returned Marshall. He struck his thin old hand on the edge of his desk. "I'll see it through. They live within two blocks of my house. Her son is an alderman; her nephew is a bailiff; two or three others of them keep saloons. They are Poles, or Bohemians, or Jews—Heaven knows what. They do business on the premises—they stick to their burrow. Yet we couldn't get a summons served by a constable. And when we finally got the matter before a court—it was continued. No defendants there—only a filthy little creature who called himself their attorney. We were never so blackguarded in our lives. Then another continuance; and a third. Roger, poor boy, makes no headway at all. He knows the law; he has a good practice; he leases and collects for me—and buys and sells. But he is getting to be almost ashamed to come here to see me about it."

"I know," assented Bingham; "a kind of *camorra*. Get a shyster; fight the devil with fire. What can a gentleman do in a justice's court? If the rats are behind the wainscot, don't stick your own hand into the hole. Hire somebody else."

"I won't!" cried the old man, stubbornly. "I want to see for myself how things actually are. I want to learn what conditions we are living under. I want to understand the things that are really going on about us. I want to see what a good citizen and a tax-payer can count upon by way of redress." He picked at his petty grievance as a child torments a sore. Yet a sore, in justice, may mean little, or it may mean much. Any physician will tell you that.

"Drop it," counselled Bingham again. "It will irritate you and exasperate you out of all proportion to its importance. And if you have been wronged in a lower court, remember that many poorer men have been wronged in higher ones. Come; keep your head clear and your temper calm, and save them for important things."

The door of the little office opened softly, and one of the important things began. The door had opened none too widely, yet sufficiently for the entrance of the thin edge of a wedge— a wedge that was to gain a tyrannizing force with each inch of advance, as is the wont.

To Bingham it seemed like another of those rats—one that had left the wainscoting and taken to the floor, regardless (in a boldness at once insolent and sly) of the presence of human-kind. To Marshall it was only an office-hand from the outer room who now entered with a handful of mail matter, which he placed, with an air not wholly guiltless of servility and stealth, upon his employer's desk.

He was a dark man of forty-five, with a black beard and a pair of narrow eyes. He looked neither of the two occupants of the room full in the face. His glance was searching and sidelong rather, not so much from the presence of anything to spy upon as from habit and instinct. One fancied a man too accustomed to the heavy foot of superiors to decline willingly any minor advantage that came his way—or any major one.

Bingham's eyes followed him out. "Whom have you there?"

"Somebody of Belden's—a new hand; some of the sediment left from the Fair."

"That's where I've seen him. He was in the Service building —draughtsman, clerk, or something. Swiss? Alsacian?"

"I don't know," replied Marshall. "He speaks German and some French." Half unconsciously he began upon his mail. "It would be more to the purpose if he spoke English—better."

Bingham reached for his hat. "Well, time's money to both of us. English is an easy thing to pick up—as witness Midway. I dare say he'll be able to express himself fluently enough inside of another six months. Good-morning."

XI

"There!" Jane had said to herself, as he stood before her small looking-glass to give a final touch to her hair and to pull out her puffed sleeves to their widest for the tenth and last time; "if I can keep in mind that I am thirty-three years old, and not a day less, I imagine I shall get through all right. Of course I sha'n't go on the floor and dance—at least, not very much. Perhaps nobody will ask me, anyway; of course I can expect nothing from Theodore Brower, who couldn't waltz any more than he could fly. No; I'll just sit in the box, and then nobody can say that I am giddy, or flighty, or trying to be too young."

She cast a last glance towards her looking-glass, which seemed smaller than ever. "I do wish I could see both of them at once. I hope Theodore will like 'em; the chances are, though, he'll never notice 'em at all."

Such had been Jane's modest and cautious programme, and she carried it out pretty closely. She sat in the box with Mrs. Bates a good part of the evening, and bowed a great many times to a great many gentlemen, young and old, whom she had never seen before and never expected to see again, and whose names, therefore, she made no effort to secure. She talked with two or three with whom it seemed possible and profitable *to* talk, and learned their names afterwards.

Mr. Bates himself spent very little time in his wife's box. He lounged on one of the springy sofas in the narrow lobby behind, or leaned over the burnished barriers of other boxes to talk murmurously with other magnates about the Stock Exchange or the volume of traffic. He was a grave and somewhat inexpressive person, with reticent eyes and snow-white bunches of side-whiskers, and a rather cold and impassive manner. His wife followed his peregrinations with an indulgent eye.

"Poor Granger," she said to Jane; "this thing tires him more and more every year. So I give him plenty of leeway. See him now." She looked over her shoulder, where, twenty feet away, her husband was talking across the bronze bar with another elderly man in the adjoining box.

"It's a conference," she went on—"it's a deal; it's on my account—he told me so himself. If it goes through it means another string to this necklace."

She suddenly became quite smileless and rigid. "Why, what's the matter?" asked Jane.

Mrs. Bates presently relaxed. "That woman who just passed," she explained; "she was wondering if these diamonds weren't imitations, and the real ones in the safety vaults down-town. Notice that other one over there; yes, the one in nile-green, with the garnet velvet sleeves. She's looking for me, and can't find me. There! she sees Granger—everybody knows *him*. And now she's quieter; she's satisfied; she has taken old Mrs. McIntosh for me, just because Granger happens to be in their box for a moment. See, the man alongside of her is smiling and looking the same way. I know what she's saying to him: 'Is *that* Mrs. Bates—that plain old woman in that dowdy gown? Well, I never!—after all I've heard and read.' And she's so happy over it. Tell me, child; *am* I plain, *am* I dowdy?"

"You are magnificent," said Jane, squeezing her hand. "Carolus-Duran is only a dauber—and a half-blind one at that!"

Jane, after the first half-hour, had become quite habituated to her new and unaccustomed environment. Her attitude was neither too self-conscious nor too relaxed; and she never lost sight of the fact that she was thirty-three. Her dress was a fabric in a soft shade of blue-gray run through by fine black lines. Her ample sleeves took full advantage of the prevailing mode, and several falls of wide lace passed between them, both before and behind. Her hair was done up high, in a fashion devised by her fairy godmother—a piece of discreet but fetching phantasy. Jane leaned back graciously in her chair, after the manner of her favorite heroines, losing in height and gaining in breadth; never before had she felt so amplitudinous, so imperial.

"Whoever would suspect," she asked, turning over her shoulder to Susan Bates, "that I was a natural-born rail?"

"Nobody," the other responded. "You never looked so well in your life."

Jane blushed with pleasure. At that moment two of the Fortnightly ladies passed—clever creatures, who could drive culture and society abreast. Jane, with the flush still on her face and a happy glitter in those wide eyes, leaned forward and bowed in the most marked style at her command. "I am here myself," she seemed to announce.

"Well," said one of the Fortnightly ladies, "where is the 'Decadence' now?"

"Ah!" smiled the other, "that's past, and the 'Renaissance' is here again!"

However, Jane was not so taken up with her literary affinities as to lose sight of her own kith and kin. She saw Rosy swim past once or twice, and was gratified by constant glimpses of an active and radiant Truesdale. Once Statira Belden drove by in saffron satin and a mother-of-pearl tiara. "And that's her daughter with her," commented Jane. "And there's that girl from New York. And there goes her son—that smooth-faced little snip. Huh!—compare him with our Truesdale!"

She leaned forward eagerly as her brother came once more

into view. "Yes," she said, "his flower is all right, and the soles of his shoes. I wonder if—" and she leaned still farther forward and drew in a long breath through her nose. "No, I can't smell it; I don't believe it's bothered him any!"

Jane, in the earlier part of the evening, had sent Truesdale to the ball as a lady sends a knight to battle. She had stopped him on the moment of his departure at the foot of the stairs, close to the grotesque old newel-post, to look him over with a severely critical eye.

"Has it got its posy in its button-hole?" she inquired, throwing open his ulster. There was a gardenia there. "Yes, *that's* all right." Then:

"Has it got its little soles blacked?" Truesdale laughed, and turned up one of his long, slender, shining shoes, while he supported himself by his other leg and the newel-post. "Yes, that's first-rate," she assented. "What else is there, now?" she pondered.

"Oh! wait one second." She ravaged his inner pocket with a sudden hand. "Has it got its 'foom'ry on its little hanky?" She drew out the handkerchief and clapped it to her nose. "Not a drop—just wait one second."

She tore up-stairs in great haste, and in a moment more she came tumbling down with her own cologne-bottle in her hand. "You'll kill yourself, Jane," her mother called.

"Here!" She seized her brother's handkerchief again and drenched it with a plentiful and vigorous douse. "There!" she said, with great satisfaction, as she restored it to him.

"Goodness, Jane!" Truesdale cried, in laughing protest, "they'll all smell this for fifty feet around."

Jane gave her brother a commendatory pat, and said no word. She felt that he was now ready for conquest. Speech was superfluous.

"No, I can't smell it," said Jane, aagin; "I think he must have exaggerated. He's going off in the other direction, anyway."

Mrs. Bates touched her elbow. "Who's that dark girl in pink? No; not to the left—straight ahead."

"Why, I declare, it's Rosy!" exclaimed Jane. "And doesn't she look lovely! She's the prettiest girl here, isn't she?"

"Yes."

"And how well that little curly-cue curl on her forehead keeps its shape! But do you think she should have worn Maréchal Niels?"

"I dare say she's had red until she is tired of them. Who is the young man with her?"

"Don't know," said Jane. "These new young men are getting to be too many for *me*."

"Well, then, I'll tell you. It's Arthur Paston."

"Arthur Scodd-Paston?" asked Jane, contributing a conscientious hyphen to the name and a laborious accent to the forepart of it. "Why, he doesn't look so very hateful and supercilious."

"Oh, he's never that. He's a nice enough fellow. You mustn't take all my exaggerations seriously. He's jolly and pleasant, as you see for yourself."

"He'd better be—with Rosamund. She won't stand any great 'I' and little 'u' from anybody. But he does look real nice and stout and healthy and rosy, and everything, doesn't he?"

"Especially rosy," said Mrs. Bates, wickedly.

"I'm ashamed of you," remonstrated Jane; and the two young people swept on, while the music swirled and crashed, and the vast illumined ceiling bent above them like a rainbow of promise.

During one of the promenades Truesdale passed by with Bertie Patterson on his arm. The decorum of the walk could not exclude all of Truesdale's lithe and swaying ease; he held his head high, and sent his eyes abroad to right or left with an assurance that some might have felt to be an impertinence and others an insolence. To Jane he seemed just descended from some heaven-kissing hill. She sniffed once or twice as he went past. "I *hope* I didn't put too much on—I'm sure I didn't. I just sha'n't worry about it any more."

Bertie Patterson kept step beside him bravely, though she knew that Jane was looking at her from one side of the house and her aunt Lydia from the other. She was striving faithfully to be worthy of her environment. To take the arm of this brilliant young personage on any occasion at all would have been a test of spirit; how much more so on an occasion so brilliant and entrancing as this—particularly when the badge upon the young man's breast connected him so closely with it, and made the connection patent to all? She fused everything, and filled him with it and it with him: the mounting tones of violins and trumpets, the sparkling quincunxes of the girdling balcony-front, the wide band of fresco which ran in unison with the arches of glittering bulbs above their heads, the circling and swaying throng—all the sheen and splendor of a vast and successful city.

"Nice little girl with your brother," said Mrs. Bates.

"A real dear," responded Jane. "She poured tea for Rosy."

"Did she, indeed?" And Mrs. Bates looked at her harder to avoid seeing the passage of Gilbert Belden and his wife.

"There's another real dear," she said, presently, "if I can only catch his eye." She held up her finger to a young man who had just conducted Rosamund back to her aunt Lydia's box. Rosy had quite scorned the antiquated usage of the balls of an earlier and less sophisticated day. "Of *course* I shall not go with any young man; I shall go with a chaperon, and if the young men wish to see me they may see me there. It's all right if Jane wants to go with Theodore Brower; they might do anything after the way they bang around together in the street-cars. And I sha'n't go even with a chaperon unless she is in a box, where I can be taken afterwards"—a declaration which led to financial negotiations between David Marshall and his sister-in-law, and which brought him to a still higher appreciation of the general preciousness of his youngest daughter.

"There! he's coming—my boy Billy. Isn't he about right?" A tall, broad-shouldered young man of twenty-five was making his way across the floor, and presently passed through the exit in the midst of the lower boxes to gain the level of the upper ones.

"College all over, isn't he?" commented Jane; "his shoulders, and the way he parts his hair."

"The best boy in the world," said Mrs. Bates, plumply. "He has been with his father for the last four years, and he's come to be a real help to him. Gets to the office at eight o'clock, rain or shine, and loves nothing better than to sit and grub there all day long. Steady as a rock. Splendid future. Holds his own nose to the grindstone like a real little lamb. I hope he asked Rosamund for supper."

The young man presently reappeared, making his way behind the long tier of upper boxes.

"Well, my boy, were you forgetting all about your mother and her elderly friends? I'd never figured on your meeting the younger daughter first. My son William, Miss Marshall. William, here's an awfully good girl; her father thinks as much of her as I do of you."

The young man bowed, but blushed and halted before this singular presentation.

"Well, I don't know," said Jane, filling up the breach in the first fashion that presented itself. "If pa had the same gift of language that you have, I should feel surer." She picked out her puffs, and then leaned back negligently with her hands crossed. She was too thoroughly grounded by this time to be discomposed by any youth seven or eight years her junior.

The youth shifted his feet.

"I saw you with my sister a minute ago," continued Jane. She knew, without looking round to see, that Mrs. Bates was smiling in the anxious, would-be-helpful way of parents who have put their offspring at a disadvantage.

"Yes—oh yes," the young man responded, with precipitation. "We had a very nice polka, indeed."

"Well," said Jane to herself, "I can talk about polkas and lots of other things." And she did. She held and entertained the young man for a full ten minutes. She found, after all, that he was in no degree constrained or backward, and she made him do himself justice.

"Well, my dear," said Mrs. Bates, as he withdrew, "you made my Billy quite brilliant. I don't know when I have heard so much real conversation!"

"That's all right," responded Jane; "I was young myself once. I haven't forgotten that."

"Only you mustn't fascinate him," protested the elder woman, with a burlesque of maternal anxiety. "I want somebody else to do *that*." She gave Jane a smile full of meaning.

"Aha!" thought Jane, and wondered if she were to see a certain little romance resumed after the lapse of so many lumbering years.

"But she didn't seem to mind Paston any. Well, why should she?" concluded Jane.

Presently Truesdale came along and asked his sister to waltz. "All right," she said; "just for a minute; but not out in the middle—yet." She wished to test herself first.

"You're awfully good to me, Dicky," she whispered, as he led her back.

"Cut it," said Truesdale; "I'm proud of you."

Jane got back to her lofty perch. "I'll do it once more—if anybody asks me; yes, I will."

In another ten minutes she was on the floor again. "Quite happy, I'm sure," she had said to Bingham.

"Only I'm no great dancer," this big and bearded bachelor had warned her.

"Neither am I," declared Jane. "I can just totter around and that's about all." She arose quickly, shook out her plumage, took his arm, and in less than a minute was waltzing again. "Lucky it *is* a waltz," she thought; "I don't want to be trying too many novelties."

Mrs. Bates moved to let them pass out. "Really," she said, "I don't want to sit here all alone. Oh, Mr. Brower, I rely upon you. Let me have your arm. I suppose"—with a resigned submission to the inevitable—"that I am expected to walk around once, at least."

Brower had returned to the box, after diverting himself for some time rather shyly in the foyer. He had given Jane a promenade earlier in the evening, and had hoped to pass the rest of the time as inconspicuously as might be. Jane had been much pleased by his efforts to do the right thing—to be correctly dressed, for example. She knew from her own experience how one thing led to another, and she was appreciative of the pains he had taken on her account. It was easy for her to fancy how dress-suits must lead to dress-shirts, and shirts to studs and collars and ties and shoes and boutonnières—but Brower wore no boutonnière; there he drew the line. "Never mind," said Jane; "that isn't necessary, anyway. He has done quite enough as it is, and he's a good fellow to have done it." She knew how he regarded all this: as a sacrifice to Mammon, if not indeed to Moloch. "On my account, too," thought Jane—"every bit of it. Isn't it splendid of him!"

Brower was vastly disconcerted on receiving this command from Mrs. Bates—it was nothing less than a command, of course, and he must obey it. He had found it something of an ordeal to lead even Jane round the floor once; how much greater a one, then, to perform the like service for Mrs. Granger Bates, whose escort could not but expect to draw scrutiny and to provoke inquiry. He was a modest man with no pronounced social ambitions; he would immensely have preferred to pass the same length of time staring into a locomotive head-light.

Mrs. Bates presently effected a clearance, and with Brower as a convoy steered straight for the open sea. She carried a bunch of plumes aloft, showed a flashing brilliant on both the port and the starboard side, and left a long trail of rustling silk and lace behind her. And as she pursued her course, other craft, great and small, dipped their colors right and left.

"I want you to see both ends of the scale," she presently said to Brower. "You are trying to bring them closer together, they tell me."

"That is a part of our object," replied Brower.

"Well, you have one end in your Nineteenth Ward, and the other here. I want you to get the good side of this."

"I should be glad to; there *is* one, I'm sure."

"To begin with, don't encourage your associates to talk about the 'butterflies of fashion,' and that sort of thing. There are no butterflies in this town, except young girls under twenty, and you surely won't quarrel with *them*. Yes, we are all workers; what could Idleness herself do with her time in such a place as this? You've got to work in self-defence. Do you see that woman up aloft there?"

"Well?"

"She's the president and responsible manager of an orphan asylum. That one over across on the other side is an officer of the Civil Federation. Do you believe in that?"

"Devoutly."

"The woman just ahead of us—the purple velvet one—is a member of the Board of Education; she helps to place teachers and to audit coal bills. Why, even I myself have got a good many more things to look after than you could easily shake a stick at!"

"And the one you this instant bowed to?"

"You mean the one who bowed to me." For Mrs. Rhodes had leaned completely out of her box, and had then looked both right and left to observe whether her neighbors had done full justice to the episode. "Oh, she's a good little woman who is—climbing.

"The fact is," Mrs. Bates proceeded, "that there are not a dozen real grown-up butterflies in town. We're coming to one now." They were skirting one range of the lower boxes. "It's Mrs. Ingles; you must meet her."

"Some other time, please," implored Brower, as Mrs. Bates nodded to a sumptuous young creature not ten feet away.

"Very well." Mrs. Bates shrugged her shoulders "Yes," she proceeded, presently, "Cecilia Ingles and her immediate set are about the only real butterflies we have. However, I'm going to take her in hand pretty soon and make a good, earnest woman of her."

"There is work for them all," said Brower.

"But don't let's be too serious just now," rejoined Mrs. Bates in friendly caution.

"Who was that young man you had with you last night?" somebody demanded of her next day.

"Mr. Brower."

"Who is Mr. Brower, may I ask?"

"A friend of Jane Marshall's." This (save that he had a trusty face) was all that she knew of Theodore Brower; but she thought it enough.

"And who is Jane Marshall?"

Mrs. Bates gave her questioner one look. "Really, you surprise me," she observed, and said no word more. Within a week Jane was known throughout the inquirer's whole set.

Truesdale presently passed Mrs. Bates with a girl on his arm. "I wonder if that's another one of the tea-pourers?" she asked herself.

It was. Truesdale was escorting Gladys—Gladys McKenna,

146

as her complete name had finally come to him. He had laughed on first hearing it. "There's a *chaud-froid* for you, sure enough!"

Gladys wore a flame-colored gown, and her eyes, curiously fringed with black above and beneath, had an *outré* and dishevelled appearance that lingered in the memory as wax-works do. She kept a strong clutch on his arm, and galloped alongside him with a persistent *camaraderie* which conveyed no hint of cessation.

"Why insist so strongly on a *quadrille d'honneur?*" he was asking her. "Wasn't a march good enough?"

"We always look for a quadrille at one of the best functions —at home."

"But why draw lines? You don't object if people meet for pleasure on terms free and equal?"

"Oh, of course if you have no celebrities here—no great figures—"

"Not one—not till you came. We are all plain people here. If any of us forget our plainness there are plenty who are glad enough to remind us of it."

"Are you plain, too?"

"The plainest of the lot."

"You don't seem so; you look awfully ornamental, with that ribbon and all." The "all" meant the wave in his hair, the lustre of his eyes, the upward flaunt of his mustache which hid in no degree the white, firm evenness of his teeth, the freshness of a second gardenia—even the sheen of his shapely shoes.

"The ribbon—you like it? Sorry I'm wearing only one. How would you have liked a second running the opposite way? Or a third pinned on behind?"

"Oh, you!—How about all these other young men; are they anybody?"

"What other young men?"

"The ones with these criss-cross red ribbons."

"Oh! Well, some few of them have what you might call position, and some are working for it, and some are not thinking anything about it; and some, after having served their purpose, will be dropped soon enough, I promise you."

"And you yourself—are you in, or out, or not thinking about it, or—"

"I?" returned Truesdale, carelessly. "I'm just a passer-by; I'm on my way to Japan."

"Oh no; not Japan!" said the girl, quickly.

"Japan, I assure you," he smiled.

She caught herself. "To escape my uncle, then?"

"Why that, in Heaven's name?"

"You have offended him."

"Dear me! How?"

"By what you said at the house the other night. About the costumes, you know."

"Nonsense. How could that have reached him?"

"Those things do get around. Do you know what he's going to do? He's going to cut your comb. My aunt—she cried like anything."

To Truesdale the girl's tone seemed preposterously confidential. "You were in the wrong," she seemed to imply; "but I am on your side for all that."

"Ouf!" said Truesdale; "this comes of trenching on Biblical ground. I'll never quote scripture again."

Truesdale had gone to the Belden house in pursuance of the invitation extended at his mother's own tea-table. Eliza Marshall had made a faint effort to dissuade him; despite Mrs. Belden's presence at her own function, his going seemed, in one way or another, too much like an excursion into the enemy's country. But the occasion was a fancy-dress ball, and Truesdale declared himself much too curious to remain away. "I must go," he said, and at once took steps to equip himself for this voyage of discovery.

He wore the dress of a Spanish grandee of the early seventeenth century—he recalled the Spaniards as famous explorers. He was in black throughout, save for the white lace of his wide collar and cuffs, and for the dark purple lining of his mantle. If the Beldens, for their part, had costumed themselves half so discreetly, he would never have fallen from their good graces. But Statira Belden (keeping her own given name in view) had based her costume upon one of the old French tapestries—the Family of Darius at the Feet of Alexander; you may see the original, a Veronese, in the National Gallery. She had counterfeited the distresssed queen by flowing robes and pearls strung through her yellow hair. She had revivified and heightened the faded ideal of the oldtime artist, and incidentally she had extinguished every other woman in the room.

But the difficulty would still have been avoided had not Belden himself so far lapsed from discretion as to put himself forward in the guise of Shylock. It mended matters little that he had abandoned the costume within half an hour after donning it. Thus it was that Truesdale saw him for the first time in four or five years; the young man had completely disdained, thus far, to visit the store. With eyes freshened by long absence, and wits sharpened by contact with the world, he saw his father's partner in a dress which seemed to throw into greater prominence every lineament of his face and every trait of his character. The young man instantly doubted, mistrusted him. His Hebraic garments suggested another character held in still lower esteem. Truesdale, at a certain stage of the entertainment, observed his host and hostess in momentary conjunction on the threshold of the drawing-room; it was then that he uttered his little jest, whimsically careless of accuracy and loftily indifferent to outlying ears.

"Ananias and Statira," he said, and his words travelled through the house like escaping gas.

"They're awfully offended," said Gladys, continuing her confidential tone. "You can't come there any more—I don't believe. I'm so glad to have seen you here—who knows where I shall ever see you again? Why wouldn't you talk to me any, that first time? Why were you so long in asking me to dance to-night?"

She seemed to be pushing the claim of proprietorship first advanced at the Belden ball.

"Well, I hope I've talked enough since."

"But where shall we talk together next time? I don't believe you can come to the house," she repeated.

She seemed to be drawing attention romantically to obstacles in the way—in their way—and to be calling on him to remove them.

"Perhaps they won't let me see you again. Perhaps they're offended by my having danced with you here." She was adding to the barricade, but he was bold and resourceful enough to level it.

"Ouf!" thought Truesdale. "Girls—they're alike, every one of 'em, after all!"

XII

It was two o'clock in the morning when Jane said good-bye to Theodore Brower in the vestibule and burst into the house. There was a light burning in the library, and thitherward Jane swept in high feather. Her father was sitting there; as she entered he took up a newspaper that he had completely read out three hours before.

"Why, poppy!" she cried; "isn't this pretty late for you? But I know what you've been sitting up for so long: to have me tell you all about the party. Now, haven't you?'

Her father looked up at her in some wonder. Jane was distinctly in a state of exhilaration. She seemed conscious of having played well her part—no mean part, either—in a large performance; one might have fancied indeed that the splendor and success of the occasion was in some degree due to her own participation. She was decidedly gay, bright, sparkling; her father felt that here at last was his daughter almost pretty.

"Maybe I was," he answered. He threw down the newspaper so as to make it cover several loose sheets full of figures. "Did you enjoy yourself?"

"I should say I did!" She seated herself on the arm of his chair; one of her big puffed sleeves almost covered his face. "Don't think I was a wallflower, either; I wasn't. I went out on the floor three times. Mr. Brower walked me around once, and Mr. Bingham waltzed with me once. And so did Truedy. Oh, poppy, he was so good to me! And he was the only young man there with violet eyes—I didn't see another one."

Her father gave vent to a low, inarticulate monosyllable; it seemed to convey little appreciation of his son's eyes.

Jane had met Truesdale for a moment just before she came away. "How's the handkerchief?" she had asked. "All right," he responded, cheerfully. He took it folded and crumpled from his coat-pocket and showed it to her. He had carried it in his trousers pocket until a moment before; but Jane never knew.

"And I went to supper with Mrs. Bates and Theo—Mr. Brower," she continued. "And the oldest Bates boy took Rosy. We all went up in the elevator together and had a table quite to ourselves. I saw Mr. Bates there too. And lots of other elderly gentlemen. I wish *you* had been there. Several of them made themselves prominent enough—no younger than you, no richer, no more deserving of notice. Poppy, you must get out that coat some time and brush it up, and go somewhere with *me*."

Marshall thrust a finger under the edge of the newspaper. "I don't know, Jennie. There are lots of other things to think about."

Rosy came home at four. Mrs. Rhodes dropped her on her own way southward. Bertie Patterson nodded sleepily in one corner of the carriage. She was unused to late hours, and had been ready to go long before. But Rosy made it plain to all involved that she regarded herself as the first to be considered; she did not design leaving a minute sooner or a minute later than her own good pleasure should will. Her card was filled to the last line, and she danced it out—with William Bates, with Arthur Paston, and with a score of other young men for whose names the present pages have no need.

In the course of a week Arthur Paston called. Truesdale, who happened to be at home, found himself regarding Paston's presence with something the reverse of complacency, and his bearing with something that distinctly approached disapproval. He recalled to mind many of the diversions in which they had participated together, and he felt offended that Paston should bring here the same jaunty, familiar, off-hand ways that he had displayed in other scenes but slightly approved by Propriety. He would have preferred a line of conduct suggestive, in some small degree at least, of the penitent, the chastened, the abashed; a laugh less ready; a smile less confident; a bearing less self-assured, less divested of any sense of his need of tolerance, charity, forbearance. "I don't precisely like his acting in that free fashion here with Rosy," thought Truesdale; "there are times and times, and there are places and places."

His thought presently turned towards himself. He had no less need, truly, of charity and forbearance than Paston, yet he was not in the habit, to any great degree, of adjusting his own manner to varying conditions. He treated other fellows' sisters just as Paston was treating his. The idealizing gaze of little Bertie Patterson was upon him; it was not precisely with reverence, certainly, that he was in the habit of treating her, for example. And the other girl with the red gown and the wax-work eyes —her he had treated almost with open derision. But that was different.

Paston's cheery laugh rang out from the parlor. Truesdale stood in the library before the bookcase, reading the tarnished titles of the few spare volumes, as he shifted his weight from one foot to another, uncertain whether to advance or to retire. Paston knew him for what he was; but Bertie Patterson, he felt sure, would never acknowledge that he could be guilty of any wrong. "Hideous thing to be poetized," thought Truesdale; "but they all do it in one way or another." He thought of the faithful little hearts that beat in the German garrison towns. " 'Byron's Poems'—I could easily be better than I am—'Lossing's History of the American Revolution,' volume one, volume two—and I must try to be. 'The Lamplighter'; 'The Wide, Wide World';

—oh, curse that fellow's funny stories!" as Rosy's ready laugh came from the next room. Truesdale blushed as he thought of some of the stories that Paston could tell, when so minded; and he stamped his foot that such a—such a—(he found no word)—should be telling his sister any story at all. "But he's as good as I am," Truesdale was forced to avow, as he passed through the hallway and ascended to his room. "And better than lots of others. What can *I* say or do?"

Rosy herself, however, would have asked for no change in Paston's manner. She found him charming, fascinating; compared with him, William Bates was far from entertaining. If Paston had attempted the chastened, the deprecatory, she would have feared that he was not enjoying himself. She would have taken but little satisfaction in deference pushed to humility. She was beginning to idealize him, as Bertie Patterson had begun to idealize her brother; but Rosy's idealization was not half so generous.

While walking on his arm a week ago, she had not felt her self in a public hall within a few hundred yards of her own home; no, she was at Buckingham Palace or at St. James's—she was not sure which. There were moments, indeed, when it was not a palace at all: it was the terrace of some Tudor house, with stone balls on all the posts, or it was the trim path of some village church-yard, bordered by yew-trees and by tombstones with cherubs' heads and hour-glasses. She was the bride of a month, and this was her first service in England. The people around them figured no longer as the swell crush of London, but as a respectful, lock-tugging, courtesy-dropping tenantry who fell off on either side as she passed out to her carriage on her husband's arm. There were side-long glimpses, too, of forgeries and murders and lost wills and stolen jewels and people drowned in wells; in one book there had been a maniac girl shut up in a room—but she should try to avoid all these superfluities; a duchess in possession of her senses would be decidedly preferable. A week later and she was deeper in Burke and Debrett than ever.

"Well, here it is finally—Saltonstall, Scamperdown, Scodd-Paston." Rosy bent her head and studied the large gilt volume with redoubled vigor. "It's pretty near the end, after all."

Rosy sat at a desk in a big new granite building to one side of a small park. Above the window-ledge appeared the tops of trees, the towers and gables of a pair of churches, the dark and dignified façade of a club-house, and the various elements that make up one of the half-dozen local views which bear in any great degree the stamp of civilization. Around her people fluttered leaves, or put books back on their shelves, or carried on the cataloguing of a large and but half-arranged library. But Rosy gave heed to none of this. "Scodd-Paston," she said; "here's a whole paragraph." And she buried herself in it at once.

She had begun with the Queen and the royal family and the order of precedence. Then she had gone through the dukes, very carefully; then through the marquesses, not so carefully; then through the earls, somewhat cursorily: "Here's one with eight daughters, the Honourable Gertrude-Adeline, and seven more." Then she had bolted through the viscounts and barons: "This one's awfully new—only from 1810." Then she slid lightly over the baronets. Then she passed on to the knights. "I don't suppose it's *here*." But it was.

" 'General Sir John-George-Alexander Scodd-Paston,'—that's a pretty good name," thought the girl—" 'born in 1835; entered Life Guards in 1855; married in 1857 to Mary-Victoria, dau. of James, Lord Lyndhurst'—I wonder if she was of higher rank than he. Oh, here we come to his own. 'Attained rank of colonel, 1869; general, 1877; served in Egyptian campaign of 1882; appointed Groom-in-Waiting to Her Majesty in 1883'—ever so many capital letters. 'C.B., 1882; K.C.B., 1885'—a lot more. Whatever do they mean? Does he wear stars and things? And here's where he lives: 'Boxton Park, Witham, Essex.' And somewhere else, too: '10, King's-gate Gardens, S. Kensington'—that's in London, I suppose. And here are his clubs: 'Whitehall and United Service.' Only two; why, lots of the others have five or six. But papa hasn't got one, even. Besides, think of *our* ever being in a book!"

She paused a moment in perplexity. "But where are his children—all the sons and daughters, and when they were born, and who they married, and everything? It tells in the dukes and earls. Never mind, though; I don't need a book for that. Boxton Park, Witham, Essex," she mused. The posts came back again with the stone balls on top of them; and a few oriel-windows; and a peacock or two strutting on a terrace. The prospect widened; ditches and hedge-rows under a low, gray sky, packs of yelping hounds, hunters following in red coats....

Rosamund went home in a thoughtful mood. It was within a fortnight of this that she was taking hurdles at her riding-school.

This involved still another horse, and a habit, and a saddle. Rosamund was teaching her father how to spend money; no other member of the family, save Truesdale, had ever attempted as much.

"Are we going on forever living in this same old place?" Rosy asked her mother one day. She had fallen into the way of making comparisons between Boxton Park and No. two hundred and whatever-it-may-have-been Michigan Avenue—just as she had made comparisons with the many fine houses where she had lately been entertained.

"I don't expect to live anywhere forever," replied her mother, tartly.

"It's so old and dismal," Rosy went on. "I declare, I hate almost to ask anybody here. And it's getting so noisy and dirty —and all those awful people over there on those streets behind us."

Eliza Marshall's thought flew swiftly towards the second-hand dealer of those purlieus who had carried away so much good, solid furniture, and then had declined to pay for it. But this did not prevent her from looking on her child now as if a viper, warmed at her hearth, had roused to life and stung her.

"Why can't we change?" Rosy proceeded; "why can't we move? Why can't we build somewhere—where we can have neighbors, and a house to invite them to?"

"What do you call the Blackburns and the Freemans?" asked her mother, severely. "Where can you find nicer folks? Why do we want to chase after a lot of new people that we don't know anything about?"

"The Blackburns and the Freemans are no company for me," Rosy declared. "All the people I know are up on the North side or down on Prairie Avenue."

"The North side!" repeated her mother, out of all patience. "I see myself moving to the North side at my time of life, after living on this side for more than forty years. I should feel as much at home in Milwaukee. And don't talk to me about Prairie, either; as long as I live, I live on Michigan, and nowhere else. I don't want to hear any more about it—no, not a word."

While Rosy assailed her mother about the house, Jane attacked her father about himself. Her social triumphs (so she regarded them) had made her more ambitious and more aggressive than ever. She was less solicitous about the family in general, which seemed to be moving on satisfactorily enough, than she was about the head of it himself, who appeared distinctly to be lagging behind.

Marshall now listened to his daughter's urgings with a more serious consideration; she was only saying to him what older and more experienced people had said already—Susan Bates, for example, and Tom Bingham. Susan Bates, in fact, had renewed the attack, and she prosecuted it whenever occasion offered. She had not scrupled, indeed, to pursue the theme within the precincts of her own house.

Mrs. Bates had not yet achieved the peculiar aboriginal function which she had outlined to Jane in the course of their first talk—the reel, the old settlers, and the young squaws to pour firewater were still in the future; but she had entertained the Marshalls at dinner, *en famille,* and she had pushed the subject with still greater insistency in her own house than at David Marshall's office.

For the occasion of the Marshall dinner Mrs. Bates put her household on a peace footing. She banished, as far as possible, all traces of social war-paint. She determined to dispense with as many of the men-servants as might be, and to have those who were left over wear their plainest liveries; she even thought of arranging to have the Marshalls' ring answered by a maid instead of a footman. So when David Marshall came, in the dress-coat that had not seen the light for over a year, and Eliza Marshall, in the plum-colored silk whose only recent airing had been at Rosy's coming-out, they had little to contend against save the house itself and its furnishings.

Jane accompanied them. "Tom Bingham is going to take you out," Mrs. Bates announced. "He is very much interested in you. He thinks you are quite a clever girl."

"All right," replied Jane. "I'm interested in him, too. I think him a person of great discernment."

"I had some notion of asking Rosy at first; Billy was so taken with her. But this is really an old folks' party, after all. Besides, Billy had a theatre engagement."

"Sorry," said Jane; "I'm sure pa and ma would have liked to meet him." Whatever little plan Mrs. Bates may have been revolving in her mind, Jane was too loyal to throw cold water on it. "So should I myself."

Susan Bates gave the Marshalls a short, plain dinner; she had no desire to glorify herself or to embarrass her guests. But Eliza Marshall learned more of contemporanics in that one evening than she had picked up in the previous decade. She learned how people received, how they set their tables and served them, how they built their houses and furnished them. She learned not only the possibilities but the actualities of splendor and luxury in the town where she had led a retired and humdrum existence for nearly a lifetime. She now thrust her head forth from her dim old cavern, and fed her eyes on the flowers and fields and skies and goodly streams of the great world outside.

While Jane supported her mother against the lumbering charges of Granger Bates's conversational cavalry, his wife engrossed Marshall's attention for her dormitory. Her plans had taken shape in her own mind, and were now beginning to take shape on paper.

"It's more than a mere dormitory, of course." She cleared a space between them, and took up a dessert-spoon. "Here's the vestibule and entrance-hall," she began, drawing with the spoon on the table-cloth; "and here's where the stairs run up. Off to this side—John, do take some of these glasses away—off to this side"—with a wider sweep of the spoon—"is a sort of parlor and reception-room—quite a good size, you see. Right next to it is the dining-room—so that they can be thrown together, when the girls receive."

"Good," said Bingham; "nothing more civilizing than receptions."

"On this side of the dining-room," pursued Mrs. Bates, "is going to be a sort of alcove—Jane, dear, just push me over that salt and pepper. There!" She planted the two bottles in her alcove; "that's the tank for tea, and this is the tank for coffee. Practical, don't you think?"—to Bingham.

"First-rate. And I suppose you have a screen that you can put in front."

"Precisely." She laid a tiny spoon across her alcove. "Hardwood floors down-stairs, throughout. Up-stairs, bedrooms for fifty girls, and each one shall have a closet, if possible. We begin the foundations in five or six weeks—as soon as the frost is out."

Susan Bates cleared a larger space, and appropriated more knives and forks and spoons, and went on in a lower tone for Marshall's ear alone. Jane strained to catch her words. She saw her father blush once, slightly, and then smile, as if partly flustered—as Jane herself phrased it.

"What a dear good old sentimental soul she is!" thought the girl. "I'll bet a cent she is asking pa to put up a dormitory for boys on the other side of the campus!"

Mrs. Bates presently carried Jane and her mother into the library, leaving the men behind to contemplate a litter of disordered wineglasses and dishevelled napkins, and to smoke themselves out, in the course of half an hour, to the women.

Mrs. Bates's talk, here as heretofore, was frankly personal. On a previous occasion she had talked to Rosy's mother about Rosy; now she exacted that Rosy's mother should talk to her about her own boy Billy.

"The best boy in the world; his father says he's making a splendid business man." She took a cabinet photograph from over the fireplace. "There; this is the latest, but it doesn't do him any kind of justice."

"Well, he's got a real *good* face," said Eliza Marshall.

"And a real good-looking face, too," rejoined his mother, quickly. "Jane, dear, run up to my room and get the one before this—that's something like; second drawer on the left. And stop eying those books; you can't get at them with anything less than a cold-chisel!

"But why should you depend on pictures?" Mrs. Bates observed, presently. "See the boy yourself. Go down-stairs next time he calls. Oh, he will call again, I assure you," concluded Susan Bates, archly.

"Tell him to inquire for ma, and send in a card for her, too," whispered Jane. "Rosy's getting awfully sticky."

" 'Sticky'?"

"Yes; fussy, stiff, critical—that's what it means, as near as I can make out. It's a word Dick brought home from London."

"H'm," said Susan Bates, "I'll remember it.

The men, meanwhile, sat round the dining-room table. Marshall smoked with the others and tried to forget his boutonnière —the first he had ever worn.

"I shall make them very small and unobtrusive," Susan Bates had said; "only a dozen violets." Marshall noticed that Bates had put his flowers into his right-hand button-hole, and Bingham his into his left. Jane saw her father hesitate; finally he imitated Bates. "Well, that's cutting it pretty fine," thought the girl; "I wonder if there *is* a right or wrong way. But think of pa with any button-hole bouquet at all! We shall budge him yet!" She smiled; she knew the forces were all arrayed against him to-night.

"What this town needs more than anything else," Bingham was saying, "is a big assembly-hall—one with a capacity of ten thousand, say. Something not too fine—we've got that already; and something not too rough—we've had that in plenty. A hall suitable for conventions, for promenade concerts, for mass-meetings, for horse shows—in short, something after the fashion of that magnificent thing in New York."

"The Madison Square Garden?" asked Bates. "You're perfectly right."

"Now that Garden," pursued Bingham, "is not exactly a paying investment—wasn't meant to be. The last time I was down East—"

"Yes—"

—"some fellows there quoted it to me as an evidence of public spirit—the spirit that we here suppose not to exist in New York at all. The men who put it up could easily have got more on their money; but there it stands, one of the most useful and beneficent features of the whole city."

"We ought to have one here," declared Bates.

"And I should like to build it," declared Bingham. "The man

who would give such a thing to Chicago, or who would even take the headship of it and make a suitable contribution, would be doing as much for himself and for the town as any one man well could."

"But don't look at me," said Bates. "My wife has drained me dry—you know about her dormitory and all her other schemes. Look at—well, look at Marshall. What is Marshall doing for the good of the city?"

Marshall lowered his eyes and fingered the broad foot of an empty wineglass. He sat between two of the great powers of the town, and he had never felt smaller. He wondered whether he had deserved his success; he wondered if he himself had really made it. After all, he had come on the ground before competition had fairly set in. He had done nothing by force or by audacity; he had been slow, cautious, even timorous, and he confessed inwardly that there were men in his own employ—men on a mere salary—who were cleverer, readier, more resourceful than he—men who, in a fair field and on even terms, could have distanced him completely. He gave the wineglass another turn or two, and did not lift his eyes.

He heard Bingham's voice again. It was declaring that in the history of every great mercantile city there was a single short period—a passing moment, almost—on which the citizen who wished to impress himself upon the community and to imbed himself in the local annals must seize. Marshall heard him instancing the Fuggers, of Augsburg, and the Loredani and Morosini, of Venice, and the Medici and Tornabuoni, of Florence, and many other names alien and all unfamiliar—merchants, most of them, it seemed, who had perpetuated their name and fame by improving the precise moment when their town, like plaster-of-Paris, was taking its "set."

"Make your impression while you may," concluded Bingham. "This is the time—this very year. The man who makes his mark here to-day will enjoy a fame which will spread as the fame of the city spreads and its power and prosperity increases. You know what we are destined to be—a hundred times greater than we are to-day. Fasten your name on the town, and your name will grow as the town itself does."

Marshall drove home thoughtfully in the new carriage, with the new horses, and August in his new cape-coat. Eliza Marshall, who had sat gingerly upon the edge of her seat in driving out, now leaned back at her ease when returning; it seemed that, with a little practice, she might easily become habituated to luxury. As she re-entered her old familiar parlor, she almost gave a gulp of mortification over its plainness and shabbiness; for the first time in years she had given herself a chance to know it for what it was.

"There, now," Jane declared loudly, "you've both seen what money and brains can do. Well, haven't *we* got money? Haven't *we* got brains? Is there any reason why *we* shouldn't be known, and looked up to, and respected?" And at breakfast next morning she opened out upon her father once more. Her lunch-room was now, thanks to her solicitings and her concert, in full running order, and moving on to a marked success. To-day she was rising to a more ambitious plane. Not a college building, not an assembly-hall; no, during the watches of the night she had risen to the conception of a working-girls' home. Her father had been listening to the mellow and flowing hautboy of Susan Bates, and to the deep diapason of Tom Bingham; but his daughter had now pulled out the coupler and was screaming shrilly above all the other voices of the organ. He felt almost deafened, stunned.

The "second girl" came in, frightened. "What is it?" asked Eliza Marshall.

"August is in the kitchen, with his face all cut and bleeding."

Jane left her father. "Let me go out and see what it is."

It was another chapter in the Van Horn matter. Roger, having become more familiar with police-court methods, had been pushing things with greater vigor and effect. During the past night two or three ruffians had broken into the stable, had shattered the windows of the new carriage and defaced its panels, and had beaten the coachman.

"There!" cried Rosy. "How much longer have we got to live down here among all these savages and hoodlums?"

Eliza Marshall made no reply, and Rosy felt that this in itself was to have gained a point.

XIII

Eliza Marshall meditated on the Bates dinner for several days succeeding, and when the following Saturday morning came round she was still busy with it. Saturday was her day for going over the antiquated accumulations of her parlor; no hands ever dusted and replaced the ornaments on her what-not save her own. She had been very chary of expressing herself about Susan Bates's entertainment, even to Jane. But now she felt that the time had come when she might trust herself to speak.

"I can't say I see the need of so many kinds of spoons," she said, as she transferred one of her gilt candelabra from the what-not to the contorted old rosewood centre-table: the candelabra were of an operatic cast—the one under removal represented (though all unknown to Eliza Marshall) Manrico and Leonora clasped in each other's arms beneath a bower-like tree. "Cut right through the middle, too—so that you could hardly tell whether they were spoons or forks."

"What could be better for ice-cream or salad?" asked Jane, who was blooming forth as an authority on matters social. She sometimes assisted her mother on these Saturday mornings— under close supervision.

"And three kinds of wineglasses," observed her mother, with some disapproval. "Sort of showy, I thought. Kind of as if they wanted to impress us, and let us see what— No!" she cried, as

165

a figure came up the front walk, carrying a tray fastened in front. "No! 'Melia, tell him we don't want any suspenders or collar-buttons; we don't wear them."

"Showy!" called Jane. "My sakes! it was the plainest thing I ever saw at their house. If you could see *some* of their doings!"

Eliza Marshall set back the candelabrum and transferred her attention to a Rock of Ages in Parian marble. "I believe things get dirtier here every year. I'm sure more dust comes in at that window than goes out." Then: "Well, I don't see but what we're as good as anybody else; I don't see but what we are as well worth taking pains for." She ran her cloth resentfully between the arms of Faith and the arms of the cross.

"Oh, dear me suz!" cried Jane; "are you trying to get the poor woman both ways? Her dinner was just right, and I am sure she took every possible pains to have it so."

"What?" called her mother, craning her neck and contorting her features. A locomotive was letting off steam opposite the house, and the noise and the vapor came across the hundred yards of dead grass together.

"I say it was all right," shouted Jane. "Don't you suppose she knows how to— Dear me! what's the use of trying to talk here?" She fell on the mantel-piece and dusted its vases in silent desperation.

Her mother accepted this dictum as final—a proof of Jane's altered status, and of the discretion with which she was carrying herself. "Of course I am not a society girl," was the way Jane turned the matter over in her own head; "I am a benevolent old maid, with a capacity for society when occasion offers." Jane had kept this point distinctly in view, and had now extricated herself from the squeezed and anomalous position which, for the last few years, she had occupied between her two sisters. "Alice thinks she knows everything, just because she's married," Jane had said to herself a year back; "and Rosy thinks she knows everything just because—well, I'm sure I can't exactly tell why.

But anyhow, between the two, I'm being pretty well flattened out. I've got to do *something*." And she had.

Jane, running on the new track she had laid down for herself, had regained the consideration of Alice, and had even conquered the respect of Rosy. Indeed, so far had she triumphed with her younger sister that Rosy was even showing civility and goodwill to Theodore Brower, whose regard for Jane had brought about his social rehabilitation. "I wonder why he never cut his beard to a point before," Rosy said one day; "he looks ever so much better. And I see that he has finally provided himself with calling-cards. Well, if he leaves one behind every time he comes, we shall soon have a fine litter."

"He won't, though," said Jane, "except when he calls on you."

"Well, he may call on me if he chooses," responded Rosy, with a gracious condescension. "I'm sure he talks very sensibly."

"Never fear," retorted Jane; "he isn't competing with the British aristocracy!"

Then Rosy would go up-stairs for a bit of pen-and-ink practice—to cover a sheet with such words as these: Lady Rosamund This-or-that; Rosamund, Countess of Thus-and-so; the Honourable Rosamund Such-a-one. She lingered fondly over the baptismal "Rosamund"; what word could match more fitly with a title, or harmonize more completely with the grand old names of the peerage? Once she wrote on the extreme lower corner of the sheet: Mrs. W. F. Bates. "Oh, pshaw!" she exclaimed, and tore the corner off and threw it into the fire.

The locomotive had relieved itself, and no noise remained save the jangling of a long line of freight-cars on another track. "Those people who repaired the carriage," resumed Eliza Marshall, now beginning on one of her Dresden figures—"those people who repaired the carriage spoke to your father about—'Melia, shoo that tramp out of the side yard; of *course* we haven't got anything for him this time of day. They spoke to your father about—"

She paused, and began to bestow an exaggerated care upon the figure now under her hands—a dancing-girl of Seville. Jane paused in her own work and waited for the rest. "Well?" she asked, presently.

Her mother wiped the head of the dancing-girl very carefully. The girl had black hair parted in the middle and laid in two wide scallops over her ears. "They told your father they were looking for a site to build a new warehouse on."

Jane's heart gave a throb. "Well?"

Her mother applied herself painstakingly to the apron and petticoat of the dancer—a petticoat striped in purple and green, and sprigged over with some species of flower wholly non-botanical. She drew her cloth down every stripe.

"They said they were hoping to find something just about in—in this neighborhood."

Jane shrank and trembled as if before a knife. "Well?"

Her mother passed on to the girl's slippers. She wiped the worn gilt of one stubby foot and then of the other. "They asked him to put a price on—on—"

"On our home!" cried Jane. There was a tear in each eye as she bowed her head over the mantel-piece.

Her mother returned to the Rock of Ages, and began to dust it again—as carefully as before.

"Well," she said, slowly, without turning round, "there's a building of that same sort a block or two south of us, already." She lingered on the short arm of the cross. "The Blackburns are talking of going, you know."

Jane bowed her head again and picked at the fringe of the mantel-covering—a foolish thing that she herself had embroidered and draped. Now, for the first time, she formulated her mother. "I've half known it all along," she thought, "and now I know it for sure." In this moment she definitely saw her mother, not as a creature of the affections, but as a creature of mere habit. "And it's been so for the last twenty years," thought the poor girl.

Eliza Marshall passed back to one of the candelabra; its cracked prisms tinkled as her broken talk went on. "Well, I don't know, I'm sure. Our last neighbors are leaving us. Business and boarding-houses all around. And Rosy wants to change. And there's so much noise and dirt, and so many peddlers and beggars. And—and—" She was thinking of Susan Bates's library, but would not permit herself a spoken reference to it. "And so much work to keep things tidy. And those miserable fellows breaking into our barn. I don't know, I'm sure."

Marshall himself, meanwhile, talked the matter over with Belden and with Roger, when Roger came in to consider the assault on the stable and the policy of employing the police. "I don't know that I should depend too much on the city's detectives," he had observed; "but I will have them go down to the house, if you say."

Accordingly, one morning a brace of young Irishmen modestly traversed the sidewalk which led around the house, and knocked with some show of decorum at the kitchen door. Each had the fresh complexion of a recent arrival, chestnut hair plastered in a scallop on his forehead, room under his nose for a large red mustache, and room under his finger-nails for a noticeable quantity of "matter misplaced." Presently they put on their derby hats again and went out to visit the stable. Then they took their departure and were never heard of more.

The next detective rang at the front door. He wore gloves and a high silk hat. He was a tough and determined-looking person, whose progress rearward the family attended with a close watch on their portable property: he seemed much more corrupt and knowing than any mere barn-breaker could be. He was more efficacious, too, than the duo that had preceded him. Even in the stable he gave much less heed to August than to August's mistress, and in the course of a few days he put his hands on the offenders. Ten to one he could have done that without having visited the premises at all.

Roger was the family counsellor in matters of investment

as well as matters of law. He had early made the observation that few lawyers amassed a fortune in the strict practice of their profession; and he had accordingly turned a prompt attention to building and to land, operating largely for himself and for his father, and to the advantage of both. Indeed, manipulations in real estate had done more for David Marshall's fortune than had the pursuit of the grocery business—just as they had done more for his son than the pursuit of the law.

"Your mother won't live anywhere but on Michigan, though," he declared to Roger.

"She needn't," the other rejoined. "Move south three miles— if you mean to make any change at all. The best houses in town are going up along that stretch—just within the old limits. And a house there could be turned into money at any time."

Roger, as a practical real-estate man, naturally put convertibility before domesticity.

Marshall also canvassed the matter with Belden. Belden listened to him somewhat coldly and impassively—with less interest, the old man thought, than one's partner rightly should. But Belden took the idea of a new house as another step in the social advance of the Marshalls. It seemed to him almost like the challenge of a rival; and a rivalry like this nettled him none the less from being so sudden, so unexpected; so impracticable, as—six months back—he would have considered it. He felt himself and his family outdone at every point. Rosamund Marshall had eclipsed his own daughter at a dozen dances; Truesdale Marshall, thanks to the half-jocular patronage of the press, was becoming in his way a celebrity, while his own son merely led a dubious existence which oscillated between the bar of the Metropole and the billiard-room of the Lexington, and conferred little distinction upon himself or anybody else; and even dusty old Eliza Marshall, almost despite herself, was being dragged up into a circle to which his own wife, notwithstanding all her lavish and industrious endeavor, remained as alien at at the beginning.

And, to crown all, Marshall himself had finally come forth as a public figure. Belden had actually been obliged to sit at a banquet-board and to hear this old man, usually so quiet and inexpressive, loudly applauded by a hundred hard-headed businessmen, who, a month before, had received an effort of his own with mere civil toleration.

This new advance of Marshall's was made partly by Jane's help, partly in spite of it. "Speak?" she had said, when her father broached the subject one evening; "of course you'll speak. You know all about the topic, if anybody does; and here's an opportunity right at your hand. I'll help you get up your speech, myself."

She did. She prepared a long address after the most approved rhetorical models: a flowing introduction which walked all around the subject before going into it; a telling peroration whose emphatic periods seemed to render any subsequent consideration of the matter a mere piece of futility; and in between, briefly and cursorily, the one or two vital points of the whole discourse. Thus equipped, David Marshall was to rise at half an hour before midnight, the last but one of a long line of speakers, to claim the attention of a great roomful of men sated with meat and drink and sodden with oratory.

But in the cloak-room the manuscript had slipped from his pocket, and at the table all its overwrought periods had slipped from his mind. And at midnight he rose to confront an expanse of disordered table-cloths and an array of wearied faces, his own face full of uncertainty, and nothing to nerve his inexperience save a desperate determination not to disappoint his daughter.

"Another old bore getting up"—from a distant corner of the smoky room. "Any idea who he is?"

"Not the slightest." A yawn. "Take another regalia."

David Marshall had forgotten everything but his main points and the facts that supported them. He began in the very midst of things. He spoke a minute and a quarter—plainly, simply; and sat down the instant he had finished.

He had spoken in his usual husky and sibilant voice. Nobody had called "Louder!" however—because nobody had really wished to hear.

On his ending, the room rang with applause—the applause of gratitude, largely.

"Well, the old fellow can say his say, after all, eh? And no blooming oratory, either."

"And sense enough to cut it short—the last man usually shows the least mercy."

As Marshall sat down his neighbor on the right shook his hand warmly. "Why haven't you been doing this for us before?"

As he was leaving the hall, the secretary of another club, present by accident, solicited an address on a cognate subject for a coming meeting of his own organization. "Why didn't you give yourself a little more time?" he asked.

Jane was wild with pride and pleasure; her father had given her the results and not the process. "I knew you could, poppy; I just knew you could. We'll start in on the other speech right away, and make it even better than this. We'll show 'em, yet!"

But it was not Marshall himself, for all the inexplicable ease of this success, who chiefly angered Belden. Nor had he any great feeling against Rosamund, having no undue interest in the social rivalries of young girls. Nor was he particularly incensed against her mother, being offended chiefly by the ostentatious and invidious good-will shown her by Mrs. Bates. But against Truesdale Marshall he nourished a hot and rancorous grievance. He did not apprehend Truesdale's attitude towards the town at large, and the young man's manner in his own house (regardless of his insolent utterance) seemed to have carried a half-contemptuous curiosity beyond all decent bounds. "That young cockerel—I'll soon find a way to quiet his crowing. What does all his singing and painting and fencing amount to, after all? He couldn't post an item into a ledger; he couldn't even tie up a pound of tea. He can't work off any of his foreign smartness on *me!*"

Truesdale readily figured himself the reverse of *persona grata* to the Beldens, and stayed away; but this did not prevent his reception of advices more or less regular from the heart of the Belden household. "What's that absurd girl up to *this* time?" he asked one morning, as an envelope, directed in a hand already too familiar, came to the door. He recognized readily enough the sprawling, half-masculine penmanship of Gladys McKenna, as readily as he divined the rôle which she must imagine herself to be playing. She was pretending herself to be a prisoner in some hostile camp—a hostage in some dismal dungeon; and, despite the close and suspicious watchfulness of those surrounding her, she was still sending her little messages, all the same, to her *preux chevalier* on the opposing side. In the end her reward would come; she and her knight. . . .

"Ouf!" cried Truesdale, who scented all this crass and forward romanticism between the trivial lines of her communications; "why does she write, when she hasn't got anything to say?"

Sometimes she *did* have something to say—a little. To her statements of the disposition of the Belden family towards her correspondent, and to her general recommendation to "beware," would be tagged indications of her own individual movements. "Poor auntie is laid up with the neuralgia, and Ethel has gone visiting in Kenwood, so I am the only one to be sent to Field's for those gloves. Auntie says the best time for the glove counter is about twelve-thirty, when the crowd is smallest."—"Yes," mumbled Truesdale, irritably; "and lunch at one."

Or: "They are going to let me go alone to Modjeska to-morrow afternoon—in the street-car; just think of it! I think I shall ask for a seat in the last row—I am so timid about fires." Sometimes she would add "destroy this," or, "burn this." "Most willingly!" Truesdale would exclaim, and throw "this" in the fire at once.

Or, again "Imagine; I am to have a tooth filled. Auntie says I needn't trouble to go away down-town—there is a very good man right on Twenty-second Street. 'Go early,' she says; 'and try to be over with it by eleven, so that you can enjoy your lunch.' Did you ever know of such thoughtfulness?"

"No, I never did," acknowledged Truesdale, grimly.

By these and other such subterfuges did Gladys keep her epistolary hand in, until the time came when she really had something of consequence to communicate.

Once or twice she also regaled him with the comments of the Beldens on the building projects of the Marshalls. Truesdale had the same tepid interest for these advices as for her other notes and comments. He did not consider himself as particularly concerned. At best he was but a bird of passage. And it seemed to him a sad error to load one's self down with so dense and stationary a thing as a house.

The conferences over this matter went on, however, regardless of Truesdale's non-participation. Jane discussed it with her father and mother; and Rosy handled it, and Roger; and Alice came in from Riverdale Park to stay overnight, and to contend with Jane and Rosy through the steak and the griddle-cakes in the morning, as well as to intimate to her father that if he would build out a little library from her parlor, her husband could pay for the carpet and furniture; and Aunt Lydia Rhodes came now and then and fluttered around the question, unsettling points that had been looked on as settled for good and all, and raising other points of her own that needed no consideration whatever. And, at the end of a wearisome and contentious month, the matter—with what seemed to everybody an extraordinary and reckless precipitation, the end once reached —was finally arranged. Tom Bingham was to build them a house in the neighborhood favored by Roger, and was to find an architect for them—a reversal of the usual procedure which afflicted Jane with grave doubts. And on the morning of the earliest day of spring, when the piano-organs were trilling through the side streets, and the flower-men were offering hurried shoppers their earliest verbenas and fuchsias from the tail ends of their carts, Jane walked down to the store to look at the signatures on the contracts for the new house.

"Ah!" she said to herself, thoughtfully; we *are* moving—faster than I anticipated, and not precisely in the direction I had fancied."

She was in no degree elated; she experienced, on the contrary, a distinct feeling of depression.

XIV

During those active weeks which followed the decision of the family to surrender their old home to business and to contrive another one in a new neighborhood towards the south, Jane had taken her full share in all the debates and consultations. Hers, indeed, was the personality which impressed itself most strongly upon the young architect whom Bingham brought forward to evolve the plans, elevations, and specifications upon which he himself was to work. In matters architectural Jane was a purist of the purists, a theorist of the theorists; she fought this young man steadily on points of style, and never abandoned her ground until the exigencies of practicalities, reinforced by the prejudices of her mother and the unillumined indifference of her father, proved too strong to be withstood. "Well," she would say, "if we have got to sacrifice Art to steam-heat and speaking-tubes...." The young man was both amazed and exasperated by her spirit and her pertinacity; he could only be kept in trim and in temper by Bingham's frequent assurances that she was a very clever girl—and a very well-meaning one, after all.

Jane saw the plans composed, discomposed, recomposed, and, finally, accepted as a working basis; then, in the interval between this and the actual commencement of construction, she turned back a diverted attention to her lunch-club.

This institution, at the start, had required her attendance and ministrations but once a week. At present she was on hand twice a week, and in the near future she was to be there still more frequently. Every kind of co-operative endeavor, whether it involves the politics of a ward, the finances of a bank, or the refreshment-table of a church social, falls in the end on the shoulders of two or three people, and Jane's undertaking was no exception. And as it became more a matter of personal endeavor, it became, at the same time, more a matter of personal pride. She frequently asked people to call and inspect it, and she was coming more and more to feel that if the line of natural evolution were followed out, then her own lunch-room for girls would be developed into a home for working-girls by her father.

"There, poppy," she said to him one evening, as she put several sheets of paper into his hands; "that's my notion of what could be done on a hundred-foot lot. I haven't drawn the front yet, but here's the plan for down-stairs, and another for one of the upper floors."

The germ of Jane's unexpected architectural facility was to be found, perhaps, in Susan Bates's table-cloth drawings; and it had developed during her long labors on those big brown sheets which Bingham's young man had brought so many times both to house and store.

"But if you really want some notion of the front," she went on, "I can give it to you fast enough." She turned over one of her sheets and began to draw on the back of it. "Pooh! architecture's easy enough! It'll be about five stories high." She sketched the five stories with five or six lines. "In red brick—Romanesque style like this." She gave a broad sweep with the pencil, grouping several rapidly evolved windows under a wide, round arch. "And the cornice will be brick and terra-cotta; no galvanized iron—*that* I will not have. And a good-sized terra-cotta panel here over the doorway, to tell who we are—like that."

She outlined a large oblong, and filled it with an indefinite jumble of curly-cues.

Her father looked at the drawing, and laid it back on the table with a wan and patient smile. "Some other time, Jennie; we'll think about it when we haven't got so many other things on hand. Isn't the new house enough for now?"

Jane studied her father's face for a moment, and then thrust the drawings aside with a sudden and remorseful sweep. For he looked tired and worn, and in the slight pallor of his face she noted the deepening of old wrinkles and the appearance of new ones. "You poor old pa!" she cried, "I didn't mean to worry you. It can wait, of course; and the more we learn about building in the meanwhile the better we shall be prepared for this when the time comes round."

She looked into his eyes; they seemed to her both haggard and appealing. "I declare, you look just dragged out. Poor pa!— just bother, bother, bother. Something at the store?"

"There's always something at the store," he said, looking away. "I haven't been feeling very well all day. I guess I didn't get my full share of sleep last night."

Yes, there was always something at the store, and this time it was an affair between Belden and the South town assessor. Belden—largely on his own account, certainly without anything like a consultation—had undertaken to secure a revaluation of of the warehouse property; and he had been so successful (through the use of arguments by which an assessor may be moved) as to get a figure even lower than that of the previous year, despite the increased value of the building. Unfortunately, he had selected the very time when the scandalous inequality in assessments was engaging the attention of an ambitious evening paper; and this paper had just printed a cut of the enlarged building in juxtaposition to some small retail grocery in a remote ward and precinct, which was assessed in a ratio ten times as great—a vivid illustration of the manner in which the rich were favored at the expense of the poor. Marshall felt himself put forward as a criminal—a malefactor; he was assured, furthermore, that a man who offered a bribe was worse than the man who accepted it.

He might have added too, that Belden was showing some disposition to divert the house from its old conservative paths into the wild courses of speculation. His dash and daring found an outlet in an endeavor to manipulate the tea market, with less eye, perhaps, to profit than to prestige—to primacy in the trade. The old man had given but a half-hearted assent; he felt the credit, if any were involved, would outrun the profit, and that the promise of profit was too little to justify all the worry and care.

Nor was Jane's own enterprise, meanwhile, wholly free from difficulties. There were distinctly days when the postponement of the millennium seemed indefinite—when there appeared to be enough human nature remaining in the world to secure the present state of things for many years to come.

"It's a good deal more complicated than I thought," she confessed to her aunt Lydia, upon calling, one day, to invite her to visit the institution and to inspect its workings. "Now, Miss Casey and Miss Erlanger, for example, get along together all right, because Miss Casey is the cashier in an insurance office, and Miss Erlanger is the stenographer for a railroad president. Both of them kind of edge off from some of the salesladies; and the salesladies are pretty nearly as bad among themselves. Miss Maddox, who sells gloves on the first floor of Bernstein's Bazaar, never quite wants to sit at the same table with Miss Slopinka, who sells bolts and padlocks in the basement. So we have to trim and fuss and compromise all the time; in fact, we've been obliged to take in another room or two. However, that makes all the more to see."

Jane then added a few words to cover what she conceived to be the etiquette of such a call. Aunt Lydia was not one of the kind to find any force in a delicate intimation; so Jane said what she had to say as plainly and pointedly as possible.

"Don't call during the rush; you'd only be in the way. And don't look at the girls as if they were natural history specimens in glass cases. And don't whatever else you do, be flip—"

"Flip? What a word! Where did you get it—there?"

—"and gushing, and effusive, and as condescending as if you had come down sixteen pairs of stairs. I lost three girls the day after Mrs. Bates brough Cecilia Ingles up. 'Why did you do it?' I asked her. 'I want her to see things,' she told me; 'I want to make a good earnest woman of her.' I hope she won't do it again. I sha'nt encourage many visitors after this. I don't think it helps a place like that to be made into a show."

"Well, I don't know," returned her aunt. "Wouldn't it be a good idea to have entertainments and things, to bring the different sections of society together? I should be very glad to help," she added, as she debated the probable participation of Susan Bates and Cecilia Ingles.

"No, I'm not going to have any picnic business," returned Jane. "That's all nonsense. I'm going to keep this thing within its own lines."

"I suppose I could bring Bertie with me," suggested the chastened Lydia. "She thinks you're a perfect little tin thing-a-ma-jig on wheels."

"Yes," said Jane, "she can come; only don't bring a whole raft with her."

"I won't," Mrs. Rhodes reassured her; "only one more besides. You wouldnt mind a third?"

"No, I shouldn't mind just one."

Then Lydia Rhodes made an immediate request of Truesdale to act as escort; *he* was her third. She took, in this malapropos manœuvre, the same delight that a child experiences through the consciousness of being engaged in some mischievous wrong.

"Lunch with us at Fields," she directed him, "and then we

shall get around in time to see Jane wiping off her tables and putting away her crockery. We go very simply—we wear sackcloth and ashes. As for the portrait—that can wait a day or two."

Then she told Bertie very solemnly that they were to begin a study of the philanthropies of a great city. But Bertie took her own view of the expedition; Truesdale's participation made it seem rather like an excursion into fairy-land. Now, more than ever, was she under the glamour of this young man's accomplishments; now, more than ever, did she feel the embellishing and decorative qualities of his presence. Not only had she heard the composer sing his own songs; she had lately seen him paint his own picture—and hers. "Why can't you do a little water-color or something of Bertie?" his aunt had suggested to him one day, upon encountering him in an attitude of graceful negligence before the exposition of his own pictures. "It would please her so much. Do you know"—lowering her voice as she looked towards the girl over her shoulder—"the dear child has been down here eight or ten times to see these things? Fancy how much it would please her to watch you actually at work—on a portrait of herself, too."

Truesdale glanced sidewise towards Bertie, who stood in painstaking scrutiny before one of the outlying pictures of his group. A pair of art students in their careless working clothes, stood a little apart with their eyes on the same work.

"Terrible knowing, ain't it?" remarked one.

"Yep," rejoined the other; "awful lot of snap."

"Just knocks it right out, doesn't it?"

"Fearfully up to date, ain't it? Doesn't need any '1893' on it!"

"Full of jump! Why can't we fellows here at home get more of that sort of thing?"

Bertie's heart swelled proudly as she heard this jargon. It was quite unintelligible to her, but she felt sure it conveyed extreme approval. She turned to look at Truesdale just as he turned to look at her.

He shook his head in burlesque deprecation of her too obvious appreciation, and then brought his attention back to his aunt.

"All right," he said; "I'll do it. I'll come down some day and paint her, or you, or the front doors, or anything else you say." He pondered for a moment, as he edged away a little from Bertie, and tried to carry his aunt with him. "I suppose I shall be expected to look the part?"

"Yes," she responded, sympathetically. "Bertie has never seen an artist, of course, but she has her ideas of how one would look. If it wouldn't be too much trouble for you to. . . ."

"Oh, I don't mind the trouble so very much," replied Truesdale, magnanimously. "I hope I can put myself out a little. She might look for a loose red tie, perhaps, and a Tam O'Shanter, eh?"

"And a velvet coat," suggested his aunt, ardently.

"Oh, bother a velvet coat; that's going a little *too* far. She would be more likely to look for a palette and a maul-stick."

"Why, certainly."

"Yes, they use those things sometimes. I wonder if she would insist upon an easel?"

"I think I could arrange that," replied his aunt. She drew on an expression of decorous and pensive sadness, and Truesdale knew that she was mentally detaching her crayon of the dear departed from that elaborate white and gold apparatus in her parlor. "And if you should care for a few Persian rugs hung up around. . . ."

"By all means!" cried Truesdale. "And a few Bedouin rifles; and a few bits of brasswork from Cairo; and a few scraps of drapery from Bombay or Trebizond; and one of those inlaid Turkish tables; and one or two stacks of old French armor. I think with all that help I could do a water-color or so."

"You're going to do her in oil," declared his aunt, stoutly.

"I am? Then I must have that table, sure. And a nargileh.

And a dozen Japanese swords, if you happen to have them about the place. And what else?—oh yes; a small bit of canvas, now I think of it."

Bertie looked round once more, and divined herself under discussion. She sidled away, past a long row of landscapes and marines, and drifted out into the hall, where she leaned over the balustrade and studied the mosaics of the vestibule below.

"Good little subject," said one of the students, looking after her. He ran a sudden hand upward through his hair, which had lately fallen from its high estate and had come to look like the hair of anybody else. "Get that profile against a red plush curtain—"

"And drape her in a red silk kimono or something."

"And have a vase of Jacqueminots to one side—a study in reds, you know."

"Yes, I know, you know." He turned on his heel. "Well, this ain't work, or anything like it. Come along up-stairs."

And up-stairs they went—through the main hallway.

Lydia Rhodes followed her protégée with a fond eye. "You know, Truesdale, that she's just the sweetest little thing in the world."

"Oh, yes, I know."

"Why don't you go into the business?" asked his aunt, impulsively, as she placed a cajoling hand upon his arm.

"The business? So I might. Well, you may pay me a hundred dollars for this commission, if you like!"

"You know what I mean—your father's business. Now that they are making it all over, they might easily find a place for you."

"Um," observed Truesdale, falling into a gloomy and chilling reserve.

His aunt saw the necessity of abandoning this new ground at once. "You'll take pains, won't you?" she said, struggling back to her former position. "You'll make it as nice as you can?"

"Well, it will be a sort of sketch, of course,' said Truesdale, still rather coldly.

"It won't, either," insisted his aunt; "it will be a real, regular picture."

"She'd get tired of it. Do you think it's any fun to pose?"

"Tired!" said his aunt, scornfully. She thrust the supposition into the outer darkness and slammed the door behind it. "How are you going to dress her?" she asked, passing on with a resolute swiftness to detail. "If you want anything of mine . . . I've got a lovely breadth of old gold satin; and then there are those Roman pearls you brought me."

"Dress her? I sha'nt dress her at all. I don't believe I shall want any of your rugs, either. If they are on the floor, keep them there; that's where they belong. No; I shall just put her before a plain wall in her every-day clothes—the black hat and jacket she's wearing now. Won't that do well enough?"

"We—ell," said his aunt, doubtfully.

Truesdale had juggled enough in his time with draperies and accessories to know how to employ them here, if so minded; but he felt instinctively that any such manipulations would now be quite out of place. "She's a good, sincere, simple little thing," he said to himself, "and she will speak better for herself than all those things could speak for her. I shall make just a sketch—but a careful one. I shall do the best I can; I shall make a very lady-like thing of it." Suddenly he flushed. "I shall tear those old things up to-morrow—they've got to go sometime." He was thinking of certain studies at the back of one of his portfolios; they were *not* ladylike. "Those models!" he muttered, in a tone at once of objurgation and of self-reproach.

Truesdale came for the first sitting in a costume discreetly picturesque, and his aunt frisked through all the preliminary preparations in a state of great glee. Bertie surrendered herself to the process with an expression of wondering self-depreciation; her large dark eyes shone with a kind of surprised humility.

"If she wouldn't look *quite* so much like one of Murillo's Madonnas," thought Truesdale. "This isn't really the most important thing that has ever happened in the universe, after all." Then he sighed lightly. "Still, I suppose she *is* a good deal nearer to a Madonna than I am to a Murillo."

Mrs. Rhodes seemed to feel the necessity of upsetting the whole apartment. She had the inside man bring up the stepladder. "What's this for?" Truesdale asked.

"To fix the curtains right. I can have them taken down, if you say. How far up do you want the shades? Are those lambrequins in the way?"

"Good heavens!" cried Truesdale, "do you want to tear the house down? Do you think I am Raphael painting the Pope?" But all this was only his aunt's way of flattering him into a good-humor, and of making him share her sense of the importance of the occasion.

As the work went on, however, his aunt's song changed imperceptibly from allegretto to adagio, and from the major mode to the minor.

The change first appeared as she studied his charcoal outline. "Well," she observed, "I think you might have put Bertie somewhere near the middle of the picture, instead of away off to the left, like that."

"They put them in the middle sometimes—yes," admitted Truesdale, cheerily waving his aunt back. "I'm leaving the other side for you," he added, with a genial impudence.

"Oh, that's it, is it?" And she half believed it true.

On the day following she was distinctly mournful. "Do you mean to tell me that you can ever work over that mass of red and blue and yellow freckles into anything resembling Bertie's complexion?—such a beautiful one, too!" Bertie blushed. "There! look at it now!" cried his aunt, with a mounting enthusiasm; and Bertie blushed still more violently. Truesdale gave her a brief glance, which he at once transferred to his palette. This was the first time in his life that he had ever lowered his eyes from a woman's face, merely because there happened to be a blush upon it.

"Work it over?" he presently inquired, as he looked up to his aunt across his shoulder. "I never work anything over."

"Is it going to stay that way?" demanded his aunt, peremptorily. Bertie's own face was overcast, with an expression of plaintive distrust.

"Of course it is. I work in the primary colors. If you should prefer something a little less advanced ..." He waved his maulstick vaguely, as if in reference to the professorial practice of Munich, or to the antediluvian school of England.

"Well, if that's the way it's going to stay ..." commented his aunt, with her face close to the canvas.

"My dear aunt," protested Truesdale, "we don't look at a painting with our noses, but with our eyes. I decompose what is before me into the primary colors. Now the thing for you to do is to step back ten or twelve feet and recompose them. That armchair over there is just about your point of view precisely—and so inviting and comfortable! Try it."

His aunt removed herself to the point suggested. "Well, perhaps it *does* look a little better from here." And Bertie Patterson breathed a tiny sigh of relief; for the last thing in the world she wished to be was a witness to her young artist's failure.

"Of course," responded Truesdale. He gave an invocatory sweep with his brush, and the spirit of complete modernity descended and perched upon the top of his easel. "Just wait; it will be so naïve; it will seem so improvised, so spontaneous— a regular little impromptu. Of course."

But the next day his aunt accompanied him to the front door when he took his leave. Her tone to-day was one of out-and-out protest.

"Now, Truesdale, this has gone far enough. You may muss

186

up the house as much as you like, but I can't let you make a laughing-stock of Bertie. When it comes to streaks of green under her chin, and purple shadows under her hair, I—I don't think it is right. And she—she admires you so much." His aunt's voice broke, and she seemed at no great remove from tears.

"Dear Aunt Lyddy," returned Truesdale, with an unruffled imperturbability and an exhaustless and patronizing patience, "you have never learned to use your eyes; you don't know how to see. Did you ever try looking at things from under your elbow?" He raised his own, as he fastened the last button of his glove, and gave her a teasing glance from beneath his arm. "You are quite transfigured," he declared; "it makes all the difference in the world. Try it some time. Well, good-bye." He gave her his hand without lowering his elbow, and then sauntered complacently down the front steps.

Bertie watched him from behind the curtains of the front window. He wore a black cape-overcoat, which swung gracefully as he moved along, and a soft Fedora hat with a brave dent in the crown. "The most becoming thing he could possibly have picked out," she thought.

Mrs. Rhodes came back to take one more look at the canvas. "It's a perfect living picture of you, Bertie, except for the color. I can't get around that." She leaned forward and twisted her neck round and looked at Bertie from under her elbow, and then looked again at the canvas and shook her head. "And as for naïveté from Truesdale..." she murmured. She would as soon have looked for sunbeams from cucumbers.

Bertie, intent upon the painting, saw nothing of these manœuvres. "I guess it will come out all right," she said, with a reviving trust.

XV

When Jane looked up at the stroke of one and saw her aunt Lydia and Bertie Patterson enter under the escort of Truesdale, she was not completely pleased. Her rooms were no place for men, anyway—especially young ones; and she had often wished that Truesdale, however worthy her admiration and the world's, were a little less ready as to bringing his fascinations into play. "If ever he comes down here," she thought, "he'll wear something too striking, and he'll want to talk to the girls about the continued stories in the magazines, or play the piano, or something; and they'll think he's trying to flirt with them. I hate anything of that kind—here," said Jane, virtuously.

Truesdale, however, conducted himself with an immense discretion, and wore nothing out of the ordinary. His hats and shoes were now quite like those of other people. His Florentine *stivaletti* had drawn so much attention in the street-cars that he had been obliged to give them up; and as for the flat-brimmed high silk hat which he had brought home from the Boulevard St. Michel, *that* he had had to leave off after a second trial: there were some things, he found, that people would not stand. And his manner to-day was utterly stripped of gallantry; it was gauged with the precise idea of meeting the approval of Bertie Patterson. "I expect I shall seem awfully insipid," he said to himself.

Jane came to meet them from a room beyond, where she left a doughnut and a half cup of coffee standing on a round-topped oak table. The regular noon hour enjoyed by most of the girls was done; two or three remained finishing their lunch or looking over the picture papers, and a couple of them, in the little parlor, were trying duets on the piano.

"I'm the only one of the board on hand to-day," Jane explained. "So I've been doing a little book-keeping and a little waiting and a little everything. This is Miss Casey," she said, introducing one of the piano-players; "and this is Miss O'Brien," introducing the other.

Miss Casey and Miss O'Brien bowed and smiled, and made a dexterous remark apiece without too apparent an effort, and presently took an adroit departure. They had already overrun their time, they explained.

"Walk around and look at things," suggested Jane. "We're pretty high up, you see, but we don't save any rent, because the elevators make one floor worth as much as another. Still, the light's good, and the air; and there's a great deal less noise."

The others followed Jane's lead with much docility. Truesdale was profoundly impressed by his sister's aspect under these novel conditions; Bertie Patterson seemed to find in her the incarnation of all the town's philanthropy; even Aunt Lydia was almost too deeply affected to chirp and chatter with her wonted volubility.

"Here's the office," said Jane, leading them into a small, lighted closet to one side. "This book is for our account with the butcher, and that one is for our account with the baker. Our supplies are brought up on the freight elevator every morning. Come and see the gas-stove, where we cook eggs."

As they passed through the adjoining room a girl sat at one of the tables with a piece of pie and a cup of tea. She was turning the leaves of one of the comic weeklies, and a slight frown of intentness upon her face indicated either a limited sense of humor or some unfamiliarity with the subjects under review. The latter, perhaps; her face and air were distinctly foreign.

"Poor Sophie!" said Jane, indulgently; "she's trying her English on those jokes. She's improving, however; and she can speak French and German like a fire-engine. I guess she's smart enough; anyway, she looks so."

The girl seemed of a type that might have come from Baden, or Alsace, or the Franco-Swiss frontier. She had a high color and an abundance of black hair. Her eyes, as she lifted them to Bertie Patterson, were dark and narrow and full of sparkle and decision, and the half-frown, which still survived from her study of the comic paper, helped to give her a look of some force and determination.

Truesdale, on seeing her, gave a sudden start, and turned his eyes and his face away at once. Then, with a quickened pace, he followed his sister's lead towards the kitchen and pantry. He smiled half grimly. "Such a thing may happen anywhere, of course," he said to himself; "but I shouldn't have chosen it to happen right here. No—not exactly."

Bertie and Mrs. Rhodes followed after, to see the gas-stove that cooked eggs. As they crossed the threshold, Truesdale looked back between them towards the subject of his speculation. She had grasped her paper firmly with both fists, and now sat with an intent stare fixed on its pages. She neither raised nor lowered her head, nor could he observe that she looked either to the right or to the left. "Ouf!" said Truesdale, as Jane lit up the stove, "you never know when a thing is at an end."

Jane presently turned off her gas-stove. "You can go back through the other room. It isn't quite so swell," she expounded, as she moved along; "but we have several grades of girls, and each one finds her own level and her own society for herself." She led the way back into the parlor, and drew a finger along the key-board of the piano as she passed by. "Anybody who wants to send a few new pieces of lively music may do so."

Two or three late lunchers had come in and were clattering their knives and forks at the table opposite the girl whom Jane had called Sophie. Sophie still sat in her place; she held her paper with a firm hand, and turned the leaves at intervals. She looked up once—as the party was passing out. Truesdale stepped over the door-mat rapidly, on the far side of Jane and Bertie and Mrs. Rhodes. He dropped his glove that he might stoop for it, and as he stooped he shot a rapid glance through the narrow door of the other room. The girl still held her paper before her face, but she sent a single look after the party athwart its side.

Truesdale stepped into the hall and pressed the button of the elevator. "It's Sophie, true enough—not a bit of doubt about it. If she didn't recognize me just now, she'll never have another chance to—here."

He handed his charges into the elevator. "Well, what do you think of Jane and her doings now?" he asked, briskly, as he stepped in after them. "Can you think of any better opening for the investment of your idle funds? Isn't she an able financier? Hasn't she got a great administrative capacity? Isn't she one of the rising young men of the day?" As he flung off this string of stock phrases from the newspapers, his eyes flashed brightly, a mounting color came into his cheeks, and a triumphant smile to his lips, and a caressing and ringing vibration into his voice. He seemed to coruscate wth all the conquering insolence of youth; Bertie Patterson had never seen him quite so handsome.

"Down we go!" he cried to his aunt, as the cab resumed its course with a sudden, breath-taking drop. "No; don't catch hold of me—I'm only a broken reed. Yes; try the door-jamb—much more satisfactory. But look out for your fingers—never get your fingers caught." Then, as they arrived at the street level: "Wait a second; don't hurry. Be sure of your footing; don't stumble and break your neck at the last minute—one poor last little chance, after so many glorious opportunities have gone by!"

" 'Sh, Truesdale!" whispered his aunt.

For there were other people in the elevator, and they looked askance at this smart volley of verbal superfluities.

He led them out to the carriage. "Here we are on solid ground once more," he continued; "best place in the world to be. No; don't ask me to get in—I'll walk on a bit. I wouldn't leave terra firma now for anything." He handed his aunt in, and then Bertie. He exacted from Bertie a perfectly superfluous shake of the hand, bowed over that hand with a sudden access of gravity, and lost himself in an abysmal reverie before he had traversed a hundred yards.

He saw before him a high-heaped assemblage of red-tiled roofs, and above them rose the fretwork of a soaring Gothic spire. A narrow river half encircled the town, and a battered old bridge, guarded by a round-towered gateway, led out into the open country towards a horizon bounded by a low range of blue hills. Trumpet-calls rang out from distant barrack-yards, and troops of dragoons clattered noisily over the rough pavement of the great square. The dragoons passed, and a colony of awnings and umbrellas sprang up in their place, and bands of stocky peasantry chattered and chaffered, and left the pavement strewn with the loose leaves of cabbages and carrot-tops. Then night came and blotted these out, and the moon rose and music played, and throngs of officers and students and towns-people sat through a long-drawn evening before the coffee-houses round-about. High towards the stars towered the columns and pediments of a vast official structure, whose broken sky-line sawed the heavens, and whose varied cornices and ledges were disjointed by deep and perplexing shadows. On each side of the great portal which opened through the pillared arcade there was stationed a mounted cuirassier, and above it there appeared in large letters—

"Marshall & Belden," said Truesdale, suddenly emerging from his reverie. He sprang lightly over the muddy gutter and found a foothold on the damp flagging. "Pshaw!" he said, rather ruefully; "in a moment more she would have come to meet me."

He looked up at the building before him. "Well, really, they've made quite a decent affair of it. But what are they doing to the sign? Oh, I see: putting 'The' to the front of it, and 'Co.' to the back. That ladder looks rather shaky. 'The Marshall & Belden Co.' Perhaps it would be civil of me to call on the new concern—seeing that I have chanced their way."

Truesdale picked his way choicely through the office, with the urbane affectation of never having seen the place before. One or two of the clerks recognized him, and a hurried word, passed from desk to desk, effected an immediate establishment of his identity throughout the room. Those who had never seen him had at least heard about him. Some of them had visited his pictures at the Art Institute, and, as devotees of the old school, if of any, had mildly guyed them. Others had read paragraphs in the "Chappie Chat" of the newspapers about his trousers and cravats—those genial paragraphs which may so easily endow a young man of parts and peculiarities with a quasi-celebrity. One of them now smiled broadly, and another so far forgot himself and his dignity as to wink; but all the rest, as American freemen by birth or adoption, united in a stolid determination to refrain from seeing, or at least from acknowledging, any distinguishing peculiarity, any differentiation—above all, any savor of superiority. The one of whom Truesdale inquired for his father was so Spartan in his brusqueness that Truesdale, despite himself, smiled in his face.

In the private office he found his father closeted with Roger. Crumpled and trampled on the floor, and with the effect of a matter abandoned or at least superseded, lay a large sheet of paper printed with the outlines of a real-estate subdivision, while a hundred similar sheets rested in a roll on the end of the old man's desk. Marshall himself lay back in his chair, with marks of the exhaustion that follows intense indignation and exasperation, while Roger paced the floor with all the vehemence and choler of younger blood.

"Yes," Roger was saying, explosively, "the bond was opened, and all they found was a blank paper—the alderman's name, and nothing more. Why do you blame *me?* What more can *I* do? What more could you do? What more could any decent man do? And if you wanted to find out how things are run here, you're doing it."

"What's the trouble?" asked Truesdale. He sat down with an engaging disposition to show himself interested.

Marshall passed his hand feebly over his forehead. "It's that police affair of your mother's," he said, in a tired voice.

"Well, I hope those two scamps have been sent to jail, or to Bridewell, or wherever they belong. August will carry that scar to his dying day."

"Jail!" cried Roger. "No ward-worker need ever go to jail. They sent for their alderman the minute they were caught. Our ward hasn't elected anything but crime-brokers for the last ten years."

"Well, what did the present crime-broker do?"

"He went bail for them. He made out the bond himself—inside of thirty seconds. He marked it so on the envelope, and the police-captain took it for what he called it. So when these fellows jumped their bail—"

"Our alderman lost—his autograph. A bad take-in for the police, wasn't it?" queried Truesdale, impartially.

"Take-in!" cried Roger. "It's easy enough to be taken in if you want to be taken in—if you lend yourself to being taken in!"

His father gave a long sigh and dropped a helpless hand on his desk. Truesdale looked into vacancy and gave a long, low whistle.

"And there you have it!" ended Roger. "You have lifted off the cover and looked in. Do you want to go deeper? You'll find a hell-broth—thieves, gamblers, prostitutes, pawnbrokers, saloon-keepers, aldermen, heelers, justices, bailiffs, policemen—and all concocted for us within a short quarter of a century." He drew his hands across each other. "I've never felt so cheap and filthy in my life."

Truesdale made no further inquiries about the Van Horns. His fastidious nature shrank back from all these malodorous actualities. He added his own footprints to those which already defaced the map lying on the floor, and asked about that.

"You're interesting yourself in buying land, I imagine."

"In selling," replied Roger, curtly.

David Marshall leaned laboriously over the arm of his chair with the intention, perhaps, of crowding the crumpled map into his waste-basket. Instead, he gave it several neat and careful folds and thrust it abstractedly into one of his pigeon-holes. It found place alongside of a bill for doctor's services handed in that morning. A porter who had fallen down three floors of the elevator shaft had been attended by one of his own friends. The bill was exorbitant—everybody concerned knew that. But it was rather less than a probable award for damages—everybody knew that, too. The excess was to be shared, of course, between doctor and patient.

"Was there anything special?" his father asked presently, with a wan and dejected glance towards his younger son. "If not, I think I'll put on my things and go home. I don't quite feel myself today."

"Perhaps you'd better," recommended Roger, taking the roll of maps under his arm. "I'll have these distributed from my office during the week."

"No, nothing special," answered Truesdale; "I just happened in. And I think," he added to himself, "that I had better lose no time in happening out. The idea of my running up against such a tar-kettle as this! Pouf!"

As he went out he passed along the front of Belden's desk.

Belden himself sat there attended, with the sort of deferential familiarity that suggests the confidential clerk, by the Swiss, the Alsacian, or whatever else, who on a previous occasion had moved the curiosity of Bingham.

This man caught sight of Truesdale as he passed, and gave him an instant glance of recognition. He at once bowed his head over Belden's desk, so as to hide his face among its papers. "A gentleman to see you sir?" he suggested with a magnificent readiness.

Belden raised his own head and met the careless nod of the passing Truesdale with a forbidding frown. "No, he doesn't want to see me. And I don't want to see him," he muttered in a lower tone.

"You know him—is it not so?" the man insisted, with a kind of smothered determination.

"Know him? Yes"—with extreme distaste. "It's young Marshall."

"Mr. Marshall's son?"

"Yes," Belden thrust some papers towards him. "Take these as you go."

The man put out his hand. "I know him, I myself, also," he said, looking Belden full in the face with a steady eye. "Ich selbst." He struck his breast and ventured on the liberty of a smile—a smile slow and sinister, one that called for an understanding and challenged co-operation.

One might have fancied such a conjunction effected when, an evening or two later, Truesdale received a "note" from Gladys McKenna. As he sifted apart its numerous sheets he tried to recall whether he had replied to her last; he could not remember having done so. "But sometimes they *will* write," he said, discontentedly, "and nothing can stop them."

Her pages led him a rough and rugged chase. She wrote a large, hasty hand, with an unstinted expenditure of ink. "I declare," he said, running several sheets over in succession, "she

gets blinder and blinder the further along she goes. And now"
—turning back to the beginning—"let's see what it's all about."

The letter assumed from the outset a mysterious and melo-
dramatic tone. "Perhaps, finally, she really has something to
say," commented Truesdale. But she went on, circling round
her theme, dipping down to it now and again, and then soaring
up and away from it altogether. "Well," asked Truesdale presently, with a slight show of impatience, "what is it?—something
she doesn't fully understand, or something she does understand
but can't bring herself to write about? She 'listened,' she says;
to very small purpose, say I." He felt one moment that she was
more or less in the dark; the next, that she was making passes
at some forbidden theme; the third, that she was asking a more
ardent recognition of her loyalty and devotion. "She speaks of
her 'position,' too. It's 'awkward,' it seems, and 'embarrassing,'
and 'dangerous.' It needn't be, though. She made it for herself,
and she can unmake it whenever she chooses. Well, I'll try all
this again, when I've got more time; it will keep. What is this,
though, it says at the end? H'm; I am to remember that if I
have enemies I also have fast friends, ever yours sincerely—oh,
that's all right." He crammed the sheets into his bureau-drawer,
drew on his gloves, selected a stick to his taste, gave himself
a last look in the glass, and sauntered out to dinner.

He had discovered a French restaurant within a kilometre
of the house, where he could dine *à prix fixe* in a *cabinet par-
ticulier* for five francs, including a *demi-bouteille* of *ordinaire.*

"That's something like," he declared. "That's what I'm used
to!" He thought with a shudder of the rest of the family going
down to supper in the basement dining-room—that time-hon-
ored, semi-subterranean dungeon. "I'm glad, I'm sure, that they
are going to have their new dining-room above-ground; for their
own sakes, that is to say—not that it will matter the least to
me!"

XVI

Truesdale airily waved the remaining coin from the plate to the waiter's pocket and rose to go. He never omitted the giving of a *pour-boire*; "it helps so much to increase the illusion," he said. The waiters, accordingly, bestowed an exaggerated attention upon his hat and coat, and had developed an almost clinging affection for his stick. They also insisted upon passing things that he could very well reach for himself, and their "bon soir, m'sieu' " was quite unfailing in its regularity. "This shaggy town may have a silver lining, after all," he would think; "but you've got to turn things inside out to find it."

Near the exit Truesdale noticed Theodore Brower sitting with a *demi-tasse* before him. "Hallo!" he called to Brower, "I didn't know you came here."

"Once in a while," returned Brower. "I shop around. I'm a tramp. I eat anywhere. And I'm getting tired of it, too." He rose. "Give me a lift with this coat and I'll go along with you."

Brower was too incorruptibly native to give a fee; usually therefore, he put on his coat for himself. "Well, what's the programme?" he asked, feeling for his inside sleeves.

"Nothing," said Truesdale; "or anything. Only, I bar law, and philanthropy, and the *Complete Letter-writer*. What have you got in mind yourself?

"I though of going up to the Consolation Club; this is their night."

"Sounds sort of soothing," observed Truesdale. "Well, what do *they* do?—nothing like the pow-wow at the Crepuscular, I hope. Are strangers admitted?"

"What do they do? They try to show that the world isn't so bad as it seems. They'll let you in all right."

"Because I'm not so bad as I seem? Thanks. They don't have a dinner, I hope."

"No dinner."

"But they give you a bite later on, don't they? I was almost famished at the Simplicity. What will they talk about?"

"Almost anything; you never can tell. Come along." Truesdale, as an individual, interested Brower but moderately; Truesdale, as Jane's brother, interested him extremely. "You state your case—that's the idea; and the worse you make it, the better the face they try to put on it."

"Do I? Well, I don't know that I've *got* a case. And if I had, I might prefer to keep it to myself. However . . ."

The Consolation Club met in an upper chamber on Erie Street, and carried on their deliberations under a large plaster bust of the prince of optimists. The patient Emerson listened to the discussion of many a burning question, and witnessed the application of many an alleviating salve. Sometimes the question was personal; they soothed the book-keeper who had been cut on the street by his employer's daughter. Sometimes it was national; they commiserated the citizen who had been intimidated at the polling-booth. Sometimes it was a question of right —like a uniform divorce law; sometimes merely a question of expediency—like the tariff. But principally they discussed the affairs of a vast and sudden municipality; they bade one another not to despair, after all, either of the city or of the republic. And towards eleven o'clock the priests of the cult saw an offering of cheese-sandwiches and beer set before their idol, and presently, in true sacerdotal fashion, they fell upon these viands on their own account.

"Oh, come," said Truesdale, shrugging his shoulders, as he cast on Brower and his circle a look half of expostulation and half of embarrassment, "I'm not entitled to annoy your friends with any such filthy trifle as *that*. Besides, I don't claim it as any grievance of *mine*." He thought, privately, that his mother's disposition to dicker with the populace was no more creditable than necessary; he could take no great pleasure in dwelling upon it too lingeringly.

"Oh, go ahead," urged Brower; "our fellows here are interested in just that sort of thing. If you should want to come in, we'll take it as your initiation."

"Do," added another member. "I believe that for every one man who leaves the polling-place with a waning confidence in the present and a clouded hope for the future, there are scores who thus leave the lower courts of justice."

"Oh, very well," replied Truesdale, throwing out his hands in his light French fashion. And he recounted the whole chain of circumstances which had so exasperated his father and baffled his brother, from the first panting appearance of frowzy old Mother Van Horn on his own mother's door-step down to the forfeiture of the fictitious bail-bond by her two grandnephews. He gave his narrative in a series of light, graphic, delicate touches. He almost saw it print itself before his very eyes, like a page from one of those beautiful little volumes made by Hachette or by Lemerre—those sprightly, broken pages, where a paragraph consists of a line or even a word, where brief exclamatory phrases abound, and where short rows of dots leave the reader to complete the meaning at his own pleasure. He even gesticulated a tiny illustration or two into the edge of the text. Seldom had these earnest and intent young men heard such a theme presented with so many nods and becks and wreathèd smiles; it seemed like the stirring of a cesspool with a silver soup-ladle.

"And what consolation have you to offer me for that?" smiled Truesdale, as he finished.

He himself appeared to share but slightly the indignation that his recital aroused; after all, these doings were alien to him —like the domestic difficulties that might be distracting some ant-hill in mid-Africa. But on the others it produced the effect that the recital of specific injuries always does—and should.

"This, for example," answered a sardonic young man, whose close-shaven black beard showed through his drawn and sallow skin: "that we are at last playing the game with all the pieces on the board, with all the cards in the pack; with all the elements, in other words, of a vast and diversified human nature. The simple hopes and ideals of this Western world of fifty years ago—even of twenty years ago—where are they now? What the country really celebrated at Philadelphia in 1876, however unconsciously, was the ending of its minority and the assumption of full manhood with all its perplexities and cares. The broad life of the real world began for us the very next year—"

"You mean with the railroad riots?" asked Brower.

—"and has been going on more fiercely ever since. Take a man who was born in 1860, and who is to die with the century— what would be *his* idea of life? Contention, bickering, discontent, chronic irritation—a régime of hair-cloth tempered by finger-nails."

"Yes," said another, "as you say, we have all the elements at last. And the elements of human nature are unchanging—like the elements of chemistry; and they combine in the same unchanging fashions. Imagine a reconstructed universe without sulphur or nitrogen; or imagine elements that combine to one purpose in this corner of the laboratory combining to another purpose in that. The same human compounds are produced through the ages, and the elements that follow one formula in the old world will follow the same formula in the new—even if they break the crucible. A generation ago we thought—poor pathetic creatures—that our pacific processes showed social science in its fullest development. But to-day we have all the elements possessed by the old world itself, and we must take whatever they develop, as the old world does. We have the full working apparatus finally, with all its resultant noise, waste, stenches, stains, dangers, explosions."

"Um," said Truesdale, to whom these observations sounded disagreeably like oratory; "how does all this bear on my case? I *call* it mine, to observe the forms," he added, with a smile to which no one responded.

"I can tell you that myself," broke in Brower. "The last twenty years have brought us elements that have never been in our national life before: a heavy immigration from south-eastern Europe, for example. The populations of Italy and Poland and Hungary—what view, now, do *they* take of the government—their government, all government? Isn't it an implacable and immemorial enemy—a great and cruel and dreadful monster to be evaded, hoodwinked, combated, stabbed in the dark if occasion offers?"

"Quite right," acknowledged Truesdale. "Why, to-day, when the peasants come into Rome from the Campagna, they always bring their pitchforks with them—you can see them any Sunday behind the Capitol. They're going to be murdered or robbed or imprisoned or something."

"And when these people have been out of the government from generation to generation, and opposed to it and mistrustful of it, is it an easy matter, on their coming over here, to make them feel themselves a part of it, and to imbue them with a loyalty to it?"

"One thing more," broke in the first speaker. "There is another element; it is imported from the nearer half of Europe, and is a more dangerous element still. I mean the element of feudality."

"Oh," said Truesdale, "now I begin to see."

"The essence of feudality is the idea of personal loyalty. Now, loyalty to another individual is a good thing in its way and in its own field and in a certain measure and at a certain juncture.

But it is not the right prop for a great republic. That requires not the idea of personal loyalty to some chief, but the idea of personal responsibility to a cause above all chiefs. This takes a breadth of view and a loftiness of ideal that only one race in the world has ever possessed—our own. The great man, politically, is the man who can eliminate the personal element from a great cause. The little man is the—well," turning to Truesdale, "there are the general data; make your own application of them."

"I see," said Truesdale; "my people are naturally against the governing powers anyway, from instinct and heredity; even when one of them does attain official position, it is only the position of the worm in the apple. And they think, too, that it is a more sane and practical thing to help one another out of a tangible difficulty than to sacrifice one another to an intangible cause. I never contended they were not human!"

"That isn't all, by any means," said Brower, determinedly. "There's just as bad behind." He resettled himself in his chair, as he claimed the attention of the room. He seemed to Truesdale as if seating himself in a saddle—a saddle on the back of some well-ridden hobby. Truesdale already heard the steed pant and champ.

"This town of ours labors under one peculiar disadvantage: it is the only great city in the world to which all its citizens have come for the one common, avowed object of making money. There you have its genesis, its growth, its end and object; and there are but few of us who are not attending to that object very strictly. In this Garden City of ours every man cultivates his own little bed and his neighbor his; but who looks after the paths between? They have become a kind of No Man's Land, and the weeds of a rank iniquity are fast choking them up. The thing to teach the public is this: that the general good is a different thing from the sum of the individual goods. Over in the Settlement we are trying to make those new-comers realize that they are a part of the body politic; perhaps we need another settlement to remind some of the original charter-members of the same fact!"

"H'm," thought Truesdale, "I believe Brower is an awfully fine fellow; but if he keeps up this kind of talk all the time with Jane . . ."

Then, as they passed out into the street a few minutes later: "I don't just see where my consolation comes in, after all."

"Perhaps they thought," responded Brower, "that you wouldn't appreciate the beauty of consolation until you had first appreciated the gravity of your case. I think their idea was less consolation than instruction."

"Ouf!" said Truesdale, who disdained instruction from whatever source.

"Do you know," said Brower, at the first crossing, "I'm going to talk to your father about this justice business."

"Well," rejoined Truesdale, "he'll listen to you if he'll listen to anybody; but he's awfully sore about it.'

"So are other people sore about it—hundreds of people much poorer and humbler than any of us, people to whom the miscarriage of justice is not a mere matter of exasperation and annoyance, but a real matter of life and death. They want care and attention—as the doctors say; they need a law-dispensary—that's about it. There are institutions that look after people's minds and bodies gratis; I want to see an institution started up that will do as much for their estates. I want to see a building for it, with an endowment and a library and a force of practitioners. To think of all the things that a man with money and ideas and sympathies might do—and should do—in a town like this!"

"You might try him," said Truesdale, doubtfully; "but I think Jane has got the inside track. You've heard about her Home, I suppose, and seen the plans for it. I should *want* to put up an architectural monument in such a ghastly town as this; I should as soon think of ramming an angel into a coal-hole."

Yes, Brower knew all about Jane's Home—much more than

Truesdale did, in fact; but this did not prevent him from asking for all manner of information about the project. He did this purely for the pleasure of talking about Jane herself; and he wondered time and time again whether he had not betrayed to Jane's brother the particular kind of interest he was developing in her. He felt that his beard offered but a slight concealment to the nervous twitching of his mouth, and that, despite the muffling of his heavy overcoat, the throbbings of his heart must be as perceptible to Truesdale as to himself. And when Truesdale presently made the ungrudging avowal that Jane was a pretty good sort of girl, after all—the *ne plus ultra* of a brother's praise—Brower was driven to thrust a trembling hand inside his coat to reduce his thumping organ to something like subjection.

His admiration for Jane had been based originally on her essential qualities; certainly he had received no quickening impulse, at the beginning, from a contemplation of her mere exterior. He had looked upon her as a valuable text put at a disadvantage by an unprepossessing binding. But now there came the issue of a new edition, in a tastefully designed cover, with additions and corrections, with extra illustrations, too—illustrations of a startling social aptitude; and with even a hint of illumination—the illumination that comes from the consciousness of a noble purpose. Brower now began to feel, with a rising pride and pleasure, that Jane was at last doing herself the fullest justice.

Jane, in the meanwhile, with no thought of a possible competition between rival collectors for a certain rare old volume, was helping Tom Bingham to build the new house. She went out southward two or three times a week, and carried a tape-line with her. As she once explained it to Bingham: "You can't be too sure of having things right at the start." So she measured the foundations with her tape-line when the distances were short, and paced them off when they were long. She kept a close eye on the work through each advancing stage, and saw that it was good.

One Sunday morning in mid-May, Jane took the street-car—one of those leisurely green ones that run to the Old People's Home—and went out to satisfy herself that the first courses of dressed stone were going into place as they should. May was speaking truly in the mildness and freshness of the air, in the slow passing of the light and expansive cumuli across the wide blueness of the sky, in the grasses and dandelions springing up among the stark weeds of last year that swayed and rustled on every vacant lot. From her stand-point among the heaps of brick and sand and yellow lumber that surrounded the site of the new house, Jane saw the fronts or sides or backs of other new houses placed dispersedly round about: their towers and turrets and porches and oriels and the myriad other massive manifestations proper to the new Stone Age. Between them and beyond them her eye took transversely the unkempt prairie as it lay cut up by sketchy streets and alleys, and traversed by street-car tracks and rows of lamp-posts and long lines of telegraph poles and the gaunt framework of an elevated road. In one direction she saw above the dead crop of rustling weeds the heads of a long line of people on their way to church; in the other direction, the distant clang of a passing gong drew her eye to the vast advertisement which glared in the sun from the four-story flank of an outlying shoe-store. "I hope the next man who builds will shut *that* out," she thought.

Presently a light buggy drove up to the curbstone, and a large, stout man within it squeezed his way out carefully between its muddy wheels. Then with a jerk he landed his hitching-weight in the roadway, clicked the catch in the end of its strap to the ring at his horse's bit, and advanced towards the house. It was Bingham.

"So you have concluded to give us a little attention, finally?" was Jane's greeting. Her tone was slightly hectoring; this was to punish him for having lately taken more of her thought than she felt him entitled to.

As a matter of fact, Jane was uncomfortably mindful that more than once within the past month she had opened the morning paper to Building Notes before giving due heed to Insurance News. She had been distinctly pleased to read that the Bingham Construction Company had just got one big building ready for tenancy, or had just been awarded the contract for another; and once, for a week, she had followed the head of it through a particularly stubborn bricklayers' strike with the most avid interest. Indeed, she had only been brought back to herself by a fire which had damaged one of Brower's companies to the extent of five thousand dollars and another to the extent of ten. After that she chained her wandering attention to such matters as short rates and unearned premiums, the organization of new companies and the bankruptcies of old ones, the upward climbing of sub-solicitors and assistant managers, the losses suffered by the companies represented by the agency of Brower & Brand, and, above all, the closest scrutiny for the name of Theodore L. Brower himself. Nothing pleased her more than to read a paragraph announcing that he had gone East to attend a general conference—except, of course, his return.

Sometimes, as she sat alone in her room, mending her stockings or taking timely stitches in the fingers of her gloves, she would further fortify herself by humming a scrap from the refrain of a song she had once heard at a concert. *"Toujours fidèle,"* she would moan in a deep contralto voice, as she drew her needle slowly in and out; *"toujours fidèle."* She paused lingeringly on the second syllable of *toujours* and on the middle syllable of *fidèle,* and repeated the phrase over and over again at short intervals—that was all of the song that she knew. And after she had chanted it a dozen times or so, her heart would soften and her eyes would overflow, and she would have to pause in her work. Then she would look at her brimming eyes in the glass, and wonder how she could ever have had a thought for any other man than Theodore.

While poor Brower would sit at his desk and bemoan the fate that compelled him to insure houses instead of building them. He had waited until thirty-five for his first affair, and he was foredoomed to take it has hard as a man may.

"Yes," pursued Jane, "you thought you would come and see whether they were building us upside down or hindside before, I suppose."

"Everything looks all right," said Bingham, serenely. "The foreman can be trusted, I imagine. What's that you've got in your hand?"

Jane held out a battered horseshoe, to which a few twisted nails were still clinging. "I picked it up a minute ago. I was thinking about laying a corner-stone—or relaying it."

"Good!" said Bingham; "the better the day, the better the deed. Do you want to put that horseshoe under it?"

"Um, h'm," replied Jane. She walked along the top of the foundation, and Bingham followed her.

Jane moved on until she found a practicable stone in a suitable angle. "About here, I think," she said, tapping the stone with her toe.

"Do you want me to pry it out?"

"If you can. There's a sort of sharp stick over on that sand-pile."

Bingham removed the stone, and imbedded the horseshoe among the sharp-edged fragments which had been worked into the course beneath.

"I want it to stay, too," declared Jane, as her eye roamed towards the half-dried mortar-bed just beyond the foundation trench. "Wait a second." She skipped across the small chasm which intervened between the foundation-wall and solid ground. She scooped up some water from a shallow puddle with a battered tin can, and began the formation of an oozy little pocket in the middle of the mortar-bed. "Now if I only had a shingle," she said, after she had reduced the mortar to the consistency of slime.

"No shingle would hold that," said Bingham, jumping across after her. "Here, give me that can."

He poured a quart or two of mortar on top of the horseshoe and reset the stone "There!" said Jane, bringing her whole weight upon it.

"Good-luck to this house and household!" said Bingham. He raised his hat; she could not tell whether he were in jest or in earnest.

"It needs all the luck it can have," said Jane. "It may be a nice house, but it will never be home."

"Oh yes, it will," said Bingham, soothingly.

"Oh no, it won't," returned Jane, permitting herself the luxury of a little woe. "Even if we *do* have wreaths of flowers in all the wash-bowls, and transoms that you can open and shut without getting on to chairs, and a what-you-may-call-it to regulate the furnace heat without going down cellar—all the same, it won't be our dear old home."

"No; a better one."

"Well," said Jane, resignedly. She lifted her eyes and pointed her finger aloft. "I suppose I shall be up there, somewhere."

"Oh, not yet," replied Bingham, bringing his eyes back from the clouds. "You look very well fitted for your present sphere."

"I didn't mean all the way up,' said Jane, smilingly dismal. "I only meant the next floor—yet awhile."

"That's better. Don't be an angel just yet; you're too useful here."

"If not ornamental."

"Too ornamental, too."

"I never claimed to be that," observed Jane, dropping her eyes. "Do you think I'm—improving?"

Jane stood there on the foundations, clad in the ample and

voluminous fashion of the day and topped off with a distinctly stylish hat. She had had a long regimen of fencing and dumbbells, and her self-imposed superintendence of the new house had led to many hours spent in the open air. Her hair was blowing airily about her face, and on her cheek there was a slight flush—produced, perhaps, by her own question.

"Decidedly," replied Bingham, promptly.

"Thanks. There's always room for improvement. It's the biggest room in the world, somebody says."

She gave another look at her corner-stone. "Well, what do they do after the last sad rites? They go home, don't they? Yes; let's go home."

"Suppose I drive you down? I'm going your way."

"I *have* got a nickel, somewhere," said Jane, "and I was going back on the elevated, for a change; but—well, all right."

And she let him help her into the buggy.

"Monstrous big house, isn't it?" she commented, as she overlooked the foundations from this loftier point. "I don't know how we are ever going to fill it."

"Oh yes, you will," said Bingham, gathering up the lines. "Your father and mother, and your brother and Rosy . . ."

"I don't know as to Truesdale; he's such a fly-about. You can't depend very much on *him*. And I don't feel any too sure about Rosy, either," she added, inwardly.

Her state of uncertainty about Rosy was shared, in fact, by all the rest of the family; it looked decidedly as if the youngest daughter were to leave the shelter of her father's roof before the completion of her first year in the world. She was a maiden choosing, and the absorbing question was—which? On the side of William Bates there was his position, his ability, his certain future, and the sentimental resumption of old family relations. On the side of Paston there was an entertaining personality and the paragraph in Debrett. The two met occasionally in the Marshalls' front parlor, and sat each other out with much civility and pertinacity—Bates somewhat firm and severe, Paston extremely gay and diverting. Jane and her mother lingered in the *coulisses* and even ventured a word now and then with the *ingénue* after she had left the boards. But the more the family found to say directly and indirectly on behalf of William Bates, the more resolutely Rosamund turned her face in the opposite direction.

"You can't influence Rosy," said Jane; "she'll have her own way—that's a point there needn't be any doubt on. And that boudoir of hers in the new house may come around to me, after all, unless *I*—"

Jane flushed vividly as she thus cast her own horoscope. Bingham at this moment drew the buggy up alongside the curb in front of the old house. A young man on the sidewalk was just approaching the front gate. "Dear me!" gasped Jane, inwardly, "what a miserable sinner I am!" Her heart sank and her appetite left her. The young man was Theodore Brower; she had invited him to dinner and had forgotten all about it.

XVII

"Well, those are my views," said Belden. He elevated his eyebrows slightly as he dropped his glance to a row of shapely nails that lay closely together on the thick of his thumb, and an imperceptible smile moved slowly under the cover of his thick mustache. "To right completely such a wrong as this there is only one course that I know of."

Marshall ceased his earnest scrutiny of his partner's face to rest his elbow on the edge of his desk and to drop his weary old face into the hollow of his hand. There were more wrinkles on his cheeks, more white hairs in the dull dry red of his beard, more signs of sleepless hours in his anxious eyes.

Belden raised his hand and swept it across his mustache. The smile beneath escaped and spread upward over his face. His nostrils, too, dilated—half triumphally.

"It's a most unfortunate affair," he observed further, continuing his series of careful modulations. "There is an error made, a false step taken; the family flee their past to begin life anew in another land; yet at the very threshold of their new life they meet the first cause of all their misfortune and misery." Belden sighed.

His sigh seemed at once to breathe a deep sympathy and to call for the meting out of justice at whatever cost—to some one else. As Belden sighed, Marshall himself almost gave a groan.

He accepted these carefully composed observations for precisely what they seemed. He was too inexperienced in the drama to detect the essential insincerity of every word, though there was not one of the lowliest of his clerks but had heard every one of these phrases bandied across the footlights time and time again.

"I must acknowledge," continued Belden, as he moved towards the door, "that her father has acted with a good deal of reasonableness and forbearance. You can imagine Leppin's anxiety, without any word from me. You can feel how keenly he looks forward to having justice done—to having complete reparation made. You know what that means as well as I do."

And he passed out, leaving his senior to ponder the matter alone.

Belden was the first person with whom Marshall had permitted himself a full canvass of the situation, the sole husbandman towards whom he had turned for assistance in garnering the first-fruits of Truesdale's career abroad. Never before had evil grazed against him and his; he had regarded it, in fact, as something appertaining principally to ill-regulated persons in a lower walk of life. He had heard of such subjects as being handled in fiction, and he had noticed them touched upon in the theatrical reviews of the newspapers. But nothing of the sinful, the vicious, the malodorous had ever, within his recollection, come to his family, to his friends, or even to any of his business associates. Yet here it had come at last, and it must be confronted.

He had quite shrunk from the ordeal of considering the matter with so nimble and experienced a person as Truesdale himself, and he was almost too Anglo-Saxon in his pure-mindedness to attempt an over-intimate discussion of it with his own wife; it took a large share of his fortitude to broach the matter even to his elder son.

"I can't talk to Truesdale about it," said this virginal old man, as he sat in Roger's office; "you've got to do it. I can't."

"Well, really, father," began Roger. He had almost the air of resenting an imputation.

"I don't mean that, Roger," said his father, in some distress. "I have every confidence in you; I believe you're all right. But—"

"Has anybody seen the girl?"

"Your mother says that—well, she says that Jane has seen her"—he brought in his daughter's name with a great disrelish —"and your aunt Lydia. She told your mother she was sure this girl was one to lend herself to—to—"

"H'm," said Roger, in a non-committal way. He always subjected his aunt Lydia's opinions and impressions to a double discount.

Meanwhile the odor of Truesdale's offence permeated the house as completely as the office. Rosy wondered what could be under way as she saw her mother and Jane seated on unaccustomed chairs in unaccustomed attitdues at unaccustomed times in unaccustomed rooms while they engaged in brief and infrequent interchanges of words, or co-operated for the production of long and eloquent silences. Jane, in fact, took the matter with the rigorous thoroughness of the complete theorist. She knew what it was to thread the mazes of a guilty conscience through half a dozen consecutive chapters; she knew how it felt to see the agonies of acknowledged sin transferred from chair to sofa and sofa to chair over the full extent of a large and well-equipped stage. How the leaves had fluttered! How the footlights had palpitated! How those people had suffered—and how she had suffered with them! How she was suffering now—and how much greater still must be the suffering of her erring and idolized brother!

"If he had only been born with eyes like other people's!" she would moan.

The actual mental state of Truesdale was, however, with Jane and with everybody else, a matter of pure conjecture. Very little, in fact, was seen of him. He breakfasted in his own room, as he had done ever since his return home. When the waitress had declined to enter the chamber with his coffee and rolls he had shrugged his shoulders and had directed to have them set on the floor outside. "*Quelle pudeur!*" he more than once observed, as her knock drew him towards the door. His lunch he took wherever he happened to be, and he dined at his French restaurant, or at a new Italian one where the *spaghetti* was unapproachable, and where everything was cheap, plentiful, and informal. He returned home at his own discretion, and sometimes was heard working upon the obdurate old night-lock at midnight or later.

Among the first of the family to have extended speech with him after the *exposé* was his aunt Lydia. He had gone to her house to put the last few finishing touches to Bertie Patterson's portrait. To his aunt and to Bertie herself the portrait seemed already finished, but it is only the artist who knows when the end has really been reached. He asked his aunt for Bertie.

"Well," she hesitated, as she looked at him with a kind of furtive and wondering interest, "Bertie is very busy this afternoon. If there is anything more to be done—and I don't exactly see that there is—it must be done without her, I'm afraid."

"Can't I see her?" he asked, brusquely. "This is the very time I need her. What is she so busy about?"

"She is packing. You know I've kept her a good deal longer already than I expected to—she can't stay into summer. Her mother has written several times, asking for her, and now, finally, she's really got to go." There was a grieving disappointment in Mrs. Rhodes's voice, and a cast of keen but discreet curiosity in her eye.

"When is she going?"

"In the morning. Then her own people will get her well before dark."

"I'm not to see her to say good-bye?—my own cousin, almost."

"Nonsense—not at all. I'll tell her good-bye for you."

"And the picture?"

"Well, *that* we may consider finished, I think." Her eyes were resting on the wall behind him. He turned and saw the portrait fastened upon it.

"So she *is* not even to have—" he began.

"Now, Truesdale," interrupted his aunt, "the picture is not Bertie's, but mine. I thought you understood that."

She followed him to the door. "You won't stay a few minutes longer?" she inquired, with an emollient intention. He shook his head.

"I won't say, Truesdale," she proceeded, with her hand on the knob, "how disappointed I am. Everything, of course, is at a stand-still now. Whether things ever go on again will depend upon you yourself. I am sure that any—any expression of regret, any promise of—of—"

"Ouf!" said Truesdale, as he descended the steps, undecided whether to laugh or to curse. " 'When I was a student at Cadiz,' " he found himself humming, half-unconsciously. "H'm! one thing learned in the study of this peculiar civilization: general badness jollied up, specific badness frowned down. What other discoveries await me, I wonder?"

Before he had taken a dozen steps a brougham drawn by a pair of blacks in glittering, gold-plated harness drew up suddenly at the curbstone, in obedience to directions given through the half-open door. In a second the door opened wide, and Gladys McKenna beckoned to him. "Get in," she uttered, in a half-repressed cry.

She had divined the situation in two swift glances. She had witnessed the moody exit of Truesdale, and she had had a glimpse of the anxious little face of Bertie Patterson in the bay-window above. Her desire to live life, to dramatize it as promptly and effectively as possible, had led her to the instant appropriation of the banned and rejected Truesdale—thus it was that she figured him.

"Get in," she repeated; "I can take you along six or eight

blocks. The coachman knows you by sight, I'm sure. But never mind; nothing matters now. My letter—did you get it?"

"Another!" thought Truesdale. He made the door fast. "No."

"I felt sure you wouldn't,' she panted, excitedly. "I gave it to that man to mail." She pointed towards the occupant of the box-seat. "He has played me false."

Truesdale smiled at her phrase. "Well, never mind; you can tell me what there was in it." He stretched out his long legs negligently under the opposite seat, determined to take this new ordeal as lightly as possible. From his point of view the girl was doing nothing towards gaining a greater measure of approval. "She never had any consideration for me," he was thinking, "until she saw that I cared for the town as little as she did; and she has waited to fling herself at me unreservedly until I have shown myself too awful for anybody else. Why did I let her pick me up? and how soon can I have her set me down?"

"You will learn now who your real friends are," she declared, casting herself energetically into a leading *rôle*; "not fair-weather friends, but friends through thick and thin. Let me tell you: there is a conspiracy against you." She laid her hand on his arm, and looked at him with a wide stare; she seemed to thrill with the consciousness of an important participation in a succession of stirring actualities.

"Is there, indeed?" Whatever one's plight, there is little consolation in the ministrations of an unwelcome hand. Considering this, that, and the other, he was now, as at his aunt's door, again midway between a laugh and a curse.

"Yes. That man—that German, or whatever—was at the house last evening, and—oh, why will Albert drive so fast?" she complained, as she made a seeming calculation of the many things she had to say and the little time she had to say them in. "Can't something be done to make him go a little slower?"

"The horses feel lively," answered Truesdale, to whom the present rapid course was perfectly agreeable; "I expect he'll have to let them go their own gait." He glanced out at a passing church or two, and frowned slightly; why did this girl insist upon doing his mathematical problems for him? Had not he himself already put his two and two together and made them four?

Gladys went on, telling him what she knew, guessed, surmised, suspected. "And they—they suspect *me*," she continued, in a mounting tone of tragedy. "And I'm—I'm going home in a few days." There were tears on the dark fringes of her eyes; he thought of a wax image exposed overnight to a heavy dew. "And all for your sake," the moisture seemed to say. Truesdale began to feel uncomfortable and a shade ungrateful. "I dare say she means well," he thought; "but I—I wish she wouldn't."

The carriage was passing between two other churches; he saw that he might alight after another square of it. "One more will be plenty," he muttered, and already his hand stole towards the handle of the door.

"You can't think how they both hate you—my aunt and uncle—and me, too, I'm afraid. They're really driving me out of the house. But never mind; I can endure even more than that for one that—for the right."

"When did you say you were going?" inquired Truesdale. It was only by asking plain, every-day questions that he could oppose this robust romanticism.

"Day after to-morrow—or the next."

"Well," said Truesdale, quietly, "I should think you would do very well at home—much better than here."

"But where am I to see you before I go? Where are we to say good-bye?"

A cable-car clanged along the cross-street immediately ahead of them, and the ten yellow stories of a vast hotel loomed up just beyond. "Right on this corner," replied Truesdale, as the carriage bumped across the tracks. "The interval is short, as you suggest, and there is no time like the present." He put his hand on the door and fixed his eye upon the corner shop; he often bought a cigar there, and meant to buy one now. He also meant this good-bye as literally final.

"You want me to let you out here? Stop, Albert. Well, good-afternoon," she said, smilingly waiving the idea of finality; "you shall know to-morrow where you can meet me. You are not deserted by everybody, after all, you see." She gave him her hand, or rather laid hold of his. "But take good care of yourself, all the same.

Truesdale stepped out. "I'll try to," he said, mumblingly; "I always have."

Being thus minded, Truesdale received but grudgingly the tenders of his brother Roger to assist in the caretaking. He admitted, however, that it would be less embarrassing to confer with one person than a dozen, and that if the whole connection were to be represented by a single spokesman, then Roger was the one that he preferred.

Roger was held by his family to be above all foibles and frailties; his aunt Lydia had once told him, on the day of a niece's hopeless return to the East, that he had too much head and not enough heart. It is certain that he had marked out a definite course for himself, and that nothing, so far, had had the power to divert him materially from it; and he had a far-reaching contempt for the man who permitted the gray matter of his brain to be demoralized by the red matter in his veins. He kept a firm hand on his own affairs and on those of his father that were not immediately connected with the business of his father's firm. His severe face was smooth-shaven, as he thought the face of a lawyer ought to be, and he could address the higher courts with such a loud and brazen utterance as to cause the court-loungers almost to feel the judges shrinking and shrivelling under their robes. His was a hot and vehement nature, but it burned with a flame blue rather than red.

"Well," he said, with a look of extreme distaste fixed half

on his brother and half on his book-shelves, "we can accept her and make the best of her. I have seen her and her father. While I can't say I admire the personal character of either, I am not prejudiced by the fact that he is only a clerk and she only a shop-girl. They are beginners here; I am willing to believe that they were something better at home. We can accept her; we shall have to, I suppose."

Truesdale reared his beautiful brazen front and flashed on his brother a haughty and disdainful smile. "You can accept her? Will you please tell me what you mean by that? And 'better at home'!" He burst into open and derisive laughter. "What new Arcadia is this, where even the lawyers walk about with their beribboned crooks and the little baa-lambs following behind them? We have been sitting in conclave, have we, on a mossy bank in some sylvan shade, with chaplets on our brows, and we have piped and twittered over the matter, and have decided that we can 'accept her'? Well, you can do more than I can," he added, abruptly. His foot slipped from the rung of the opposite chair and fell to the bare floor with a contemptuous clump.

"You've got your own character to clear, haven't you?" asked Roger, with a severe brevity.

Truesdale replaced his foot on the rung of the other chair and slid down into his own as he thrust his hands deeper into his pockets. "Dear me," he said, in affected apprehension, "am I in any danger? Well, well; if such a thing can hurt a young man, I shall be glad to know it—I never knew it before. Now, là-bas, for example—"

He drew out one of his hands and waved it vaguely; he seemed to be conjuring up a wider and more liberal world—the only one he had learned.

"It can," insisted his brother; "it will. Both you and your family."

Truesdale's thought flashed back to Bertie Patterson and the unfinished picture. It came to him all at once that his brother might be better worth listening to than he had been disposed to concede.

"And your family," Roger repeated.

But Truesdale's thought, lingering over the picture, made little of this second point. He did scant justice to the mortification of his mother before her church-members and her few remaining neighbors, or that of his sisters within the circle which they had lately constructed for themselves. Nor did he yet realize, even with Bertie's picture in mind, the hundred checks and bars that awaited him in a society of whose primitive purity he had made a jest whenever occasion came.

"Dear Roger," he presently rejoined, in his most genial and winning voice, "you mean well, I am sure—well by me and by the family and by everybody. And I dare say you do very nicely in your own narrow field; but as for knowing life—well, really now, do you think you understand what it is to live?"

"Live!" cried Roger, with a sonorous contempt. "Who *does* understand what it is to live, then—the man who has all his work and worry done for him by some one else?"

Truesdale smiled, serene and unabashed. "The world is wide," he said, with an exquisite tolerance. "It is a very comprehensive subject. You must take it up one of these days—you've hardly made a beginning on it yet."

"The world!" cried Roger again, with a vibrant indignation at this impertinence. "Who *are* the world if not my father and I and all the other earnest men who work to make the frame of things and to hold it together? *We* are the world, and you—you are only the rubbish strewn over the top of it!"

He collected this rubbish and constructed from it a Frankenstein monster, with a heart of cork, a brow of brass, and a triple-plating of self-conceit. Then with a harsh laugh and a wide-flung arm he scattered it apart again.

Perhaps Truesdale took these words and gestures merely as an example of Roger's forensic eloquence. For—

"My dear brother," he began, quietly, while Roger beat his

foot upon the floor, stung to increased indignation by the conscious artificiality of such an address—"my dear brother," said Truesdale, "you don't quite get my position in this trifling episode. Every little *conte drolatique* has its Monsieur X, of course—myself, in this instance, and rightfully enough. But is Monsieur X the only gentleman involved? Let us see. Who comes before Monsieur X? Why, Monsieur W, to be sure. And who before Monsieur W? Monsieur V, *n'est-ce pas?* And there is somebody still in front of Monsieur V. And if we go far enough back, we may come at last even to Monsieur A. Now, why are all these worthy gentlemen passed over in favor of *ce cher* Monsieur X? Well, perhaps Monsieur W, for example, is a captain of dragoons and already mated. And maybe Monsieur V is a young baron whose family won't stand any nonsense about him—families are different. And as for Monsieur A— well, let us put him down for a poor devil of a student who cuts no figure at all. But Monsieur X—ah, that is different! he is pounced upon in the bosom of his family. It is Monsieur X who has the scrupulous and strait-laced mother—"

"Truesdale!"

"And the little coterie of lily-sisters who never—"

"Truesdale! For shame!"

"And the over-conscientious and supersensitive father with millions and millions stored away in bursting money-bags somewhere or other. Oh, those money-bags, those money-bags, those money-bags!"

"Truesdale, what do you mean? Are they adventurers? Are they after black-mail?"

Truesdale threw back his head, closing his eyes and twirling his thumbs. "I knew them there; I know them here." Then he opened his eyes and gave his brother a glance of satirical approval. "*Complimenti*, Roger; you are ending where I should have expected you to begin."

"It is not the end," cried Roger, savagely. He saw that he had allowed his view of the matter to be wrongly colored by the impressions of his father and the representations of Belden; and Truesdale's comments lacerated his self-esteem as with griffins' claws. "Haven't I told you that they have taken legal advice, and that—"

"And that the whole grovelling tribe of Leppins, outnumbering the Van Horns, possibly, are ready with oral testimony and a shower of depositions, and what all besides. Ouf! not an inch do I yield. *J'y suis; j'y reste.* Not an inch should anybody else yield. Well, thank me, Roger, for having given you this little glimpse into the great big world. It's full of interest." He rose suddenly, stiff and straight and slender as some young fir-tree. "Come, Roger, put on your hat and go with me to Japan."

He looked over into the half-open drawer of his brother's desk. "More of those maps, I see."

"Other maps; another subdivision. I can do my work without trotting over the whole globe; Cook County is big enough for me."

"H'm; you seem to be branching out quite extensively. Only, don't get in too deep." Truesdale gave this valuable advice in a patronizing tone of which he alone was master. "Yes, I should think Cook County would do very well for you—until you have learned to spik something besides ze Engleesh." He picked up his hat and moved towards the door.

"English will do for *me!*" retorted Roger, savagely.

"Well, turn the thing over in this new light," continued his brother, pleasantly. "And one thing more—a little suggestion: you have some notion of the man who comes before Monsieur X; give a bit of attention, now, to the man who comes after. He could be of the greatest service to us—permanent service. *Comprenez-vous?* Find him; find Monsieur Y—and arrange it that he shall be the last!"

And Truesdale sauntered airily out of the room.

XVIII

"You might have thought it no great concern of his—you might have imagined all our efforts as only a part of a play, and his interest merely the interest of a looker-on." There was an indignant rasp in Roger's voice, and he looked across to his father with a protesting scowl. "He almost made me feel as if I had never learned the alphabet."

David Marshall fixed an intent and anxious gaze on his son's face, and ran his hand tremulously along the arm of his chair. He knew about how Roger felt; Truesdale had more than once made him feel the same way himself.

The old man had remained at home throughout the day. Too ill and nervous for the store, and too resourceless for the house, he had worried through twelve hours as wearing as any he could recollect. He had never been more unfitted for business, yet never (as he made it seem) more demanded by it. He imagined himself as still the king-pin of the Marshall & Belden Company—indeed, he found in that belief some consolation for his difficulty in reconciling himself to the style and title that the course of the business had finally evolved. He tormented himself with thoughts of odds and ends of work left over from yesterday or from last week, or with the apprehension of some fresh step taken, some new course entered upon by the younger and more ardent men of whom the company was largely composed. He had laughed more than once over the joke of business acquaintances who told him they had had to take young men into partnership because it was impossible to pay the salaries they demanded; yet something more radical had happened to himself: the young men had not only come in, but they were showing a disposition to get things into their own hands. Their former manager, their credit man, several heads of departments—all these had rallied under Belden, and together seemed to be trimming the sails to as speculative a course as a craft essentially conservative in its nature could well be made to take. Marshall had not formulated so clearly as this the practical primacy of Belden, but he felt the necessity of his own presence, and chafed under the temporary withdrawal of his own guiding hand.

But more than the course of affairs at the store, more than the avalanche of complicated minutiæ involved in the progress of the new house, more than the dawning risks attendant upon Roger's widening operations in land, more than the amiable persecutions of friends whose ambitions for him were greater than his own, did the courses of his younger son and all their threatening consequences disturb his days and harass his nights— haunting alike the hours set apart for work and for sleep, and even the few brief intervals between. He would rise in the morning haggard and dry-eyed after a sleepless night; he would toil through the weary and perplexing hours of a dragging day; and he would spend his evenings, usually, in a miserable and solitary contemplation of all his thickening annoyances and ills.

"Poor pa," Jane would say to her mother, as she watched his bent and lagging steps moving towards the recess of the bay-window; "there he goes worrying, all off by himself again."

Her mother, over her sewing or the evening paper, perhaps, would check the girl's impulse to follow. "Don't chase after your father, Jane; he's got enough things to bother him already." So that, except for the occasional charitable moment when

Jane, unimpeded, perched on the arm of his chair and attempted to divert his wearing thoughts from their ever-deepening channel, the old man spent his evenings largely—too largely—alone.

The rare visits of Roger, never highly ameliorative, were none the more so now; the grisly wrestling with realities does little to promote the exudation of balm. Roger was tough and technical and litigious; his was the hand to seize, not to soothe.

Roger had had a second and more explicit interview with Truesdale, before Truesdale had taken an airy and irresponsible flitting from town. He had also prosecuted various inquiries of his own in various directions, and these inquiries had resulted in his coming to look up Truesdale's frothy suggestion with more seriousness, and upon Truesdale himself with more consideration, if not with more respect—*that* he still withheld.

"He isn't a complete fool, after all," admitted Roger.

"I never thought he was," responded his father, dully.

"He has some little sense, I acknowledge."

"If it were only common-sense," said the old man, with a mournful, dragged-out smile.

Roger looked forth streetward, pondering. A long passenger-train shifted its line of glimmering squares rapidly southward; two or three couples passed by on the pavement, respiring the suave air of an early June evening.

"It means money," said Roger, presently.

"As much as is necessary," replied his father, tremulously; "though I never could spare it worse than now."

"And more—well, more dirty work for me." He thought of the Van Horn matter, now as good as abandoned. "Never mind, though; I'm getting used to it."

"You are the only help I have, Roger—the only one to save us from this disgrace."

There were tears in his eyes, and a feeble tremor ran through the fore-arm and fingers that he advanced towards Roger's shoulder.

"Father is not the man he used to be," thought Roger. He

felt that his sympathy was largely qualified by the impatience and aversion which must always move a young man when he observes the first signs of physical and mental impairment in an older one, and he regretted that it was so. And he was almost ashamed to feel relieved when his father withdrew his hand.

Besides Roger and his father, only Mrs. Marshall and Jane were at home. Rosamund was in Wisconsin, and no one was sorry to have her away. She was a guest of Mrs. Bates at Lake Geneva—the central figure of a house-party, in fact. Mrs. Bates's fondness for nature did not stop with flowers; it led her to the fields and woods where they grew. No sooner was the back of the winter fairly broken than she began to preach the gospel of country life. She took the cream of June, and left to later comers the skimmed milk of July and August. She always saw that her Wisconsin place was ready for her by the middle of May; then for the next five months she passed back and forth between town and country, according to the nature of her engagements and the character of the weather.

Truesdale was in Wisconsin, too—but not of the house-party. "You know, my dear," Mrs. Bates said to Jane, "I had meant to have your brother, but—"

Jane bowed her head and never thought of venturing to ask her how she *knew*. That same night Jane slowly tore her plans for the working-girls' home into long strips and burned them in the gas, one at a time. "Pa'll never listen to a word about anything like this now."

Truesdale left behind no precise indications of his movements. The only person to whom he announced anything like a programme was Arthur Paston, who met him on the way to the station, with his bag in one hand and his kit in the other.

"Off, are you?" called Paston. "Don't you begin the season rather early?"

"Just for a few days," replied Truesdale; "a little sketching tour up North. Change of scene and air, you know."

"Where are you going?"

"Oh, 'most anywhere. I shall be at Bellagio to-morrow, and at Pontresina the day after. Then I shall dip down towards Scheveningen. And Zante, if possible—I have always wanted to try Zante." He smiled jovially. "I hear there's a lovely ruined abbey at Fort Atkinson—everybody does it; and they say, too, that the capitol at Madison is a grand old structure."

He gave a hitch to his light valise and moved on with a diminished smile.

"Of course you've got your Cook's ticket and your meal coupons?" called Paston, grinning broadly.

"Don't," protested Truesdale, turning back; "you never looked less like a gentleman."

"I hope your ticket takes in Geneva," said Paston, in no degree offended. "If it does, I may meet you there; I'm going up to stay over Sunday."

"I can't tell without looking," replied Truesdale; "it's away at the bottom of my trunk." And he moved on. "Rosy's there, though," he called back. He did this largely under the promptings of a sense of justice: Paston was as much entitled to push one project as he himself was to push another.

"Yes, I know," said Paston.

This ubiquitous and ever-welcome person made his presence known throughout Geneva with no loss of time. He caused himself to be remembered by Mrs. Bates for a small dance on Saturday night, and also secured himself from forgetfulness in connection with her steam-yacht excursion for Sunday morning. This active and well-intentioned woman was the prime mover in a poor children's camp which was in process of construction near the far end of the lake. She could not expect her dozen young people to take an absorbing interest in her middle-aged philanthropies; but she knew that an excursion was none the worse for having an objective point, and she did not feel that she was likely to please her guests the less by giving a little incidental pleasure to herself.

"I've got to have something to *do*," she explained to Paston. "I couldn't be content to come up here and pass the summer in mere idleness." They were sitting on a pair of camp-stools up near the bow. Paston, looking backward, saw Rosamund and William Bates together near the stern.

"It must be a terrible thing to be cursed with ambition and executive ability," observed Paston. "I'm awfully glad *I* haven't got any."

"Well, there it is," she responded. "I've got to have something on hand. I've got to engineer. I've got to manage."

Paston brought back his eyes from William Bates and Rosamund. "Everybody knows what a capable manager you are." He said this, as he said so many other things, with a frank and bold directness that made any suspicion of an *arrière-pensée* almost an impossibility.

"Well, don't commit yourself until you get there; then you can make your own observations." She took his remark as almost anybody else would have felt obliged to take it—just for what it sounded. Nobody understood better than Paston the deceptive quality resident in a truth plumply told.

"Shall I see Cecilia Ingles there?" Paston was stopping with the Ingleses, and had rowed across immediately after breakfast. "I think I heard them speak about driving down. I say," he added, "it's a rum go for her."

"I don't see why," rejoined Susan Bates, disputatiously. "She is old enough to take things seriously; she has got far enough along to begin to be in earnest. The first thing she asked me was how much money I wanted. 'I dont want any of your money at all,' I told her; 'for such a cause as this I can scoop up all the money I want by the shovelful. No; what I want is your personal interest.' That's about the hardest thing *to* get in cases like this."

"Well, I believe you've got it," declared Paston, hitching about on his seat. "She has given up all hope of escaping from you. You're a tyrant—an inexorable tyrant, she says. She's going to do as you direct."

"All right," returned Susan Bates; "only don't be so sticky about it." She pronounced this epithet very distinctly and deliberately; she had long meant to use it with Paston, some time or other—ever since Jane had imparted it to her, in fact.

"Sticky!" cried the young man. "Me—sticky?"

"Yes—fussy, critical, disagreeable, censorious." She moved her fingers as if disentangling them from a sheet of fly-paper. "It's one of your own words, isn't it?"

"Yes, but what it means is stiff, poky, awkward; and nobody else has ever called me that!"

Susan Bates, with a slight touch of mortification, at once set the whole matter aside. "Cecilia is good enough at heart," she went on, instantly. "No, I don't want her money," she ploughed rapidly ahead, "except as a visitor. Every visitor must give something, and the first must give the most. You are the first."

"I?" stammered Paston, with an uneasy laugh.

"All of you, I mean." She waved her hand over the whole yacht. "Feel for your dollars; you will find a contribution-box fastened to the first tree, at the landing."

"Really?" said Paston, vastly ill at ease.

Susan Bates merely laughed, feeling that she had regained the upperhand. She had not been so tickled since the day when Minnie Peters had put into her hands the official notification that she was at length a member of that obdurate and exacting musical society. "But, poor fellow," she said to herself, "I mustn't tease him!" She looked back the length of the boat towards Rosy; Rosy, at the same moment, was looking forward the length of the boat towards her. A pause had apparently come in William Bates's careful enumeration of the country-seats which covered the wooded slopes of either shore. Many of them were the residences of people whom Rosy had met for the first time during the past winter, and their interest was therefore biographical as well as topographical. But now the interest, of whatever kind, was running a bit thinly; Rosy gave a careless word now and then to another young girl beside her or to a new young man sprawling at her feet, but her eyes turned every few minutes towards the bow.

"You catch the idea?" Mrs. Bates was saying. "We bring them out on the train in two hours, and give them a ride on the public steamer to the camp; we keep them a week. We start in with a fresh lot every Monday morning, right through the summer."

"Where do you get them?" asked Paston, making talk industriously. "Do you set traps for them? Or perhaps you go to the Bureau of Child Labor and say: So many tons of orphans, to be delivered on the fifth instant, at nine-thirty A.M., sharp; eh?" He had quite recovered his spirits.

"Get them? Dear me, there are plenty to be got. I expect we shall have to enlarge the dormitories before the summer is half over."

"And what is Mrs. Ingles to do with them after they *are* got?" he asked, with his eye on the foam and bubbles of the wake. "Is she to take the kinks out of their hair every morning by early candle-light? Is she to wash all their little porringers and hang them up in rows on their little hooks? Is she to keep tab when they go in paddling and check them off as they come out, to see how many have been carried away by the undertow?"

Mrs. Bates declined to consider the undertow. "See; there it is." The yacht had rounded a small wooded promontory and now approached a shallow shore, where a gingerly landing was to be effected at a rude and rickety little pier.

A grove of oak and maple came almost to the water's edge, and within it a number of barrack-like structures of clean yellow pine were taking shape and substance. The odor of the pine mingled with the earthy smells of the grove; now and then a little pile of sawdust was taken swirlingly by the breeze, and here and there a long, fresh shaving was seen caught upon the prickly branches of some June rose.

Paston helped Mrs. Bates out on to the pier with a cautious gallantry, and immediately betook himself to the younger members of the party; he considered the courtesies due from a guest as now amply accomplished. He attached himself at once to Rosamund; he helped her over the loose litter of lumber; he steadied ladders for her at every fresh feint of mounting; he bestirred himself to a rapacious culling of wild-flowers for the mere opportunity of tying them together with a shaving. Once he sprinkled them over with a handful of sawdust, after the manner of a florist extemporizing a heavy dew. Rosy laughed and nodded, and thrust the flowers into her belt.

"You will never be serious," she protested.

"Oh yes, I shall. I am always a good deal more serious than people suppose." He bestowed upon her a look serious enough to match his words. It was as serious as any one could have wished, and Rosy dropped her eyes and was distinctly pensive for a minute or two.

Presently the Ingleses came picking their way through the grove in a surrey. Cecilia Ingles alighted with the air of one somewhat at sea. She greeted Rosy quite pleasantly, but seemed to be looking about for the captain. The dry, shrewd, middle-aged face of her husband adjusted its expression readily enough to the matter before them. He was a born manager and manipulator. When he could not juggle with a dollar for profit, he was content to juggle with a penny for pleasure.

Susan Bates hastened up to his wife at once, and kissed her roundly. "So good of you to come! And on Sunday, too!"

"Never mind," said Ingles; "we can put twice as much on the plate next Sunday."

Mrs. Ingles at once appropriated William Bates for a walk through the framework of the unfinished dormitories. Ingles followed with Mrs. Bates.

"Things are going first-rate," declared Susan Bates. "We shall be under cover in a week, and ready for the painters."

"No plaster?" asked Ingles.

"Dear me, no. Two coats of paint will be quite warm enough."

Rosy, meanwhile, sat upon a pack of shingles under a young maple-tree which grew within a few steps of the water. Paston lay at her feet and dug in the sand with a split shingle drawn from the pack, while the other young people tramped and frolicked with shrill cries through the dismantled grove and unfinished buildings.

"It was at her house, you remember, that I first met you," said Paston. He nodded to Mrs. Ingles, who was just moving by with the reluctant William Bates.

"And a handsome house, too," declared Rosy. "Still, I suppose that hers, or even Mrs. Bates's, can't be compared with some in London."

"Don't be so sure," rejoined Paston. He thought of "10, King's-gate Gardens, S. Kensington"; he would have been the last to force a comparison between that and the town-house of Cecilia Ingles. "A house is no better for being more than a home," he said, somewhat ruefully.

Rosy was far from subscribing to this. Her ideal home was one that had been immemorially a palace and a show-place, with troops of servants to show the troops of tourists through.

"All these places around here are nice enough," she acknowledged, "but—new. That one over there, now." She pointed across the lake to the roofs and gables of a large country-seat set on a wooded hill-top. "They have had to stain it green to make it look old and mossy."

"Sometimes the appearance of age is to be preferred to the reality," observed Paston, thoughtfully. His mind was on "Boxton Park, Witham, Essex," and he was wishing devoutly enough that means were available for keeping that in a state of fresh repair equal to the state of the house where he was now staying.

But Rosy was entertaining her own vision of Boxton Park. It was a spacious and glorious domain, and its noble manor-house was a perfect commingling of old-time picturesqueness and modern comfort. And the peacocks paraded again on the terrace.

Rosy shifted her seat on the pile of shingles in order to take a more general view of the landscape. She shrugged her shoulders slightly. "No lanes, no hedge-rows, no weirs, no coppices..."

"What's the matter with these maples?" asked Paston, abandoning himself to the American idiom. "And where are there handsomer elms than right here in Wisconsin? And what have you against those hills?" He thought of the wide flatness of Essex; what would not Boxton Park give for a foothold on such a shore, a prospect over such a sheet of rippling blue?

But Rosy had her own conception of Essex. In some miraculous way it combined the sweetness of Devonshire, the fatness of Warwick, the boldness of Westmoreland, the severity of Cornwall. And through this enchanting tract the fox-hounds ever sped in full, re-echoing cry.

Paston gave a sudden dig with his shingle, and a lump of damp sand fell with a splash far out upon the water. "But, after all, it's dear old England," he said, plaintively.

"The dearest land in all the world, I'm sure," sighed Rosy, sympathetically. She dug her toe at a single tuft of coarse grass in the midst of the sand, and wondered over his "after all."

"Indeed, it is. You would like it, I'm sure."

"I know I should. I shall never be happy until I've seen it."

"But think of me—four thousand miles away from it."

"I do," said Rosy, softly.

"We younger sons," sighed Paston, in a tone of great self-commiseration.

"We younger daughters," echoed Rosy, with an implication that all the drawbacks were not on one side.

The rest of the party came flocking down to the shore; the Ingleses among them—to see the others off.

"I suppose you go back as you came?" said Ingles, to Paston.

"Pretty nearly," replied Paston, in the cheery tone he usually adopted for general converse. And back he went, with this small difference: that on the return he occupied the place of William Bates.

XIX

Truesdale returned home from Wisconsin after an absence of ten or twelve days; he came back without having visited Geneva. He had visited Madison, however.

His feeling, as he traversed the streets of that pleasant capital, was distinctly one of pique. To be hemmed in, to be barred out, to be shut up, to be cut off, to be turned aside—any and all of these things seemed to have been suffered by him; he felt them as stripes or as fetters applied to the degradation of an inexpugnable personality. "I shall not take it so passively as they think," he said.

His friendly but tempered interest in Bertie Patterson had risen to a higher pitch in view of the insensate safeguards thrown around her by her friends; besides, he felt himself at a juncture where he must not permit himself to falter in the maintenance of his own dignity. "I shall not be balked so easily as they imagine," he said.

He paused before a large, white frame-house which stood on a kind of banked terrace; the house was shaded by a number of evergreens, and was shut in from the street by a picket-fence. "This must be it," he said, as he clicked the latch of the gate. Patterson, as one of the large retail dry-goods merchants of the town, was of course a "prominent citizen"; his residence was easy enough to find.

"Mrs. Patterson is at home?" he uttered with the appropriate inflection, and extended his card. He made this tender to a firm-faced woman of forty in a plain black dress, who came to the door with a half-hemmed towel in her hand.

"I am Mrs. Patterson," she said. She read the card; there was no doubt of her appreciation of his identity. The more picturesque and decorative phases of his character had been presented to her, doubtless, by the docile and transparent Bertie— by letter, possibly. The less approved side (concerning which Bertie's own conception was in all likelihood darkling enough still) had probably come to her—also by letter—from Bertie's conscientious but disappointed guardian.

Truesdale dexterously insinuated himself into the house; he had instantly perceived, with a pang of mortification, that no formal encouragement to enter was likely to be extended.

"My daughter," said Mrs. Patterson, coldly, in answer to his inquiries, "is visiting friends in Watertown." This was true. "She is to remain several days." This was not true; Bertie was expected home on the morrow. But it was made true, for all purposes, by an instant message which permitted the girl to extend the period of her visit.

Truesdale bowed himself out of the house with no apparent diminution of grace and prestige. "How inexhaustible are the beauties of nature," he thought—"Wisconsin nature. I must make another sketching-tour before long."

Four or five days later he sat in his bedroom, looking over a number of water-colors that covered the counterpane and largely obscured the pillows—views of Green Lake, scenes from the rocks and gorges of the upper Wisconsin. "I've done very well," he thought—"very well, indeed." He was trying to make himself believe that he had successfully accomplished the principal object of his trip.

Rosy also returned from Wisconsin at about the same time; with an air of calm decision she announced to her mother her engagement to Arthur Paston. She regarded this statement as definitive—an admission towards which the others of the family advanced with a doubting reluctance. Jane, by reason of the place and of her own participation in the hopes of Susan Bates, thought the proceeding characterized by indelicacy, if not by disloyalty. Truesdale, on receipt of the intelligence, vented a jarring laugh. He saw little reason why Paston should have succeeded at Geneva when he himself had failed at Madison (he was conscious, here, of forcing the terms in order to compass a striking antithesis); and that it should have been his own sister whose hand Paston had won seemed to him a triumph greater and more discordant still.

David Marshall himself heard these tidings with a grave concern. It all seemed like another weight added to the load under which he was already staggering. He debated with himself on the subject of this proposed new household: where was it to be established, of whom was it to be composed, by whom (above all) was it to be supported? Marshall, in his most prosperous and least careworn days, had never acquired the useful and agreeable art of spending money; the outlay of any considerable sum had always afflicted him as with a physical pain. How much greater, then, was his shrinking dread to-day, when demands upon him were doubling up so finely, and when the last demand of all was on behalf of an alien who might well attempt to make an alien of his daughter too? He talked with Rosy about her future in a hesitating and perturbed fashion. Rosy would set her lips, and eye him coldly, and tell him that he did not love her. In the meantime the new house progressed towards its ridge-poles, and it was Jane's daily speculation whether the boudoir designed for Rosy would ever be occupied by her— or by somebody else. By somebody else, she was afraid; for since that luckless Sunday dinner, Theodore Brower had called but twice, and had been as distant as if he had not come at all.

A few weeks after the intrusion of Paston upon the board,

another piece was happily removed. This removal involved, as is often the case in such manipulations, a certain amount of sharp playing and a large element of sacrifice. Truesdale, when the recital was made to him in his brother's office, showed a scant appreciation of the sacrifice, but listened interestedly enough to the detailed report of Roger's endeavor.

"So you have found Monsieur Y, after all? And do you hold him fast?"

Roger contemptuously ignored this revival of his brother's flippant Gallic formula. He contented himself with giving a brief and stern account of the processes that he had been driven to employ. He had prosecuted his inquiries through one of those extra-legal agencies which even the highest respectability may be compelled, upon occasion, to fall back on, and he had arrived at an acquaintance with the Leppins, in all their grovelling ramifications, equal to the previous one which he had achieved with the Van Horns. His close inquiries had extended through the ranks of all their associates and connections, and in the end he had lighted upon one individual whose disposition towards Sophie Leppin and her family could be made to serve the end in view. This young man was the foreman of a tailor's establishment, and Roger wasted no more consideration upon him than upon the rest of them. Before the assembled horde he made his proposition with a blunt, business-like brutality which almost startled him at the moment, and which disgusted him with himself for a fortnight to follow.

"And they accepted it. More shame for me, more shame for them, more shame for human nature. But *you* are safe." He viewed Truesdale with an undisguised scorn, and Truesdale did not attempt to withstand it.

"I attended the ceremony," Roger said, grimly. "I presented the bride with a bouquet. For the matter of that," he continued, in a scornful jest of himself, "I was the one who took out the marriage license."

"Did you pay the minister his fee?" Truesdale asked this principally for the purpose of reasserting himself.

"Minister!" cried Roger, half shocked. "No; I had a justice of the peace. I was the guest of honor," he went on, with a savage irony. "With good reason; it was I who paid the bride's dowry."

Truesdale sat with his eyes on the floor. "The check; was it— was it a large one?" he asked, in a low voice.

"Check!" cried Roger again. "I paid them in hundred-dollar bills." His fingers played back and forth many and many times.

"Not so much as that!" exclaimed Truesdale, his eyes opening widely.

"More," said Roger. "I put the notices in the newspapers, too. And now, Truesdale," he said, with a final brief phrase of dismissal, "think what your father and I have had to do for you, and try to be a man." And he turned away towards other matters.

Truesdale passed out, crestfallen for the first time in his life. Not over his own follies, not over the anxieties and expenditures he had caused his father, but over the fact that Roger had treated him like a boy—and had done it all so briefly. He blushed, too, for the vulgar ending of the episode (if ended, indeed, it were); for it seemed to outrage all literary and artistic precedent. No farce at the Palais Royal had ever developed so grotesque a dénouement; no novel of Véron, of Belot, of Montépin had ever come to so sordid an ending; no Mimi, no Musette could have ever followed a line of conduct so little *spirituel* as that taken by Sophie Leppin. What, then; were the books wrong, and only life true? No; it was the fault of America itself. "*Quel pays!*" reflected Truesdale; "equally without the atmosphere of art and the atmosphere of intrigue!" This observation pleased him; he felt that he had pierced the marrow of a complicated question, and he passed along the street holding a higher head.

He drew a letter from his pocket and creased it thoughtfully in his hands as he walked on. The envelope, from which he did not draw the enclosure, was addressed in the hand of Gladys McKenna. He had parted from her just as he had meant to part—at the carriage door. She had forgiven this, and was now writing in terms no less ardent and clinging than before.

"Poor Gladys!" he said, half aloud. "I haven't treated her any too well; yet she is about the only one who cares for me or understands me or appreciates me. I'm glad, though, she's back home; I should be guilty of some horrible *sottise* or other if she were here."

All the same, he made her absence seem another deprivation; he included it in the catalogue of his injuries and woes. "I declare," he said, "take it all together, and it's enough to drive a man to—business. It wouldn't surprise me very much to be talking with father about that very thing within a month or so. For what can a man of leisure do, after all, in such a town as this?"

But the summer moved onward, and Truesdale still considerately refrained from harassing an anxious and overburdened father with the further task of contriving a harmony between such a son and such a *métier*. The old man was left to recover from the sting inflicted by the Leppins, to study over the future of his youngest daughter, to keep a careful eye upon his business associates, and to combat—as one combats the alkali dust of the Plains—all the insinuating minutiæ of house-building. The new home of the Marshalls moved on with the summer, and reached in due course the stage when such elemental features as walls and roofs gave way to the minor considerations involved in the swinging of doors, the placing of gas-jets, and the arrangements of pantries. Eliza Marshall now began to appear more frequently on the scene, and to confound both architect and builder after the fashion possible for the experienced and accomplished house-keeper. She usually exacted the support of her husband, with a pertinacity the greater for the smallness of the point at issue; and David Marshall, wearied and borne down with more important, more vital affairs, wished daily that the new house had never been undertaken at all.

Thomas Bingham stood Eliza Marshall's annoying picket-fire with the patience proper to a friend of the family; and he took advantage of the same position to press further upon her husband his own continuing sense of a rich man's duties towards the public. Marshall may be said by this time to have fixed himself in the general eye. He had made a second public address —the skilful product of Jane's literary knack and of his own previous experience. As a consequence of this he had been asked to sit on one or two platforms, and to sign two or three addresses and petitions; and though his indifferent health and his many preoccupations had somewhat impeded his advance, yet his well-wishers felt the marked disposition shown to concede him the place that they held him entitled to take.

Bingham experienced a personal interest in Marshall's maintenance of the foothold thus won. As the two toured through the half-plastered rooms or stooped to consider the question of sewerage amid the litter of the basement, Bingham, with a tactful seriousness, would urge the old man, as he had urged him often enough before, to crown his career and perpetuate his memory by the erection of some enduring structure for the public good and use.

"All of my experience is at your disposal," he would say. "And all of your own"—with a wave of the hand over the chaos prevailing about them.

The old man would give him a non-committal sidelong glance, half smiling, half protesting "I'm glad to have you acknowledge, Bingham, that there is some experience involved in building a house. There's a good deal more than I expected."

"You're not having a hard time of it," returned Bingham. "You don't realize how easy I've been making it for you."

But Marshall was coming to develop a firm reluctance towards turning the knowledge gained in his private building to the erection of some larger and different building for the public good. With every month of the past year had his estimate of the public and its character been modified by the kind of treatment that he had suffered from certain of the less worthy members of it. The Van Horns seemed to have passed the goad on to the Leppins, and it was largely under these merciless proddings that he had formed his conception of the new town which had evolved itself during the past twenty years. To these personal grievances he added the general grievances of a tax-payer under the present loose-geared régime, and there were days when he thought he saw the legitimate outcome of democracy as applied to large capitals: the organizing of criminals for the spoliation of the well-to-do. And if Bingham had pushed him too hard, he might have precipitated the blunt declaration that a man's best use for his own money was to protect himself and his interests from the depredations of an alien and rabble populace.

"But Babylon itself was built of mud bricks," Bingham would rejoin. "And the noblest mountain in the world, when you come right down to details, is only a heap of dirt and rocks strewn over with sticks and stones. But if you will just step back far enough to get the proper point of view—well, you know what the painters can do with such things as these."

"I can't step back, Bingham. I started here; I've stayed here; I belong here. I'm living right *on* your mountain, and its sticks and stones are all about me. Don't ask me to see them for anything else; don't ask me to call them anything else."

Then he would say to Bingham what he said later to Susan Bates when she came with Jane to view the wainscotings and the panelled ceilings of the long succession of rooms: that the man who met all the legal exactions of the community and all the needs and requirements of his own flesh and blood was doing quite enough for the preservation of his own credit. And when Theodore Brower cautiously suggested that the bitterness of certain experiences might be turned to sweetness by the institution of a bureau of justice for the poor and unfriended, the sensitive old man shrank back as if from contact with a nettle. Indeed, it is probable that so unconventional and untravelled a road to philanthropic renown would have proven uninviting to his feet at any time. And Jane, who, after the failure of her own idea, had transferred her support to the idea of Brower, now made a second transfer and came to the support of the idea of Susan Bates. If she could do nothing for the cause of labor, and nothing for the cause of justice, she was willing to accomplish what she could for the cause of education.

Under such urgings as these, David Marshall began irritably to impugn the motives of those men whose philanthropic disposition had earned for them the approval of the well-disposed. One was actuated by vanity and vainglory; another by political ambitions; a third took to philanthropy as to the current fad.

"There might be worse ones," Bingham would retort. "Sixty or seventy years ago the fad hereabouts was scalp-raising. Isn't the present one an improvement on that?"

"You bring up Ingles," the other went on; "he's simply philanthropic as an additional vent to his own energies. You talk about Bates; he merely makes all those benefactions to please his wife. And so with others."

"Is that a bad motive—the wish to please one's wife by a generous deed?"

"I have *my* wife to please," returned Marshall. His observation came out with a sort of raw and awkward directness. It seemed to convey the odd implication that the way to please this wife would be not to do a generous deed, but to refrain from doing it. And Bingham, who appreciated the saplessness of Eliza Marshall's sympathies and the narrowness of her horizon, made no effort to give his friend's remark a more favorable aspect.

Marshall derived support not only from the narrow selfishness of his wife, but also from the fastidiousness of his younger son, who met with open derision any project involving the accomplishment of a piece of actual architecture. He improvised an ornate and airy edifice of his own, which he allowed them to dedicate to art, to education, to charity, to what you will. Then he festooned it with telegraph wires, and draped it with fire-escapes, and girdled it with a stretch of elevated road, and hung it with signboards, and hedged it in with fruit-stands, and swathed it in clouds of coal smoke, and then asked them to find it; that was the puzzle, he said. His view of the town's architectural conditions—as too debased to justify one's serious endeavors towards improvement—was so nearly in harmony with the view that his father's inflamed mind sometimes took of the town's social conditions that the two were dangerously near to the common ground upon which they had never yet met.

Bingham would have completely dissented from all this, of course; and he agreed with Marshall no better as regarded the precarious condition of his affairs—being disposed to assume that the old man's depression over his business was due largely to the multiplied checks on his own control of it; nor any better as regarded his unusual domestic expenses—present, just past, or just about to come. He was mindful of the house-building, but looked upon it, with Roger, as an investment. He knew of the thousands extorted through Truesdale, but made the loss less than might have resulted from a maladroit barter in real estate, for example. He could anticipate, too, the demands foreshadowed by the coming marriage of Rosamund; but a considerable expenditure for a favorite daughter at the most important juncture of her life was not unprecedented. He even found some ameliorating circumstances for the persistent pressure which Roger and his affairs were now coming to bring upon the paternal estate—Roger, who had served so valiantly his father and his family, and who was now demanding a compensatory assistance amid the thickening risks and dangers of his own business operations. Not only had he extricated Truesdale from his difficulties, but he had supported his father in his demand for the dismissal of the unseemly Andreas Leppin from the business.

"He shall go!" cried David Marshall, with a trembling voice and a shaking hand, which, without reinforcement, would have constituted but a feeble demonstration.

"He shall stay!" returned Belden, with a cold insolence. "He is useful to me. Besides, he has suffered enough wrong from you already."

"He shall go!" cried Roger, rising into a threatening savagery over the brazen hypocrisy of such a pretence. "If he is here another hour, I will drag him out with my own hands." The young man seemed to tear out all his powers from his own person, as one draws a sword from its sheath, and to wield his vehemence and indignation over Belden's head as one might sweep a burning brand. He exercised the compelling power that is to be attained sometimes only by the free and impassioned employment of all one's energies; he seemed capable of an instant physical violence in more directions than one, and he carried his point.

Another outbreak of passion followed when he applied to his father for assistance during a precarious passage through the risks and dangers of an expanding business, and was met with reluctant excuses that seemed the very acme of ingratitude. He hurled forth an indignant reminder of all the services he had performed for the family—services at once degrading and gratuitous; and he demanded if a year's dabbling in such delectable detail were not a sufficient warrant for asking the help that he now required. In fact, he hectored his father as unscrupulously, as unceremoniously, as he had browbeaten Belden.

David Marshall met as well as he could the demands of his choleric son; never before had he been trampled on rough-shod by one of his own children. He almost seemed to see the moral fibre of Roger's nature coarsening—perhaps disintegrating—

under his very eyes, and he asked himself half reproachfully how much this might be due to tasks of his own imposition.

All these things had their place in his mind as he followed Bingham through the new house, scuffling over the plaster-encrusted floors, watching the adjustment of window-weights, or drawing back before the long, thin strips of moulding brought in by carpenters. No, his children did not love him. There was Rosy, who had learned her lesson of selfishness from the world all too early, and who now, in her preoccupations for the future, had less thought of him than ever. There was Alice, who saw him often enough if she saw him half a dozen times a year, and whose infrequent comings always disclosed some petty motive of domestic finance and economics. There was Truesdale, a flippant and insolent egotist, who had neither affection nor respect for his own parents, his own family, his own birthplace. There was Roger, who hewed roughly his own independent course, and who did not scruple to turn his powers against his own father if crossed in his desires or balked in his ambitions. And there was—

No; not Jane. "She is the only one of them all who really loves me," he said. He was standing in one of the upper rooms under the crude light of a northern window. On the yellow ground beneath him a workman was stacking up sheets of blue slate in regular piles, and from some remote quarter of the place came the sharp, metallic hammerings of the last remaining plumbers. The searching daylight lit up cruelly the hollows of the old man's eyes, and brought out from his whitened chin and cheeks the last few threads of dim and dulling red. His tall, thin figure shrank away from its loose coverings; never before had he seemed so detached, so impersonal, so slightly poised on any mere physical basis.

He turned to Bingham. "This will be *her* room—Jane's room. It must be right, whatever the others are. Jane—cares for me. She has always been a dutiful daughter; never a trial, never a

247

disappointment—nothing but a comfort. There must be no shortcoming here, Bingham."

Bingham, standing beside him at the window, fixed an intent regard upon the sheets of shifting slate. There was a moist smile in his eyes, and a warm glow of sympathetic appreciation permeated his whole being.

"There won't be," he said.

And Jane's chamber took on shape and finish in the minds of the two men who stood there side by side overlooking the slate piles and saying no word further; and neither recognized in her the first cause of all these changes and of the many trials and difficulties proceeding from them.

XX

The approaching completion of the new house did little towards diminishing the rigors of the daily routine within the old
one; no greater insistence upon detail could be encountered at
Gibraltar or at Ehrenbreitstein than that which prevailed under
the direction of Eliza Marshall, to whom the near breaking of
camp was no reason for the slightest break in discipline. Nor
was there any relaxation because the garrison happened to be
on a mere peace footing; it made little difference that both
Rosamund and Truesdale were spending the better part of the
summer in Wisconsin. Rosy had resumed her round among the
country-houses of her friends; she expected to repay these attentions in the near future by an elegant and lavish hospitality,
whose time, place, and method still remained more or less inde-
terminate. Truesdale, too, had made a second and longer excursion northward—Waukesha, Geneva, Oconomowoc, and
again, Madison. Jane alone remained at home, and it was she
who helped her mother through the thirtieth and last of the
annual jelly-makings. For the first time in all these years the
entire supply of currants had come from outside; the last of
their own bushes, which had put on faintly its customary green-
ness in May, had peaked and dwindled through June, and had
died at last in the early days of July.

"That reconciles me, Jane," said Eliza Marshall, as she viewed the dead bush while flapping one of her ensanguined cloths from the kitchen window; "I shall be ready to move when the time comes."

Jane sighed softly for reply; she was beginning to realize what all this change might mean.

David Marshall himself bowed to the same stringent discipline that ruled the others. Though he felt his powers weakening beneath days of worry and nights of broken rest, he would have been surprised by the smallest concession, and would even have considered it a weakness to ask for any. That his rest was broken did not postpone the early breakfast by a single five minutes; that his health was failing did not alter the somewhat primitive and rigorous character of the dishes set before him; that he returned home jaded and exhausted by the day's doings did not entitle him, any more than ever, to smoke a quiet cigar within doors. He smoked without, upon the sidewalk, according to his wont; but he never paced very far up or down, nor very long. The old routine went on—a little too inexorably. And though many of his nights were coming to be sleepless throughout, and though the strain of it all was obvious enough as his thin, drawn face bent over a breakfast for which he could find no relish, yet the tradition that he was above all physical frailties and exempt from all natural laws clamped its curious hold upon his family and even upon himself. Eliza Marshall had almost come to regard him as she regarded his business: each was a respectable and estimable abstraction which held its own without too direct a heed from her; each an admirable contrivance that had accomplished its purposes so long and with so trustworthy a regularity that the thought of hitch, lapse, failure never presented itself as a really tangible consideration. Each day he grew a shade paler, a degree feebler, but the change came too gradually for the unobservant and over-habituated eyes of his wife.

Rosy noticed it, however, when she came back to town, to

begin seriously her preparations for her wedding. "I don't think papa looks very well," she was contented to observe.

"Of course he doesn't," returned Jane, anxiously. "He ought to go off somewhere for a change and rest. I've told him so a dozen times. *You*"—to Rosy—"ought to know plenty of places. If I had my way about it, he would start off to-morrow."

"Well, I don't know," observed her mother, slowly. "He never *has* gone off. And if you don't happen to feel first-rate, I don't know where you can be better taken care of than right at home."

"You might go to Geneva—both of you," replied Jane; "I wish you would, if only on my account. Mrs. Bates is just about getting tired of asking you, and I'm 'most worn out with making up excuses for your not going." Jane had been giving an occasional attendance on Susan Bates's dormitory and children. Mrs. Bates herself had bowed to Rosy's preference with a resigned reasonableness, and had abated not one jot in her friendliness towards Rosy's family.

But to Eliza Marshall a summer's outing could easily be made to seem superfluous, impracticable, revolutionary; nor did Jane succeed any better with her father himself. He seemed to take a pathetic pride in standing at his post; he almost appeared to be imbued with the fatalistic notion that there was, indeed, no leaving it. He continued to smoke his cigar outside, to cover haltingly sheets of paper with figures under the library lamp, and to yield himself to hours of depressing and harassing reflection within the shadows of the bay-window.

When Truesdale came home his father's decline was even more noticeable. Truesdale commented briefly on his appearance, suggested as briefly a little trip into the country, and after these few passes at filial duty he concentrated his attention upon his own personal affairs.

On his second visit to Madison he had met Bertie Patterson face to face. He had encountered her in one of the broad and leafy walks before the Capitol, and she was in company with another young man. "One of those students," thought Truesdale, as he noted the smooth face and slender immaturity of her escort. "They swarm. The town is full of them. What chance has anybody else against them?"

Bertie showed him a little face at once surprised, startled, puzzled. She bowed slightly and gave him a smile which seemed to him timid, shrinking, and amusingly deferential; but she showed no disposition to pause, or even to slacken her pace. "She doesn't know, after all," he thought; "she is imagining some vague horror or other that is too dreadful to be true, or even possible."

Bertie and her youth passed on through the contending sun and shade of the path. "Can they be engaged?" thought Truesdale, upon whom certain fine shades in posture and address were not thrown away; "he looks hardly a junior." He presently met a senior of his acquaintance who told him he understood they were. "Ouf!" commented Truesdale, further; "a mere boy-and-girl affair." And he pleased himself with thinking how his own participation in such an affair would give it a much greater maturity and weight.

But as regarded this particular one, he definitely withdrew from all participation whatever. He had now done enough to satisfy his curiosity—or his interest, as he might have preferred to have it called—and fully enough to preserve the dignity so absurdly jeoparded by the fantastic scruples of his aunt Lydia. He presently dismissed the whole matter, and fell to bestowing an exaggerated care upon the tips of his brushes. "The rest of the summer I propose to enjoy," he declared.

As for David Marshall himself, he employed the rest of the summer in a laborious attempt to form the acquaintance of his coming son-in-law. Scodd-Paston presented to him an assemblage of qualities towards whose scheduling and comprehending he received but little help from his familiarity with the ordinary workaday type of local young man. Paston was uniformly gay, jovial, companionable, definite sometimes as regarded particulars, indefinite always as regarded generals. He stood constantly in a lambent flicker of humorous good-nature, and he baffled the old gentleman as one is baffled by the play of sunshine over a rippling pool. Marshall would ask himself whether the depth of the pool was a finger-length or a fathom, and would speculate on what there might be lying at the bottom of it—strange deposits, perhaps, representing the social and business developments of another age, or at least another civilization. He sometimes questioned his daughter's capacity to cope with the classification of such a collection—supposing so exacting a task ever to devolve upon her.

He sometimes canvassed the matter with Theodore Brower, as the two sat smoking together on the door-step through the long summer twilights, while other warm-weather loungers scuffled aimlessly over the cindered paths of the dingy grass-stretch opposite, or, lying on their backs, crossed their legs self-indulgently and lifted over-worn brogans towards the contemptuous stars. He opened himself unreservedly to Brower, as to a friend of the family; and Brower could not but feel that his two years' attendance at the house, with thus far no definite outcome, had given the head of it ample warrant for considering him as he did. Once or twice, while Brower was counselling with Marshall on the door-step, another man—Tom Bingham—had been entertained by Jane within the breezy recesses of the bay-window. It was then that Brower realized with a kind of muffled desperation how completely he and Bingham seemed to have changed positions. One had begun as the friend of a single member of the family, to become in the end the common and equal friend of all, and to sit discussing now with the head of it as one gray-beard with another. The other had begun as the general friend of the household, and had now advanced to the stage where he could fill in the dusk of an early September evening with the talk and company of the one young woman in the world whose talk and company were in any degree worth considering. Brower crunched his cigar between his teeth, and replied to Marshall's observations with a brusque carelessness for which he rebuked himself as being neither respectful nor civil.

"I had never thought," said the old gentleman, looking lakeward through the smoky twilight with a kind of vague wistfulnes, "but that all my girls would marry Americans." He spoke slowly, musingly, in his huskily sibilant tones.

"Um," said Brower, moodily, from the depth of an absurd jealousy. The man whose voice was coming to them with a certain deep indistinctness from the bay-window was an American —decidedly so.

"And not only an American," pursued Marshall, "but a Westerner."

"Um," said Brower, with an increasing gloom. The man who had just provoked that last clouded response from Jane was a Westerner, truly.

"And not only a Western man, but an out-and-out Chicago man; one who knows the town, one who is in sympathy with it, one who has done a little something to make it what it is."

"Um," said Brower once more, with a deeper despondency. Who had done more to make the town what it was than Bingham had done?

"Then I should undestand his ideas and ambitions," the old man proceeded, in a tone of plaintive yet unavailing protest. "I should know better about his connections and belongings. I should be able to foresee the future in some degree. I should have a clearer idea of what to expect. I should know, perhaps, where he—where he meant to live." Marshall ended this discourse with a feeble and helpless sigh.

There was nothing indefinite about Bingham, thought poor Brower; there was no doubt as to where *he* would continue to exist.

"You mean to say it isn't decided yet where they are going to live?" Brower's inquiry was prompted by civility rather than by interest. It was the first observation of any length that he had made for some time. Jane, who had been straining her ears during the last ten minutes for the mere sound of his voice, leaned back in her chair with an approximate comfort.

"I don't know, just exactly," replied Marshall, rather dismally. His tone made him say that he did not know at all. "I've talked with Rosy and I've talked with Arthur. . . ." He lapsed into a comfortless silence, and ran his thin old hand over his blanched and furrowed forehead.

"When are they going to be married?" asked Brower. His eyes were on the bay-window, through whose curtains there showed the face of Bingham, his own look anxiously fixed on Marshall.

Jane caught indistinctly the muffled tone of these few syllables. She made them mean a dozen different things and finally nothing at all, but she was glad of the opportunity to do even that.

"In a month," answered Marshall; "early in October. Rosy lays great stress on an October wedding—that's the only right sort, it seems." He sighed with a full sense of the imminence of the inevitable. The voice of Bingham came with a slow, deep gravity from the bay-window, and Jane's voice, responding, mingled nervously with her father's sigh.

"Not from the new house?" said Brower.

"Hardly. It will be almost finished, but far from furnished. Perhaps they will have their receptions there, if they decide to—to come back."

"Come back?" Brower spoke up loudly; a jangling freight train had paused opposite, and the locomotive was blowing off steam.

"To America," the old man explained. He laid his hands to his temples. "Do you sleep well?"

"Always."

"Rosy thinks the new house ought to be hurried more. But why should she object to being married from the old house she was born in? Most girls would be pleased with such a thought as that." He placed his hand over his weary old eyes. "You do, do you—always? I don't; I can't. These trains—they keep me awake. I slept hardly half an hour last night, and none at all the night before. Do you know anything about chloral?"

The voice of Bingham came to a pause, and that of Jane was presently distinguished in response—trembling, apprehensive, lapsing away into little breaks and pauses.

"I know it's dangerous," replied Brower. "And morphine, too. And all such things; they're not to be used except in the last extremity. So they are going to England for their wedding-trip, then?"

"To England, yes." He smiled half sorrowfully, half bitterly. He was thinking how easy it might be for Rosamund to give up her old home and her old friends altogether; and he was asking himself, too, if he had really toiled through these many years only to have the results squandered at last by a stranger in a strange land.

"To England, yes," he repeated. "Arthur has postponed his vacation until late in the fall, and he hopes to be able to spend as much as two or three weeks at home. At home; he is a British subject, you know—he has never been naturalized."

The air quivered with the quick pulsations of the locomotive of a passing suburban train. As it moved away Brower heard again the voice of Bingham slow, grave, earnest—a voice of warning and alarm, one might have thought.

"Some of them are here for years before they take out their papers," rejoined Brower. "And lots of them never take them out at all."

"I don't know what's to be done," said Marshall, with a fretful anxiety. "I've given up coffee; some tell me that I ought to give up smoking, too, but others say it really doesn't make any difference. But I must do something; I must have better rest.

I can't work without my sleep, and I—I can't let myself fail—now."

Jane was speaking once again—more steadily, more coolly, more composedly, it seemed. "Poor pa;—it can't be so serious as that," the listener thought he understood her to say.

"I've heard of bromine," said Brower. "That's simpler, isn't it—and safer?" Jane's voice had ceased, and silence maintained its sway within.

"She will meet all his family," the old gentleman went on. "She seems to expect to find them very fine people—finer than any we have here. And she will see the place where they live —a very much handsomer place, I make out, than any in this part of the world." A drawn and weary smile passed lightly over his face.

There was a movement in the bay-window, and presently a solid footstep in the hall.

"There's nothing like finding things out for yourself," said Brower, colorlessly.

Bingham appeared on the door-step, just as the tail of loco-motive smoke swept over the front yard. "Will you smoke with us?" asked Marshall.

Brower smiled, though neither of the others seemed conscious of any secondary meaning in this simple question. "Thank you, no," replied Bingham. "I am moving on to an appointment, and am a little late as it is." He looked down on Marshall with an expression of friendly solicitude, and shook hands with him in a long, slow clasp. "Good-night; you are entitled to better care than you are giving yourself." And he moved down the footpath towards the front gate.

Marshall looked after him wistfully. "If I were only in that man's shoes! If I but had half his health and strength!" Brower heard nothing of this; he was straining his ears for a further sound from within.

"I must get rest," cried the old man, pitifully. "I'm wearing out. I stay up till midnight and after, every night, and even then it's sometimes daylight before I have a minute's sleep, I can't stand it; nobody can."

There was a sound inside, as of scuffling among the furniture. It was Jane, feeling her way through the dark, listening for the sound of Theodore Brower's voice, and murmuring tremulously with her own, *"Toujours fidèle; toujours fidèle!"*

"What can I do?" asked the old man, with an appealing grip on Brower's arm. "What doctor can I see? Where can I go for a change and for rest? Or how," he groaned, "can I go away at all? They are crowding me down; they are wrenching my business from my hands! I can't give way at such a time as this!"

Brower hardly heard him; he was listening for Jane, who was now doubling the newel-post just within, and whose quavering undertone broke at the turn as she chanted once more her phrase of hope and reassurance. Brower heard her intonation, and wondered over its meaning; but he would have found no meaning in the words themselves, even if they had been distinctly audible, for he knew no French.

Jane crooned the same brief snatch of melody many a time as the preparations for her sister's wedding moved along—particularly during those hours when she sat in her own room and directed the invitations. It was the only bed-chamber which she remembered ever to have occupied—the same furniture, the same fireplace, the same outlook, the same familiar curtains, gas-jets, door-knobs that had been known to her tomboy childhood, to her formidably plain girlhood, to her ambitious and philanthropic spinsterhood. The very air of it seemed thick with her varying hopes and plans and dreams and projects and ideals. In this retired bower she had slept for her whole life, and no fairy prince had ever penetrated to it to awaken her. One had come for Alice and one for Rosy, but never a—*"Toujours fidèle!"* moaned Jane, in her deepest contralto, and fell to work with renewed zeal upon her envelopes.

There were hundreds and hundreds of them. Rosy had imagined a function of the first magnitude, and it was not to dwindle for mere lack of material. She had determined upon a ceremony in church and a large reception at the house, with everything in the way of music, flowers, functionaries, and supernumeraries that the most approved forms could incorporate. She stood out for a bishop, a surpliced choir, a wedding-breakfast after the English manner—in short, for the utmost attainable in the way of spendor, thoroughness, and distinction. The preparations moved on with a swirl and a sweep, and involved the whole household to the exclusion of all else.

"But, for Heaven's sake," demanded Jane, "how are you going to get all these people into the house?" She had already disposed of Paston's short list, and had even found a certain pleasure in the quaint and complicated addresses that abounded throughout it. But the other list, compiled by Rosy and her mother, seemed to pass all bounds; not her mother's part, which was limited to certain old-time friends and connections, but Rosy's own, which dealt with "society" almost in its entirety. Jane appreciated now, for the first time, the comprehensive thoroughness of Rosy's year of social endeavor.

"Here, let me have it," said Rosy, brusquely snatching the list from Jane. She fixed her eye upon the part of it that was written in her mother's cramped and antiquated hand. "Who are these Browns?"

"Why, don't you remember the Browns? They were old neighbors of ours; pa used to think everything of them. They sent Alice a beautiful present."

"Never heard of them in my life," declared Rosy. "They needn't come; they can just have announcement-cards. Who are the Grahams?—here's four of them."

"Why," faltered Jane, "they used to have the pew right behind us in the old church. Ma and Mrs. Graham had a booth together at the Sanitary Fair."

"The pew behind, eh? I haven't the slightest recollection of them." She marked the name off altogether.

She made a thorough revision of her mother's list. Then she

turned to her own. "Now, *these* people—I *know* all of *them*, and am indebted to them, and expect to have relations with them after I come back. They've all got to stay on."

"Very good," said Jane, meekly. What else could she say? Was it not to some such social triumph as this that for a good six months she had bent all her own endeavors? She tried now to make the triumph seem as glorious as it should, but she could not feel that she was succeeding.

Another stage in the proceeding arrived when the gowns began to come home from the dress-maker's. Jane then laid aside her pen to find pins, to contrive ruchings, to catch up the loose ends of draperies, while her mother and her sister Alice and her aunt Lydia circled and fluttered and swooped and chattered through a hundred suggestions and amendments and alterations. Then Jane would stand upon the threshold, and blink tearfully and indignantly into the gloom of the hall. "Nobody thinks of *me*," she would say, chokingly; "nobody cares for me; nobody seems to imagine that I've got a heart, too!"

And, lastly, the day itself;—when Truesdale, decorated with a daring and wanton orchid, followed Paston out into the middle of the chancel of a crowded and buzzing church; when his father, despite his failing powers and an innate repugnance to the conscious dramatization involved in the ceremonial side of life, led Rosamond up a long aisle with the tremulous embarrassment of an invalid and a novice, and parted from her in front of a broad pair of lawn sleeves; and when Cecilia Ingles scattered a wide shower of rice over the broken flagging of the old front walk, as Mr. and Mrs. Arthur Scodd-Paston, of Boxton Park, Witham, Essex, England (as one of the newspapers took the trouble to put it) passed out through the rusty old front gate into married life.

A few days later David Marshall, to the surprise and dismay of the remaining members of the family, took to his bed.

XXI

"Where are you, Jane?"

Eliza Marshall's voice sounded impatiently in the hallway, and presently her nervous hand was placed on the knob of her daughter's door.

"Well, here you are, finally. And what is the matter, for the land's sake? And where is the pillow you went to get for your father?—we can't keep him waiting out in the carriage on such a day as this. Come, get up; you'll catch your death of cold yourself."

Jane was lying on the bare floor of her stripped and emptied room, with her head pillowed upon the window-sill. She wore her sack, but her hat had fallen off and lay at her side. In her hand she held a stiff and curling width of paper just torn from the wall, and her body shook with sobs as she lifted her wide and welling eyes to her mother's face.

"I am to blame," she cried, wildly; "I am to blame for it all! If it hadn't been for me we should never have left our old home and given up our old life, and Rosy wouldn't have cut all our friends and gone to England to live; and Truesdale wouldn't be talking about starting off across the Pacific for somewhere or other, and we should never have made enemies of those Beldens, and poor pa wouldn't have lost his business, and wouldn't be going off to die inch by inch in that big cold place out on the prairie. I'm to blame for it all; but I—I meant as well as anybody could!"

"'Sh, Jane! Rosy hasn't gone to England to live, and your father isn't dying. How can you talk that way?"

"And my old room!" Jane went on with a stringent cry, as her eyes roamed despairingly over its dismantled walls. "I never lived anywhere else, and I don't want to, and I can't! I don't want to live at all! And this old house isn't ours any longer, and those carriage people will begin to tear it down to-morrow. They'll take away the barn and chop down the trees, and there won't be a single thing left to remember it all by." She bent her head on the window-sill again, and sobbed more vehemently still.

"Oh, Jane, Jane!" cried her mother, protestingly, "how can you act that way when there is so much to be done, and when your father is feeling so much worse than usual? Where were those pillows left, anyway? Come, come!"

Jane rose to her knees and tried to wipe her face with the piece of wall-paper. Then her mother lifted her up and led her out through the hall.

It was a chilly day in early November—a high wind lashing the gray and foaming lake—when David Marshall, wrapped in shawls and bolstered up with pillows, was driven carefully over the three miles of flinty macadam which led from his old house to his new one, and was put to bed again in a large, half-warmed apartment, fitted up scantily and provisionally with an old chamber-set that had escaped the auctioneer. His own illness and his daughter's marriage had almost brought the furnishing of the new house to a stand-still, while the anxiety of the purchasers of the old place to get their foundations in before the real cold weather had made it impossible for the family to remain a single day beyond the stipulated term. No new furnishings had been attempted beyond carpets and curtains, and for the first few days that the old man lay in these new quarters he had little to assure him that he was not in some hotel or in some hospital, save the echoing tread of the hard-finishers in other rooms about him. The first slight flurry of snow dusted the dead weeds of the open spaces round the house, and the reflections from it passed through the clear, broad panes of the windows to strike a grimmer chill from the shimmering surfaces of ash and oak. Never before had the world seemed to him so empty and so cold and so unsympathetic. And when his own wife had said to him, in accents almost of reproach, "Oh, David, David, how could you take such a time as this to be sick, with all the worry of moving and furnishing and Rosy's wedding and everything else?" he felt as bare and chill and numb as a naked sailor cast ashore on some alien and inhospitable coast.

Susan Bates appeared at the new house almost immediately; she felt its need now, if ever, of being habitable. She stuffed her carriage with rugs and draperies; she sent an expressman out with her favorite easy-chair. She brought alcohol lamps and chafing-dishes. She seldom came without fruit or flowers. She set fire-screens and adjusted window-shades. She went deeply into the subject of opiates, and she talked by the hour with Jane and her mother about symptoms and remedies.

Marshall, while grateful for her attentions, was almost embarrassed by them—not that they should come from her rather than from his wife (or at least more copiously and spontaneously), but that they should come at all. Never before in his life had he received such minute and solicitous ministrations; he felt with a shy self-depreciation that he must be making himself a great burden. If Susan Bates threw back her bonnet-strings and suggested to Jane a lowering of the window-shades, he would almost protest against the girl's laying aside her book or her sewing; and the preparation of any special dish, such as is an invalid's due, would even now still cause him that sense of guilt which he had always felt on breaking in upon the household routine of his wife. "Poor man!" Susan Bates would say; "how must he have lived all these years! Why, I could hardly get him even to let me oil the door-hinges!"

She would sit by his bedside and try to soothe and divert this wan and weary and half-desperate old man. He enjoyed but the most fitful slumber, and even that only by the action of narcotics. Through the lagging hours of the day and through the maddening watches of the night his mind, ticking like an unstillable clock, beat for him an incessant rhythmical reminder of the impending ruin of his house and of his own powerlessness to avert it. He reviewed again and again the whole course of his life and his business—they were one: his lowly beginnings, his early struggles in the raw but ambitious prairie town, the laborious stages of endeavor by which he had developed and strengthened his business—his. Then, as the house had grown, others had insinuated themselves, or imposed themselves; and these were now banded together to dominate it, and to check and circumvent him, its founder and their benefactor, and finally to bring it to the very brink of ruin, and to make the labors of his whole lifetime come to naught. And he in bed here—with his feeble hands working desperately at the hem of the sheet, and his aching head throbbing unavailingly through the cruel, open-eyed watches of the night. He raged over the world's injustice and his own impotence; the thought was never absent from him—he was coming under the disastrous domination of the *idée fixe*.

He spoke of these things to Susan Bates with such an increasing frequency and insistency as almost to transfer the rack of them from his own brain to hers. Once or twice, in an interval of semi-delirium, he bewept the ruin not only of his business, but of himself and of his family and of all his belongings. He infected her with his own dread and panic; she saw his property dispersed, his home in others' hands, his family in the depths of despairing poverty.

One morning she appeared at Roger's office; Minnie Peters

accompanied her. The one carried a large leather bag in her hand; the other had a large brown-paper parcel under her arm.

"Your poor father!" said Susan Bates, advancing straight towards Roger with moistened eyes and with a nervous tremor in her voice and body alike. She set her satchel on the corner of Roger's desk and began tugging at its catches. "You open yours too, Minnie," she said; and Minnie Peters began working at the knots in the cord that bound her stiff brown bundle with a tight-drawn tension. Roger looked at both his callers with a great surprise.

"Poor David!" said Susan Bates, with her lips twitching; "to think of his toiling and slaving so many years, and of everything going all to pieces in the end, like this! It can't be! It sha'n't be!—not if I can help it."

She thrust her hand into the top of Minnie Peter's package. She drew out a heavy folded document and followed it with others. "There! that's the abstract; and here are the leases, and here is the insurance." She threw out a sheaf of policies; the one on top was for ten thousand dollars. "I didn't know just what you would need; I brought everything connected with the whole building—here's the receipt for last year's taxes. Now, I want you to put a mortgage on it right away. It's clear, Mr. Bates says."

Roger glanced at one of the leases and placed the building in an instant. It was a vast structure in the dry-goods district, occupied by half a dozen firms of the highest standing.

Mrs. Bates now thrust her hand into her own bag. She drew it out time and time again, until she had covered the top of Roger's desk with packages of securities—bank stock, railroad bonds, State and county issues of all kinds; there was even one bright-green batch of water bonds from a far town in North Dakota.

Roger looked up at her very gravely. "Is this with Mr. Bates's approval?"

Susan Bates answered him pantingly, all a-tremble with nervous excitement. "Mr. Bates is a just man, and not an ungenerous man, but—but"—She clasped her hands and leaned forward anxiously. "Mr. Bates and I have always stepped along together. He has always done whatever I have asked him to do. He has never disappointed me. But—oh, Roger, he never knew your father in those early days; if he had, could he stand by and see him on the edge of ruin without making some effort to save him?" She waved her hand over the disorder of Roger's desk. "That's everything I've got; use as much of it as you need."

She began to cry a little. Minnie Peters, who always cried when she could, pulled out her handkerchief and frankly sobbed aloud.

Roger studied the two women with some perplexity and with a slight shade of pique.

"It is true," he began, very proudly and much too coldly, "that the affairs of the Marshall & Belden Company are moving towards the hands of a receiver, but the affairs of David Marshall himself are in the hands of his son; and they were never in better condition than they are to-day."

This was Roger's song of victory over his recent success with the largest operation (on behalf both of his father and of himself) that he had ever undertaken. It seemed as if all the world must know of that—must ring with it, in fact; yet it was this very hour which Benevolence had now chosen for the precipitation of her golden shower.

Susan Bates gave a little gasp. "Then—then you don't need it?"

"Never less," replied Roger, with a quivering nostril and a high, slow bow.

Susan Bates looked sidewise at Minnie Peters and asked her to behave herself. But she gave a few hysterical sobs on her own part, and Minnie Peters echoed them with a faithful promptitude.

"Just like a woman," thought Roger, as he sat alone after Susan Bates's departure. He drew a hundred lines on an imaginary sheet of paper with a dry pen. "Like a woman; yes," he added, under the promptings of a feeling for more exact justice, "a woman in ten thousand."

A few mornings later, when this woman in ten thousand was standing in the bleak porch of the new house to await the return of her horses from their last walk up and down, another carriage slipped into its place and another woman alighted on the curbstone. Susan Bates immediately squared her shoulders, banished all expression from her face, and began the descent of the steps with her eyes fixed upon the gaps in the broken building line over the way.

"That woman! She has never entered *my* house, and she never shall; and she should never enter this."

Statira Belden had come to do the decencies; Eliza Marshall received her with the grim inexpressiveness of a granite bowlder.

"My husband is resting quietly to-day," she said, in response to Mrs. Belden's inquiries. He was—unconscious under chloral, after three nights of open-eyed torment.

Mrs. Belden passed one of her large, smooth gloves over the other and praised the house.

"It is one of the handsomest on the street," replied Eliza Marshall, firmly. "And one of the best built. We feel completely at home in it already."

But, in truth, the poor soul was homesick, heartsick, as lost and forlorn as a shipwrecked sailor on the chill coast of Kamtchatka.

Mrs. Belden smoothed down her yellow locks and deplored, in her thickly sweet accents, the unfortunate condition of the business.

"My husband's own affairs are going very well," returned Eliza Marshall, looking forward with unblinking eyes. "My son has charge of them. There was a full account of his success in the Sunday paper."

Her tone was one of brazen triumph. Yet Eliza Marshall abhorred speculation with all the dread of the middle-aged female conservative. One dollar through legitimate trade rather than ten through such paths as Roger had of late been so fearfully treading.

Mrs. Belden had heard something of Truesdale's intended departure for the Orient. "He finds Chicago uncongenial, no doubt."

"Truesdale is at home everywhere. He will have adventures everywhere. He is handsome. He is clever. He can interest wherever he chooses. Sometimes he interests too easily and too deeply; sometimes in spite of himself and to his own annoyance."

Eliza Marshall shot out these remarks like bullets from behind a breastwork. At the end she set her jaws firmly, and stared at Statira Belden with a proud defiance. Many a night had Truesdale's courses wet her pillow with tears of sorrow and shame; she now wondered if it were really she herself who had just celebrated his profligacy, and had seemed to glory in it at that. She had surmised her son's disdain for the importunities of Gladys McKenna, and she had joined with him in a ringing derision when the Beldens had accused him of encouraging her in her folly that he might employ her as a spy upon the happenings in their house. "My son," she concluded, "will return at his own pleasure, and will always be welcome under his father's roof."

Statira Belden's eyes sought the floor. It was she who had made it sure that knowledge of Truesdale's transgression should reach the ears of Susan Bates; yet her own son had just established relations with a "baroness" who still lingered behind on the scene of the late national festivities, and at the climax of an insane extravagance had been openly cast off by his family.

"And Rosy?" said Statira Belden, presently, with a reconquered sweetness. "One would expect to find her home at such a time as this."

Eliza Marshall planted her standard upon her breastwork, and flaunted it with a firm and magnificent spirit.

"My daughter Rosamund will be with us inside of a week.

She has been detained longer than she had expected among her husband's family." The old lady rose with a stiff, slow motion, and transferred a large panel photograph from the centre-table to Statira Belden's hands. "This reached us yesterday."

It was Rosamund. Her proud and splendid young beauty was set off by a court-train, an immense bouquet, and a nodding group of ostrich-tips.

"Presented at court!" exclaimed Statira Belden, involuntarily, and bit her tongue a second after.

Eliza Marshall answered neither yes nor no. She let the photograph speak for itself.

"Rosamund," she went on, presently, "may return a little too late for her first reception, but the others will be held here, and she will entertain a great deal during the winter."

Statira Belden was cowed at last, and Eliza Marshall's heart beat high to see it. This was her only compensation for the tears shed over the delayed return of a selfish and unfilial daughter, for the anticipated ordeal of the gay social happenings which were to follow that return, for the besetting thought that some dread misfortune might displace all this future festivity by a worse alternative, and make the lightest diversion a black impossibility.

"She kissed the Queen's hand?" palpitated Statira Belden with an interest that she could not stifle; and again Eliza Marshall answered neither yes nor no.

Rosamund had not kissed the Queen's hand, but her husband's family had been so fascinated by her beauty, so amazed by her genius for dress, and so confounded by her boundless aplomb, that one of them had suggested that she attire herself in a costume which had served a daughter of the house at a Drawing-room some six months before, and others had demanded that she be photographed in it. This was the pleasantest impression that Rosy brought back of her husband's family—their generous and unbounded appreciation of herself.

Her other impressions were less acute. Boxton Park itself she had found comfortable, but not at all splendid; and as for its occupants, they were, in the main, staid and serious people who were doing what they could to justify the favors that fortune had bestowed upon them. Rosy sometimes felt that, in general terms, they might have appreciated Jane quite as fully as they had appreciated her. They were not gay, they were not lively, they were not like Arthur. Paston had truly described himself as the youngest, and he was by far the most jovial and blithesome.

Rosy had not delayed her return on account of any presentation at court—though the achievement of the photograph may have accounted for a few days more or less—but on account of the fox-hunting, which had completely fascinated her. Horse, habit, and country were all in perfect accord; her prosaic and hum-drum practice at home was now transmuted into the purest poetry, and under the promptings of this new afflatus she developed a grace and a daring which accomplished the final and irrevocable conquest of all her husband's family.

Rosy's continued sojourn in England cost her husband his position and prospects in America, where he was not of enough importance to assume such liberties. But this mattered nothing to his wife. She had lived for more than a fortnight at the seat of a county family, she had breathed the air of deference that exists for the gentry of the shires, and she was far from any thought of a permanent submission to the rasping crudities of provincial America. She had already developed the fixed determination to return to London for the "season," to accomplish an actual presentation at court, and to make England her future home for the rest of her days.

One thing more was lost by Rosamund's delay in Essex—all chance of a last recognition from her father. When she finally reached home he was in a state of slight delirium, and when he passed from that it was to enter into unconsciousness. His ideas ran incessantly on gifts, on philanthropic endeavor. To-day he built an asylum; to-morrow he endowed a hospital. He strewed promises over the counterpane with indefatigable hands, and babbled unending benefactions among his hot and harassing pillows. Jane, half mad with anguish and remorse, found an added pang in the recollection that during one of his conscious and least uncomfortable hours he had yielded to her solicitations and those of Susan Bates, and had set apart a certain portion of his estate, with the approval of Roger, for a collegiate building which was to bear his name. "He will be remembered now," said Jane, for all her poignant sorrow, and she was glad that Roger had co-operated to make this step a possibility. She tried not to see too plainly that her father had made no pretence of a keener sense of his duty towards the public, or of a kindlier disposition towards it. Whatever he had done was on personal grounds—for the pleasure of a daughter and of an old friend.

One morning, a week after Rosamund's return, a bow of crape was hanging upon the door-bell, Susan Bates was busy with Eliza Marshall up-stairs over certain sombre-hued apparel, and Roger was writing down a list of names and addresses for Theodore Brower upon the dining-room table.

"We must have eight out of this list," said Roger to Brower, "and we ought to know by night which of them can serve."

Whose names have you put down?" asked Jane, reaching for the paper. She read them over. "Give me that pencil." She wrote down half a dozen more. "There!" she said, with a sort of frenzied and towering pride, as she passed the sheet on to Brower. "Those are men that my father knew, and they are men who must help us now." Roger glanced at the names; each was a household word to every soul throughout the city. "Try *them*," said Jane to Brower, "and if any of them refuse you, they will have to refuse me later." And she walked straight out of the room, without turning her head an inch to right or left.

"Shall I?" asked Brower, abashed.

"Why not?" demanded Roger, with a laconic severity.

Brower was a quiet, retiring fellow, and entered upon his day's work with a full consciousness of the ordeal. It meant to lean over the desks of bank presidents, to intrude upon the meetings of railway directors, to penetrate to the retiring-rooms of judges, to approach more than one of the magnates whom, with an imposing vagueness, we call "capitalists." But Brower, carrying the thought of Jane with him into all these presences, accomplished his task with modesty, tact, and discretion, and finally, from the few simple types of greatness that the town possesses, evolved a list which the pride of the dead man's daughter was willing to accept.

The list of occupants of the carriages Jane made out herself. "In the first one, mother and Roger and Alice and her husband. In the second, Arthur and Rosy and Truesdale and me. In the third, Aunt Lydia and the Bateses—it will be full if Lottie and William both come. I can do *that* much for Aunt Lyddy," concluded Jane, with a rueful yet whimsical smile.

"Where do you put me?" asked Brower, with an inviolate sobriety. They were alone in the dining-room together.

"In the fourth. You and Mr. Bingham and—"

"I don't want to go in the carriage with Mr. Bingham," interrupted Brower.

"Why, Theodore, what do you mean? Mr. Bingham is one of our best and oldest friends. Who is there that has been kinder to poor dear pa, and to ma, and to me—?"

"Nor in any carriage occupied by—friends," he went on, in the same tense undertone. He took a firm grip on the back of the chair beside him; Jane saw the swelling veins of his hand and wondered what it all might mean. "I want to go in one of the carriages for the family. I want to go in the carriage that *you* go in. Do you understand me?"

A sudden consciousness had swept over him, with the mention of Bingham's name, that he himself, as well as any other, filled measurably the dead man's ideal of a husband for one of his daughters. He had waited too long already before making this discovery; he must not wait so long before declaring it.

She did not understand from his voice, which was strained and muffled to conceal an emotion all unconcealable. But she understood from his eyes, which looked into hers with an immense and endless kindness, and from his hand, which had left its heroic clutch upon the chair to take a very human hold upon the hand which hung so limply by her side. "Do you understand me?" he asked again; and his voice was gentler than before.

"I do," answered Jane, feebly, and her head fell upon his shoulder. Nothing ever seemed to happen to her as to anybody else; but if happiness chose to come to her swathed in mourning bands, none the less kindly and thankfully must it be welcomed. And as she reclined against him she breathed a sigh of thanks that not he, but Bingham, had been concerned in the laying of her ill-omened corner-stone.

He stood beside her at the open grave, and supported her there, too, as the rattling sand and gravel rained down upon the coffin. The grave had been set round with evergreen sprays, and the raw mound of earth beside it had been concealed in the same kindly fashion. But Jane, in a self-inflicted penance, would spare herself no pang; she clutched Brower's arm and stood there, motionless, until the grave had been filled in and the overplus of earth had been shaped above it. "Put those lilies at the head," she directed; "they were from Mrs. Bates." And then she walked away.

She read the next day, with a chastened satisfaction, the newspaper accounts of her father's career. A new and careless public was carried back once more to the early day whose re-vivification is always attempted for a preoccupied and unsympathetic community upon the passing away of another old settler. Then the frontier village lifts once more its bedraggled forlorn-ness from the slime of its humble beginnings, and the lingering presence of the red man is again made manifest upon the grassy horizon. Again the struggles of the early days are rehearsed, again fire deals out its awful devastation, and once more the city grows from an Indian village to a metropolis of two millions within the lifetime of a single indivdual.

One morning, the second after the funeral, Truesdale stood at the front parlor window, while the first snow-storm of the season swirled over the long reach of the street and across the straggling paths that traversed the wide stretches of broken prairie land round about. On the chair beside him was a news-paper containing the statement that the affairs of the Marshall & Belden Company were to be wound up, all thought of continuing the business having been abandoned. And on the table beside him lay the cards which announced the marriage of Bertie Patterson.

"No business," he said; "no bride." He feigned to himself that he had really designed going into his father's office, and that he had had a serious intention of asking Bertie Patterson to become his wife. He looked out through the wide, clear pane, and thought of the view, of the weather, of the hideous hubbub of the whole town. "Ouf! What a prospect, what a climate, what a human hodge-podge! Everything unites for me in saying —Japan."

David Marshall's will was opened this same day. It made Japan possible for Truesdale, and England possible for Rosamund. A codicil, added in Roger's hand at the latest practicable moment, revoked the bequest for a collegiate building and transferred the whole amount of it directly to Jane.

"This mustn't make any difference," said Jane to Brower. "It shall go for that, after all. My father was a good man, and he deserves to be remembered."

Brower bowed quietly. He appreciated the gravity of this their joint sacrifice, but he would not dispute the justness of it.

THE END